ĐELIA WHITE
BOOK THREE OF THE WINGED

T.K. PERRY

Scarlet Note Publishing, LLC
308 East 4th Street
The Dalles, Oregon 97058
scarletnotepublishing@gmail.com

Cover art by: Angela Bruggeman
www.facebook.com/annysart3
www.instagram.com/annys_interior_design

To my darling daughter:
Every day you inspire me to change for the better.

Table of Contents

Prologue

"She did *what*?!" Tearing the crown from his head, King Danaus, First King of The Winged Realm, flung it across the room. The golden circlet clattered against the throne room's stone wall before coming to rest silently on a plush rug.

"I know you heard me," Queen Annabella muttered, her eyes down. When he didn't respond, she made her way across the excessively furnished room and retrieved his crown.

He followed her, his orange and black wings twitching angrily. "She can't be married!"

"She is."

The king shook his head furiously. "Well, I cancel it! It's cancelled!"

Sighing, the queen sat atop one of the room's many ottomans that were clustered about like grazing sheep. "She's already pregnant. They flew down to Scio and were married by the village bishop weeks ago," she explained as she attempted to bend the crown back into its proper shape. "Can't you start throwing something else when you get angry?"

"I'm not angry; I'm livid!" He kicked the ottoman beside her, sending it skittering into a bookcase.

Still holding the bent crown, the queen covered her ears as her husband's rant crescendoed.

"I found her *four* proper suitors, brought them all the way up the mountain, and she married the *gardener's boy*?! I'll be the joke of the kingdom! I'll have half-breed, peasant grandchildren!"

"Perhaps we can keep it quiet," she interjected, still covering her ears. "Hide her away somewhere."

"*Someone* will spread the rumor! Someone always does!"

The queen set down the misshapen crown on a delicate, wrought-iron table. "We can say she died."

"And then have her killed?"

The queen leapt up, her brown-streaked orange wings flailing behind her. "Of course not! What is the matter with you?"

The king clutched his thinning hair, probing for the crown he had already flung. "You know Dana copies everything her twin does! What's to stop her from marrying a gardener or even a sewer sweeper when she comes into season?"

"*You* will! Change the laws, confine her to her room, make all the unsuitable young men leave the mountain. Surely you have plenty of options without seriously contemplating killing your own child? Dana would *never* forgive you for that. She would leave the moment she had wings, marry someone unsuitable just to spite you, and then I would never see *any* of my grandchildren!"

Some of King Danaus' ire cooled as he began to pace around the dais, his long robes catching on his throne each time he passed it. "All the in-season peasants should be banished together and not allowed to return until they're married."

"That's absurd. And Dana still might fly off and join them."

"No, because everyone would have to have *my* permission to marry."

The queen scoffed. "Are you going to banish yourself as well, then?" *Be certain to take your mistresses and half-breed children with you,* she thought bitterly.

"No." The corner of his mouth twitched into a smug grin. " I'll make one of the Viceroys do it."

"You're being petty. It's been almost two decades since he courted me; how can you still hold a grudge?"

The now wicked smile enveloped his entire mouth as he halted his pacing. "I don't. I just think Lord Viceroy has a *natural* understanding of the lower classes."

"You know his family line is as pure as your own! Nothing but hybrid blood all the way back to the creation." She took a deep breath and blew it out slowly. "I won't let you bait me. Your plan will fail because every bishop, priest, pastor, and reverend will just perform weddings in secret so the in-seasons can avoid banishment."

He resumed his pacing with a snarl. "Then I'll banish them, too! *I* am the authority in this land. If these religionists attempt to put themselves above me, they can leave or they can *die*."

"Don't be an insipid despot. Half the kingdom will follow their religious leaders into banishment. *I* might even consider it."

"You?" the king sneered. "You wouldn't last one day as a religious refugee. The moment you ran out of money, you would be back begging my forgiveness."

A spasm of hatred momentarily twisted her still lovely features. *It's my money! I paid for this ridiculous mountain-top castle! I pay for each golden crown you fling from your head! How dare you threaten to take my own money away from me!* She pressed her lips together to suppress the old argument. Though he had squandered most of her family fortune, she had managed to hide the remainder. If he wanted to continue living extravagantly, he could raise taxes on his unfortunate subjects. Breathing out slowly, she forced herself to listen to his twisted reasoning.

"The people will adjust; they always do. And I can start a new religion. Everyone can worship *me*."

"That's sacrilegious."

He cast her a look of baleful annoyance. "I was only joking."

"It wasn't humorous."

The king frowned. "You have no sense of humor. And your daughters simply have *no sense*."

"They're your daughters, too."

"No, I have *one* daughter; the other is dead."

The queen controlled her breathing with difficulty. "You're not still thinking of killing her?"

"Tell her she has one hour to get off this mountain, and I *never* want to hear from her again."

"That too harsh. She's pregnant; she shouldn't be traveling at all!"

The king again stopped his pacing, his expression icy. "You're welcome to go with her."

What a horrible person he has become. Feigning calm, she rolled her eyes and turned toward the bookshelf. "Must you always be so dramatic?"

"Are you going?"

She shuddered at the contempt in his voice, then selected a book at random. She couldn't leave a daughter behind, but she couldn't let one go, either. "Of course not," she lied, her voice barely tremulous as she thumbed through the pages without absorbing any of the words.

"Are you going to tell her or shall I?"

The queen shut the book and shelved it with a forced sigh. "I will do it. You have a religion to manufacture after all."

"I *said* I was joking."

The queen turned with a cold, artificial smile. "As was I. What happened to your sense of humor?" She swept from the room without waiting for his answer. In the hallway, her stately walk gave way to a panicked jog that the servants pretended not to notice. The moment she had long anticipated was upon her: she would collect her daughters and disappear. He could rage, threaten, or throw a thousand crowns, they would never willingly return.

Chapter One

It was the angry tirade that snagged her attention, and Delia stilled her spade to better hear it. Even the gulls quieted their plaintive cries as if they, too, were filled with morbid curiosity. The strident sound rang out across the meadow, and she tipped her head back to find it's source. Against the azure sky, a pink-winged woman shouted obscenities as she flew beside a green-winged man. Delia's mouth fell open as she recognized her brother, Nap. His clipped, irritable words were impossible to distinguish from the crash of the nearby surf as he dodged away from the pink-winged woman, who shrieked as she flew at him. Delia called out a warning as the woman grabbed for Nap's wing, but it was too late. She tore his forewing, separating the delicate panels before letting go. He bellowed in pain, then began a spiraling plummet into the trees at the edge of the meadow. Delia jumped up, her roots and spade forgotten as she ran to intercept his fall. It was a rhododendron that broke his descent, its lovely white blooms shedding a snowstorm of petals at the impact.

"Nap!" Delia shrieked, her blonde waves trailing out behind her. She reached the broken bush just as her brother was extricating himself from it, tearing his wings further. "Hold still!" she insisted, standing on her toes to help him lift an impaled hindwing off a broken branch.

Nap's expression was grim, perspiration running down his sunburnt face. "Doesn't matter. I won't be flying again."

Delia hugged her brother as tears ran down her face. "Who is she? Why did she do this to you?"

"Let go, Delia," Nap grumped, gently pushing her away.

The pink-winged woman landed gracefully beside Nap, her height matching his own. "Why were you hugging my husband?"

"She's your *wife*?!" Stunned, Delia eyed her sister-in-law. The woman was lovely; her imperious eyes the same rich chestnut color as her hair. Both her clothing and bag looked expensive and well-made. But her appeal ended there. She was utterly unrepentant. Delia turned to her brother. "You married *her*?!"

1

"I suppose you think he should have married *you*," the pink-winged woman drawled poisonously.

"I'm his *sister*," Delia announced, her hazel eyes full of furious tears. "Why did you attack him?!"

"He's fine. I just clipped his wings."

Nap growled as he glared at his bride.

The woman gave him a calculated smile as she ran her fingers through her thick tresses. "Now, where is this house of yours? I need a bath, an excellent lunch, and a decent bed."

Delia erupted in an outraged scoff, her fists tightening to match her brother's white knuckles.

"Well, don't just stand there staring at me. It's rude," the woman explained with cloying condescension.

Delia's chin jutted out. "You could have killed him, and now you're demanding our hospitality? Funny."

"I only tore one panel; if he's hurt himself by his bad landing, it's certainly not *my* fault."

Delia's rage gave way to an ominous smile. All her life she had known the precise words to emotionally devastate those around her. She could perceive their greatest fear, even if they were ignorant of it. The challenge was keeping the horrid words to herself; when provoked, she did not always succeed.

Nap noticed her foreboding smile and grabbed her arm. "Don't, Runt."

Delia warmed at the nickname. No one but Nap called her Runt. She was the smallest of her quadruplet siblings, and Nap had always enjoyed mocking her for it. His face was hard and urgent now, his grip tight. Delia dropped her gaze to his hand on her arm. Bloody rhododendron scratches marred the back of it and ran up his sunburnt arm. Delia opened her mouth.

"No!" Nap warned, his gray eyes stern as he squeezed tighter.

"Ow!" Delia slapped at his hand until he let her go. "She deserves it," she murmured, rubbing her sore arm, though her tanned skin hid the mark.

"Dina is my *wife*."

The weary resignation in his tone made Delia's eyes refill with tears, but a quick glance at her brother's face showed how little he would appreciate her sympathy. Shaking her head, Delia trudged back to her roots and spade. She could hear Dina's mocking tone behind her, but she gritted her teeth and tried to close her ears off to sound. It never worked very well, but at least the sound of her own rushing blood blocked some of her sister-in-law's words.

"...little spitfire...imagine what she'll be like in season!"

Delia flinched at her reference to the curse of the whites. Anyone with a white-winged father underwent a personality change with their wing birth. It only lasted while they were in season, but during that time, they were uncharacteristically aggressive and angry. It made finding mates very difficult. Delia frowned and scratched her shoulder blade. *Stupid sand fleas*; she would have to be more careful at the beach. After another vigorous scratch, she took up her spade and thrust it into the earth vehemently, wincing when she felt it pierce the carrot-like root of the yellow dock she was unearthing. Sighing, she pulled the root free, its bright yellow interior exposed in an angry gash. Her father would be disappointed at her carelessness; but then, he would probably be too upset by his new daughter-in-law to mention it.

Chapter Two

"But this is cold, and it doesn't taste good," Dina remarked.

Delia's eyes widened as she met the shocked expressions of her family members, then returned her gaze to her sister-in-law. Dina's words had been tossed carelessly as if she were telling a funny party joke rather than insulting the woman next to her.

"Well, I think it's nice," Delia's father Ned praised; his sing-song tone sounded stilted in the tense atmosphere.

Delia had purposely made herself late to lunch to avoid further conversation with her newest family member. Now she wished she had skipped the meal altogether. The wet noises of clam chowder consumption were only interrupted by alternating insults and praise for her mother's cooking.

With a petulant sigh, Dina set down her spoon. "This is as bad as the food on the mountain."

"Dina!" Nap finally snapped.

"What?" She gave him a look of wide-eyed innocence. "I was only kidding. Of course the food is fine." She laughed to herself. "Just cold. You should probably fire your cook."

"We don't *have* a cook." Nap glared at his bride, then pushed back from the table. "You're insufferable," he announced, then stalked out of the room, the shaking of his ragged wings adding weight to his words. A moment later, the front door slammed.

"Well, I am certainly looking forward to the end of *his* season. What was he like before? More like you, Ned?" Dina flashed a charming smile at her new father-in-law, who blushed and mumbled something unintelligible.

Delia's mother released an outraged laugh and leaned forward, bringing all eyes to her. "Nap was more like Delia, actually. Do you get along well with her?"

"Hmm." Dina made a sound that was part laugh and part song.

Delia shook her head emphatically, surreptitiously scratching at her shoulder blade again.

Her mother, Lila, shifted on her stool, her wings falling open in lovely autumnal hues. "Perhaps you and Nap should live separately for now. Where is your home?"

Dina's polished smile slipped a moment, and her lip twitched when she pasted it back on. "Lila, you sound just like Nap! No, I won't be going home. This is my home now, and my husband will remain *with me*."

Lila pushed her plate aside and folded her hands together. Delia stilled; she knew that move— her mother always assumed it when announcing a punishment.

"My son has married you, and he will spend the rest of his life supporting you, but I will *not* sit by and watch you abuse him under my own roof." Ned tried to interrupt, but Lila merely held up a hand to stop him. "Nor will you abuse any member of my family."

"Abuse?" Dina's smile widened with her delusory laugh.

"When you rip my son's wings apart, especially *while* he is flying, you *abuse* him. You could have *killed* him."

"Well," Dina began with a patronizing smile, "that's not really what happened."

"Delia." The force with which her mother said her name made Delia jump in her seat, her itchy back momentarily forgotten. "What did you see?"

"Uh...she was yelling and swearing at Nap while they were flying over the meadow. Then she reached out and grabbed his forewing with both hands and tore it nearly in half just as they reached the trees," Delia pantomimed as she spoke, the horror of watching her brother fall making her voice break. "Then he fell out of the sky."

"Which is just how Nap explained it to me. Unless you can provide me with a *fantastic* explanation as to why you would do such a thing, you *may not* live here."

Delia's father tried to speak again, but her mother gave him a quelling look, and he sat back in his seat, his lime green wings drooping.

"Fine. You can buy us a lovely beach house, and we'll live there."

This time Lila barked a mirthless laugh before answering. "We can't afford that, and my son does *not* want to live with you."

Dina's bottom lip trembled, but her eyes remained dry. "He *can't* leave me; he married me."

"Oh *yes*, he most certainly *can*."

Delia started at the force of her mother's words. Oddly, "most certainly" was the scariest phrase in her mother's vocabulary, and each word was spoken with an intensity that cowed even the boldest.

"But, I'm pregnant." Dina spoke to her bowl now, and despite her complaints, it was empty.

Delia's eye's grew wide, but her mother looked unperturbed.

"My son made me aware of your situation. We will pay for your return to your family."

Dina's head shot up, her face full of fury and fear. "But they're *your* grandchildren!"

"No, they are not," Lila replied.

Delia gasped, staring first at her mother, then Dina; neither woman would meet her gaze. The two seemed locked in a battle of wills that required steady eye contact.

"You will leave in the morning." Lila's tone was final as she stood and began gathering dishes.

Dina looked at her new father-in-law for support, but he merely mumbled and looked at his hands.

"Wait," she commanded, then softened her tone. "Wait." When everyone looked at her expectantly, her eyes fell back to her empty bowl. "I can't go home," she mumbled.

"Why is that?" Each of her mother's words snapped like fire consuming sap as she set down the dishes she was carrying.

Dina shifted in her seat, then glanced around the table with a false laugh. "That's a little nosy, don't you think?"

Ned made a startled noise while her mother breathed out an angry sigh and took a moment to consider her words before speaking.

Delia couldn't resist anymore. The words bubbled up her throat like a bath running over. "Everyone will—" she began, but stopped when her mother held up a quelling hand.

"I haven't insulted anyone. I'm merely pointing out the obvious." Dina tossed her chocolate-brown locks against the brilliant pink of her upper wings. "*Someone* needs to be a little less sensitive," Dina sang in an undertone.

Delia laughed unpleasantly, "Everyone will abandon—" she got out before Lila covered Delia's mouth with her hand.

"Dina, you have exactly one more minute to provide sufficient reason why we shouldn't send you home." Lila slid the hand covering Delia's mouth to her shoulder and gave it a warning squeeze.

Dina frowned, her dark eyes flashing. "You can't just ask me that. You barely know me."

"50 seconds."

"You have no right to treat me this way!"

"45 seconds."

"Where is Nap? He won't stand for this treatment of his wife!" Dina stood, dramatically knocking over her stool with a well-aimed kick.

"40 seconds."

Dina's eyes abruptly filled with tears. "How can you be so horrible to a pregnant woman?"

"35 seconds."

"Nap!" Dina called, running to the front door, then calling for him from the front yard.

"That's decided, then. Help me with the dishes," Lila requested, releasing Delia's shoulder.

"Well," Ned hummed. "That was pretty interesting. Hmm. Thanks for lunch," he added, then picked up the bag of roots Delia had set next to his chair and headed back to his apothecary shop in town.

"How could he have married *her*?" Delia demanded, collecting the dishes roughly. "You should have let me truth-bomb her."

"Oh? And what would you have said?"

"That everyone is going to abandon her and she'll be alone, with no one to care for her, because no sense of obligation is strong enough to make anyone endure her." It was a relief to finally say the words, but now that they were out, Delia's self-righteous satisfaction transformed into guilt.

"Oh, Delia, how could you say such a thing?"

"I didn't!"

"You would have."

Delia frowned and scrubbed at the dishes more vigorously than was needed. "She's an awful person."

"You just met her."

"Did you not *see* Nap's wing?!"

"Of course I did. And I'm very upset with her behavior, but we have no way of knowing if she's like this all the time."

Delia scowled at her mother's wisdom and sped up her scrubbing so she could get back outside. Ocean breezes combined with digging in the dirt always calmed her ire. Her father had taught her about the local plants, and how and when to harvest them. It was her job to replenish the family's apothecary shop when plant ingredients ran low. Since school had gone on summer hiatus two weeks ago, Delia had been out foraging nearly every day. It was easier not to miss her three siblings—Chloe, Nap, and Pearl—and her best friend, Coli, when she spent her time tromping through meadows and forests in search of flora. Coli's wing birth had been a month ago, and Delia missed her sorely. Her sunny nature and easy laugh were always infectious; life just seemed more pleasant with Coli around—as long as her brothers weren't there, too. Ora and Talis were as unpleasant as Coli was charming.

Delia sighed and handed Lila the final dish to dry. "I'm going to go dig up some dandelion root for Dad."

"Why don't you stay here and help me make Nap's room nice for Dina?"

Delia gave her flea bites a quick and vicious scratch while her mother's back was turned. "I thought you were kicking her out?"

"She will probably need to stay here at least one night before we can send her back to her family."

Delia grimaced. "I really don't want to."

"Neither do I, but we're going to."

Delia spent half the afternoon helping her mother clean and reorganize Nap's room, move Chloe's furniture in, change the linens, and make the room more feminine and welcoming. Delia hated it, but a few sharp looks from her mother had stopped her grumbling. When they finally finished, Lila sent her daughter out to the garden to cut fresh flowers for Dina and harvest vegetables for dinner. With a smirk, Delia chose chamomile for the former; she had just finished arranging them atop Nap's dresser when Dina walked in.

"What are you doing in here?"

Biting back a rude retort, Delia stepped aside and pointed to the flowers.

"What a charming weed."

Delia bristled, but took a calming breath of chamomile-scented air before speaking. "They're chamomile."

"Looks like scrawny cheap daisies to me. I don't want them."

Delia's mouth fell open in a shocked laugh. She had simply never known anyone so awful before. Coli's brothers were easily angered and full of rotten pranks, but they were never so perfectly spiteful and demanding as Dina. Shaking her head, Delia retrieved the flowers and left.

"Close the door behind you," Dina commanded.

Delia left it open.

Chapter Three

"Dina is staying," Nap announced. His heavily damaged wings twitched as he stood at the foot of the table, but his posture was rigid.

Delia stopped with her spoon midway to her mouth and stared.

"I thought we had already decided," Lila chided, generously slathering her homemade bread with honey.

"No." Nap gave a mulish shake of his head, then irritably flipped his platinum bangs out of his eyes.

"So what has changed your mind?" Lila asked, her piercing green eyes meeting his until he looked away, his complexion suddenly florid.

"Is Dad working late?" he asked instead of answering the question.

Lila sighed and gave her son a knowing smile. "Yes, he is."

Delia's eyebrows rose as she shifted in her chair. Her father often worked late when her mother was upset.

"Did she at least give you a good explanation for her behavior?" Lila demanded.

Nap nodded, still blushing furiously.

"Well? What is it?" Lila prompted.

Nap cleared his throat, some of his heightened color fading. "Dina would like me to keep that confidential."

"No," Lila answered simply.

Nap shifted again. The sunlight streaming through the windows highlighted the punctures and tears in his pale green wings. "Dina says," he began, but his mother cut him off.

"No. If she would like to remain here, I require an explanation."

"But I..." he began.

"Nap, you are welcome to live here always. Your wife mistreats us all verbally and brutalized you. She is not welcome here unless she explains herself."

Nap frowned. "She doesn't want to."

"Then *you* will or you'll have to find someplace else for your bride to live."

"Mom," he complained, his cadence almost a whine.

Delia smirked. It was lovely to see evidence that her brother's personality was still alive inside his grumpy shell. Before his season began a month ago, Nap had been a whiner. Even now his irritated face looked more sulky than forbidding. *Maybe his season is ending*, she thought, surreptitiously using her fork to scratch her back.

"Oh, I'm very serious," Lila warned, and both siblings tensed. Their mother never backed down after those words were spoken.

Nap growled and sat down in his usual place across from Delia. Instead of explaining, he piled his plate high with food. He managed to shovel an enormous bite past his sunburnt lips before his mother could speak again.

"Well?"

Nap chewed while they stared at him, Lila in impatience and Delia in amusement. When he finally swallowed, he reached for his glass of juice.

"*Now*, please," Lila insisted, the please merely ornamental in her command.

Nap cleared his throat and glanced around the room as if he expected to find his wife hiding behind a plant. "Dina's father kicked her and her pupa sister out at Dina's wing birth," he whispered.

"Why?" Delia asked, perplexed.

"Dina's wings made it clear she wasn't his daughter."

"What did her mother have to say?" Lila asked.

"She drowned when Dina and her twin were only three."

"Ohhhh," Delia intoned, suddenly feeling pity for her unpleasant sister-in-law.

"After talking their way into free passage on a cargo ship, Dina traveled to the base of the Mating Mountain on foot so her twin Ria could stay with her. They sold most of their belongings to pay for food and board until Ria finally got her wings a couple of weeks later, and they flew up together." Nap took a few rapid bites and a gulp of juice before continuing. "They'd grown up wealthy, so Dina was looking for a mate that could provide that lifestyle. She found a nobleman, but he got her pregnant, then refused to marry her."

"And that's where you stepped in," Lila supplied.

Nap nodded and resumed his dinner.

"But why did she tear your wings?" Lila prompted.

Nap sighed and finished chewing. "We didn't get along well, so I suggested we live apart until my season was over. She didn't want to go home to her father—though she hadn't yet told me why—so I told her she could stay here and I would get a job as a crown agent. She objected, but I had made up my mind, and told her so. She knew I wouldn't be able to get the job with a damaged wing. So..." he trailed off, his involuntary shudder drawing unwanted attention to his tattered wings.

"Did she at least apologize?" Delia blurted.

Nap glared at her and returned to his meal.

Lila released a long sigh. "Can she behave better?"

Nap licked honey off his thumb as he considered the question. "I don't know."

Delia rolled her eyes and pushed back from the pine table.

Nap scowled at her, then turned back to Lila. "Dad and I talked this afternoon. He's going to help me buy the Checkerspots' field and build a house on it. That way I can still stay in town and work with Dad, and you and Dina will have a little distance."

"That will take all summer," Lila observed, frowning, "and cost a lot of money."

"I have some saved."

"And in the meantime?"

"She'll stay in my room." The blush crept back up Nap's cheeks until even his forehead burned.

"What? And never come out?" Delia teased, enjoying her brother's furious blushes.

"Oh, I forgot." Nap picked up Dina's empty plate and piled it high with food then hurried to his room.

"The food has gotten cold," Lila warned, but her only answer was a closing door. "Is he going to do that all summer?"

"I don't mind if it means Dina stays in there," Delia admitted.

"I do. This is getting ridiculous."

As if to illustrate his mother's words, Nap burst out of his room, sprinted to the table to retrieve his wife's glass, poured out water from an earthen carafe, then speed-walked back to his room without a word.

Delia's laugh rang out as soon as the door was closed, but Lila merely frowned.

"It's better this way," Delia argued, scratching at her shoulder blades again. "She avoids us and I don't say something awful to her...everyone's happy."

"If she isn't going to have any relationship with us while she *lives* here, just how much do you think we'll see of Nap after they move out?"

"Well, I'll still work with him," Ned mused, stepping up to the table.

Delia and Lila both jumped. Neither had heard him return from work.

"When did you get home?" Delia asked, sliding food dishes closer to her father as he sat down.

"Hmm, just now," he smiled. "This looks good."

Lila ignored the compliment and pushed her plate away. "How are we going to pay for the Checkerspots' field and a new house for Nap?"

"Oh, we'll figure something out," Ned said vaguely, smiling as he served himself.

"You know we can't afford it. You should have discussed it with me first." Lila angrily tossed her napkin aside and stood up to clear the dishes.

"Mmm, this is so good," Ned praised. "Did Nap and Dina already eat?"

"They're eating in his room," Delia answered as her mother let her plate clatter noisily in the kitchen sink.

"Oh, hmm." Ned smiled conspiratorially at her. "Maybe I should go eat in there, too."

"Don't you dare!" Lila fumed, coming back to the table for another load. "This family will eat our meals together while we're still under the same roof," Lila announced, giving Nap's door a dark look.

Ned pointed his fork at the food in front of him. "This is a really nice meal."

Delia watched her mother's lips twitch and decided it was time to intervene. "Well, I probably won't be under this roof much longer," she blurted, then forced a casual shrug under her mother's baleful gaze. "Clearly my wings are going to burst out any minute." Delia twisted to look at her back as if she expected some sudden change.

Lila shook her head, but her mouth softened.

"Just checking." Delia whipped her head around as if she might see wings there if only she were fast enough. "Whoa, I thought I saw some wing peeping out for a second. False alarm."

Lila rolled her eyes, but chuckled.

Delia and her father exchanged a smile and returned to their meal. Though Delia was the second born of her quadruplet siblings, she was the only one still in her wingless pupa state. It might have worried her if she were not also the smallest child. Delia was petite like their mother, whereas Nap, Pearl, and Chloe took after their father in both size and coloring. Pearl and Chloe had matured within an hour of each other and flown to the Mating Mountain two months ago. Chloe was now married and expecting, but Pearl was still at the Old Castle looking for a mate. Delia missed her sisters—not the irritable malcontents they had become with their wing births, but the girls they had been before their hormones

17

altered them. Chloe's letters had turned kind and thoughtful again with her pregnancy, but Pearl's infrequent missives were still bitter and resentful. Delia frowned as she remembered the last one and gave her back a zealous scratching.

"Delia, you're bleeding." Lila seized her daughter's hand, examining her bloody fingers and nails for injury.

Delia touched the bare skin of her back with her other hand, gingerly feeling the dampness. "I think I made my back bleed. Stupid flea bites."

Lila got up and lifted the back of Delia's shirt. "I thought you were joking! But your wings really are coming!"

"What?! I *was* joking. They're not flea bites?"

"No."

"And my wings are coming right now?!"

Ned got up to look as well. "Well...hmm...I'd say within the next day or so."

"Yes!" Delia leapt up and ran to her room to haul a bag out of her closet. When her sisters had matured two months ago, they had behaved so badly out shopping that Lila had sworn that was the last time she was shopping with an in-season child. A week later, she had taken both Nap and Delia shopping for all their winged clothes and migration supplies. The two siblings had been embarrassed to be shopping without wings, but their mother insisted. She said if they outgrew them, she would simply go exchange the sizes without them. Nap hadn't needed to, and Lila was still congratulating herself for her foresight. Now Delia laid out all her winged clothes with a grin.

"Don't try them on now," her mother cautioned from the doorway. "You're still bleeding and blood is miserable to get out."

"But what if they don't fit anymore?"

Lila lifted the back of her daughter's shirt again. "We could bandage them."

"Will that hurt my wings?"

18

"If you're still wearing the bandage when they burst? Probably."

Delia frowned, then held one of the tops against her, pressing it to her sides to test the fit. "A little tight, but not too bad." She tossed the top aside and ran to the mirror, removed her shirt, and tried to examine her back over her shoulder. "Eww!" Where Delia had been scratching, the skin was red and torn, oozing bloody fluid. She quickly pulled her shirt back on with a little shudder, noting the stains dotting the back of it.

"Don't scratch anymore," Lila warned.

"Of course I'm not going to!" Delia snapped, her eyes going wide as she heard herself. "Sorry, that was rude." Delia nibbled her lip and poked a toe at the homemade rug on the floor. "Does that mean it's starting?"

Lila sighed. "I think so."

Delia looked up at the sorrow in her mother's voice. Lila's eyes shone with unshed tears as she wordlessly held out her arms for a hug, and her daughter quickly filled them.

"It'll be okay," Lila soothed, clutching her daughter tightly. "You know who you are. You are a *good* person. You love helping people, and you have a delightful sense of humor. Just hold onto that. Remember, if you can't behave the way you want to, make it up to whomever you hurt as best you can, ask God to forgive you, and forgive yourself. This is only temporary. You can stand anything for a short time."

"I don't want to be cruel," Delia mumbled into her mother's shoulder. "I'm afraid I'm going to be."

"You probably will be," Lila admitted, pulling back. "Your sister Chloe is one of the nicest people you and I have ever known, but she screeched at all of us after her wing birth, and even threw a plate at Nap. I'm not going to pretend I understand what it's like to be a white, but I am confident that you can get through it. Just . . ." Lila stopped to peer out into the hallway, then stepped back in and shut the door behind her. "Just kiss as many guys as you can."

"What?" Delia laughed. "Are you serious?"

"Shh...yes. I did, and I'm not sorry. I wish I would have kissed more."

"Mother!" Delia chortled.

"Kissing is fun, and you might end up married to a man who doesn't even like it. Your father hates kissing."

Delia blushed in the midst of her laughter. "This seems like really bad advice."

Lila laughed merrily. "Maybe," she conceded, "but I did make you laugh. And if you're still laughing, you're not in season yet. And since you're not, let's get the serious discussion out of the way." Lila pulled out a little polka-dotted stool and sat.

"Uh-oh, that sounds ominous," Delia said, her smile abruptly disappearing. She quickly gathered up her winged clothes and stuffed them back in her new bag.

"Oh hush, it isn't." Lila hesitated and lowered her voice even more. "Don't marry a white."

"What? Why?" Delia asked, sitting so heavily the bed creaked.

"It's not what you think. I'm not going to warn you that they're dangerous, though they can be...*anyone* can be. Or that it will be so hard for your children, though you're about to discover that for yourself. It's just that you can't know their personality or if you're compatible."

"Are you saying you and Dad aren't compatible?" Delia's forehead creased with worry and she unconsciously held her breath.

Lila cleared her throat and kneaded her hands. "We're okay," she said, looking at the rug.

"What does *that* mean?!" Delia fairly shouted.

"Shh. It's just that when your father was in season, we got along really well. He was so opinionated and spoke his mind forcefully. If I yelled, he yelled. And we worked it out."

Delia shook her head in bemusement. Her father quietly made his own decisions, but he never raised his voice to his wife or truly argued with her. Most of his conversation was deferential mumbling.

"His season ended two months after I married him." Lila took a deep breath and slowly let it out. "It was a hard adjustment for me."

"Wait. Are you saying you don't love him?" Delia's volume unconsciously increased with her growing alarm until her head seemed to ache with it.

"Shh! Of course I do. You can learn to love anyone with time. I just had to start over when his season ended. He's not the man I fell in love with."

Delia sat further back on the bed, letting her head lightly thunk against the wall. "So you're saying you liked Dad better when he was *mean*?" She absently began to massage her temples, trying to make the sudden pain go away.

Lila wrung her hands searching for words. "He wasn't truly mean. Can you even imagine your Dad mean?"

Delia shook her head, then immediately regretted the movement as her headache intensified.

"He was just assertive and outspoken."A faint smile flitted across her mother's mouth, then disappeared. "So if you find a white you like, understand that his personality will disappear with his season." Lila hesitated, her lips twitching with unspoken words.

Delia frowned. "Somewhere, my future husband is probably hearing this exact same lecture from his parents. I'm doomed."

"You're not doomed! You're pretty and men are very visual. In the beginning, appearance usually matters more to them than personality."

"That seems insulting."

"You know I think you're wonderful," Lila reminded her, "but the hormones are going to change you."

"Excellent pep talk!" Delia quipped, eager to escape the conversation. Her shoulder blades still begged to be scratched and her temples throbbed in time with her heart. Holding her head like a fragile thing, she gently laid down on her pillow. "Can we be done now? I don't feel very good."

"Headache?"

Delia meant to nod, but the movement increased the pain, and she merely whimpered.

"That's how *my* wing birth started. Let's get you on your stomach."

Delia allowed herself to be moved, then felt the bed being pulled away from the wall as her mother grunted with the effort. Then Lila's perpetually cold hands gingerly touched her itchy back. It was soothing, like letting ocean waves lap over your feet. And then the pain was blinding. Delia could hear her own screams like they were a living thing leaping into the room without her permission. She had the sudden illogical urge to get up and run as if the agony were something she could escape. Delia could vaguely hear her mother's voice, but the words seemed irrelevant.

"Shh. Don't scream, it's not that bad. Everyone goes through it." Lila had to yell to be heard over her daughter's shrieks. Ned, Nap, and even Dina rushed to the room and hovered, useless and fascinated as Delia's back broke open. Orange tissue emerged, bathed in the pink fluid that drained out around it.

"Towels!" Lila shouted twice before Nap recovered enough to obey.

When the pain subsided enough for Delia to open her eyes, she saw Dina standing in the doorway to her room with a troubled expression on her face.

"Are you adopted?" Dina asked.

"No," Lila answered for her.

"She doesn't really look like any of you, and those wings . . ."

Delia wanted to look, but she was too exhausted to lift her head. The pain had stopped, but it had robbed her of all her strength. Rather than participate in the conversation, she simply closed her eyes.

"She looks like her grandparents," Lila snapped, still watching Delia's wings unfold. "And she's petite like I am. This is ridiculous. I remember when she was born; of course she's mine." Lila watched Dina turn to Ned, a question on her lips. "And *his*, too," Lila asserted before Dina could ask.

Everyone was quiet while Delia's wings continued to unfold and expand. The vivid yellow and orange veined with black seemed to belie Lila's protests. All three stood unnaturally still, until Dina clutched her stomach and ran from the room. Nap glanced after his wife, then back at his sister's wings. Reluctantly, he drifted after Dina.

"Hmm, well, they're very pretty," Ned declared, then wandered away.

Lila smoothed back her daughter's damp locks. "Just sleep, sweetheart. Get your strength back," she whispered.

Delia meant to nod, but sleep captured her before her neck muscles could comply.

Chapter Four

Delia woke in a fury. Her entire body trembled with rage as she lifted up from her soiled bed. Her shirt was bunched above her exposed stomach, and she gave the offending clothing a futile yank, then furiously tore it off when she realized it was caught above her wings. The alarming sound of ripping fabric did nothing to deter her, and she flung the torn remains, growling when they hit her mirror and left a damp smudge. She marched up to her besmirched reflection and examined her new anatomy. There was some white on her upper wings, but it was heavily veined with black and smeared with golden color. She turned and looked awkwardly behind her. *There* was the white. When she opened her wings—which felt wonderfully odd—she could see the meandering pattern of dark veins outlining starkly white panels. They looked like a children's coloring book picture just waiting for paint. She closed her wings again and turned sideways. Dina was right; with just her underwings showing, she didn't look like a white. The thought of Dina had her fisting both hands and gritting her teeth. Her wrath even felt justified as she enumerated Dina's infractions. A wicked truth bomb formed in her mind and Delia stomped out the door to deliver it, then remembered she had torn off her shirt. Growling, she returned to her room and rummaged through her new bag. Much of the clothing had been chosen to complement the white and pastel wings of her father and siblings. And every pair of her pants were some earth-matching shade of brown. Delia glared at her black-rimmed wings with their bright yellow and vivid orange. They were so completely unexpected—and beautiful. With her wings closed, she could pass for a sulphur. *Could be useful*, she thought, then yanked out a pale yellow top and was soon sweating and swearing trying to maneuver around her new anatomy. She had never had a foul mouth before, but suddenly the distasteful words were always in her head, marching their way into every thought and begging to escape her mouth. Delia pressed her lips together. *That's not who I am.* With the sleek, stretchy material finally in place, she vented her exasperation by flinging everything else from her bag. Her room now looked as if a small hurricane had hit it. Sighing, she retrieved the store bag and filled it with all the unsuitably colored new clothes she had flung. She repacked her travel bag with the remainder. Then she threw her door open and went tromping through the house to raid the kitchen. Though it wasn't yet midnight, her rumbling stomach demanded food. She slammed cabinets, banged pans, and clattered dishes as she cooked, relishing the disruptive sound.

"Hey, keep it down," Nap groused, rubbing sleep from his eyes. "You'll wake everyone up."

"Don't care."

Nap's lips betrayed the slightest of smiles. "Even Dina?"

Rage vibrated through her again and she stilled, willing it to pass.

Nap made a noise halfway between a humph and a laugh as he pulled a bar stool up to the kitchen counter and sat.

"Not looking for company just now," Delia warned.

"Don't care," Nap imitated her, swiping a bit of bacon before she could smack his hand.

Delia gritted her teeth and glared at him, but he met her look with a satisfied smile.

"I *like* being around angry people," he admitted. "It makes me feel calmer."

"That's stupid."

Nap nodded, the smile persisting. "It is."

"That's why you like Dina?"

Nap didn't speak for a full minute, then glanced out toward his room before lowering his voice. "She was screaming and pounding on a door when I saw her. She called that aristocratic jerk that got her pregnant the foulest words I've ever heard. She looked mad enough to start tearing chunks out of his door with her teeth." He smiled and shook his head. "I have never been so attracted to any woman as I was at that moment."

"You're an idiot."

He nodded his agreement. "I kept creeping closer until I could smell her, make sure she was a pheromone match. When I caught the scent of spicy lilacs, I just walked right up and grabbed her arm before she could pound on his door again, and told her to marry me."

"That is the dumbest love story I have ever heard."

"You expect yours to be any better?" he demanded.

Delia shoved a plate of pancakes at him. "No," she growled. "Why did you want to leave her if you like her temper so much?"

"Because," he fairly shouted, then lowered his voice with a wary glance out into the darkened house. "Because mostly she *doesn't* yell. She says unpleasant things, but she *keeps* her temper. After she agreed to marry me, she didn't yell at me once until right before she tore my wing."

"And will you like her temper when your season ends?" she asked, slathering marionberry preserves on her pancakes.

He shrugged irritably. "I have no idea." He shoved an enormous bite of buttered pancakes into his mouth and chomped angrily.

Delia stared at her brother until he swallowed. "Doesn't it bother you that someone else got her pregnant?"

"You can't just ask that! It's invasive and rude."

"I don't care," Delia admitted, putting a dainty bite into her diminutive mouth.

"You will later."

"But I don't now. So just tell me."

Nap scowled. "I want kids."

"Not what I asked."

"But I don't want *white-winged* kids."

"Ah."

They ate in silence for several minutes, both irritated at the sound of the other's chewing. Delia grimaced and chewed louder only to be matched in sound and expression by her brother. Several minutes in, they sounded like barnyard animals enjoying a feast.

"Why are you making such horrible sounds? Don't you have any manners?" Dina asked, emerging from the darkness of the dining room with a delicate yawn.

"You should go back to sleep," Nap said around a colossal mouthful of food.

"Well, I would, but *somebody* is being a little too loud for that to be possible." Dina delivered her reproof with a charming smile and head tilt.

Delia concentrated on chewing while little tremors of fury ran up and down her arms and her grip on her fork tightened.

Swallowing, Nap frowned at his wife. "Go back to bed."

"No, I don't want to," Dina smiled, wiping food from the corners of his mouth with her thumb. "Besides, how will I get to know my new sister-in-law if we never talk? She is your personality twin, is she not?"

Delia turned away, packing her bag as quickly as possible.

"She's in season now, Dina. She's going to act just like I do."

"Surely not as fearsome as that. She's a *girl*, after all."

Delia bit at her lip to keep the words in as she finished stocking her bag and quickly left the room.

"Well, that was rude," Dina complained.

Delia could hear her brother hushing his wife, and the desire to truth-bomb Dina only intensified. Fighting the temptation, Delia grabbed the shopping bag from her room, then pounded on her parents' door.

"What is it?" Lila called sleepily.

"I'm leaving."

"Now? Can you fly?" All traces of sleep had left Lila's voice by the time she threw her door open.

Delia looked at the low ceilings and shrugged. "Don't know."

"Well, you should at least practice in the yard first, then have breakfast with the family."

"No. I ate."

Her mother's eyes filled with tears and she held out her arms. "I need a hug."

Delia cringed, but allowed it. She had never minded her mother's hugs before, but now being confined in someone's arms felt unbearably restricting and Delia had to fight the urge to shove her away. When her mother finally let go, she released the breath she hadn't realized she had been holding.

"What if it's windy?" Lila worried.

Delia listened carefully for a moment, but only managed to overhear Dina and Nap's latest argument. "It's not," she asserted, though she had no idea if that was true. Her father joined her mother in the doorway and handed Delia some money.

"It's not much," he apologized, giving her shoulder a brief squeeze.

"Thanks," Delia managed, tucking it away.

"I love you so much. Don't forget what I said," her mother urged, wiping at her eyes.

"We love you," Ned echoed in his soft tone. "It'll be okay," he added.

Delia tried to smile, but it was as if her mouth had forgotten how. "Love you too." Her words sounded forced, and her mother's face crumpled at the gruff tone. Turning away quickly, Delia strode from the house.

She could hear the roar of the ocean as a salty breeze pulled at her wings. She closed them tightly and trudged into the wind as it whistled around the darkened buildings of the seaside town. The Fritillarys' store wasn't far, and their home was attached to the back of it. The store was dark and closed, but she could still see light inside their living quarters. Delia pounded on the window that betrayed the insomniac within.

Mr. Fritillary's cross face appeared at the window a moment later. They exchanged glares for a moment, then he nodded toward the shop and walked away from the window. His shop was an eclectic combination of fishing gear and clothing. Mr. Fritillary's passion was the former, but the latter paid the bills. Since his wife was a hypochondriac, his bill at the Whites' apothecary shop was steep. Thus, whenever the family needed clothing, they shopped from the Fritillarys' store on trade.

Before Delia reached the shop door, Mr. Fritillary had flung it open. "Well, git in here before the wind breaks your wings!" he scolded. "I told your mother not to buy your winged clothes before your wing birth. I knew there'd be a problem. Are they too small now?"

"Wrong colors."

"What?"

Delia opened her wings to display their bright colors, then handed him the bag of pastel tops. Her mother had insisted they would look beautiful whether she sprouted pale green wings like her father's or white wings with pale gold markings like her sisters'. Delia glared at the predominately pink clothing as Mr. Fritillary took it out.

"Oh," he said, glancing back and forth from her wings to the tops. "Well, go ahead and pick some new ones, then." He shooed her away and began to inventory her returns, giving the white and black backside of her wings a double take as she passed.

Delia irritably sifted through her choices, occasionally holding out a wing to compare color. Mr. Fritillary's store was not large, and the selection was quickly exhausted. With a scowl, she gathered up the acceptable clothing and dumped it atop his open ledger.

"Serve you right if you just got fresh ink on your new clothes," he reproved with an exaggerated shake of his head.

Delia lifted the pile off the ledger and checked for stains. "They're fine," she growled, as he moved his bookkeeping out of the way.

"Because you can't return them stained, you know."

"I know!"

Mr. Fritillary jumped at her vehemence and dropped the red shirt he had been folding. "Still a white despite those colorful wings," he muttered, picking it up.

Delia bit her lips to keep the cruel retort in and yanked the half-filled bag from his grasp while scooping the remaining items off the counter. She was out the door before his next reproach could get beyond an angry recitation of her full name.

The cold wind that bit at her rosy cheeks did little to cool her inner fire. She marched up the dark street shoving her purchases into her travel bag and verbally skewering Mr. Fritillary under her breath. Her insults lasted all the way out of the little seaside town of Hamlet. The moon was bright in the sky, but the heavily forested mountains in front of her hid it. There was something about the way the moss-covered trees curved over the little country road that had always made Delia lower her voice, and their inky darkness stilled her muttering now. It seemed like a place of secrets, and most people quieted themselves to hear them. Delia listened now, pleased she could no longer hear the wind. She fanned her wings in time to her steps, using her wings to maintain her balance despite the rocks and weeds she stumbled over. The sound of a branch breaking in the forest sent her into the air before she realized what she had done. Not yet trusting her flying, she stayed just above the road though it wound through the coastal mountains in switchbacks. Outside the protective canopy of trees, the wind slowly stilled, and Delia began to practice her landings. The first couple brought her to her knees, but her pants already matched the color of the dirt and left no real evidence behind. Delia brushed at her knees with a grim smile. Years of fetching plants from the forest had taught her the importance of clothing that matched the soil. All her pants were practical shades of earth...until now. She had exchanged some of her pastel tops for black pants to match her wings. The thought bothered Delia a moment until she remembered the Mating Mountain was a volcano; wasn't volcanic soil black? A tight smile graced her lips. Delia attempted to broaden it and felt her upper lip thin and tighten.

"That must look attractive," she muttered sarcastically, an irritable frown absorbing the awkward smile. She rubbed her face with her hands, hoping the quick massage would restore her face to its normal expression, then felt it settle back into its sour lines. "Great!" she shouted. "Now I'm foul-tempered *and* ugly!" Delia took out her frustration in furious wingstrokes all the way up to the forest canopy, then through an opening. She was immediately sorry. It was impossible to see the road through the trees, and the coastal mountains still blocked her moonlit view of the Mating Mountain. Retracing her flight, she once again found the break in the trees and flew back down to the

31

road. For the next few hours, she alternated flying and walking to rest whatever hurt the most. The still nighttime air of late spring warmed as Delia traveled inland, and she was soon overheated. She twisted her wavy locks into a messy bun and mopped the perspiration from her face with her sleeve. Her tan skin was suffused with an uncomfortable red that she was grateful the darkness hid. The permanent glacier atop the Mating Mountain now glinted in the moonlight. Renewed by having her goal within view, she ignored her back muscles that screamed at her to stop. Instead, she guzzled water from her canteen and ate cold pancakes from her bag while she flew.

She hadn't meant to stop in the little town at the western base of the mountain, but the pancakes had made her thirsty and her water was soon gone. Despite it being the middle of the night, Firwood still had an open store and hotel for its in-season customers. Delia landed next to a public well spigot and filled her canteen, then immediately guzzled a third of it, letting a liberal amount spill down the front of her. The water was cold and sweet, and she wished she was bathing in it. She looked down at the spigot as she refilled her canteen and wondered how she could get her head underneath the spout without bending her wings.

"Thirsty?" The question was followed by a forced guffaw.

Delia turned toward the voice, her nose wrinkling up at the stench of rotting meat. A tall, lanky young man with spiky hair approached her, the artificial light from the shops backlighting his hair like a halo.

"Hi," he said, lifting his eyebrows and fanning his wings in syncopation.

"Never do that again. It's creepy," Delia advised, sniffing. "Are you carrying dragonwort or old meat?"

"What's dragonwort?" He stopped fanning his brown wings, but his eyebrows still danced on his forehead, punctuating his words.

"A poisonous plant that smells like dead things when it blooms." She turned away from him dismissively and refilled her canteen.

"Why would I be carrying that?" he asked, bemused.

"I don't know. You're superstitious and fear snakes?" Delia asked as she attached her canteen to her bag.

He shook his head in confusion. "That doesn't make any sense."

"Never mind." She took a few running steps away from him before launching into the air.

"Hey," he called, quickly joining her. "I was talking to you."

Delia gritted her teeth and increased her speed, but he still flew circles around her, his large wings backed in a lovely seafoam green.

"Why did you think I was afraid of snakes? I'm not. I'm not afraid of anything."

Delia rolled her eyes. "Some people think dragonwort wards off snakes."

"And why did you think I had some?"

She turned to glare at him, tempted to bare her teeth like a territorial dog. "Because you reek of it!"

He looked momentarily abashed, but then resumed circling. "Dragonwort smells bad to you?"

"It smells bad to everyone. It's also known as the *stink* lily."

"Why do you know so much about plants?"

"My dad's an apothecary. I find medicinal plants for him." *Now go away*, Delia thought.

"Why are you so grumpy?"

Delia's little hands tightened into fists and she let out a breath through clenched teeth instead of answering him.

"Seriously. Is there something the matter with you? Or do you just hate me?"

"I'm a white, you moth brain," she snapped. "Now go away before I hurt you."

He threw back his head and laughed. "I'm twice your size! You *can't* hurt me."

"Let's find out." Delia flew at him, and he deftly winged out of her way chortling.

"You are so angry! Are you always like this?"

"No!" she shouted, darting at him again only to be foiled by his speed. "Don't you know about whites? We get crazy mean during our season!"

"Really?" The information surprised him enough that she momentarily caught up to him and grasped a handful of shirt before he twisted away.

The horrible dragonwort smell seemed to be everywhere, and Delia clutched her nose and mouth with both hands, then flung the hand that had touched him as far from her nose as possible.

His grin faded as he noticed her response. "You really don't like it?"

"You really have to ask?!"

"Hm, guess we're not compatible." His voice was laced with genuine regret.

"What are you talking about?" she demanded irritably.

"My pheromone scent. What are *you* talking about?"

Delia dropped her other hand in surprise. "*That's* your pheromone scent?" She could still catch traces of the unpleasant odor, but it was quickly fading.

He shrugged.

"That's only allowed on the mountain," she scolded.

"Look down," he pointed. "We *are* on the mountain."

Delia shook her head. "We just barely left Firwood. You violated the display laws."

He looked around at the empty air space. "Who cares?! Nobody's around."

"I care! It was *annoying*."

"Well, sorry for being interested!"

Delia spoke through clenched teeth. "You can be interested without *torturing* me with your pheromones!"

"How would *you* know?! It could be involuntary!"

"I doubt it is."

"It was the first time!" he admitted, then beat his wings with such force that it blew back the wavy tendrils of hair that had escaped Delia's bun.

His sudden burst of speed rapidly increased the distance between them. Delia watched him go with relief, then regret. She replayed their conversation in her head, chastising herself for her rudeness and vowing to apologize when she had the chance. Fortunately, his seafoam wings were visible in the moonlight. Pushing herself, she kept him in sight, not just to apologize, but because he seemed to know the way. The large mountain loomed in front of her, and her directions—just below the tree line on the northeast side—were beginning to seem inadequate. She followed him for hours, the exertion making sweat run into her eyes until she closed them for a long blink. When she opened them again, he was gone. She searched the tree line for any sign of the Old Castle. Nothing. Spewing colorful language, she neared the treetops, looking for an opening or a trail he might have landed on. Sweat streamed into her eyes and her back muscles screamed with each wing beat, but she persevered. When the trees continued solidly beneath her, she shrieked her frustration.

"What's the matter?"

Delia followed the voice to an opening she hadn't noticed and landed in mud.

"Why are you following me?" he asked, his voice genuinely curious. "Did you change your mind?"

"No, *Dragonwort*, I haven't."

"It's Bul Leafwing," he retorted. "Why are you following me?"

"Because I *assumed* you were going to the Old Castle," Delia snapped. "Was I wrong?"

He mumbled something as he started up the path.

Delia swallowed down her fresh irritation and followed him. "And I'm sorry." She had meant to sound meek and repentant when she apologized, but it came out as more of a challenge.

Bul turned to stare at her. "What is your *problem*?"

"I already told you. I'm a *white*, and I'm *trying* to be nice to you." She finished the sentence speaking through her teeth.

He snorted out a laugh. "You're terrible at it."

"Well, I'll stop trying, then. Would you like my brutally honest opinion of your hair or your flirting first?"

"Ha. No, thanks," he said as he resumed his steps. "You just shouldn't talk...at all," he advised. "You smell nice, and you look . . ." he glanced back at her and revised his statement. "Well, your hair's kind of a mess, but you looked decent in Firwood."

"Thank you for your unsolicited advice," she seethed, self-consciously yanking her hair from its battered bun. She freed her brush from her tightly packed bag and viciously yanked it through her tangled, sweat-soaked hair. Next she dumped the last dregs of her canteen into the palm of her hand and rubbed her wet, salty face. Her entire head seemed to pulse with each heartbeat and she longed to wade into the chilly ocean waves at home. Distracted, she didn't notice he had turned to watch her and she walked into his chest.

"What are you doing? Get away from me." She shoved him, annoyed when he barely moved. The trail had widened to admit more moonlight and she could see the grin on his face.

"Now *that* is a scary expression," Bul commented, walking backwards while he appraised her.

"No one asked you!"

"And that one is scarier. You really need to practice a neutral expression."

"And you need to shut your mouth!" Delia pressed her nails into the palms of her hands, fighting the urge to attack him again.

He cackled, then tripped over a root and fanned his wings to avoid a fall. Delia's face lit with a malicious smile, her hands relaxing as he fluttered and finally regained his footing.

"And that one just makes you look psychotic," he said, pointing at her face.

"Maybe I am," she snapped, flying over his head.

"Are you?" he asked, flying after her. "I mean, what are you like when you're not all..." he hesitated, searching for the right word, "...hormonal?"

"What do you care?" she shot back at him.

"You are the prickliest person I have ever met. And since I don't know your name, I think I'll call you Thistle. Thistle White."

"It's Delia!" she growled.

"No, I think I like Thistle better; it suits you."

She spun around in the air and punched him in the chest before he could move away. "Delia, Delia, Delia," she shouted, punctuating each repetition with an additional punch.

Bul's surprised laughter quickly carried him into hysteria, forcing him to land. He bent over, hands on his thighs, laughing until tears streamed from his eyes. "It's like being attacked by a duckling," he chortled, wiping his eyes. His laughter renewed when he saw her face.

Delia stood in front of him, hands on hips, waiting for Bul to stand up straight so she could punch him again. Her fists ached from the last volley, but the violence had been satisfying, and his reaction assuaged her guilt. When he leaned forward with a fresh peal of laughter, she let out an exasperated huff and left him behind. Her anger fueled her march until her feet reminded her she had already walked plenty today. Grimacing, she changed her pace to a mincing walk that favored her blisters. She glared down at her new lightweight shoes that had turned out to be horrific for walking. Delia considered ripping them off her sweaty feet and flinging them at Bul's head. She could still hear his stupid laugh. His long legs were making short work of the distance between them. With a pained grunt, she flew again; though her back was in agony, it was still faster than traveling on foot.

"See you at the castle, then," Bul called in farewell.

"Hopefully not," Delia muttered. She flew in the direction Bul had been going, hoping she was aiming for the castle. The tree line was beneath her as she skirted the mountain. Icy breezes from the permanent glacier atop the volcano chilled her overheated body. By the time she spotted ghostly pale stonework jutting out from the mountainside in the predawn moonlight, goosebumps lined her uncovered arms. The forest abruptly stopped to make way for a stone-paved courtyard dotted with empty tables and chairs. Bul strode between them singing a song Delia had never heard before. When he turned to scan the starry sky, she ducked behind a douglas fir, then flew along the treetops hoping he couldn't see her.

"Where did you go?" Bul called. He had stopped at the massive entrance doors. "I don't think you can open this." He grunted and dragged one door open. "It's really heavy. Come on. I'll let you hit me again."

Delia gritted her teeth, but stayed silent.

"Fine!" Before Delia could change her mind, Bul went inside and pulled the heavy door shut behind him.

Already regretting her obstinance, Delia flew to the door and tried it. It didn't move. She tried again, her toned arms straining. No movement. Delia kicked the door, then hopped around in a rage holding her injured foot. She could hear laughter, but it wasn't coming from inside the castle. Her wounded foot forgotten in a new flush of rage, she flew toward the sound of mirth. Where the courtyard clearing met forest, she stopped and tipped her head to listen. Hesitantly, she began to pick through the undergrowth for a trail. She was certain the laughter had come from this spot, but the trail wasn't forthcoming. She heard a muttered oath, and moved toward the sound.

"Nice work, Delia. Now the guard knows I'm here."

Delia jumped, then flew just as someone stepped out of the shadows and grabbed her waist.

"Don't fly here! See these branches? You'll tear your wings."

Delia beat at the shadowed figure until he released her.

"It's Ora! Don't you recognize my voice? Calm down!" he whispered urgently.

Delia landed awkwardly, Ora's hand steadying her until she shook it off. "Ora?" She peered at him, but was able to discern no more than his close-cropped curls. "Where's Coli?"

"Asleep."

Delia shifted her weight, suddenly feeling foolish. "What are you doing out here?"

"Shh! I'm getting revenge."

"For what?"

Ora stepped closer and pointed up at the castle. "See that balcony with the guard?"

Delia followed the line of his arm, her cheek grazing his wiry muscles as she strained to see where he pointed. Three stories up, the shadow on the balcony was the wrong shape, then it moved.

"He's guarding the woman that stole Coli's boyfriend and broke Talis' wing." Ora's voice was filled with venom as he whispered the words.

"What?!"

"Shh! Now she claims she's *Princess Lexi* and she took over as governor so she won't have to do dungeon time for breaking Talis' wing."

"And the old governor just let her?"

Ora nodded. "She must have blackmailed him or something."

"Are Coli and Talis okay?"

"No. Talis has been here too long; his wing can't heal before his season ends. That arrogant wench turned him into a life servant!" Despite his venomous fury, Ora's voice broke on the word *servant*. Everyone feared losing their ability to fly before they could leave the mountain; the sheer cliffs virtually guaranteed a crippling fall, and even if you survived, a lengthy prison term was often your reward. Lifelong service on the Mating Mountain was legally required of those unfortunate enough to have their season end while still at the Old Castle.

Delia pitied Talis, but she knew him too well to believe he was an innocent victim. And she was sufficiently familiar with Ora's love of exaggeration to believe Talis' life servitude was certain. "But Coli's okay?"

"Of course not! She was in love with that cheating scum, *Tiger!*" he spat the name out derisively, then shook his head. "He met Coli for dinner reeking of some other girl, and when Talis called him out for it, the fake princess—and source of the stench— showed up and broke Talis' wing."

Though Talis' broken wing was upsetting, it was Coli's hurt that enraged Delia. "So what are you going to *do* about it?"

"Exactly what the so-called *princess* deserves: I'm going to break *her* wing."

Delia found herself nodding beside him, her seething anger making his plan seem reasonable. "How?"

"First, I have to get rid of that guard." Ora held up a bag and pulled something out. "Now that you're here, you can help." He placed a rough stone in her hand that covered her entire palm. "I know from playing horseshoes with you that you have rotten aim, but it doesn't matter. Just get him to chase you out here so I can get in the door."

"I do *not* have bad aim," Delia argued irritably. "But I'm not a very fast flyer yet; what if he catches me?"

"He can't fly at all. He's a life servant. When he chases after you, he has to go inside, walk down two flights of stairs, then come out the front door. You'll be long gone."

"And if he sees me?"

Ora shook his head dismissively. "Too dark. Just throw from here."

"But..."

"Don't be a coward! Coli's been crying herself to sleep and Talis is going to be a slave. You really want this haughty minx to get away with it?"

Delia's jaw set. "I'll need another rock."

Ora handed her two. "Don't start throwing until I do," he warned as he crept away.

"Where are you going?" Delia hissed.

"To get closer." Ora leapt into the air as soon as he left the trees, his yellow wings looking white in the moonlight.

Delia's grip tightened around the stones until her fingers began to ache. She couldn't see Ora anymore. How would she know when he started throwing? She glanced up at the shadowy guard and lifted her arm. She didn't want to hit him. He was just some poor life servant doing his job. And what if she hit Ora on accident? Or worse, his wing? She heard a resounding thunk, and the guard clutched his forehead. That was the signal, but Delia lowered her arm instead. The irrational anger that had spurred her on was quickly dissipating. The guard cried out in pain as another rocky missile found its target, and Delia dropped the rocks.

"You!? Of course you're protecting your tramp!" Ora called angrily. He was wrestling with a larger man in the air above the courtyard. The other man forced him to land, but Ora continued to fight. "You thought you could just cheat on my sister without paying for it? I'm going to break your wings and then your girlfriend's, too!"

"Ora, stop!" the other man shouted, subduing Ora with a heavy crack to the jaw. Ora fell to his knees in a daze.

"It's fine now. Mr. Swallowtail got him," the guard called from above.

"Got who?" a masculine voice asked.

"The brother of the guy that got his wing broken yesterday," the guard said, pressing a white handkerchief to his forehead.

"He threw rocks at you?" a female voice questioned.

Delia stared up at the balcony, but could only see the guard walking into the open room. She glanced back at Ora. The man who had hit him was tying Ora's hands together while he swayed woozily on his knees. Delia glared back up at the balcony just as another guard stepped out and began to close the doors.

"Wait," the same female voice commanded.

The new guard opened the doors wider and Delia could see a tall woman with long dark hair.

"Is Tiger injured?" the tall brunette questioned, trying to see past the guard. The room's lantern backlit her large wings, betraying an intricate pattern.

Some of Delia's anger rekindled. This was the woman who had hurt Coli. Delia clenched her empty fists and cursed herself for dropping the rocks. Bending over, she frantically searched through the ferns at her feet trying to recover them.

"Didn't look it. He took the attacker inside the castle," the new guard said.

Ora was gone? Delia abruptly stood and stared out at the empty courtyard, then glanced up at the balcony just as the new guard shut the doors with the woman inside. Delia growled and kicked at the ground, her unfortunate toe finding one of the hidden rocks. Cursing under her breath, she skirted the tree edge until the castle hid her from the guard's view. Then she darted across the open side yard and slunk back around the castle until she stood once again before the enormous doors. Taking a deep breath, she yanked, and it opened. Delia scowled. *Stupid Dragonwort must have held the door shut from the other side!* She slipped quickly inside, and straining, pulled it closed behind her. *What a jerk!*

"You're not a guard! You can't take me to the dungeon!" Ora shouted.

Delia couldn't see him, but she followed his voice down a hallway. Her nose turned up at the stench of sulphur and mold; *Ugh, does it always smell like this?* Clamping a hand over her nose and mouth, she hurried after them.

"This isn't justice! She can't get away with this! And neither can you!" Ora yelled.

Delia could see them now. Ora was squirming futilely in the larger man's grip. *That must be Tiger.*

"I'll make you both pay! I'll stick my fingers in those pretty orange wings of hers and shred until there's nothing left! Then she won't be so high and mighty!"

Tiger's tightly folded yellow and black wings quivered at Ora's last threat. Before Ora could speak again, Tiger lifted Ora by the arm and knocked his shoulder into the stone wall. Ora's closed wings vibrated at the jarring collision, but appeared undamaged.

"You idiot! She's a *princess*! That threat was probably a capital offense. Shut your stupid mouth and stop making the situation worse." As if he could feel her eyes, Tiger glanced down the hall behind him and frowned at Delia, then he dragged Ora away.

Delia trailed them from a greater distance, hoping Tiger wouldn't look back again. Ora's vitriol had deteriorated into incoherent threats, and Delia began to wonder if he had a head injury. She could hear badly played music ahead, and the hallway was dotted with couples talking, kissing, and arguing. Tiger deftly navigated Ora through the light crowd, everyone shifting away, then leaning in curiously after they passed. Delia had to fly to see them now, and when they disappeared around a corner, she flew directly over a cluster of people blocking the hallway.

"Hey! Come down." A tall man with beige wings and a minty scent leapt up and grazed her thigh as she flew over him. Delia kneed him in the face. She heard him sputter and several other people laugh, but didn't bother to look back.

When Delia rounded the corner, Tiger was headed down a stairway, and Ora was no longer visible. She landed at the top of the stairwell to an overwhelming stench of hot sulphur. Breathing through her mouth, she took a few steps, then gagged at the taste of it, reflexively gasping a breath in through both her nose and mouth. She gagged again, her stomach contents surging as she ran back up the steps and partway down the hall to stop the vomit. There she bent forward, gulping the fresher air and struggling to calm her stomach.

"You gave me a bloody nose!" Brown-clad legs wearing dirty boots walked into Delia's limited view.

"And you sexually assaulted me," she growled, not bothering to look up. Despite her aggravation, his minty scent immediately began to soothe her stomach.

"That's not what that...I wasn't..." The dirty boots shifted and a small clump of dried mud fell onto the stone floor.

Delia noted the mud's dark hue with satisfaction, lifting her own shoe to ensure it matched. A grim smile raced across her lips and was gone. The dirt wouldn't show on her black pants after all.

"You can't just knee people in the face!"

Delia took a deep breath to contain her sudden resurgence of rage. "Sure I can," she said, glaring up at him without straightening.

He started back at her venomous gaze. His sleeve fell away from his nose, betraying a smattering of blood. "Hey, are you a white?" He took a few steps back, his gaze traveling from the backside of her wings to her face and back again.

"Does it matter?"

"Yeah." He let out a nervous laugh and backed away. "Hey, I didn't mean to start anything. I'll just leave you alone and you leave me alone, okay?" He stumbled in his retreat and another clump of dried mud fell off his boot. "Okay?" He held one hand out as if he were trying to both placate and ward her off.

"Gladly." Delia's anger cooled with her dismay. He was genuinely frightened. As she watched him back awkwardly around the corner, she closed her wings tightly. Maybe admitting she was a white wasn't such a good idea. She glanced back at the vivid yellow and orange that dramatically smeared the underside of her wings. The little bit of white on her upper wings was hardly noticeable. Experimentally, she raised, then lowered her shoulders, forcing her upper wings to relax more fully behind her lower. It was an awkward posture, but the white disappeared entirely. Satisfied, Delia attempted walking with the white hidden. After a few minutes, her back muscles protested stridently, reminding her that she had flown all night, and it was time to rest. She glanced wistfully at the stairs; she knew it was unlikely Ora would return. The horrible smell alone seemed to mark the lower regions as a place of punishment. But surely Tiger would return to his new girlfriend? When he climbed the stairs, she would confront him, demand answers, and possibly revenge on Coli's behalf. She nodded in grim satisfaction, then turned to see a tall brunette with enormous orange and black wings flying toward her. Delia was almost certain it was the same woman from the balcony, but without her guards. The woman who had broken Talis' wing and stolen Coli's boyfriend. Delia huffed out righteous fury, planted her feet, and blocked the stairwell.

The brunette's tangled hair tumbled around her shoulders as she landed. "Please move." The polite words sounded like a command.

Delia took in her haughty mien and agitated impatience, then stared at the woman's distinctive monarch wings. *Ora is an idiot*, she thought. The probable princess and the new governor towered over her, but it wasn't right that this woman would use her position to break wings without consequences. Delia's hands tightened into fists. She would be the consequences.

"Wing-breaker," Delia began, the devastating words she would say coming into her head like a wave crashing onto the reef. But the brunette leaned over her menacingly, and Delia's next words died on her tongue.

"Get out of my way." The words were spoken quietly, but with a tone of pure wrath and an expression that promised harm.

Alarmed, Delia shuffled aside, her wings falling open under the brunette's icy gaze. No one had *ever* spoken to her or looked at her like *that*. Not even Talis or Ora in their foulest moods were that frightening. She shivered as the princess inspected her in passing. Were all the royals like this? Delia looked up to see two males in black shirts barreling toward her. *The princess' guards?* Delia didn't wait to find out. Interrogating Tiger was not worth dealing with guards or their intimidating princess. Delia shook her head as she bolted; she needed to talk to Coli. Maybe no revenge was required. Delia frowned at her cowardice as she hurried past the knots of people outside the room with the horrid music. She shoved a man that didn't move out of her way. When he turned to complain, she recognized the mint-scented man

45

with the bloody nose. Wordlessly, he made way, giving her the widest berth possible. Delia glared at him as she hurried past, but then closed her wings tightly and dropped her shoulders to make the white vanish altogether. The previously empty hallways were now filled with other women sleepily headed in the opposite direction. Delia watched them pass with a growing sense of discomfort; was she supposed to join them? The steady stream died out as she reached the two-story entry with its grand front doors and Delia slowly turned a full circle. There was only one open door and she headed toward it. The room within was brightly lit by a solar lantern and consisted of a single broad desk. A white-winged man sat behind it, his left upper wing in tattered shreds that reminded Delia of her brother.

"Hello."

Delia dragged her eyes away from the damaged section of his wing to the open countenance beneath it.

"What's your name?"

"I just got here." *Lie.* "Am I in the right place?" she asked instead of answering him.

"Sure are. Name?"

"Delia..." she hesitated, holding her wings tighter a moment before finally releasing them. "Delia White."

He looked over her wings carefully. "I wouldn't have guessed," he admitted, then lowered his head to write. "Age?"

"Nineteen."

"Father's name?"

"Ned White."

"Mother's maiden name?"

"Lila Copper."

"And where are you from?"

"Hamlet."

The white-winged man finished writing, then slumped on his stool with a sigh. "Because you're a white, I'm supposed to ask about internships, work experience, and special skills." He looked up at her apologetically. "It's not fair, but because a higher percentage of us whites get stuck here as life servants, they like to be prepared."

Delia scowled. "I'm not going to get stuck here."

"That's what I said."

Delia looked at his tattered wing again. "Who did that to you?"

"My girl's brother."

"Did he get punished?"

He nodded. "Month in the dungeon, then he got married and went home."

"That's not fair."

"No, it's not. But then, not a whole lot is fair when you're a white in season." He shrugged. "I'm Malan White, by the way. If I can help you while you're here, let me know. If you get in trouble, I'll stand in for Nap."

Delia's brows shot up.

"Yes, I know your brother and your two sisters. I know everybody. How's Nap doing with Dina?"

Delia scowled.

"Hm, thought so. That's too bad." He poised his pencil over the paper. "So, I'm guessing you worked in the apothecary shop, too?"

Delia gave him a brief nod.

"Bookkeeping? Sales?" he guessed.

Delia shook her head. "I find and harvest medicinal plants."

"Oh." Malan frowned, his pencil hesitating over the paper. "We don't have anyone up here that knows how to do that." He set the pencil down. "If I write that, some of the life servants will be rooting for you to get stuck here; they might even make it harder for you. They made it harder for Nap."

47

"What did they do to my brother?"

"Kept asking him for medical advice and medicine, then locked him up in the dungeon twice for no good reason."

Delia swallowed, her nausea returning as she remembered the stench of the dungeon stairwell. "What are you going to write?"

"Some of them already know about the apothecary shop and that your sister Pearl helped with bookkeeping. I could write the same for you."

"I hate bookkeeping. So does Pearl. Neither of us helped. Is that what she told you?"

"No," Malan's voice took on a chiding tone. "That's what *I* *suggested* to her after she told me she makes medicine."

"Oh." Pearl was a brilliant chemist and always finding new and better ways to distill and compound the plants Delia harvested. If she had agreed to lie... No, she still couldn't. It would grate on her. "Just put nothing. They shouldn't be asking, anyway."

"They'll just come ask you themselves. And you'll have to deal with the question over and over."

Delia pressed her fingernails into her palms. "Then write that I'm a forager or a gardener."

Malan picked up the pencil and met her gaze steadily. After a moment, he wrote *bookkeeping* under her name.

Delia released her fists with a conciliatory huff.

"*If* you get stuck here, you can tell them about your skills then. Now, room assignment."

"Could I share a room with my sister Pearl or with Coli Sulphur?"

He shook his head. "Whites get single rooms. I have a life-servant room available."

"I don't want a life-servant room."

"They're warmer—which is great if you don't mind the smell of sulphur."

Delia swallowed back a gag. "No sulphur."

"Hmm, let's try 308, then. Here's a map."

Delia glanced at the sloppily drawn map with its crooked walls and found her circled room. "Thanks." She tried to show her gratitude with a smile, but it felt more like a grimace.

"And remember what I said: If you get in trouble, come find me."

Delia blinked back the tears that suddenly threatened. "Thanks," she repeated, hating that her voice sounded curt. "Wait, where are Pearl and Coli's rooms?"

"Hand me your map." Delia passed it back to him, and he wrote Pearl and Coli's names over their respective rooms.

"Thank you," she said as he handed it back. "I mean that."

Malan smiled. "I know."

Delia glanced at his tattered wing one last time, and Malan wiggled his shoulder to wave it at her. "Sorry," she said, a slight blush showing beneath her tan.

Malan shrugged. "I'm used to it. I am a cautionary tale for all the new in-seasons."

Delia took one last look at his tattered wing before she turned and left. *What was the caution? Don't be a white?* She closed her wings tightly, glancing back to make sure no white was showing. *There. Now I'm a grumpy sulphur.* Delia smirked, then set out to find her room.

Chapter Five

A scarred wooden door creaked a welcome into her dark, windowless room. The solar lantern that hung from the ceiling was in desperate need of a charge and only produced the dullest of glows. Delia tucked her map into her bag, then flew up and detached the waning lantern. Back out in the hallway, she chose the brightest lantern and swapped it out. She glanced around guiltily as she did so, spotting a guard in fancy livery marching toward her.

"Have you seen Princess Lexi?" he demanded.

Ah, more proof that Ora was an idiot. "Yes."

His glare softened into eager surprise. "Where?"

Delia briefly considered misleading him. If the princess was without her guards, she was more likely to get what she deserved.

"Where?!"

His little fit of temper spurred Delia's own. "Follow your nose. When the stench of sulphur makes you gag, you're almost there."

"Do you mean the dungeon?"

Delia hugged her bright lantern and shrugged.

The guard shook his head at her disapprovingly and hurried away.

"You're welcome," she called after him sarcastically, then muttered a few insults under her breath before slamming the door to her room. The door hinges' protesting creak followed by the resounding thud of heavy oak was immensely satisfying. Delia was tempted to open it so she could slam it again. But the fully illuminated room quickly robbed her of her glee. The bed was covered in a stained sheet and hole-ridden blanket. The pillow was heavily water-stained from drooling sleepers and missing its pillowcase. A rickety three-legged table sported a coat of dust on its crooked surface and the little stool was crisscrossed with spider webs. A round, cracked mirror was attached to the back of the door, too high for Delia to see while standing. Her room at home had never been anything impressive, and she had shared it with her two sisters, but this room was simply disheartening. With the door closed, the scent emanating from the bed pervaded the room. Delia wrinkled her nose, but took a deeper breath; the scent was familiar. "Skunk cabbage," she said aloud. Had someone had the plant in here or simply been unfortunate enough to smell like it? She sniffed about the room, even looked under the bed. No, the smell was coming from the bed itself. With an impatient yank, she stripped the bedding and sniffed the mattress. There the scent was only faint. She lifted the pillow to her nose and grimaced. Someone had been sleeping on it without a pillowcase. She flung it to the floor with the dirty sheet and blanket, then retrieved her map. "Laundry," she said aloud as she searched the lazy reproduction, snorting when she found the partially illegible word "lawndery." *Close enough*, she thought as she stowed the map, then gathered the corners of the dirty blanket to form a makeshift sack of the used bedding. She nearly tossed it over her shoulder before she remembered her wings. Breathing out a relieved sigh, she waddled awkwardly, holding the cumbersome sack in front of her. At the door, she managed another hearty slam before making her way through the empty corridor. Down two flights of stairs, Delia found an open doorway with steam billowing out. A middle-aged woman stood in the middle of it fanning herself with a graying apron. As Delia approached with her bedding, the woman dropped her apron and glared down at Delia.

"Why aren't you at breakfast?!" she demanded, refusing to step aside so Delia could enter.

"Because I wanted to have a picnic right here," Delia retorted, dropping her load at the woman's feet.

The woman inhaled deeply through flared nostrils, then bent to gather the bedding. "High and mighty in-seasons think you can just order us around," she griped as she straightened. "We used to *be* you! And you're not safe! Tomorrow, you could be one of us!" She shifted the bedding to point a scaly finger in Delia's face.

Delia opened her mouth, happy to enter a verbal battle until she looked at the women's hand. Her knuckles were red with scabby patches that made Delia's brain switch into apothecary mode. *Eczema*, she thought, *treatable with chamomile flowers*. Her father and Chloe were far better diagnosticians, but the case was fairly obvious.

"So go demand your breakfast, you little ingrate. I hope you find mealworms in your mush!"

Delia's medical interest faded to the background with the woman's continued invective. And then the devastating words were there in her head. Delia pressed her lips together trying to distract herself with chamomile-flower preparations.

The woman leaned further forward making a bulging blood vessel on her forehead visible. "Go!" she shrieked.

Delia's resolve crumbled. "You wanted everyone's pity so badly that you wrecked your own life to get it. Is it all you hoped it would be?"

The woman's mouth worked in apoplectic rage while her ruddy hands reached for Delia's wings. Delia leapt backwards and flew out of the woman's reach, her own heart pounding at the near miss. She *had* to control her tongue; it was dangerous not to. And that unpleasant exchange meant she didn't have bedding. It also meant it was wise to get away from the castle until the woman had calmed down. With only the smallest regret over her missed and possibly wormy breakfast, Delia headed outside.

The sun had risen during Delia's misadventures and seared her eyes after the dim castle lighting. Blinking spots, she flew northwest, away from the sunny brilliance. The muscles beneath her wings quickly reminded her that they were exhausted, but landing only made her blisters burn. After a few steps down a forest path, Delia felt the sudden fluid of one of her large blisters popping. She stopped to remove the offending shoe only to discover her foot was polka-dotted in blisters. Groaning, she gingerly removed the other shoe to find the same condition. Delia growled. Mr. Fritillary had claimed the shoes were so good that he even used them for fishing.

"As what? Bait?" Delia yelled. She wanted to tear the shoes in half, but they proved annoyingly durable. With frustration-driven fury, she flung her new flying-friendly, lightweight shoes. She watched them arc above the path with a grim smile that turned to dismay as they fell into the forest underbrush. Delia hurried down the path, her bare feet smarting. Around the trunks of towering douglas firs, the forest floor was dominated by the spiny leaflets of holly grape overshadowed by dead elderberry branches ready to snag her wings. Delia cursed her idiocy, her wretched hormonal temper, and the heavy, practical boots she had left at home. She rummaged through her bag and extracted her dancing slippers, then hesitated at the pristine sand-colored leather soles. She glanced at the muddy path, then shoved them back in her bag. Taking to the air, she grimaced at her aching muscles, promising them a rest after a short flight.

As she returned, barefoot, to the castle courtyard, someone swooped down from the castle roof. Delia jumped, fearing it was a guard or Coli's ex-boyfriend come to drag her away to the dungeon, until she registered what the squeaky, androgynous voice was hollering.

"New arrival! Incoming!!"

Delia's eyes narrowed, and she backed away as the small male landed where she had been standing. She glanced around the courtyard. A single guard was watching from the princess' balcony, but no one else was in sight.

"You're just my size!" the small male crowed approvingly, closing the distance while Delia continued to back up. "Name's Pyrgus, but you can call me—" Pyrgus stopped dead and gagged. "Ugh, it's like someone shoved a pinecone up my nose."

"Well, it would improve your face," Delia retorted. His freckled face wasn't unpleasant, nor was the spicy scent of golden currant flowers that seemed to emanate from him, but his belligerent disgust certainly was.

"Hilarious," he snapped, rubbing vigorously at his nostrils as he backed away. "Just keep your distance."

"Likewise."

He jumped into the air, his checked wings seeming to fan her scent away as he returned to his perch. "My eyes are still watering!" he complained loudly.

Delia was tempted to yell back, but the princess' guard was still watching. With a start, she realized it was the same guard that had tackled Ora and thrown him against the wall on the way to the dungeon: Coli's ex-boyfriend. Did he remember her from this morning? Just then, the princess' balcony door opened and there was the intimidating princess herself. Delia panicked. She was flying before she even realized it, and she didn't stop or look back for a long time.

It was the lake that made her want to stop. Before that, she had contemplated flying to the base of the mountain for comfortable boots and maybe even some bedding. But now her canteen was empty and the lake was a serene oasis. The dense coniferous forest allowed only a narrow fringe of shoreline before plunging into the frigid mountain water. Delia landed in the shallows, scattering the resident salamanders. Her relief was immediate, and her feet were blissfully numb in seconds. She splashed feebly at her angry back muscles before deciding a proper bath was in order. She removed her bag and canteen and tossed them on a small sandy beach, then waded deep enough to swim. The temperature stole her breath and turned her partially submerged wings numb almost immediately. *Uh-oh.* She needed to be able to fly back to the Old Castle or to a town or somewhere. Delia waded back to ankle depth as she indulged thoughts of home, and her comfortable boots waiting by the front door. She wiggled her frozen toes in the silt. It almost seemed worth going home until she imagined her mother's confused questions that would quickly morph into irritation.

"That's right, Mom, I'm home because I committed a crime with Ora, infuriated a princess, lost my bedding to a life servant who wants to break my wings, and threw my only pair of outdoor shoes irretrievably into the forest...all because I lost my temper. Also, I'm not sure the mating thing is going to work out as I apparently smell like a nostril-scraping pinecone." Delia snorted at her own dark humor, then got to work washing in earnest. Despite the warm sun, her icy bath had her shivering. After a hurried scan of the sky and shore, Delia stripped off her wet clothing and draped it over nearby branches. Teeth chattering, she rummaged through her bag for her warmest clothes, settling on a black long-sleeved top and matching pants. She glared at the visible dirt beneath the trees as she dressed; it was ruddy-brown, not black. *You're not here to dig up plants,* she reminded herself. *You didn't even bring your spade.*

Out of habit, Delia searched the forest periphery. White-petaled trillium flowers caught her eye. "Better than mealworms for breakfast," she shrugged, gingerly crossing to the flowers and removing the new leaves from the stem. She itched to dig up the root as well, knowing how many medicinal uses it had. She forced herself back to the lake and filtered some water to drink and some more to wash the trillium leaves. When she finished, she made quick work of her leafy breakfast, enjoying the nutty flavor. Then she paced in and out of the shallows, fanning her wings in the sunshine and idly watching ducks swim across the lake. She was bored in seconds. Shaking her head, she retrieved her dancing slippers and made peace with destroying them. She then spent the next two hours harvesting plants with makeshift tools. She knotted one of her new shirts until it made a passable bag and loaded her harvest. Once her wings were dry, she meandered back to the castle, harvesting more plants along the way. *So much for bookkeeping.* She arrived back at the castle exhausted, filthy, and happy.

Just outside the courtyard, Delia paused to check the princess' balcony, pleased to see a guard with blue wings that she didn't recognize. Closing her wings to hide the white and tucking her makeshift bag of herbs under her arm, Delia boldly marched through a dozen people lazily enjoying conversation at the rusty metal tables. She was almost to the door when someone caught her arm. Delia whirled, instantly furious.

"Whoa, Delia, calm down!" Coli's cornflower-blue eyes widened in alarm at the expression on her friends's face, and she scooted back on her stool. "You look as scary as Pearl!"

"I don't look scary," Pearl snapped from the other side of Coli's table, then nodded a greeting at Delia. Pearl's perceptive gray eyes paused on her sister's brightly colored wings.

Coli glanced at Pearl's scowl, then threw back her head of golden curls and laughed. "Sit down, Delia. Your wings are beautiful! But why are you so dirty?"

Delia stood there awkwardly for a moment. Should she hug her sister? They hadn't seen each other in two months, but Pearl had dropped her eyes to glare at the table in front of her, idly scratching off rust with her nail. Delia made a move to hug Coli.

Coli laughed and put up a hand. "*After* you bathe." She glanced at Pearl, then added, "and if you still feel like it." Coli smoothed down her pink dress, the color an exact match to the trim of her yellow wings.

Delia glanced around, then slid her bag of plants under the table.

"What's that?" Pearl demanded, leaning back to look under the table.

Delia shifted uncomfortably. "Just some supplies."

Pearl leaned close to her sister, her platinum hair grazing Delia's shoulder. "If you've been gathering *medicinal* supplies, I'm going to kill you," she hissed, then grabbed Delia's hand to examine her nails. "You've been digging. Didn't Malan explain things to you?"

"I'm not a *bookkeeper*," Delia hissed.

"Neither am *I*. Don't you understand anything?!"

"Malan wrote that I was."

"Yes, I know. He told me. Now *act* like one or we'll both end up slaves!" Pearl leapt up, bumping the table and knocking over her stool as she flew away.

Some of Delia's anger dissipated in shock. "Am I like that?"

Coli smiled sadly. "I'll let you know."

"Are you okay? I heard about your break up. And I know about your brothers."

Coli glanced at the other tables. "They're listening. Let's go talk somewhere else."

As they both stood, Coli took the makeshift bag from under the table as if it were hers, but held it carefully away from her body to avoid the dirt-smeared fabric.

"Did you ruin one of your shirts?" Coli asked as they entered the castle.

Delia shrugged. "I didn't have room left in my bag."

Coli chuckled. "I missed you, Delia."

Delia's mouth twitched in a feeble smile, but her eyes filled momentarily with tears. "I missed you, too."

Coli waited for two giggly girls to pass them in the hallway, then spoke in an undertone. "I talked to Ora after your little *adventure* this morning. I can't believe he got you caught up in that! And now both my idiot brothers will probably be life servants." Coli shook her head angrily. "I should have stopped Talis, and I should have known Tiger was involved with our new *governor*." Coli spat the title, then laughed ruefully. "Now *I* sound like a white. No offense."

Delia shrugged.

Coli opened a door, peered in, then quickly shut it again. "My new roommate is in there. She's an awful gossip and not very nice. I try to avoid her. Where is your room?"

Delia took out her map, reoriented herself, then led the way.

"You killed your shoes. Why don't you change to another pair?" Coli asked.

Delia's eyes narrowed, but she swallowed back her irritation. "Don't have any."

"You only brought *one* pair of shoes?"

"No," Delia's steps turned to stomping, little bits of brown and black earth dropping off with each step.

"Delia," Coli chided, walking faster to catch up. "I know you're feeling all hormonal, but try to be yourself for a minute. I've had a bad few days and I want to complain about them and have you tell me how stupid everyone is. And since both my brothers are in the dungeon, I've been trying to make do with Pearl, but it is *not* working, and I need you."

Delia made herself stop. "I had a tantrum and flung my other shoes into the forest."

"Really?" Coli started to chuckle, then covered her mouth.

"Really."

"Can we go get them?" Coli's words still sounded of suppressed laughter.

"Not with wings." Delia stopped and threw her door open. Rather than the bright lantern she had expected to see, her room no longer had one. Delia grabbed yet another lantern from the hallway and went inside. The table and chair were gone. The rusty metal bedframe was empty; someone had taken the mattress.

"Are you sure this is your room?"

Delia checked the number carved into the door. "Yes."

"Was it like this before?"

"No."

"Who did this?"

Delia shut the door and put the lantern back. "I think I'm in trouble."

"What did you do?"

Delia fought the idiotic wave of anger that washed over her. "A couple of things..."

A brown-winged male walked toward them, giving Coli a lazy grin and nod. She gave him a tight smile, then pulled Delia in the other direction.

"Hopefully my brothers' room hasn't been reassigned yet," she whispered. Coli led her down a flight a stairs, then knocked on the first door on the right. "Hey guys, coming in," she called casually, smiling at another passerby, then pulled Delia inside.

The room was lit with a barely glowing lantern and permeated with a sharp but pleasant smell. Coli flew up to the light fixture and turned it brighter. The room was strewn with clothes, hedged in by two crooked beds with blankets trailing across the floor.

"Pigs!" Coli set down Delia's makeshift bag, then kicked at the clothes on the floor until she found Ora's bag and started packing it. "It won't be so bad once I clean it up. You can at least nap in here. Unless it smells horrid; does it?"

Delia shook her head as she inhaled deeply. It was something familiar. "You can't smell it?"

Coli shook her head. "Family can't smell family; what's it like?'

Delia inhaled again. "It smells like mustard."

Coli wrinkled up her nose. "I hate mustard."

"Lucky you can't smell it, then." Delia took off her bag, and stretched her back.

Coli dropped her brother's packed bag by the door and flopped on one of the beds. "Okay, tell me what you did after you and Ora attacked the princess' guard."

"I didn't throw any rocks," Delia clarified.

"Glad you haven't completely lost your mind."

Delia stuck out her tongue.

"That's the Delia I know," Coli laughed.

"I *would* have, but I felt bad for the guard and then I couldn't find a rock when the princess came out."

"The princess came out? Her worshipfulness, the-high-and-mighty-Lexi was out on her balcony when Ora attacked?"

"No." Delia wriggled out of her dirty clothes and shoes as she talked. "Your ex-boyfriend had tackled him by then."

Coli rolled her eyes. "Stupid Tiger. He should have just told me he liked her. But no, he spent days convincing me that she was 'just a sister' to him. What a liar." Coli punched a pillow, then folded it under her arms. "I knew something was wrong."

Delia fought a clean shirt into place, speaking through the fabric of the elongated neck. "How long was he your boyfriend?"

Coli shrugged. "A couple of weeks."

Delia's head finally popped through the tight neck-opening. "Are you in love with him?"

Coli stared at her hands, then looked up at her friend. "That is such a weird shirt."

"It's the right color," Delia argued, pointing to the matching orange of her wings. The subject change was abrupt, but Delia had no intention of mentioning it. *Poor Coli.*

"Points for color coordination," Coli nodded. "I've never seen a white with such colorful wings."

"Me neither." Delia selected a pair of brown pants that exactly matched the soil outside the castle and slipped them on. "My new sister-in-law asked if I was adopted."

Coli rose up to her knees. "Oh! I heard she was awful. Why did Nap marry her?"

"Apparently he likes women who yell."

Coli winced. "It's just the hormones. He won't like it later."

"And she broke his wing *while* he was flying."

"Why?!"

"She didn't want him to be a crown agent."

Coli let out a low whistle. "Is Nap okay?"

"He can't fly anymore."

"What did your mom say?"

"Kicked her out, but she wouldn't leave. She hides out in Nap's room and he brings her food there."

"No!"

"Yes!"

"Sounds like we both had a bad couple of days." Coli laid back down, her eyes still wide.

Delia nodded and laid down on the opposite bed, the mustard scent enveloping her.

"And you still haven't told me what you did."

"I followed Ora and Tiger. Ora was fighting and threatening the princess until Tiger slammed him into the wall."

"He did *what*?!" Coli was back up on her knees. "Oh, he and I are going to talk."

"Right now?"

Coli forced herself back down. "No. Finish telling me."

"I couldn't follow them down to the dungeon; it reeked so bad I started gagging. So I waited at the top of the stairs so I could yell at your ex for hurting you and Ora, but the princess showed up. So I blocked her way and called her a wing-breaker."

Coli gasped and jumped back up to her knees.

"I was going to do my truth-bomb thing and tell her how she would always be a horrible leader because she abuses her power to get what she wants, but she leaned over me all menacing." Delia flew to her feet to demonstrate. "And said 'get out of my way!' I seriously thought she was going to kick me down the stairs and lock me up forever." Delia shivered involuntarily. "So I let her pass, and gave up on yelling at Tiger when her guards came. But I will now, if you want. We can go together."

"No." Coli jumped to her feet and paced the small room. "If the princess was mad enough to strip your room, she's probably going to lock you up. I don't think Ora would have told anyone you were with him. Did Tiger see you?"

"He saw me following them to the dungeon."

Coli shook her head. "We might need to hide you. Or maybe you should go home for a while."

"No! Dina is there. Besides, the princess might not be responsible for my room."

"Who else would have done it?"

"Well, there was this life servant at the laundry who yelled at me when I brought my dirty bedding..."

Coli stopped pacing. "Did you truth-bomb her?"

Delia nodded. "I may have told her that she brought her misery on herself in order to get pity and asked her if it was worth it."

Coli winced. "What did she do?"

"Tried to break my wings."

"That sounds about right." Coli tapped her fingertips against her chin. "We need information. And I think I know how to get it. You stay here. Don't go out for lunch. Just eat one of your plants and nap. I'll be back as soon as I can."

Coli headed for the door, then turned back and hugged her friend. Delia barely hesitated before returning her affection.

"The door doesn't lock, but try wedging one of the beds against it," Coli advised as she lifted her brother's bag and slipped out the door.

Delia moved the bed she had been lying on as soon as the door shut, then unpacked all of her harvested plants and hung them from the light fixture to dry. It wasn't ideal, but better than letting them molder. Besides, she might be taking them home to her father tonight. Delia's back muscles ached at the thought, and she laid down to rest them.

Chapter Six

A jarring screech awoke her.

"Is that the bed? Ugh, it's so heavy. Delia, can't you just wake up and help me?"

Delia felt like she had been tumbling in the surf. Turning her head, she squinted at the vertical sliver of light just as the room went dark. "Coli?"

"Oh, hi!" Coli's cheerful voice was muffled by the now-closed door. "No, everything's fine. Just cleaning up my brothers' room."

Delia could hear the low timbre of a male voice.

"Yeah, it *was* unfair," Coli agreed.

The unintelligible voice sounded again and Delia closed her eyes. Maybe she was back on the beach. "Sand fleas," she murmured, the words drifting into a sonorous snore.

"Delia!" Coli hissed, then kicked the door. "You are impossible to wake up."

No I'm not, Delia argued, then realized she wasn't speaking.

The horrible screech of metal across stone felt like it was scraping her brain.

"Delia? Please wake up." Coli's voice quivered, then cracked on the last word. "Tiger left," she sniffed. "Can you please get up and open the door?"

Delia dragged herself up noting the pain in her back and feet. She stumbled toward the partially opened door and rammed her shin into the barricading bed frame. "Ow."

"You're up! Let me in before someone sees me," Coli urged, her voice sounding wrong.

Moving the bed was much harder with the light off. Delia flew up to turn it on and a trillium root fell on her head. Disoriented, she returned to the door and hit her other shin. "Okay, now I'm awake," she announced, shins smarting. Her second try at the light was more successful. Then she cringed as she dragged the bed. *Was it this loud before?*

As soon as the bed cleared the door, Coli slipped inside. "I need a hug," she quavered, and grabbed hold of Delia. She broke into trembling, noisy sobs into her friend's hair.

"No snot," Delia warned, patting the taller girl's arm.

"No snot," Coli agreed, letting go. She wiped her reddened eyes. "He left with her. He didn't say goodbye. He just left me. Part of me still thought we were going to get married." Coli shook her head, her golden curls bouncing. "I loved him." Coli covered her face. "I love him," she corrected.

Delia hugged her friend again, her thoughts moving sluggishly. "Wait, the *princess* left?"

Coli nodded, her pointed chin tapping the top of Delia's head. "Someone beat up the old governor and broke his wings before he could fly down the mountain. He has to stay, so she made him the governor again and left. And Tiger went with her." Fresh tears ran down Coli's face. "I'll never even see him again."

Delia retrieved her bag and rummaged inside. "Here," she said, handing Coli a handkerchief.

Coli took it and blew her nose. "Now tell me how stupid everyone is."

"Everyone is stupid," Delia yawned.

Coli smiled through her tears. "No. You're supposed to tell me how stupid *he* was to cheat on me and leave me."

Delia nodded. "He's stupid."

"He grew up at the palace, you know. He takes care of the horses there. Guess they'll go back and live happily ever after." Coli blew her nose again. "I can't really compete with a princess."

66

"She's an *awful* person."

"She's his best friend. They grew up together."

"Then he must be an awful person, too."

"He's not, really. I miss him." Coli climbed onto one of the beds. "This room needs stools."

Delia nodded her agreement and climbed onto the other bed.

"But you can stay here until Talis is out of the dungeon in a couple of days. Nobody knows you were with Ora; he didn't talk. But that life servant you truth-bombed is in charge of the laundry. She's probably the one that stripped your room, but she's not admitting it. Officially, you're banned from using the laundry and no one's supposed to give you bedding or wash your clothes. I don't know what happened to your mattress or how you would get a new one. And I wouldn't leave anything in your assigned room because I've heard the laundry mistress is a thief."

"All because I was rude back to her?! Why does she have so much power? She's just a miserable life servant! Can't anyone make her stop?"

"I'm sure the governor could, but I hear he's too beat-up to see anyone."

"Perfect!" Delia yelled sarcastically, her stomach adding its own complaints.

"Shhh! You're *hiding out* in here, remember? Do you have anything left you can eat? You slept through dinner."

Delia looked up at her wilted plants and scowled. "Nothing that doesn't taste horrible. But I can go foraging again."

Coli shook her head. "It's dark outside."

Delia growled. "Then I will fly down to Firwood, get some food and decent shoes, and fly back."

"You really think your body is up to that?"

Delia rolled her shoulders, feeling the muscles cramp and protest at the small movement. Could she even find Firwood in the dark? Or the Old Castle again if Dragonwort weren't leading the way?

Coli sagged. "Normally I would ask Tiger to help or try to manipulate my brothers into it." She shook her head, then brightened. "We could go to the pool and try to charm some food out of the guys there."

Delia looked askance. "I am currently incapable of charm."

"Fine, I'll do it. I need to cheer myself up, anyway." Coli handed Delia the used handkerchief, then pulled it back before Delia could take it. "Never mind. I'll wash it. Just come with me to the pool and look pretty." Coli scrutinized Delia's mildly irritated expression. "That's not bad, but what if you open your eyes a little more and lift your brows?"

"So I look surprised?"

"No, let me show you." Coli dragged Delia over to the back of the door. "There's no mirror in this room? Ugh. Fine. I'll be your mirror. Right now you look like this." Coli crossed her arms and glowered.

Delia smirked at the unnatural expression on her friend's face.

"A little better. Now tell me about your best plant find since you've been up here."

Delia flew up to the light fixture and retrieved a smooth, oval leaf. "Queen's cup leaf," she announced happily. "The flowers hadn't bloomed yet, so it was a tricky find."

"And what's it for?"

"Helps stop bleeding," Delia answered as she flew up to replace the drying leaf.

"You look like your beautiful self when you talk about plants. So just imagine every guy you see tonight is a plant."

Delia narrowed her eyes skeptically.

"I can be a plant, too, if it helps. I'll be a dandelion."

"You're not a dandelion. They're too common and bitter."

Coli laughed. "Thank you. I'm going to go put my swimsuit on and come back for you," she announced, then opened the door a crack and peered out into the hallway. She waited a minute, then hurried out, closing the door softly behind her.

Delia changed into her suit, then paced, listening to her stomach growl and cursing herself for agreeing to Coli's plan. Every fourth turn, she flew up to the light and took down one of the Douglas fir tips she had gathered, grimacing at the flavor as she chewed.

"Now I will have fir needles in my teeth *and* smell like a nostril-scraping pine cone," she growled, jumping as the door flew open and Coli slipped inside.

"Ready?"

Delia picked up a bar of soap and waved it.

"No shoes?" Coli asked, eyeing Delia's blistered and dirty feet.

Delia gave her a withering glower.

"That's right," Coli laughed, "you flung them. Just be careful where you step at the pool. The volcanic rock is rough on the feet."

Delia glanced at her mud-caked dancing slippers, and Coli shuddered.

"I would tell you just to throw them away, but since you don't have any other shoes..." Coli sighed. "You can just share mine."

Delia looked at her friend's long slender feet and snorted.

"They're not that big," Coli objected, then opened the door a sliver. "Hallway is empty; let's go."

Delia followed her friend, her foot smarting as another blister broke. "This doesn't seem like a good idea," she blurted.

"What? Getting clean?" Coli teased.

"No, trying to charm food off strangers."

"Especially not when you still have your last meal showing in your teeth," Coli chided.

"I do?" Delia sucked vigorously at her teeth. "Did I get it?"

Coli nodded. "It's a good distraction even if you aren't hungry any more."

"Sorry, I forgot we were distracting you," Delia apologized. "And I'm kind of hungry."

"I am, too. Dinner was lousy, as usual."

"What was it?"

"Watery pea and mushroom soup."

"What kind of mushrooms?" Delia asked, automatically running through the likely varieties in her head.

"I knew you were going to ask that! And I have no idea."

"What did they taste like?"

"Couldn't tell you. Gave mine to Pearl."

Delia frowned. "Pearl doesn't like mushrooms."

"I guess she was hungrier than I was." Coli slowed her pace. "That's the door to the bathing pool up ahead. Let me see your charming smile."

Delia rolled her eyes.

"Okay, I will smile, and you will look neutral. No, that's irritable and a little threatening. Think of plants. Better." Coli nodded and pulled open the door.

A light mist of sulphurous steam greeted them and Delia gagged.

"It smells like the dungeon."

"Hush, it's not nearly as bad."

Delia gagged again. "I'm going to stay out here."

Coli's eyes filled with tears. "Please? I'm not okay."

Delia set her jaw, then trudged inside.

"Plants," Coli reminded her, then blazed her sunny smile at the pool's occupants.

"Ladies! Welcome!" an orange-winged man shouted from across the room. "Join us!" He motioned them over to where he stood, chest-deep in the water with two other orange-winged men.

"It's a little deep for me," Coli responded, her smile dulling as she glanced around the pool.

Four solitary males and the gregarious group of three were the only occupants. Two of the solitary males appeared to be sulking and the other two gave them suggestive smiles.

Delia glared at the latter two until one of them dropped his gaze. "Why are we the only women in here?" Delia whispered, continuing to glare at the unruffled smiler who was moving closer.

"Luck, I guess," Coli shrugged and waded into the water.

"Who's your friend, Coli?" the undeterred smiler asked.

Coli laughed merrily without looking at him. "She's not interested, Holis."

"She might be," Holis argued pleasantly.

"Not after I tell her about you," Coli laughed.

Holis' expression soured as his dark wings closed. "I guess Tiger made a good choice."

"What did you just say to my friend?" Delia demanded, splashing into the water between them. Her blistered feet slipped and tore against the rough surface, but she was too furious to care.

Holis let out a surprised chuckle. "Fiery," he commented letting his gaze stray down Delia's body, "I like that."

"And yet, no one likes you," Delia snapped. "Apologize."

Holis leaned closer and a musky scent filled the air. "Or what?"

"Or," Delia began, letting the acerbic words dance off her tongue, "I'll tell everyone what a terrible coward you are so they can despise you for the right reasons instead of just hating you for your arrogance."

Coli groaned while chuckling erupted around them.

All humor had left Holis' face. He cleared his throat and muttered an apology as he quickly left the pool. When the door closed behind him, the chuckling broke into raucous laughter.

Coli sighed. "He's a jerk, but that was too harsh."

71

Delia sagged while some of the other bathers congratulated her. "I know, but that was a really cruel thing to say to you."

"I thought I wanted you to truth-bomb him, but now I just feel guilty."

"Fine. I'll do something nice for him later," Delia conceded as she waded to the shallower water to examine her stinging feet.

"Be careful. He's gotten a lot of girls pregnant."

"Eww! And I'm supposed to feel bad for him?" Delia demanded as she gingerly prodded her now-bleeding feet.

"Oh! Sorry, I forgot!" Coli hurried to her bag and retrieved a second pair of shoes. "Stand on those."

Delia took them gratefully. They were much too large for her tiny feet, but a relief to stand on.

"Hey, were you Tiger's girlfriend?" One of the sulkers had drawn close during their conversation, his somber eyes seeming to apologize for the question as he asked it. "I'm not asking to be rude; it's just that I was Princess Lexi's boyfriend...fiancé actually."

Coli eyed him with curiosity and pity. "You're Cam?"

He nodded as he stared down at the water, his long lashes casting shadows.

Coli reached out one hand to touch his arm. "I'm sorry."

"I'm sorry, too. Not that she's— I mean—I'm sorry they hurt you, too."

Coli nodded, blinking back tears.

"Anyway, I just wanted to say, if you needed to talk about...what happened, I'm here. I mean, not tomorrow, I'm going to town for food, but after that..."

"Thank you," Coli managed, her voice tight with emotion.

He nodded solemnly, and stepped around them to exit the pool.

"Cam," Coli called after him, waiting until he turned to look at her. "If you need to talk, I'll listen."

He gave her a sad smile that made dimples alight in both cheeks, then left, his brown, orange, and gold wings drooping behind him. Both girls watched him go.

"He's better looking than Tiger," Delia said. "Seems a lot nicer, too. I would question his taste in women, but I think he likes you."

Coli let out a dismissive laugh.

"Now that you ladies have cleared the pool, why not come join us?"

Delia glanced around the pool, surprised to discover the other two loners had left and only the group of three remained.

"We won't bite," the same speaker assured them. One of the other males in the group made a quiet comment and they all snickered.

Coli turned to look at Delia. "Do you want to talk to them? They're the governor's illegitimate relatives, but that's all I know about them."

"Princess governor or beat-up guy?"

"Beat-up guy."

Delia shrugged. "They've already seen my temper, so I don't have to pretend."

Coli laughed, then turned to the governor's relatives. "You're welcome to join us. Delia's not tall enough for that part of the pool."

The men laughed and moved toward them.

"I can swim," Delia protested.

"With wings?" Coli reminded her.

"Don't feel bad. Vic's too short for that part of the pool, too." Vic began splashing the speaker violently, but he only chortled and continued. "He dragged a big old rock in here to stand on."

Vic dunked the speaker and held his head under the water. "Archi here was standing on his tiptoes, and Roy was crouched on a little ledge," Vic tattled with a wicked smile.

Archi fought back to the surface, his gasp of air quickly turning to laughter as he wiped the water from his eyes.

Coli laughed with him, but the sound was stilted and uneasy.

"I'm Archi," he announced.

"She knows. Vic already told her," Roy barked irritably. "I'm going back to my room."

Delia watching him go. His black hair fell into the bluest eyes she had ever seen, but he walked past her as if she were invisible.

"Roy's a little grumpy," Archi acknowledged, "but he's our cousin, so..."

Delia looked back and forth between the two men with their identical mischievous blue eyes, dimpled chins, and broad smiles. "So, you're twins."

"Not identical, obviously, I'm much taller and better looking," Archi laughed as Vic splashed him again.

"And a shameless liar," Vic added, attempting to dunk Archi a second time.

Coli laughed nervously and backed away from the tussle.

"Quit that; you're bothering the ladies," Archi chided, protectively herding Coli a few steps away.

Delia searched her friend's face for signs she needed rescuing, but Coli was smiling more genuinely now, and she laughed when Archi whispered something in her ear. Delia relaxed her grip on her soap and began to wash.

"She won't need rescuing," Vic assured her. "Archi is a good guy."

"Or you could be biased," Delia suggested, arching back to wet her hair. When she lifted her head, Vic had moved closer.

"I could be," he said with an easy laugh that made his eyes sparkle.

Almost as blue as Roy's, Delia thought and examined him more carefully, liking the sprinkling of freckles across his nose. "Are *you* a good guy?"

His cheerful expression faltered, and she could see him rubbing the knuckles of his right hand under the water. "Not as good as Archi," he conceded.

"And why is that?"

"Uh, I have a bit of a temper," he admitted, his cheeks coloring slightly.

"Better or worse than mine?"

He chuckled. "Based on the few minutes that I've known you, I have no idea."

Delia felt a smile creeping onto her face. "That's a good answer."

"I was hoping you'd think so." He stepped even closer until only a foot separated them.

A familiar scent caught Delia's nose and she inhaled deeply. It reminded her of an afternoon in her father's shop.

"Do you want to have a moonlight picnic with me?"

Perhaps she *was* still capable of charm. "Do you mind if Coli comes, too? And Archi, of course." Delia glanced over at them and her mouth fell open. They were kissing.

Vic snickered. "Smooth."

Delia scowled. "She's vulnerable, and he's taking advantage."

"She seems to be enjoying herself." Vic grinned as he watched them. Archi cradled Coli's face in his hands while she gripped his biceps.

"You shouldn't watch," Delia chided, grabbing Vic's chin and turning his face away from the amorous couple. His lightly stubbled jaw felt rough in her hand, and her stomach dropped at his proximity. Vic's grin faded as his eyes fell to her lips and he leaned forward.

Gasping, Delia fell out of her borrowed shoes as she backed away. "You don't even know me! We just met. You can't just kiss me."

"Sorry."

An awkward silence ensued, punctuated by the soft kissing noises of their companions. Delia resumed her washing, trying to nonchalantly locate her shoes while she did so. Her searching toes met with nothing but rugged volcanic rock.

"Would that have been your first kiss?"

Delia felt her face heat and she rinsed her hair to hide it. When she finished, he was close again.

"I could show you how," he offered. "Then when you're ready for that first kiss, you'll know what you're doing."

"That's stupid." Despite her dismissive words, her heart began to race. There was that smell again. Why was it familiar? She closed her eyes, seeing herself at the family apothecary shop rummaging through the rare items on a day too stormy to look for plants. She remembered the little glass vial with the richly scented amber liquid. *What was it called?*

A soft pressure met her lips, and she leapt back, eyes wide. "Did you just kiss me?!"

Confusion clouded Vic's face. "You closed your eyes and leaned into me. I thought you wanted me to."

Fury flooded Delia until she shook with rage. "Didn't I just say that you couldn't?" She marched toward him and he stumbled back.

"Delia? Are you okay?" Coli asked.

"He just stole my first kiss!" Delia snarled, digging her nails into the bar of soap as she advanced.

"It was just a kiss! What's wrong with you?" Vic demanded as she lunged for him and missed.

"Delia, stop!" Coli warned. "Just truth-bomb him and we'll go."

"No!" The rest of Delia's words were lost to a mouthful of sulphur-flavored water as the pool deepened. She coughed out as she began to swim, her wings awkwardly dragging behind her.

"Welcome to the deep end, you psychotic prude," Vic muttered.

Guttural wrath erupted from Delia's throat as she swam at him. He had retreated back to his rock, but now he looked around nervously as she splashed closer. He was trapped at the edge of the pool, unable to get out without turning to expose his wings. Just as she reached him, a firm hand on her arm pulled her back.

"You remember how bad the dungeon smelled?" Coli reminded her, towing her back to the shallower water. "You attack him, you might end up there with my stupid brothers. And I *know* you are smarter than they are. So use that clever brain of yours and calm yourself down!"

Shame was now battling with Delia's anger as she watched Vic climb out of the pool. His eyes never left hers as he gathered his belongings. The knuckles of his right hand were bloody; had she done that?

"Is she a white?" Archi asked Coli, who ignored him.

"She's crazy!" Vic accused as he hurried out of the room, dripping like a storm cloud.

Delia glared after him, her anger flaring back up.

Archi eyed Delia curiously. "Are you a white?"

Delia started to close her wings tighter, then let them drift partially open in the gentle current. There was no point in hiding after that display of temper. "Yes," she hissed. "Isn't it obvious?"

Archi tried to hide his smile. "It kind of is."

Delia wanted to snap at him, but his face was just so utterly good-natured, especially now as he attempted, but failed to contain his amusement. "Your brother is a jerk," she mumbled and wiggled out of Coli's grasp to search for her shoes.

"He can be," Archi admitted, "especially when he's embarrassed."

"Are you okay now?" Coli asked.

"Yeah. Just lost your shoes," Delia muttered.

Coli squelched a grin. "You lost another pair, huh?"

"I'll find them," Delia grumbled, her feet protesting with each probing step.

77

"That sounds like a story," Archi said, his smile evident in his voice.

"Can I tell him?" Coli asked.

"I don't care," Delia lied. It could be part of her penance. They would laugh together, and the strained look of feigned happiness on Coli's face would go away again. Delia gritted her teeth as she listened to Coli's retelling, then resisted covering her ears when they laughed.

"Oh, blisters on this rock? That's gotta hurt. I'll help you find them," Archi volunteered, getting out of the pool to peer down at the water. "There's one on your left, I think."

Delia located the errant shoe with a sigh of relief and stood atop it with both feet.

"Can you see the other?" Coli asked, coming up beside her to join the search.

"Uhh..." Archi ran around the pool. "What about there?"

Coli laughed and walked to where he indicated. "Nope."

"But I see it!"

"You'll have to show me," Coli teased.

Delia rolled her eyes as Archi returned to the water and the new couple made a game of it. Instead of helping, Delia finished washing, including soaping her offended lips until it got in her mouth. She turned to tell Coli she was leaving, but they were kissing again. Clenching the single recovered shoe between her toes, Delia hopped across the pool and climbed out. She set Coli's shoe next to her bag and slipped through the door, grateful it didn't squeak. Her torn feet left bloody marks on the stone hallways, but flying wasn't an option with soaked wings. Back in her borrowed room, she changed, then stared up at her gathered plants. She could treat her feet, but she needed bandages. Collecting her map, she gingerly made her way to the infirmary. Inside, the sharp scent of thyme pricked her nose and she idly wondered if they grew their own to make disinfectant. The long room was predictably full of cots that were barely visible in the low light. The single shining lantern was inside a corner office, lighting up a pair of yellow and black wings as their owner bent over his books.

"What do you need?" the medic called through the open door without looking up.

"Bandages," Delia said simply, peering around his office to look for medications. There were none. Likely locked inside those cabinets, she thought. A stone mortar and pestle with a heavy coating of dust sat on the desk where he had been reading.

"Let me see the injury," he said, pointing to a cot.

"I can treat them myself; I just need bandages," Delia clarified, trying to keep her irritation at bay. Her father had let her treat her own minor injuries since she was twelve. Only a major injury required a visit to a doctor.

"I am not going to give you medical supplies; we have far too little. Now please show me the injury."

"It's my feet," Delia conceded through gritted teeth.

The medic stared down at her bare feet. "Yes, I see you've bloodied my clean floor. Lay down, Miss..." he examined her wings, then walked around her to view the back side. "White," he finished, once again pointing to a cot and turning on the adjacent lantern.

Delia glared at him, but complied, feeling foolish and exposed.

"You need to wear shoes in the pool, and walking around the halls without them when your feet have open wounds will only lead to infection."

"I *know* that," she snapped. "My only pair are filthy inside and out."

"Then you need to *wash* them," he retorted, as he fetched a bottle from the office cabinet. "The laundry ladies can help you."

"They won't," she argued, then gasped as he applied the bottle's contents to her feet. It burned like a jellyfish sting.

"Just go to the laundry and Phasia will give you a bucket of water and a brush."

"I'm not allowed in the laundry, and what are you using that's so painful?!"

"Oh. You're *that* Miss White."

"Yes, I'm truly horrible," she scoffed. "Now *what* are you using?!"

"Alcohol."

Another wave of liquid fire poured over her feet. "Why?!"

"It's all we have," he admitted, returning the bottle to his office.

"You don't have soap and water?"

"You want your feet to get infected?" He punctuated his words with the screeching of a rusted metal stool across the stone floor, then sat heavily.

"Don't you have any yarrow? I know you have thyme, I can smell it."

"That's the floor cleaner."

"Of all the moth-brained quackery!" Delia leapt to her knees, making the cot groan. "Give me those bandages," she demanded, ripping them from his hands. She started to sit on the bed before remembering her wings. Back up to her knees, she closed her wings and awkwardly reached back to apply the bandage.

The medic's mouth twitched with amusement as Delia strained to wrap her feet. "Do you want my moth-brained help now?"

"No. Just give me your stool so I can sit down and do this," Delia huffed.

He shook his head and crossed his arms.

Delia flung the bandage awkwardly around her right foot in a messy wrap, then gasped when her hamstring cramped. "Fine! Help me!"

"Leg cramp? Lay down and stretch your leg like this," he instructed, taking the bandages back. "Are you an apothecary apprentice like your brother?"

Yes. Delia let out a sigh as the cramp released. "Not exactly."

"But you're not just a bookkeeper," he guessed as he unwound her bandaging debacle.

"I'm not a bookkeeper *at all*," she snapped, immediately regretting her words.

"Malan's idea? He likes to coddle all the whites. He thinks we treat you unfairly."

"Don't you?"

The medic took a moment to answer, methodically wrapping her foot as he thought about his answer. "We treat you realistically. One third of all the life servants are whites."

Delia shuddered involuntarily.

The medic finished bandaging her right foot and started on her left. "So, what did you do at your dad's apothecary shop? Compounding?"

"No," she mumbled. Pearl was going to kill her for even having this conversation.

"Wait," he said, his voice going higher in his excitement. "Are you a wildcrafter?"

"What is that?" Delia asked, genuinely curious; she had never heard the term before.

"A forager of wild medicinal plants."

"Oh." *Wildcrafter,* she mulled the word. *That's perfect...and so much better than bookkeeper.*

"Is that what you do?" He walked around to look at her, an irrepressible smile on his face.

She wanted to return his smile, but the thought of Pearl's fury kept her silent.

"Yes!" he pumped a fist in the air, correctly interpreting her silence as assent. "We're going to have a decent dispensary again! There must be a ton of medicines growing all over this mountain."

Did he expect her to start working for him immediately? "I'm *not* a life servant and I don't plan to be one."

"Nobody does," he shrugged. "But I'll make you a deal. You work for me, and I'll find you some decent shoes and get your other pair washed."

"That's a terrible deal."

"Fine. What do you want?"

"To be left alone," Delia groused just as her stomach growled.

"You want food? I can get you food."

"I can forage for it myself," Delia said, turning to go.

The medic caught her arm. "Please. The governor hasn't cared enough to keep the infirmary stocked. Now that he's badly injured, he's furious we don't have the medicine to take care of him. He's been threatening the attending medics with the dungeon if we can't get him out of pain. We paid an in-season to fly down to Pine Hollow and buy medicine, but we don't expect him back until tomorrow afternoon, and who knows what he'll bring. Just get me something for pain and swelling, and I'll try to undo whatever the laundry mistress has done to you. Knowing her, I'm sure it's bad."

Delia nodded, her pity too strong to refuse. "I already have what you need. I'll get them now."

"Are you serious? That's wonderful! I'd come with you, but I'm not allowed to leave the infirmary unattended."

I will NOT become a life servant, Delia vowed to herself as she left the infirmary, walking as quickly as her painful feet would allow. Back in Talis and Ora's room, she took up her makeshift shirt-bag, then stared up at the light fixture well out of reach to her wet wings. Wincing at the horrible sound, she dragged the bed over, then jumped, pulling down a few plants with each bounce. By the time she had retrieved them all, her feet were throbbing. Hobbling, she loaded up her bag, then hurried back to the infirmary where the medic was pacing excitedly. Delia spent the next hour teaching him about the plants and telling him what she could remember of her father's preparations. The temptation to find Pearl and quiz her was strong, but common sense kept her from acting on it. Before she left, she showed him how to treat her feet with cottonwood leaf bud resin.

"Thank you," Delia said when he finished.

"No, thank you, Miss White."

"Delia."

"Only the life servants get called by their first names. I'm Zelic."

"Zelic, could we keep this just between the two of us?"

"I can try, but when the other medics see all the raw medicine, it won't take them long to figure it out."

"Maybe just the medics, then?"

Zelic nodded. "But if I keep your secret, I doubt I'll have enough leverage to get Phasia to stop punishing you."

"Phasia is the laundry mistress with the eczema all over her hands?"

Zelic nodded. "I don't have anything for it. I think she's been stealing lotion from the in-seasons, but it's not working."

"Chamomile and pigweed would help. I'll look for some tomorrow," Delia announced before she could catch herself. Guilt kept her from taking it back.

"That's very generous considering how she's probably treating you."

Delia shrugged uncomfortably. "I let her goad me into being cruel."

"You're a white; could you have resisted?"

Delia hesitated. *Could I have resisted?* "I *should* have resisted," she answered. *No more truth bombs*, she promised herself, knowing it was a promise she would probably break.

"You're a nice person, Miss White, despite all the hormonal rage."

Delia turned away quickly, her eyes filling with tears. Not trusting her voice, she waved as she walked away, hoping the gesture passed for a sufficient response. She was almost to the door when guilt bade her stop. Clearing her throat, she turned around. "Sorry I was so horrid before."

Zelic grinned. "You mean you don't think I'm a moth-brained quack?"

Delia's face heated. "I'm really not doing a good job of handling my hormones."

"No one really expects you to."

"*I* expect it."

Zelic's smile dimmed. "Sometimes happiness lies in lowering our expectations."

Delia knit her brows. "No."

He laughed.

Chapter Seven

Delia stared down at her feet, the bandages getting dirtier with each step. She needed shoes *now*. Though it would be lovely if Zelic found her some, she had called his offer a bad deal and brought him the plants without agreeing to a specific exchange. She wanted to berate herself for the oversight, but giving him the plants felt like the right thing to do. *Was the right thing to do*, she corrected herself. If only she had brought her foraging boots. Her mother had convinced her they were too worn, ugly, and heavy to bring to the Mating Mountain when they had shopped for her winged clothes two months ago. Part of her mother's vehemence on the subject was due to the heavy boots Pearl had insisted on taking. Delia stopped abruptly in the hallway. *Pearl's boots!* They were a size larger than hers, but the bandages would make up the difference. Delia fumbled with the map she had stuffed into her pocket and found Pearl's room. At her sister's door, she paused with her fist raised to knock. Pearl had always shared her clothes with her sisters growing up, but she was a little odd about her shoes. Any money their father paid Pearl for compounding went into her boot collection. She had even installed special shelves to display them in their room. She did wear most of the thick-soled, bright-laced footwear that she collected, but no one had ever asked to borrow them, not even Chloe, who had the same shoe size. The boots Pearl had brought to the Old Castle were her favorite. Delia shifted her feet as they began to ache again and knocked.

"What?!" came the irritable call from within.

Delia eased the door open and attempted a smile. "Hi."

Her sister glared at her from the bed where she was reading a book. "Let me guess: Coli found a new boyfriend and flitted off, so now you're talking to me again."

Guilt and confusion warred in Delia's face. "You got mad at me for collecting plants; I didn't think you'd want me around, especially when we're both all hormonal and liable to tear each other's wings off.

"Is that what you're here to do? Tear them off? Go ahead; I'm not using them," her sister snapped, her eyes returning to the book while her angry breathing belied her indifference.

"Why are you sitting in here reading and feeling sorry for yourself anyway? Shouldn't you be looking for a husband?"

Pearl threw the book across the room, making them both wince when the spine broke, scattering pages. "Look what you made me do! I'm not even supposed to have it."

Pearl flew across the room and gathered up the pages while Delia rescued the abused book. Together they laid it out on Pearl's little table, working together to restore the pages. By the time each page was back in its proper place, they were both calmer.

Delia pulled out the little stool from under the table and sat, relieved to take the pressure off her feet. "I didn't mean to neglect you. I've mostly been sleeping."

"Have a seat. Make yourself comfortable," Pearl intoned sarcastically.

"Sorry, my feet started hurting again."

Pearl looked down at her sister's bandages. "What did you do?"

"It was Mr. Fritillary's horrible fishing shoes! He swore they were the most comfortable water shoes he'd ever worn, but they gave me more blisters than any shoes ever have."

Pearl snorted. "He tried that on me, but his daughter told me he accidentally ordered fifty pairs instead of five. He wore them once and decided they weren't 'fit to stand in,' but it didn't stop him from singing their praises to anyone that would listen."

"What a weasel! I can't believe he did that."

Pearl's second snort sounded more like a chuckle. She patted Delia on the head. "You're just gullible, little sister."

Delia pushed her hand away. "I was born nine minutes before you!"

"But you're so wee," Pearl teased, sounding like her old self.

"There's nothing wrong with being small!" Delia protested. This was an old argument, and she drew comfort from its repetition rather than feeling any ire.

Pearl smirked at her, then laid back down on her bed. "Is that what the plants were for?"

"Yes; they're magical make-me-grow-taller-than-my-annoying-sister plants," Delia deadpanned.

Pearl snorted. "No, your feet, you moth-brain."

Delia nodded at the floor, hating the half-truth. "Cottonwood leaf bud resin for my feet and some food."

"Do you have any food left?"

Delia shook her head just as her stomach growled again.

"That big bag of plants and you already ate them all?" Pearl narrowed her eyes. "*And* you're hungry?"

Delia shrugged and ran her fingers over the ill-repaired book. "I've missed all my meals so far; that bag was all I had to eat."

"Why have you missed all your meals?"

Delia sighed and told her sister all of her misadventures since coming in season, carefully leaving out her visits to the infirmary.

"Where'd you get the bandages?"

Delia swallowed, composing her face before looking up. "Coli got them for me."

"I thought she was with the governor's illegitimate brother?"

Delia cleared her throat. "She got them before we went to the pool so I could apply them when I got out."

"Mm-hm," Pearl intoned, her skepticism obvious.

"What? I was afraid to go anywhere myself because I was worried the princess or the laundry curmudgeon were going to put me in the dungeon. I've literally been hiding in Talis and Ora's room." Delia took a breath, evaluating her sister's face for signs of softening. *Don't ask for the boots yet; time for a subject change!* "I wonder if this is what Dina feels like hiding in Nap's room."

"Dina is hiding in Nap's room?"

Delia nodded and launched into a full account of Dina's misdeeds, grateful to have such an effective distraction. Pearl jumped to her feet when she told her how Dina had broken their brother's wings, then paced through the rest of the story.

"Well, that ruins everything," Pearl growled when she finished.

"Why? You don't have to live with them. It's sad for Mom and Dad, and really sad for Nap, but why would it be sad for you?"

"Why?!" Pearl marched back to stand over her sister. "Because it's another lost option, Delia! I've been here too long. I'm going to get stuck unless I leave soon. And all of my relationships have ended horribly, and right now I have *no* prospects. And I just want to go home and work. I miss Mom and Dad, I miss the apothecary and compounding, and I'm not sure I even want children."

Delia's mouth fell open, but she quickly closed it.

Pearl resumed pacing her small room. "I never met Dina. I thought the rumors about her were exaggerations."

"You didn't go to the wedding?

Pearl shook her head. "Nap and I weren't getting along, and they got married and left fifteen minutes after he proposed. He left me a note, though. Honestly, I was planning to go home the day you arrived."

"Are you still?"

"I don't know! I certainly can't handle Dina while I'm in season; I couldn't even handle Nap!"

"Wow," Delia managed. "I don't know how to fix that."

"It's not fixable," Pearl snapped. "And then you come up here toting your plants and arguing with Malan about calling yourself a bookkeeper, and what I thought couldn't get worse suddenly did!"

Delia jumped to her feet, ignoring the pain it caused. "I *knew* you didn't want me around. You pretend to be all upset that I didn't come talk to you before now, but that's what you *wanted*!"

"I don't know what I want!" Pearl shouted, glaring at her sister for a moment before she opened the door and marched out of it.

Delia followed her out into the hallway. "You're just going to leave?"

"It's better than saying something I will regret," Pearl yelled over her shoulder.

"Haven't you done that already?"

Pearl stopped and turned to glower at her sister. "Don't follow me."

"Fine, but I'm stealing your boots."

"What?! Why?"

"Because I don't have any shoes."

Pearl fumed, her head shaking minutely. "Is that why you came to talk to me?"

"Partly," Delia admitted, hoping that was the right answer.

Pearl blew out a loud breath. "You can *borrow* them if you promise not to go tromping around in the forest with them."

"That's what boots are for!"

"Not *my* boots! Do you promise?"

"Ugh! Fine! I promise," Delia conceded. The chamomile and pigweed would have to wait until she got some boots of her own.

Satisfied, Pearl resumed her march, then turned back. "And wear *socks*, Delia!"

"I didn't bring any," Delia called back.

"Then borrow those, too!" Pearl shrieked before stomping away. Delia watched her go, marveling at the unpleasant transformation. She missed the pre-season witty and wise Pearl with her low laugh and teasing manner. *And she probably misses the old me*, Delia thought. Full of bittersweet memories, she laced up her sister's boots.

Now that she had shoes, it was time to tackle the next problem. All the way to Malan's office, she rehearsed what she might say and hoped he was serious when he offered to help her if she got into trouble. She stopped just outside the clerk's office when she heard voices inside.

"I swear if Coli cries herself to sleep again tonight, I'm going to smother her," the female voice griped.

Delia fisted her hands, feeling the half-moons of her fingernails digging into her palms. It had to be Coli's gossipy roommate. Delia peered around the door frame to see a blue-winged girl in a very short dress.

"I could probably move you back into your old room now that the princess is gone," Malan suggested. "Clodi is probably lonely."

The female snorted derisively. "I don't know which is worse, Clodi's snoring or Coli's tears. At least my old room is bigger, and I like watching for new arrivals from the balcony."

Malan laughed. "You and Gus."

"How does he manage to be *that* excited over new arrivals when he's been here for three months?"

"Irrepressible hope, I think."

The blue-winged girl shifted her weight and lowered her voice. "I could use some of that."

"I think you're too jaded for anything more than guarded optimism," Malan said wryly, then laughed when she hit him.

"You made me what I am," she accused, then leaned forward reaching for Malan, her blue wings blocking their faces from view, but the soft sounds were unmistakable.

Is everyone constantly kissing up here?! Malan can't be in season, he's a life servant! Delia turned away, her emotions a tangle of embarrassment and confusion. She needed to talk to Coli. Delia checked the pool first, then Talis and Ora's room, then her own empty room, then Coli's. There she knocked on the door, hoping Coli's roommate wasn't inside.

"What?!" the same female voice from the clerk's office yelled through the door.

Delia sighed. "Is Coli there?" she shouted to be heard through the solid wood door.

"No."

As Delia walked away, she could hear the door open behind her. She turned to look, and Coli's roommate gave her an evaluative stare before shutting the door once again.

"Charming," Delia huffed. *No wonder Coli doesn't like her.* Scowling, she pulled the folded map out of her pocket again. *Where would Coli and Archi be? Amphitheater? Library? Ballroom?* It must have been outside the ballroom where the minty jerk had grabbed her thigh. Delia clenched the map, knuckles white at the thought. Folding up her map again, she marched toward the ballroom, ready for battle in her sister's heavy boots.

The ballroom crowds grated against her like coarse sand on a sunburn. The air was a cacophony of scents with the underlying note of sulphur escaping from the nearby dungeon. Worse was the error-ridden song that the life-servant musicians were playing on makeshift instruments. Delia covered her ears and breathed through her mouth, attempting to navigate the room without being touched. Despite the late hour, the ballroom was full and dancers crowded the air while envious watchers cluttered the floor. Random apologies were tossed her way as elbows, wings, and even a slipper-clad foot collided with her. Delia tightened her wings behind her. *How did anyone's wings survive this onslaught? And why would anyone choose to come here?* She searched for Coli's golden wings, but flashes of yellow clothing and wings swirled throughout the room.

"Delia!"

Did someone call me? Relenting, Delia lowered her hands, letting the wave of sound hit her unfiltered.

"Delia! Over here!"

Delia followed the voice to the spot near the band where Coli and Archi were dancing, her friend waving enthusiastically for her to join them. Recoiling, Delia pointed outside the room, then turned to exit, her hands once again covering her ears. Out in the hall, the music and loud conversation was a mere irritant and Delia became aware that people were staring at her. Self-conscious, she dropped her hands and took a breath through her nose again. Three dark-haired men with identical wings gave her shy smiles as they passed by, making the air catch fire with their spicy scents. Delia gasped a breath through her mouth, her eyes running as she hurried to increase the distance between them.

"Delia, wait!"

Delia turned back at Coli's voice, but her eyes were swimming, making the blur of people indistinguishable.

"Have you been crying?" Coli was next to her now, trying to pull her into a hug. "What happened?"

Delia pushed her back, wiping her eyes. "Smells like angry pepper and bitter onion."

Coli's laugh rang out. "Is that all?"

Delia could hear Archi's pleasant chuckle, but she kept her eyes shut as they continued to stream.

"Let's get you further away. I can smell it, too, now. That's just awful."

Delia let Coli lead her down the hall.

"Are you wearing Pearl's boots?" Coli asked. "Did you have to steal them?"

"She let me borrow them as long as I promised not to go into the woods."

"That's going to torture you," Coli laughed.

Delia took an experimental breath through her nose, then opened her eyes, wiping away the last of her reflexive tears. "I'll get some more shoes tomorrow."

Archi stood ten feet away, watching Coli with a happy smile on his handsome face.

"Do you want us to go with you?" Coli volunteered.

Hmm...you've become an 'us.' "Not unless you want to."

Coli looked back at Archi, a silly smile spreading across her face. "I love looking at him. And he's so cheerful. And I really like kissing him." Coli giggled. "Sorry, what were you saying?"

"Didn't the princess' ex-fiancé say he was going to town tomorrow? What was his name?"

"Cam. But you don't know anything about him; we can go with you."

Coli was staring at Archi again. "Is that what you wanted to talk about?" Coli dragged her eyes back to her friend. "Where did you go anyway? Were you with Pearl this whole time? We looked for you. Archi made us a big picnic. Vic has a ton of food, and Archi talked him into sharing it even though he was in a terrible mood. I think Vic really liked you. Are you still mad at him?"

"He called me a psychotic prude."

Coli gasped. "No wonder you attacked him! That is so not okay; I take back my pity and my matchmaking. What a horrible thing to say!"

A high nasal laugh drew their attention back to Archi and the two identical gray-winged girls that were flirting with him. One of them tried to whisper in his ear, but he danced back with an uneasy laugh and gave Coli a "help me" face.

Coli chuckled. "I know I don't really know him yet, but he's making me feel so much better. When I'm with him, Tiger doesn't exist and I don't feel like I wasted an entire month of my season." Coli's brows contracted before she shook her head, making her golden curls bounce. "So what have you been doing?"

"Gave my plants to one of the medics."

"You didn't! Oh, Pearl is going to kill you."

"Not if you don't tell her."

"Of course I won't. But that is going to get out, Delia. How is the medic going to explain your plants?"

"I told him he could tell the other medics."

Coli sighed. "That won't stay a secret for long. The life servants are bored; they live for gossip. And Pearl is going to break your wings when she finds out."

Delia ran a calming hand over her face, trying to soothe down her own alarm. "Did she tell you she was planning to leave? Just give up and go home?"

"Pearl? No. She has a guy that follows her around a lot. She says he's only a friend, but I think she'll marry him eventually."

"Hmm. Oh, and I kind of met your horrible roommate."

"Psyche? Were you looking for me?"

Delia nodded. "I saw her kissing Malan."

Coli gasped so loudly that Archi turned to look at her. "No! He's her old boyfriend, but he's a life servant now; why would he even want to? Oh." A deep blush suffused Coli's cheeks. "They must have mated when he was still in season...if he's still attracted enough to feel like kissing her. What kind of kiss?"

Now Delia colored. "Sounded like you and Archi at the pool."

"You couldn't see them?"

Delia shook her head. "Her wings blocked their faces, but she leaned forward and reached out, and then the sounds." Delia's color deepened and she shifted from foot to foot.

"In my room?!"

Delia shook her head. "The clerk's office."

"Oh." Coli's relief turned to concern. "They're going to get caught."

"They *did* get caught."

"Yes, but *we're* not going to tell anyone."

Delia nodded her agreement. "I think she's moving back into her old room; was she rooming with the princess?"

Coli nodded. "Until the princess kicked her out."

Delia quelled a shiver. "The princess is even scarier than Psyche."

"Yes, she is," Coli agreed emphatically.

"Everything okay?" Archi asked, making both girls jump. They had been too engrossed in their conversation to notice his approach.

Coli laughed nervously. "It's fine."

"Want to dance a few more songs before bedtime?" Archi held out a hand and Coli took it with a partially suppressed giggle.

"You should come with us, Delia," Coli urged. "We can find you a partner easily."

"No. That room is a torture chamber."

Archi laughed as if Delia had a made a joke.

Coli hesitated. "Do you mind if I go?"

"Of course not. That's all I wanted to talk about."

Coli looked perplexed, but relented as Archi tugged on her arm. Delia watched them disappear back into the crowd and didn't bother to suppress her shiver. Hopefully that would be her first and last time in the ballroom.

Chapter Eight

Delia once again stood outside Malan's office, listening to assure herself that no one else was inside. Satisfied, she slipped in.

Malan grinned at her. "You look like someone in need of my big brother services."

Delia started to argue, then frowned. It was true.

"I didn't even know Phasia could get that angry! She piled your mattress on top of her own, and she swears you won't have a comfortable night of sleep or clean clothes as long as you're here. Did you really throw your bedding at her feet and demand she wash it while you waited?"

"No! I would never say that."

"What *did* you say?" he asked, his face lit up with delighted curiosity.

Delia scowled at him, remembering what Coli had said about the life servants loving gossip. "It doesn't matter. It wasn't nice."

Malan nodded knowingly. "You must have really humiliated her, so she's lying about what you said."

Delia colored.

"Do you need a place to sleep?"

Delia hesitated, not wanting to tell him where she was sleeping nor Coli's part in it.

"Coli's roommate is moving out as we speak. So if you want to sleep there, I won't say a word."

Delia breathed a sigh of relief. "Thank you."

"Was that all you needed?"

"No. I need room numbers."

Malan nodded and looked down at the papers on the desk before him. "Whose?"

"Uh, Cam, the guy who was the princess' boyfriend. And..." The blush that had yet to fade now invaded her forehead and neck. "...Holis," she finished, hoping he was the only in-season with that first name.

Malan whistled. "Cam Crescent is in 217, but Holis...that's not a good idea."

"I need to apologize to him."

"What did you do?"

"I wasn't nice to him, either."

Malan chuckled. "I think I need to witness some of these conversations."

"No, you don't," Delia assured him, handing him her map. "Could you mark both their rooms?"

Malan hesitated. "Nap wouldn't want you talking to him."

"I doubt he'll be willing to talk to me. I'll just apologize and go."

Reluctantly, Malan marked a second room. "Does this mean you want Phasia's room, too?"

Delia shook her head. "She tried to break my wings. I'll do something nice for her, but I'll keep my distance."

Malan stilled. "She did? Did she actually touch you?"

Delia pulled her map out from under his hand, eager to escape. "No, I moved just in time."

"Do you want to report it? She's not allowed to do that."

Delia stopped her retreat to consider the question. "Won't she just retaliate more?"

Malan scratched his head, making his shredded wing bounce with the movement. "She'd try, but the governor doesn't tolerate life servants attacking in-seasons, especially pretty young women. Normally, he'd give Phasia dungeon time, but he's a little preoccupied just now."

"Don't report it."

"You're sure? You don't owe her anything. Rude words don't justify violence."

Delia shook her head. "I was cruel. Don't report it," she repeated as she hurried out the door.

"You couldn't help it," Malan called after her.

Yes, I could have...I think. Delia shook her head and tried to smooth out the map she had clenched in her hand. It didn't matter *if* she was responsible or *how* responsible; God could sort that out. She would just make up for it as best she could. Delia wiped sudden tears from her eyes as she arrived at Cam's door and knocked.

She could hear fumbling around in the room for a full minute before the door opened and he stood, shirt inside out, wiping the sleep from his eyes.

"Yeah?"

"Sorry to wake you up."

Cam blinked blearily. "You were with Tiger's girlfriend, right?"

She nodded and held out her hand. "I'm Delia."

He grasped her hand, his long fingers even more calloused than her own. "Cam, but you probably know that. Sorry, I'm not awake yet." He let go of her hand to smooth down short-shorn auburn curls.

"Are you still planning to go to town tomorrow?"

Cam nodded and hid a yawn.

Delia shifted her weight, suddenly feeling ridiculous. "I need shoes."

He glanced down at her borrowed boots.

"These aren't mine."

"Do you want me to buy shoes for you?"

Delia held out the money her father had given her. "I need a good pair of work boots for hiking and digging," she explained. "And some water shoes. And a spade." Her face colored. "And I'll pay you for your time, of course."

99

He shook his head. "I'm going anyway, it's no trouble."

"Yes, it is. Good work boots are heavy," she insisted, still holding out the money.

He chuckled as he looked down at her feet. "Not in your size, they're not. Do you wear children's shoes?"

Delia frowned. "Sometimes."

Cam grinned, making a dimple appear in each cheek before he wisely hid his amusement. "What size?"

"Five in a women's shoe, but size three in a men's shoe."

"Isn't that a child's size?" he asked, the humor evident in his voice.

She thrust the money at his stomach with a light punch, and he finally took it, laughing openly as she walked away.

"And where do I find you when I get back?"

Good question. "I'll find you," she called over her shoulder. "Thank you."

"You're welcome," Cam replied, his chuckle cut off by the closing of his door.

Delia pulled out her map and found Holis' name. Beneath it, Malan had written *???* and Delia ground her teeth in annoyance as she marched back to the clerk's office.

"Malan!" she shouted, not caring who or what she interrupted as she turned into his office. She strode past a man standing at the clerk's desk, and slapped the map in front of Malan. "Actual numbers this time."

"What's wrong with you?" the waiting man demanded.

"The same thing that's wrong with you," Malan chortled. "You're both whites in season."

Startled, Delia examined the man closely. His wings were heavily lined in black and suffused with gold. The small sections of white looked unfinished, as if they were still expecting color. She walked behind him, ignoring his protest as she examined the back of his wings. Like hers, they were white, though more heavily edged in black. She walked back around to stare at his face. Icy blue intelligent eyes stared back at her from small, deeply tanned features. His hair was a short, bland brown, his lithe height average.

"You don't look like a white," Delia blurted, wishing she could recall the foolish words the moment they left her mouth.

"Neither do you," he smirked, aware of the effect he was having on her.

Delia could detect an exotic sweet and spicy scent in the air now, and it somehow made it harder to look away.

"Hey, now. Don't signal in my office!" Malan complained. "Here," he offered, writing on Delia's map. "Take it! Just stay out of his room." He waved the map at her until Delia took it, her face burning.

"Mine?" the white-winged man asked, confused.

"Yours, too," Malan said, then made shooing motions at Delia. "Go before he signals you again."

Delia forced herself to turn and walk away.

"I can control it," the white-winged man protested in an undertone.

"Can you?" Malan asked mockingly. "Did you mean to do it the first time?"

At the door, Delia glanced back, delighted to discover he was still watching her with those intent eyes.

"Go!" Malan implored.

Delia hurried through the door, but outside, she eavesdropped.

"Here," Malan said irritably. "You're in room 205."

"What's her name?" the white-winged man asked.

Delia thrilled at the question, a triumphant burble of joy rising up her throat and erupting in a silent laugh.

"You're both whites; it's not a good idea," Malan advised.

"I don't think that's up to you."

"I've *been* you. Be wise; take some advice."

"No, thanks."

With a wave of panic, Delia realized the conversation was over and she could hear footsteps nearing the door. With a leap, she flew to the balcony above, hoping the white-winged man wouldn't look up. But he landed beside her seconds later. Her previous blushes had been nothing to the volcanic shame that stained her skin now.

"Did you wait for me?" the white-winged man asked.

Delia shook her head, desperate for a plausible lie. "I was just going to visit a friend."

"It's okay," he said. "I'm glad you waited."

"I really do need to visit someone," Delia stuttered, hating the way she sounded.

"The guy whose room Malan told you to stay out of?"

"He's not my friend," Delia snapped, grateful to let anger overtake her humiliation.

The white-winged man nodded his head. "Good. Then you don't need to visit him."

Delia opened her mouth to explain, then realized she didn't want to.

"You can help me find my room," he said, as he took her elbow and turned her down the hallway.

Delia looked down at his slender fingers on her arm and wondered why she didn't mind. The air smelled of sweet spice again, and she found herself leaning closer to him as they walked. He was thoroughly sweaty, his shirt damp with it. Delia drew her brows together; it was odd that it didn't bother her.

"What's your name?" he asked, letting his hand slide to her wrist.

"Delia."

"I'm Len. And this is my room." He stopped in front of a door and opened it, the hinges protesting the movement with a loud creak. "Do you want to come in?"

All the reasons that she shouldn't crowded into her brain and fought for expression. Her lips fell open, but when his piercing eyes met hers, she forgot what she wanted to say.

He pulled her into the dimly lit room, then released her arm. "Sit down," he directed, pointing at a little table with a stool. He pushed the door shut, then began to unfasten his bag.

She should leave. *Why did he close the door?* Instead of sitting, she turned to the door.

"Wait!"

Hand on the door handle, she looked back. Len had removed his shirt, and the sight of his lean chest set her face aflame. She quickly opened the door.

He pushed it shut, then leaned against it, preventing her escape.

Delia froze, feeling his breath on her wings. She shivered lightly as the room swam with his pleasantly spicy scent. "I need to go," she finally managed.

He stepped away from the door. "I need to sleep, anyway."

The indifference in his tone was enough to make her look up at him. He answered her confused expression with a long, hard kiss, then climbed onto his bed. "I'll find you when I wake up. You can let yourself out."

Delia opened the door, her face so hot she could feel her pulse in her cheeks. *What just happened?! Why did I let it happen?!* Belated fury rose up to war with her humiliation as she shut the door behind her. *Another stolen kiss,* she thought, tempted to open the door back up and yell at him. Instead, she kicked it, then flew away in a panic that he would open the door and she would have to explain herself. *What's wrong with me?* Wrath returned when her own question reminded her of the one Len had asked when she first met him. *Stupid men!* Delia ran the whole incident through her mind. She shouldn't have gone inside his room. She should have listened to Malan. *Stupid me!* It was Len's intense blue eyes and his pheromones that made her stupid, she decided. She took a deep breath and blew it out. She would just have to stay away from him. Vic's blue eyes flitted through her mind as well, and she growled. Maybe no more blue eyes. Shaking her head, she took out her map and found Holis' room. *At least his eyes aren't blue*, she grumbled to herself, then felt irritated that she had noticed. At his door, she rapped hard enough to make her knuckles smart.

When he opened the door, his sleepy face soured. "What are *you* doing here?"

"I'm sorry," she snapped, then tried to school her tone. "I shouldn't have been cruel to you."

He sniffed, a look of confusion on his face. "Does your mate know you're here?"

"What? I don't have a mate."

Holis leaned forward and took a deeper breath. "Your boyfriend, then."

"I don't have a boyfriend, either!" Delia asserted, stepping back. "Stop smelling me!"

"Hard to avoid," Holis scowled. "Some guy marked you."

"What? I don't even know what that means." *What did Len do?*

Holis sighed and crossed his arms, his biceps bulging as he did so. *Stop noticing!* Delia chided herself.

"Some guy signaled enough times while he was near you to let all the men on the mountain know you're *his*."

Delia sniffed her hair and clothing. The unmistakable spicy-sweet smell of Len saturated both. Snarling, she stamped her foot, her blisters answering with immediate pain. "You horrible men!"

Amusement quirked Holis' face. "You want me to fix it for you?"

"No!"

Holis was grinning now as he stepped back and invited her into his room. "It'll only take a minute or two."

"No!" she shrieked, clenching all her muscles to stop herself from attacking him.

Chuckling, Holis went back into his room and shut the door.

Delia stomped all the way back to Talis and Ora's room, the pain in her feet somehow relieving her rage. Inside, she stripped off her clothes and boots, and yanked on her still-wet bathing suit. Muttering violently, she glared down at her bandaged feet, then put her sister's boots back on. Giving her aching feet a rest, she flew to Coli's room.

She knocked softly, worried that her friend was already sleeping. "Coli?" Delia put her ear to the door. "Psyche?" Relieved when she received no response, Delia opened the door a crack. The lantern shone brightly in the tidy room. Coli's belongings were neatly hung and stowed. The other side of the room was empty, mattress stripped, and pillow missing. Delia frowned as she slipped inside and shut the door. She was glad Psyche was gone, but why take the bedding? Four pairs of shoes were lined up under the hooks that held Coli's clothing, including the pair that Delia had worn at the pool and lost. A small metal table and stool were tucked neatly into the corner behind the door. Setting her soap on the table, Delia dragged out the little stool and sat, quickly swapping out Pearl's boots for Coli's water shoes. She stuffed her unwound, blood-stained bandages into her borrowed socks, then hid them inside the boots, lining them up neatly beside Coli's other shoes. With a nod, she retrieved her soap and left the room.

Chapter Nine

Someone had propped open the door to the bathing pool with a large rock, and the room had aired out until the sulphur scent was barely detectable. There were two girls in the water this time, one who gave her a friendly smile and the other an insincere one. At the back of the pool, where Archi and his family had lounged, stood three brown-winged males, laughing raucously. Despite the similarly colored wings, they looked nothing alike. Delia groaned when she recognized the spiky light-brown hair.

"Thistle!" Bul shouted in greeting. "I see you finally made it through the door."

"I know you held it shut, *Dragonwort*," Delia accused, making her way into the water as far away from both groups as she could manage.

More raucous laughter was her only answer as they began to drift nearer. Delia quickly dipped her hair in the water and began to wash it vigorously.

"Phew! That's some strong-smelling soap," Bul commented.

A brown-winged male with dark hair hit Bul's arm and whispered something to him.

"No! She hasn't even been here a day," Bul argued.

"How long do you think it takes?" the same brown-winged male asked in an undertone and snickered.

Delia plunged her head under to rinse, grateful the water distorted the sound of their voices and their dissonant laughter. When she stood up, she surreptitiously sniffed her hair. The spicy scent was faint now, but still there. Delia gritted her teeth and began washing her hair all over again.

"Do you have a mate already?" Bul asked bluntly. The two other males had moved back to the other side of the pool.

"No."

"A boyfriend, then?

"No!"

Bul drew his light brows together. "Why do you smell like some guy, then?"

"He *marked* me without my permission or knowledge five minutes after I met him!"

Bul nodded his head sagely. "Want us to beat him up?"

"He's a white."

"Your size?"

"Nope. Yours."

"Hmm."

"Yes, hmm...so if you and your friends are done laughing at me, you can go away now," Delia snapped.

Bul scratched his eyebrow with his thumbnail and looked back at the two brown-winged males. "Sorry," he whispered, then hurried to rejoin his group.

What? Delia's brain stumbled over the unexpected apology and she dropped her soap. Cursing herself, she searched with her feet while peering down at the volcanic rock. *Why did I bring brown soap?!* An accidental kick sent it skidding along the bottom and heightened her frustration. *Because it doesn't make your hair tangly,* she reminded herself as she chased it.

"Need some help?" Bul offered.

"No."

Bul wandered closer. "What did you drop?"

"My soap," she admitted, then forced the words out. "Sorry I was rude."

"Don't you usually yell your apologies?" he teased, then turned back to his companions. "Rus!" Bul called. "Come fetch."

"Why don't you?" Rus called back.

"Because I don't want to break my wings on the bottom of the pool."

Rus rolled his eyes. "What am I fetching?" he asked as he drew closer. His brown wings angled out rather than up, extending only a few inches above his heavily muscled shoulders.

"Brown soap," Delia answered.

Rus turned to look at her, his warm brown eyes a contrast to his feigned attitude. "Where is it?"

"I don't know; I kicked it somewhere over there." Delia pointed, suddenly aware that her hair was a mass of unrinsed suds.

"Why'd you do that?" The wry expression on Rus' face said he didn't expect an answer.

"Quit teasing her and just do it," Bul chided. "It can't be harder than moving the rock."

Delia glanced back at the propped open door wondering if it was Vic's perching rock that Rus had moved; she hoped so.

Rus submerged; the back of his wings a vivid orange beneath the water. Bul's other friend was drifting toward them now, already laughing unpleasantly, and Delia ducked her head under the water so she wouldn't have to hear what he thought was funny. This time when she finished rinsing, the unwanted scent was gone.

Rus finally broke the surface, his light brown hair plastered to his face until he shoved it off. "Thanks," he said. "I needed some soap."

Delia's mouth fell open as Rus began to move away while Bul and his other friend cackled.

"No, I need that!" Delia protested, following them until the water was too deep to walk. She started to swim, but Coli's shoe immediately began to fall off. Moving back into the shallower water, she tried to calm down. *He's just teasing*, she reminded herself, *and he did fetch the soap.*

"You guys are such brats," a female voice scolded.

Delia turned to see the girl that had smiled genuinely get out of the pool and walk around to where Bul and his friends were grinning. Her vivid green wings were rimmed in brown that almost matched her reddish hair. She stood over them, one hand on her hip and the other held out expectantly.

"Hand it over," she insisted, sounding like a mother chastising her naughty children.

The boys tittered, but Rus reached up and set the soap in her hand.

"Aargh! What is that?!" Rus complained, clutching his nose.

Bul's other companion laughed uproariously. "Every time. I swear, it burns my eyes."

Bul frowned, disconcerted. "Does everybody hate it?"

The green-winged girl smiled over her shoulder as she walked away. "I don't."

"Are you serious?" Bul asked.

She looked back and nodded coyly. Bul scrambled out of the pool to follow her while his companions shouted ribald encouragement. The green-winged girl sauntered around to the shallow end and waded back in. Bul splashed into the water right behind her. Delia could smell the foul dragonwort aroma now, and began to worry it would cling to her.

"Here you go," the green-winged girl chirped as she handed Delia her soap.

"Thank you," Delia said, relieved tears pricking her eyes. "That was kind."

The green-winged girl waved a dismissive hand and turned to Bul. "I'm Rubi."

"You really don't hate it?" Bul asked, a cloud of his putrid scent seeming to follow him.

"Bul, please stop!" Delia complained, moving away to wash her hair once again.

"Oh, quit complaining. You got your soap back, didn't you?" Bul said, his eyes on Rubi.

Rubi leaned into him and inhaled. "You smell like steak to me."

Bul chortled and turned to look at his friends who snickered at his reaction. Unperturbed, he returned his gaze to Rubi. "Want to join us?"

"No, you should stay over there, Bul," Rus called.

"Just a second. Got to take care of something," Bul told Rubi, then headed for Rus.

Rus clapped a hand over his nose. "No, I want to live!" he yelled, then laughed hysterically as Bul came at him. They wrestled and splashed at the deeper end of the pool while their dark-haired companion shouted encouragement.

"We're going to break our wings," Rus warned between laughing fits.

Bul pushed away from him with a hearty splash. "Steak! I smell like steak!" he asserted, then turned back to Rubi, who was once again standing with her friend.

"I'm Bul."

Rubi and her friend giggled.

Delia again put her head under the water to rinse, effectively blocking scent and muffling sound. Her fingers caught in the tangle of her over-washed hair, and she mentally added marshmallow root to her foraging list. When the need to breathe forced her above the water, the dragonwort scent was faint. The other occupants of the pool had clustered together in jovial hilarity. Delia slipped out of the pool, hoping the water cascading off her wasn't as loud and noticeable as it seemed.

"Bye, Thistle!" Bul yelled just as she passed through the door.

"Bye, Thistle!" the group echoed.

Eyes narrowed, Delia quickened her pace.

"Wait, I thought her name was Delia. Bye, Delia!" Rus called, his low voice carrying down the hall.

Her lips twitched in the faintest hint of a smile.

Coli's room was still empty when Delia returned the shoes. The neatly organized space was a closet compared to the lavish bedroom Coli had at home, but her friend had still managed to make the room feel uniquely hers. Delia rebandaged her feet at a snail's pace, hoping Coli would soon return. It seemed thoughtless to simply move into her friend's room without asking her permission first. *And you are a white,* Delia reminded herself bitterly. *Maybe you need to be alone.* With that sour thought, she laced up her borrowed boots and returned to her borrowed room.

The mustard scent had faded from Talis and Ora's room, and Delia idly wondered if it now smelled like her. With a sigh, she put her nightgown on. She wasn't tired, not really, she just didn't have anywhere to go. *Pathetic,* she thought, then began to tidy the room with her irritable energy. Her belongings had migrated from her bag and seemingly flung themselves about the room. It had always irritated Pearl (who was just as messy) when they still shared a room. The two of them would quibble over who had made the room untidy while Chloe selflessly cleaned up. A pang of homesickness hit Delia at the thought, and she climbed into bed longing for salty coastal wind and the plaintive cry of seagulls.

"Five thirty, testing time! Ladies report to the infirmary!"

The words broke through Delia's dream and then blended with it. The test was at her old school, and she panicked as she realized she had not studied. The other students were laughing at her. She ran from the room only to hear a chorus of "Bye, Thistle!" jeered behind her. Delia moaned in her sleep and covered both ears before drifting into less troubled dreams.

"Delia? What are you doing in my bed?"

Delia groaned and shifted her head to the other side. *Not another nightmare,* she thought.

A dry chuckle was followed by a tousling of her hair. "You always were impossible to wake up."

Memories of sleepovers at Coli's house suddenly collided with reality and Delia jerked awake. "Talis?"

He stood above her, the lantern highlighting his cherubic curls.

Delia leapt up to her knees and then stumbled off the end of the bed, swaying as she rubbed her eyes. "Sorry. I thought because the dungeon and Ora, but I didn't throw rocks, and she took my mattress." Her sleep-slurred words jumbled together like an overturned jigsaw puzzle. "And I like mustard."

Talis snorted laughter. "You're lucky I know this story or I would be very confused right now. Coli didn't tell us she hid you *here*."

Delia yawned and blinked. His yellow wings looked wrong...unmatched. She stared hard at his left forewing, finally seeing the healing frame for what it was. "She broke your wing."

Talis' face darkened. "I can't believe she's a *princess* and halfway home to her palace with her horsey boy. I *knew* he wasn't good enough for Coli. She should have let me break his wings. Now Coli's heartbroken and all three of us will probably end up life servants."

Talis' vitriol hit Delia like an icy winter wave. She shifted on her bandaged feet, wishing Pearl's boots weren't behind Talis and that she hadn't slept in her nightgown.

"The governor knows it's totally unfair; that's why he let me out of the dungeon a day early. He may be a lecherous creep, but at least he has some sense of justice. You should tell him what the laundry mistress did to you; I bet he'd make her give your mattress back."

"I don't think he's talking to in-seasons just now."

"Right. I heard that he got beat up. It was probably his illegitimate relatives; they *hate* him."

Delia stilled. "Do you mean Archi, Vic, and Roy?"

Talis nodded. "I overheard them a couple weeks ago. They asked the governor for life-servant meals—which are *way* better than the slop they feed us. They figured they were entitled to a perk or two from their half-brother."

Half-brother and cousin, Delia corrected, but said nothing as she thought of Vic's bloody knuckles.

"But the governor just threatened to throw them in the dungeon and gave them some outraged speech about his 'superior pedigree,' and then sicced the guards on them. Bet they got their revenge, especially since whoever beat him up took his food."

"I need to find Coli," Delia blurted before he could continue. "Could you go outside so I can change?"

Talis glanced at her nightgown and his face warmed. "Uh, yeah. Um, I can just," he said, pointing at the door, then trying to get around her.

Delia flew up to the bed to make space for his open golden wings.

"The break hurts when I close them," he explained, the blush spreading to his ears. "I'll just wait out there." Talis opened the door and turned sideways to exit, then carefully closed it behind him.

Delia dressed in a whirl as she reviewed everything the governor's half-brothers and cousin had said. *Could they have done it?* It was difficult to imagine Archi being violent, but not Roy and maybe not Vic either. *Poor Coli!* The last thing she needed was another troubled romance. Dressed, she stuffed her belongings into her bag and headed for the door. Whether or not Coli wanted a roommate, she had to move out. Outside the door, Talis waited.

He glanced at her bag. "You don't have to move out. We could sleep in shifts or I could move my mattress to your room," he blurted, then colored. "I mean, I'll make sure you have a place to sleep. You're kind of like my sister, but not my sister, because obviously I can smell you. The room smells way better now."

"Did *you* just wake up?"

Talis laughed self-consciously. "This is so weird. Because I've known you all my life, and you and Coli were usually tattling on Ora and me and you two stopped some of our best pranks before we could pull them off." He rubbed his neck. "You were kind of obnoxious. And then I find you in my bed after a really bad couple of days, and I just feel—happy, and I...I don't want you to leave."

What do I say to that?! "Um, thank you, but Coli's roommate moved out last night and Malan said I could sleep there. I just wanted to ask Coli first, but I didn't get a chance last night." Delia took a step into the hall, but Talis stepped forward as well, forcing her to step back into the doorway to maintain a comfortable distance between them.

Talis laughed, the sound turning bitter as he put a hand up on the doorframe. "It's the broken wing, right? You figure the governor won't let me get married until it heals and my season will probably end first, so you don't want to get involved with me." He nodded, lips tight. "That's smart."

No, I don't want to get involved with you because you're not very nice, and we've never gotten along well. "I'm sorry about your wing. I'll see what I can find to make it heal faster."

"I could fly with it now; it's just painful. Maybe something to numb it?"

"I think that would make it even harder to fly. You should give it a chance to heal."

"In two weeks? I've been here for two and a half months. My father's season only lasted three."

"Yours could be longer. I'll do what I can." Delia eyed his wings, wondering if she could push past the uninjured set without hurting him.

Talis noticed her gaze and stepped forward until she backed into the room. He winced as he closed his wings just enough to make it through the doorway without turning away from her, then shut the door with his foot. The unmistakable scent of mustard filled the room, and Delia glared up at him.

"Let me out." Each measured word was a warning that Talis seemed determined to ignore.

"Listen," he said, his tone conciliatory and wheedling. "I might be your best option."

Delia bristled at the tone and spoke through gritted teeth. "Move away from the door, Talis."

"You're a *white*, Delia. Coli told us how you've been acting. But *I* know that's not what you're really like. With me you could live by your parents, even help Nap take over the apothecary shop when our kids are grown. And you know you'd never want for anything. My dad's entire shipping company will fall to me now that Ora's going to be a life servant. And who cares if the governor won't marry us; my family would keep the secret. I'm very good at keeping secrets. No one has to know you were with Ora when he attacked the princess' guard."

Delia poked him so hard in the chest that her finger ached. "Don't you *dare* try to blackmail me into mating with you, Talis! You are a spoiled, rotten little pupa in the shape of a man. For Coli's sake, I will not rip your broken wing right off your back, but know that I'm thinking about it, and being a white, who's to say whether I can control myself or not? So if you value that slim chance of not becoming a life servant, you will leave me *and my secrets* alone. Now, will I be tearing off that wing right now or will you let me out?"

"You don't have to be such a shrew about it," Talis said sulkily, but flinched and took refuge between the beds when Delia jerked forward threateningly.

"I can't believe you did that," Delia chastised as she walked back to open the door. "I'm telling Coli *and* I'm going to write a letter to your mother." Delia slammed the door on his protests and flew down the hall, heart pounding. *That was not my fault*, she assured herself. *Coli knows what he's like.* But at Coli's door, she hesitated, hand raised to knock. A trill of laughter sounded from behind the door followed by Archi's throaty chuckle. *How wonderfully awkward.*

Delia knocked before she could talk herself out of it, and the laughter immediately quieted. "Coli?"

Coli opened the door just wide enough to stick her head through. "Delia, I didn't see you at breakfast or pregnancy tests. I thought you went shoe shopping with Cam."

Delia shook her head. "There was a pregnancy test?"

"Every morning."

Delia scowled. "Can I talk to you privately?

116

Coli rolled her eyes before stepping out into the hallway in her bare feet and shutting the door. "We were only talking."

Delia grabbed her friend's elbow and pulled her further down the hall, glancing suspiciously at the few people passing by. "Talis overheard Archi, Vic, and Roy talking about how much they hate the governor a couple of weeks ago. They asked him for better food and he threatened them with the dungeon."

Coli's thin brows knit together. "So?"

"So Vic's knuckles were bloody, and where did he get all that food?"

Coli glanced back at her door frowning. "Archi's knuckles aren't bloody. He couldn't have done it. He wouldn't be a part of that."

"Are you sure? You haven't known him very long."

"He wouldn't do that, Delia. I talked to him half the night. If Vic did it, then Archi doesn't know."

"I hope you're right. And I hope he doesn't get punished anyway, since the rules seem to be whatever the governor says they are. He let Talis out a day early."

Coli looked down at Delia's bag. "Talis kicked you out?"

"No, he said he wanted me to stay and tried to blackmail me into mating with him."

Coli laughed merrily, mistaking the truth for sarcasm.

Delia frowned and dropped her voice. "Ora told him I was there when he attacked the guard."

Coli's mouth fell open, all traces of humor gone. "He didn't!"

"I truth-bombed him and threatened to rip his wing off if he didn't let me out of his room." Delia lifted her hair and sniffed it, annoyed when she detected mustard. "Great. It stinks. If I got marked again, someone is going to die."

"Marked *again?*"

"I met a white, five minutes later he kissed me and marked me."

"Delia!"

"I hate this place. The next guy that tries to kiss me or mark me or trap me in a room is losing a wing."

Coli hugged Delia, then pulled away when she didn't return it. "I'm really sorry about my brother; I'll take care of it. And you can stay in my room," Coli tugged Delia's bag away from her. "Just let me deal with..." she glanced back at her door and sighed, "...Archi. And then I'll come find you, okay?"

Delia's stomach rumbled. *How many meals have I skipped?* "I'm going foraging."

"I thought Pearl said her boots weren't allowed in the forest."

Delia swore and stared down at her sister's pristine footwear. "I'll clean them really well, and hopefully she'll never know. I just can't be here right now. I'm going to hurt someone if I stay."

Coli took a step back.

"Not *you*. I have to go." Delia took her bag back, and strapped it on as she walked away. An unending stream of expletives paraded through her mind despite her fight to dispel them. Her pace increased until a hand-holding couple blocked the hallway. Their syrupy words grated on her like a sand-filled shoe. Grumbling, she flew over them. At the entrance, a propped-open door aided her escape, and she breathed easier as the cool breeze hit her face. The mid-morning sunshine dappled the beckoning forest a golden green. Delia flew faster, ignoring the chattering courtyard occupants.

"No boots in the forest!" Pearl yelled.

Delia groaned, her disappointment a sinking force that brought her to the ground on the courtyard's outer edge. Her escape was so enticingly close! Guiltily, she turned back to her sister. "I will wash them *so* well," she promised.

"No!" Pearl leapt up from her seat and marched over. The man she had been sitting with turned to watch them with an amused expression. "Those are my favorite boots! Stay in the castle or take them off."

"Fine." Delia yanked a rusted stool out from under an equally rusted table and sat on it. She unlaced and ripped off the boots and socks, setting her feet afire with her violence. When she leapt into the air, one bandage dangled behind her.

"Are you insane?" Pearl demanded, collecting her beloved boots before following her sister into the air. "You're still going?"

"If I don't get away from people, I'm going to hurt someone."

Pearl nodded. "Swearing in your head?"

Delia looked at her sister in surprise.

"Thought you were the only one? I think it's a white thing, though Chloe never admitted to it."

They were quiet as they flew over dense evergreen forest, the wind pulling at their hair and wings. Delia took deep breaths of the clean air, grateful the ever-present sulphur scent of the castle was behind her. *Flying is lovely*, she thought, grateful that the expletive stream was finally drying up.

"You're going foraging, aren't you?" Pearl accused.

"I'm hungry and my hair is all ratty because I had to wash it a million times after I got marked," Delia snapped.

"What were you *doing*?"

"Nothing. I didn't even know he marked me."

Pearl snorted. "You kind of smell like it happened again."

"I knew it!" Delia raged. "Stupid Talis trapped me in his room and tried to blackmail me into mating with him."

"Talis? I thought he was still in the dungeon. And what's he doing trying to mate with you when his wing is broken? Do you even like him?! I can't believe he marked you *twice*! And how is he blackmailing you?!"

Delia's mouth twitched into a partial smile at her sister's furious volley of questions. "No, I don't like him, and he only marked me once. Some other guy did it, too."

"Oh, I would have hurt someone. I would have hurt several someones."

Delia's twitch grew into a smirk.

"You know what?" Pearl asked rhetorically as she yanked off her shoes, then offered them to Delia. "Here. These can get dirty. You got marked twice, you deserve a day of foraging."

Delia accepted the awkward in-air transfer. "Thank you."

Pearl nodded and turned back. "If you find marshmallow root, get some for me, too," she called over her shoulder.

Delia smiled as she clutched her sister's shoes. A golden day of solitude lay before her with an entire forest of plants to discover.

Chapter Ten

Delia returned to the castle at dusk with a serene, dirt-smudged smile. Two shirts had become makeshift bags this time, and both were overflowing with her wild harvest. She had dined well in the forest, and found herself pitying the in-seasons their meager menu. A single person sat out on the patio, arms across his chest, his familiar dark-tipped wings blending into the shadows.

"You didn't tell me you were leaving the castle," Len said as she landed in the courtyard.

Delia put a hand up to smooth her tangled hair, then let it drop. "And you didn't tell me you marked me."

"Marked you? I don't know what that means."

Delia blushed. "You made me smell like your mate."

"Oh." He shifted forward, his hands falling into his lap. "That wasn't intentional."

Delia began to move past him, but he stood and bent toward her, his lips grazing her cheek and making sparks flash down her side.

"Why do you keep kissing me?!"

He took a step back. "You don't like it?"

Delia's blush deepened. "You should ask first," she grumbled.

He stepped too close and bent down, his mouth almost touching hers. "Well?" he asked, his blue eyes mocking.

Delia's breath hitched and she stumbled back a step. "That's not how you ask."

"Tell me how, then."

Delia's face felt hot in the cool evening breeze. She could smell his spicy-sweet scent, and couldn't seem to revive her indignation. "I don't know."

He let out a low chuckle. "Then how do you know that wasn't the right way?"

"When someone asks me properly, I'll let you know," Delia snapped, pushing past him.

He followed her, still chuckling as she yanked the heavy door open and stepped inside.

"So is this all food?" he asked, pointing to her makeshift bags full of roots, stalks, leaves, and flowers.

"Some of it is," she conceded, as he pulled the heavy door closed behind them.

"What's the rest of it?" he asked, keeping pace with her.

None of your business. "Poison for my enemies," she quipped.

He smirked, then pulled out a reddish root that protruded from one of her makeshift bags. "Can I eat this one?"

"No!" She yanked it away from him, then tucked it deeper into one of her bags. "It tastes horrible and that much would kill you."

"It's a medicine?"

Stop asking questions! Delia glanced uncomfortably around them, but no one seemed to have overheard.

"Did you work at an apothecary?"

Delia threw up her hands as two men passed them in the hallway. "Didn't Malan explain to you about not advertising your skills, especially to the life servants?" she whispered.

"No."

"What's your apprenticeship?"

"I'm a teacher's assistant."

"Ah," Delia said, nodding her head. "I guess that wouldn't matter."

He frowned. "That's rude."

"It wouldn't matter because it's not a skill they need among the life servants. Mine is."

"Oh. Why are you doing life-servant work? You're in season."

Delia sucked in a big breath and blew it out slowly. "Foraging calms me down. People do not."

He snorted. "What are you going to do with all the plants, then?"

Penance? Trade? "I'm going to...help people."

"Why?"

Delia stopped walking and looked at him, perplexed. "Why *not*?"

"Because you're in season. You're here for yourself."

Delia rolled her shoulders as if shrugging off an uncomfortable sweater. "I don't like that."

"Why? Because it's true?"

Delia shook her head at him. "No, because it's selfish. People always need help...even when they're really annoying...*especially* when they're really annoying."

"People need to be independent; figure it out for themselves."

"That's funny, coming from a teacher."

One side of his mouth curved up into a wry grin. "I like talking to you."

You're enjoying this conversation? "Thanks. I need to make some...deliveries."

"Helping people?"

She nodded.

"And then what?"

Delia looked down at her soil-lined nails self-consciously. "And then a bath."

"I'll meet you at the pool," he said, then gave her a quick kiss before she realized what he was doing.

Momentarily stunned, she watched him walk away, his long stride purposeful. "You're supposed to ask first," she mumbled belatedly. What was it that she had threatened for the next man who tried to kiss her? Wing loss? She sighed and touched her lips.

She dropped off some marshmallow root in her sister's empty room, grateful that Pearl wasn't there to see the state of her shoes. Delia looked down at her feet—dirty bandages peeking out from mud-caked shoes—and shrugged. The plants she had found on the riverbank had been more than worth it. She found herself excited to tell Zelic about today's finds. It was a shame Pearl wasn't willing to help process them, but she and Zelic would make do.

Delia opened the infirmary door, an almost-smile on her face, and froze. A tall, lanky man with yellow wings and a crown of golden curls stood across the room with his back to her. Zelic's yellow and black wings were barely visible behind him.

"Just take it off!" Talis was shouting. "It's not that bad of a break. Let me see if I can fly with it."

Zelic sucked in an audible breath, then spoke in a pedantic tone. "That will jeopardize its healing."

"It's not going to have time to heal," Talis snapped. "Now take it off before I rip it off myself."

"That would not be advisable. You're likely to further damage your wing."

"But I can fly *now*! You have no right to make me stay here. What is it you want? Money? Fine, I'll pay you."

"You can't bribe me into doing something medically harmful." Zelic sucked in another audible breath that betrayed his fraying patience. "Listen, you still have a good chance of flying away with healthy wings. If I take off the frame right now and you *can't* fly, your chance is considerably reduced. I know you're panicking, but decisions made out of fear are always the wrong choice."

"It's *my* choice!" Talis fairly shrieked as he reached for the frame with both hands.

Delia darted into the room and grabbed Talis' arms. "Stop it, Talis, you giant, moth-brained pupa!"

Talis' momentary surprise gave way to anger. "What do you care, Delia? You don't want me anyway,"

"Quit feeling sorry for yourself and *think*. I found you medicine to make it heal faster, but I *will not* give it to you if you don't leave that frame alone!"

"Technically, I'd be obligated to treat him with it either way," Zelic said.

Delia turned to glare at Zelic, her hands still gripping Talis' arms. "Then I won't give it to *you*, either." Delia turned back to Talis, her forage-filled bags smashed between them as she clung to his arms. "Now sit down!" she commanded.

Talis sat on the nearest stool.

"You have an excellent bedside manner," Zelic deadpanned.

Delia dug a plant with white flowers out of one of her bags and handed it to him. "That's chickweed; it increases circulation. Make it into a poultice."

Zelic frowned at her command, but took the plant back into his office.

"And you," Delia said, once again stabbing a finger into Talis' chest, "will not do anything else to upset your sister."

"Why do you think I want to leave so bad? Coli said she can't bear to look at me, and that if I bothered you again, she'd tell our mom. You didn't already write to her, did you?"

"Of course," Delia lied.

"Don't send it! You didn't already send it, did you?" Talis began to stand in his agitation, but Delia pushed him back onto the stool.

"Calm down. I didn't even write it."

Talis' shoulders slumped, but he kept wary watch as Delia emptied her plants onto one of the cots. "Are all of those for me?"

"No."

"Why'd you get so many?"

"Are you *bothering* me?" Delia asked pointedly.

Talis frowned. "No, but I don't think that's what Coli meant."

"I do."

Talis' frown deepened. "No, she meant not to ask you to marry me again."

Delia flung the plants she was separating. "You did *not* ask me to marry you."

Talis shrugged. "Same thing."

"Blackmailing me into *mating* with you is *so not* the same thing."

"I wouldn't actually tell anyone what you did, just like you didn't actually write the letter to my mom."

Delia was in his face, his shirt twisted up in one hand before he finished the sentence. "You *deserve* for your mother to know what you did. I do not deserve to be forced into mating with you just because I happened to be there when Ora was doing something stupid."

An impish grin lit Talis' face. "The medic is behind you."

Delia gasped and turned, but Zelic was still in his office grinding the chickweed with his mortar and pestle.

Talis snickered, and Delia grabbed his chin to stop the annoying sound. "You are the worst person I know," she hissed.

"Must be really annoying to be so attracted to me, then."

"I'm not!" Delia protested, tossing his chin away as he laughed gleefully.

"Your pheromones say otherwise."

Oh please let him be lying. "That's not true. That can't be true."

"It's true. Your scent just got *much* stronger."

Delia backed away. "I'm just sweaty from foraging all day."

"Then why are you touching me so much? And begging me to let my wing heal? No wonder you were so upset about just *mating* with me; you want to *marry* me!"

126

"I want to *kill* you," Delia growled as she gathered up her plants.

Talis laughed so hard he nearly fell off his stool.

Eyeing him balefully, Delia spun and marched into Zelic's office.

"Go treat him before I kill him," she warned, then dumped her plants unceremoniously on Zelic's desk. "I'll label all the plants with their uses and what preparations I remember."

"You're not actually involved with him, are you?" Zelic asked.

"No! We're from the same town. His sister is my best friend."

Zelic looked out the open door at Talis and then lowered his voice. "Is he mentally ill?"

Delia looked up from the plant she was labeling. "I don't think so."

"His moods change very quickly," Zelic commented, a thoughtful expression on his face as he stepped out of the office.

Delia stared after him, then at Talis, considering. Talis caught her glance and winked at her, a smug grin crossing his face.

"Ugh!" Delia rolled her eyes and slammed the office door.

When the door opened, Talis was gone.

"Are you finished?" Zelic asked.

"Almost," Delia answered absently while she continued to write.

"Where did you find shoes?"

"Borrowed them from my sister."

"Looks like it's time to change your bandages."

"I'm going to bathe. I'll come by afterwards. There, I'm done," Delia announced, standing.

Zelic moved out of the doorway to let her through. "The governor was very pleased with the new medicine. He stopped threatening to throw us in the dungeon. Thank you."

Delia nodded and collected her makeshift bags from the cot.

"Um," Zelic began, and cleared his throat. "Phasia found a new mattress in your room and took it. Sorry. If you'll let me tell the governor about your skills, he'll make her stop."

Who put a new mattress in my room? "No, it's fine," Delia said. "There's some chamomile and pigweed in your office; a poultice of that will help her eczema."

"Can I tell her it's from you?"

Delia snorted. "Would she use it if you did?"

"Probably not," Zelic conceded. "But then why get it for her?"

Delia shrugged. "Just because she's vengeful doesn't mean I wasn't wrong. This is my way of making it right."

"You would make a great life servant."

Delia glared at him. "No more plants for you."

"I didn't mean that as an insult or that I think you'll become one, just that you would handle it better than most of us." He sighed. "I'm sorry; please bring more."

Delia gave him an inscrutable look.

"You can skip pregnancy tests, like you did this morning, and we won't report it. We didn't report you today."

"They're *mandatory* tests?"

Zelic shrugged. "Can't have children growing up on the Mating Mountain. If the test comes back positive, you have to leave within an hour."

No wonder Dina was so furious, she thought, seeing her sister-in-law's predicament in a new light.

"And I'll do your laundry," he offered. "And if you show me where to find some of these plants, I'll...I'll give you my meals, too."

"Keep your food, but I do need some clean clothes." Delia unknotted the shirts she had used as bags and retrieved her dirty clothes from her main bag. She set them on the same cot her bags had been sitting on, then pulled up the sheet and knotted it around her dirty clothes. "There."

"And you'll keep bringing plants?" Zelic asked as he reluctantly accepted her bundle.

Delia nodded.

"Then we have a deal."

I would have brought you plants without the laundry service. "Deal."

The pool was uncomfortably empty except for Len, his steady gaze unnerving her the moment she walked through the door. Her black bathing suit was modest, but Delia suddenly wished she had worn clothing over it. Len's spicy-sweet scent overpowered the sulphur, even from ten feet away.

"Did you mark the whole room?"

Len shrugged, making little undulations in the water. His wiry chest looked pale in contrast to the tan of his face. "It smelled bad. Now it doesn't."

Delia stepped carefully into the water, minding her steps in Coli's larger shoes. She had borrowed them without asking, but Coli wouldn't care; she had brought four other pairs.

"Your deliveries took a long time," Len said, his handsome face betraying irritation.

Delia waded out to where he stood. "There were a lot of plants."

"Did you keep any for yourself?"

Delia shook her head and began to wash herself, feeling the blood rush to her face. Despite the well-lit public room, their privacy felt intimate.

"Does that mean you're foraging again tomorrow?"

"Probably," Delia admitted, putting her heated face into the cooler water and scrubbing it.

When she lifted her head he was scowling. "It's a waste of your time."

Delia clenched her soap, her nails making deep grooves. She opened her mouth to protest, but he was already speaking.

"It's the governor's job to make sure we have medicine and food here, and the king's job to use our tax dollars to pay for it. If they squandered the money somewhere else, it's certainly not your job to make up for it."

"But they didn't have any medicine in the infirmary and the governor was going to lock the medics in the dungeon if they couldn't get him out of pain," Delia argued, belatedly wondering if she ought to have kept that information to herself.

"So you saved the governor from the consequences of his actions?"

Delia ran a wet hand through her tangled hair. "No, I didn't mean...I was just trying to help the medics."

"By perpetuating a broken system."

"I hadn't thought of it that way," Delia conceded.

"If the monarchy wants to control the courtship of the lower classes by making us fly up here to find a mate, the least it can do is provide us with decent meals and medication." Rant over, Len glared at the water.

Something about his sullenness reminded her of Nap just before dinner. "You're hungry, aren't you?"

"Of course I am," he admitted testily. "All the meals today were watery soups."

"And if I take you foraging with me tomorrow and feed you, will that count as perpetuating a broken system?" she asked archly.

He shot her a piercing glance before breaking into a silent chuckle. "No, because if I come with you, you'll be using your time wisely."

The laugh transformed his face, making him appear good-humored and open. Delia unconsciously moved closer. "So feeding *you* is a wise use of my time, but feeding or medicating everyone else isn't?"

"That depends," he said, the grin settling into his face like it belonged there.

Delia felt his arms slide around her waist, pulling her closer.

"On what?"

"How many people you're trying to seduce at once," he teased.

She shoved at his chest, but he held tighter, a single bark of laughter ringing out.

"I'm not trying to seduce anyone!" she protested, trying to wriggle away from his iron grasp.

"It's a solid strategy. Kiss them, then offer them food."

Delia's face reddened. "I did not kiss you! You keep kissing *me*!"

He bent toward her, another silent laugh enveloping his face before his lips brushed hers, then waited for her to reciprocate.

"I am *not* seducing you," Delia griped.

His lips brushed hers again and sparks danced through her body. "Come on, Delia," he murmured, "kiss me."

"No," she whispered, letting his lips move hers until she found herself kissing back.

"See? You're seducing me."

Delia pulled back and smacked his chest, the slap sounding sharp against his wet skin. Rather than let go, he lifted her from the floor of the pool, one hand snaking around her neck to hold her head. Before she could protest, he kissed her so violently that her face smarted with the pain.

"You're hurting me!" she cried out, pushing ineffectually at his chest while her legs kicked out wildly, rarely catching their target. His fingers dug into her neck as he smashed his face harder into her own.

Still clutching her bar of soap, she wielded it like a weapon, bashing the side of his head. "You're hurting me!" she screamed against his mouth.

With two more blows, he finally released her and backed away, breathing heavily. A red hand print marred his paler chest and the skin around his left eye was red and beginning to swell. Delia ran a hand over her aching jaw, her lips felt swollen and she could taste blood. Her tongue found the cut just inside her lower lip.

"You made me bleed!" Delia stumbled as she backed away from him. "Why didn't you stop when I said you were hurting me?!"

He ran his hands over his face, then through his short hair. "I don't think we should see each other again."

"Oh, you think?! What's the matter with you?!"

Avoiding her gaze, he climbed out the side of the pool and left without a word.

Delia shivered violently despite the warm water. She took a step to wade deeper and noticed her shoes were missing. Looking down into the water, her vision blurred with angry tears. She felt around for Coli's shoes half-heartedly. *How did that just happen?*

Someone opened the door and she spun to look, her wings protesting the weight of the water.

"You did not! I saw you!" Bul laughed, shoving someone coming in behind him.

Delia turned away, wiping her tears and nose.

"What is that smell? Thistle, what have you been doing?"

She could hear the titters of his friends, a murmured comment, and then raucous laughing. Delia resumed the search for Coli's shoes in earnest.

"Hey, who took my rock?" Rus complained. "Bul, come be the doorstop."

"Rude! The rock's probably back in the pool. Maybe Thistle is standing on it; I definitely don't remember her being that tall."

There was splashing now, and Delia tensed, her shoe search turning frantic.

"Hey, what's the matter? Shouldn't you be telling me how tall you are and beating my chest by now?" Bul asked as he waded in beside her.

Delia turned away, hiding her face behind a curtain of hair. She could still taste blood, and her face and neck ached. She splashed a little water over her mouth, hoping any blood there would wash away, but her lips felt misshapen under her fingers.

"Are you okay?" Bul asked. He touched her shoulder, but she flinched away from him.

"I'm fine," she lied.

"Did that guy mark you again?" Bul asked.

Delia sniffed her hair; *of course he had.*

"Offer still stands to beat him up," Bul said.

"Who are we beating up?" Rus asked, coming up beside them.

Delia shook her head. Abandoning Coli's shoes, she turned to walk away, but Bul's dark-haired friend was blocking her path.

"What happened to your face?" he asked, his expression alarmed.

Oh, no. Delia bent her head and pushed more hair forward.

Bul was walking around her now, and trying to pull back her hair. She swatted his hand.

"It's nothing. Leave me alone." Her steps were less careful now and she winced as her feet tore. A quick touch of her lip confirmed the split had widened with her wince.

"Her mouth's bleeding," the dark-haired friend reported as she hurried past him.

"Delia, stop," Bul said.

Her feet were afire as she stepped out of the pool.

"Her feet are bleeding, too," the dark-haired friend said.

Will you shut up?!

133

The door had been feebly propped open with someone's bag. As Delia pulled the door wider to escape, Rubi and her friend came partially through, blocking her exit.

"Thanks!" Rubi said brightly, then her expression faltered. "You have a little blood there," she said, brushing her lips. "Did you have an accident?"

No! Delia wiped her lip, and tried to slip past them.

"A white beat her up," Bul said from behind her. The girls gasped.

"He didn't..." Delia began, her shoulders sagging. It wasn't a sentence she wanted to finish.

Rubi grasped Delia's arm. "Are you okay? Do you want me to take you to the infirmary?"

"I'm fine," Delia lied again, twisting out of her grasp.

"I'll take her," Bul volunteered.

"No one is going to take me. I will take myself."

"I found her shoes," Rus called, tossing Coli's shoes at Bul's feet.

"Ouch! Don't throw them at me; you're going to break my wings!" Bul complained as he kicked the shoes to Delia.

Delia slipped them on gratefully, then stared defiantly at the two girls until they moved aside. The relatively unscented air of the hallway calmed her agitation as she hurried out, and she breathed deeply. Len's spicy-sweet scent was still emanating from her half-wet hair, and she yanked it up into a knotted bun as she cursed him. Her own wet footsteps seemed loud in the empty hall until she realized she was hearing a second set. Panicked, she spun around, her soap raised like a club.

Bul put up his hands defensively. "I just want to make sure you're okay."

Delia willed her heartbeat to slow as she dropped her soap-wielding hand to her side. "I'm *fine.*"

"You don't *look* fine. Where is the guy that did that to you, anyway? What if he tries it again?"

Delia shook her head as she resumed her steps. "He won't."

"You need to stay away from guys like that," Bul urged, easily matching her pace with his long strides.

"You mean I need to stay away from *whites*?" Delia snapped.

"Well, yeah, actually."

Delia turned to glare at him.

"You've got enough of a temper for two people. You need someone mellow."

Delia thought of her mother's disappointment over her father's out-of-season mellow temperament and scowled.

"Rus is easygoing, and he likes you."

"Rus is a brat," Delia said, remembering him taking her soap.

"He was trying to flirt with you; he's just not very good at it. You should talk to him."

Delia stopped at Coli's door, hesitating before opening it.

"You're not going to the infirmary?"

"I am, but I'm not going dripping wet," Delia said, stepping inside. The room was still empty and just as she had left it. With a relieved sigh, she shut the door.

"You want me to wait?" Bul called from the hallway.

"No. I didn't want you to follow me in the first place," Delia retorted, changing rapidly and inwardly cursing non-locking doors.

"I'm just being nice!"

"Well, stop it."

"Fine!"

Delia finished dressing, hoping the silence meant he had really left. At the door, she caught sight of the mirror and examined her face. There was a smear of blood on her chin from the steady trickle of her split lip. Her lips and nose were both swollen.

"Lovely," she said, then grimaced at the flash of bloody teeth when she spoke. *No wonder everyone looked so alarmed.* She took a swig from her nearly empty canteen and swished it around her mouth, then groaned when she realized she had nowhere to spit it. She swallowed, trying not to taste the blood and ignoring the persistent sting from her cut lip. Using the last of her water, she cleaned off her chin, then wiped her fingers on her black pants, grateful they would hide the blood. As she opened the door to the empty hallway, she touched a hand to her hair, regretting the hasty bun that left her nothing to hide behind. She began to take it down, but the scent of Len overwhelmed her, and she hastily twisted it back up. Raising her hand to her face, she covered her mouth as if she were deep in thought, and then headed to the infirmary. No one she passed made any comment, and she kept her eyes on the floor to avoid any stares.

In the blissfully empty infirmary, Zelic was seated in his office pouring over her notes.

"Can you read them?" Delia asked.

"Mostly." Zelic glanced up at her then did a double take. "Were you in a fight?" Then he sniffed. "Or something else?"

"Something else."

Zelic stood and examined her face. "You'll probably bruise. Did he hit you anywhere else?"

Delia colored and rubbed her neck. "It wasn't a hit."

"Headbutt, then. Let me see your neck." He probed it gently until Delia winced. "More bruising, I expect." He sighed. "I'm supposed to report fighting and *other kinds* of injuries. Was it consensual?"

Delia's face flamed. "No."

"Did he rape you?"

The flush of humiliation crept down her neck. "No."

"Did you injure him?"

"I don't want to discuss it."

"Who is he?"

Delia ignored the question, slipped past him, and began selecting plants. "I'll treat myself."

"You know he'll just hurt someone else or you again."

Delia's brows contracted. "Fine. Len White. And I probably gave him a black eye," she added, hearing the satisfaction in her own voice.

"With your fist?" Zelic asked, glancing at her knuckles.

"Soap," she said, her lips pulling into a smile until her lip smarted.

"Did you hit him before or after he injured you?"

"With the soap? After." Delia thought of the red hand print on Len's chest. "But I slapped him before," she admitted.

Zelic groaned. "You whites need to stay away from each other. Now when I report it to the governor, you might get dungeon time, too."

Delia's stomach turned, the memory of the sulphur stench making her gag. "I can't. Don't report it."

"And if *he* reports it?"

Fury filled Delia until she began to shake again. "What would he report? That I slapped his chest so he was forced to smash my face?"

Zelic gave her a pitying look, and pulled a whistle out of his pocket. "If the governor sentences you to dungeon time, I'll tell him you're the one supplying his pain medications."

"No. Don't..." she began, but Zelic was already blowing on the shrill whistle as he walked out to the open hallway door. Panicked, she rushed past him, the plants she had just selected still clutched in her fist.

"It's better if you stay," Zelic called after her, then blew the whistle again.

Delia fled down the corridor, cursing her wet wings and aching feet that slowed her. She ran first to Coli's room and packed up her meager belongings, leaving no trace of herself behind in the tidy room. At the door she hesitated; she couldn't fly until her wings dried, and a dark walk through the forest had no appeal. She just needed somewhere to hide until morning. Delia unfolded her castle map and stared at it.

Cam! He was probably spending the night in town; his room would be empty. But would Malan tell the guards she had asked for his room number? *Maybe he won't remember.* Peeking out into the corridor, she rushed to Cam's room, grateful that it was nearby. At his door, she gave a frantic knock as she tried to remember if there had been one or two beds in his room. Had she even looked? *What if he shares the room with a brother or a cousin?* She glanced furtively up and down the hall, then opened the door and stepped inside. The room was dark and her eyes were slow to adjust. But the smell was familiar. *Oceanspray flowers,* she decided.

"Uh, Cam? Cam's relative?" Hearing voices in the hallway, Delia shut the door quietly behind her. She felt her way to a bed, praying that she wasn't about to touch a foot. She worked her way up to a pillow without encountering anything but a blanket. Then she reached out to where another bed might be, and touched clothing. She froze, listening. *You would be able to hear them breathing,* she reminded herself. Gingerly, she followed the clothing upward to a hook instead of a face. She released a shuddering breath of relief. Her eyes slowly adjusted to the dim light from beneath the door until she could make out a table and stool. She set her bag on the table, then drew out the plants she had taken from the infirmary and began to treat her feet and face. When she finished, the exhaustion of her busy day and adrenalin-fueled evening had caught up to her. Squelching the yawn that tore at her split lip, she crawled onto Cam's bed, hoping he would forgive the imposition or better yet, remain ignorant of it.

Chapter Eleven

Delia awoke cradling a pillow, a sleepy smile gracing her face. The dark room made the time of day impossible to determine, but the light from under the door was just sufficient to fly up to the hanging solar lantern and turn it on. She blinked in the bright light, temporarily blinded as memories of the previous night bombarded her. Delia touched her face cautiously; only her mouth was still swollen, and she could feel a scab where her lips touched.

"Why did you do it, Len?" she whispered, wondering if he was in the dungeon, and if she was about to join him. That alarming thought had her scampering across the room, feet smarting with each step. She retrieved yesterday's filthy bandages and Pearl's mud-caked shoes before her mind registered the shiny object. Propped up beside her bag was a lovely new spade. Both bandages and shoes were quickly discarded in favor of the garden tool. She gripped the wooden handle, testing its weight as her distorted image smiled back at her from the smooth metal. *Thank you, Cam,* she thought happily. Then, the significance of what she was holding penetrated her sleep-addled mind. He was back, he had been in this room, and she had slept right through it! Delia groaned. Where was he now? She owed him an explanation and an apology, but it would have to wait. Neatly lined up beneath the table were brand new workboots and water shoes. She eagerly tried them on. The water shoes rubbed her newly healing blisters, but would be adequate for the pool. The boots were heavenly, despite her injured feet, and she indulged a few turns around the room walking in them. If they kept the water out, they would be perfect. Delia hugged herself in delight, acknowledging that if Cam were here, she would be hugging him instead. She swiftly packed up her belongings, then peered out into the hall, shutting the door quickly when she saw people walking by. *What time is it?* She counted to fifty, then peeked out again. This time the hall was empty and she darted out, Pearl's dirty shoes swinging in one hand. She had promised to wash them, and she would *eventually*, but she assumed her sister would rather have them back dirty than go another day without them. At Pearl's door, she opened it just wide enough to toss the shoes in and quickly shut it. Then she flew away, bracing for a tirade that would draw everyone's attention to her. When she made it to the castle door without a confrontation, her worry eased.

She was pushing open the heavy door when she heard a voice behind her.

"Miss White?"

Delia closed her wings, hiding their telltale backside, and pretended she had not heard.

"Miss *White*, the governor would like to speak with you."

Fear slid down Delia's throat, stopping the lies bubbling up. The door was open just wide enough to slip through now, but the heavy footsteps behind her were drawing closer. Would she be in more trouble if she fled now? Delia thought again of the sulphurous torture that was just the *stairs* down to the dungeon and her decision was made. She slipped through the door and into the air.

"Miss White! You're making a mistake."

When she was out of reach, Delia glanced back at the stocky guard with his balding head and white wings.

"He doesn't like it when anyone ignores a summons, and since he summoned you last night, he's getting pretty grumpy about it," the guard said.

Staying out of reach, Delia circled back to listen.

"Now, you could bat your eyelashes and say, 'Oh Governor, I had no idea you wanted to talk to me! I came the moment Beck told me!'" The guard finished his falsetto and grinned at her. "That would probably work, especially since you're the one that got him out of pain."

Delia glanced around to see if anyone had heard him, her heart beating in her throat.

"Yeah, Zelic told him; and now Malan's in the dungeon for writing that you were a bookkeeper."

Delia sank, landing heavily at the edge of the courtyard. *Poor Malan.*

Beck took a few steps toward her, but stopped when she backed up. "I won't lie to you, the governor *is* in a foul mood, but he has a long history of leniency with pretty girls. Just tell him what happened last night, then explain that it was Malan's idea to write bookkeeper, and clear up whatever happened between you and Phasia. If you can keep your temper through all that, you can stop running from guards and furious laundry mistresses. Between you and me, Phasia is scarier than most of the guards."

Maybe I should just go home. Delia glanced at the inviting forest behind her, the early morning sun still hidden behind the trees.

"But if you don't come now, the governor will just assume all the accusations are true, and you *will* get dungeon time."

Delia's head whipped back to stare at the guard. "What accusations?"

Beck glanced up at one of the balconies with an open door. "Good morning, Miss Blue. Does your dad know you're back in the queen's suite?"

A muffled expletive accompanied the shutting door, and Beck chuckled as he turned back to Delia. "I don't want to shout them across the courtyard."

Delia took a few reluctant steps toward him and let him advance without retreating.

"Psyche is a terrible gossip," the guard explained, "so you don't want her to hear this."

"Hear what?" Delia snapped, her patience wearing thin.

"Now keep your temper; I'm not your enemy. The governor wanted to spring the accusations on you, but I know what it's like to be a white. So I'm going to tell you now, and then you'll have time to calm down before you talk to him."

"*If* I talk to him."

Beck raised his ginger-colored brows. "You want to go straight to the dungeon instead?"

"I want to go home." A sudden lump formed in Delia's throat at the thought of her parents, Nap, the apothecary shop, and the sound of the sea. *Now* she understood Pearl wanting to leave.

The guard nodded. "I can understand that. Thought about it myself a time or two, but I just couldn't figure out how I would tell my parents that I gave up on a wife and family. And even if I could find the words, I think they would have sent me back here to try again."

Delia swallowed the lump. That was *exactly* what her parents would do. "Fine. Tell me."

"Mr. White said you attacked him with a bar of soap while you two were kissing passionately. He suggested any injuries *you* sustained were self-inflicted to get him in trouble for rejecting you."

Delia blinked rapidly as rage colored her vision.

"Don't take it out on me," Beck warned, backing up. "Remember *who* wronged you, and figure out the best way to right the wrong."

Delia released a stuttering breath and tried to force herself to calm down.

"Now, Malan said it was his idea to say you were a bookkeeper, so you'll only have to confirm that. But Phasia is *now* saying you assaulted her and demanded that she get 'that stinking mattress' out of your room, and that you stole someone else's mattress while she was trying to find you one, so she was just holding on to it until she could find the rightful owner."

It was so absurd, Delia's fury began to morph into incredulous humor. "Does anyone believe her?"

Beck chuckled. "No. The only difficult part is going to be the incident with Mr. White. The governor will want details; if you can answer *all* his questions without yelling at him, you should be okay."

Delia's fury surged back in like a tide. "I'm not sure I can do that."

"Here, practice question: It smells like you mated with Mr. White; did you?"

"No!"

Beck grimaced. "You yelled."

"I can't do this!" Delia hissed, her gaze straying back to the trees.

"You're an apothecary apprentice, right?"

142

Wildcrafter, Delia thought, but only nodded.

"The governor is a battered mess right now. He doesn't want anyone to see him like this. I think he's making an exception for you because he thinks you can help him. If you think of him as a difficult patient, maybe even offer to treat him, he won't want to punish you, even if you did cosh Mr. White without provocation."

"I *didn't!*"

Beck chortled as he lightly took her elbow. "This is going to be an interesting day."

Delia yanked her arm out of his grasp.

"Still thinking of going home?"

"No."

"Don't want to be touched?"

Delia covered her arm where he had held it. "Not particularly, no."

Beck nodded. "I remember that. Just walk beside me, and if I see a life servant, I'll hold your arm until they pass by, then let go. That way no one will complain to the governor that I'm not doing my job." He turned and began to walk back to the castle, Delia trailing him.

"Why are you being so nice?" she asked.

The stocky guard turned back to grin at her as he pulled the still-open door wider. "I *am* nice. Can't have Malan getting all the credit."

Delia passed through the door and waited for him to close it. "How long will the governor keep him in the dungeon?"

"It was two days last time."

"Malan got caught doing this before?"

Beck shook his head as they passed the clerk's office. "No, when he started as a clerk a couple months ago, he would ask *everyone* about their apprenticeships, even though he was only supposed to ask the whites. When the governor told him to stop, he gave him this great speech about how it was unfair to plan for anyone to fail, deciding their life-servant position long before they got stranded here." Beck smiled at

143

the memory. "Some of the guards even applauded. Okay, it was just me that applauded, but it was a really great speech."

"And the governor put him in the dungeon for that?"

"And me for clapping!" Beck took her arm and nodded at an older woman as she passed them, then released her. "He was in a *really* bad mood that day."

"Like today?"

Beck met her gaze, his expression encouraging. "It will be okay. Just pretend he walked into your dad's apothecary shop. Treat anything unpleasant he says as a symptom of what's wrong with him."

"I'm not a medic. I'm not even a very good diagnostician. I mostly just found wild medicinal plants," Delia confessed. "Nap and Chloe worked the counter; they're better with people."

"And you're not?"

Delia sighed. "People tell long stories that aren't relevant or they say really obvious things about the weather or they want to gossip. I just want to focus on the problem and tell them how to solve it."

"So you were grumpy even before you were in season?" Beck asked, chuckling.

Delia scowled. "No, just... not very good at hiding my impatience."

Beck chortled. "And what happens when you lose your patience? Soap bludgeoning?" He laughed jovially at his own joke.

"No!" Delia glared at him, but his laughter had an infectious quality that made it difficult for her to remain annoyed, and her expression softened. "I truth-bomb people."

"Truth bomb? What is that?"

Delia waited until he finished laughing. "Usually the thing that people least want to hear about themselves."

"Okay, let's hear it then. Truth-bomb me."

Delia pondered for a moment before the words came. *You could have had everything you wanted if you had only learned to control your tongue. But you sabotaged your hopes more thoroughly than any enemy could have.* She shuddered inwardly at the harshness of it. "No, it's mean."

"I can take it. Go ahead and tell me that I'm balding or getting pudgy," he said, poking his middle.

Delia only shook her head.

"Did you truth-bomb Phasia? Is that why she's acting like this?"

Delia nodded sadly.

"Oh, so they're really *bad* truth bombs. I changed my mind, I don't want to hear mine." He grasped her arm again as they approached a door with four guards outside it. "And whatever you do, don't truth-bomb the governor." he added in an undertone.

Delia pressed her lips together, afraid of what was about to fall out of them.

"Look who found the elusive Miss White!" Beck announced.

"Where was she? I looked all night," one of the guards whined, giving Delia an appraising glance.

"Sneaking out the front doors just like I told you she'd be," Beck crowed. "You're losing your touch, Avell."

Avell glowered at them, but moved aside as another guard rapped an odd-patterned knock at the door. The heavy door creaked open just wide enough for a bulbous nose to protrude through.

"Beck found her," the guard reported.

The nose sniffed, then withdrew as the door closed.

"Where did you hide all night?" Avell demanded.

"Just an empty room."

"*Which* empty room? I searched them all."

Delia fought to appear calm as the guards all turned to look at her. "Guess you missed one."

Beck snickered and two of the other guards grinned, one giving Avell a shove.

"I *know* somebody hid you," Avell accused. "Who was it? That broken-winged sulphur?"

Talis? "No one *hid* me," Delia snapped.

Bulbous nose reopened the door and motioned Delia in. "Just the girl," he said when Beck tried to follow.

Inside, the large room smelled like an apothecary, and Delia could pick out the scent of several plants she had procured. The long table to her right was littered with teas, broths, and soaking poultices. A young woman with bark-colored wings was busy fussing over the latter. To Delia's left was an expansive bed that was absurdly tall. Sprawled across it was a young man nearly obscured by the healing frames attached to both wings. The bulbous-nosed guard pointed to the stool beside the bed, then took his place next to the door with another guard. Delia smoothed the rumpled clothing she had slept in and crossed to the stool. She could see the purpose for the high bed now, as sitting gave her an easy view of his bruised and bandaged face.

"Miss White," the governor greeted her, his overly formal tone feigning dignity from his pillow. "It has come to my attention that you have been involved in two altercations and a deception, despite your short time here. The accusations made against you are serious enough to warrant dungeon time unless you can convince me of your innocence."

Delia nodded, distracted by the angry red cut over his eye. *Looks infected; what did they treat it with?* Delia glanced over at the woman in the room, presumably a medic, and longed to ask her.

"First, I am informed that you assaulted our laundry mistress when she refused to replace your mattress."

Delia fought the desire to roll her eyes. "I didn't touch her nor did I ask her to replace my mattress. The mattress was fine. The bedding was dirty and I brought it to be washed. She was standing in the doorway and annoyed that I wasn't at breakfast. When she wouldn't take the dirty bedding or let me into the room, I dropped my laundry at her feet.

Then I said something rude and she reached for my wings, so I flew away."

The governor raised a dark eyebrow, then winced as it pulled at the crusty cut.

"Do you want something for that?" Delia asked, touching her brow.

"Graci," the governor called peevishly, "isn't it ready yet?"

The woman looked back at them with a sigh. "I don't know; I've never worked with these medicines before."

Delia stood and went over to the table, belatedly wondering if she ought to have asked permission first.

Graci pointed to a poultice soaking in a bowl of water. "I don't know how long to soak it."

Delia shook her head, lifting the herb-laden cloth out of the water. "These plants are fresh, you can apply them directly to the skin. Soaking is for when they're old and dried."

"Oh," Graci said, her pretty face crumpling.

"They'll still work," Delia said, offering them to her. "Just wrap his head with a bandage to hold them in place."

"Thanks." Graci hurried back over to the governor, then looked back at Delia. "Could you help?"

"I haven't washed my hands," Delia protested as she came nearer.

"Just hold the wing frame like this," Graci instructed as the governor groaned. "Sorry, Limen," she added, then colored deeply.

Delia held the frame while Graci placed the poultice on the cut over his eye, then wrapped it in place with a bandage. When Delia lowered the frame, the governor groaned again.

"Did you put any on his wing breaks?" Delia asked.

Graci looked blank. "I haven't, but I wasn't here when they put on the frames." Graci dipped down to look at the governor's face beneath the frame. "Did they put anything on the breaks?"

"I don't know! I was unconscious!"

"Hmm, I'll ask Zelic when he wakes up," Graci said, then trotted back to the table and noisily began gathering dishes.

The governor cleared his throat and Delia sat on the stool again.

"Clearly you are not a bookkeeper," he began.

"I never said I was," Delia interrupted.

"But you allowed Malan to record that you were."

"How could I have stopped him?" Delia demanded, "I told him exactly what I do."

The governor's single visible brow contracted. "I realize that you have trouble controlling your temper, but you *will* speak to me respectfully."

Delia took a deep breath and blew it out. "Sorry."

The door opened and Delia glanced up to see Graci exit.

"And now to the matter of last night: did you assault Mr. White with a bar of soap?"

"He was hurting me. I told him so and tried to push him away, but he wouldn't stop. So I hit him."

"Zelic reported your injuries; were any of them self-inflicted?"

"Of course not!" Delia's hand strayed to her neck, gently rubbing the bruised skin before she dropped her hand.

"Did you treat your injuries yourself?"

Delia nodded.

"You seem to be healing well. Did you give Zelic the same plants you used on yourself?"

"Yes."

"Good. I'm assigning you as a provisional medic. You will provide the infirmary with medicinal plants and train the other medics how to use them and where to find them."

Delia's mouth dropped open. "But, I'm in season."

"You were also with Mr. Sulphur when he attacked Princess Lexi's guards. So you can serve a month in the dungeon for that and your other infractions, or you can work in the infirmary for that same time period."

"That's not fair," Delia whispered, her face drained of color. "I didn't throw any rocks."

"I know that. If you had, you wouldn't be given this option."

Delia gripped the stool beneath her, suddenly having difficulty remaining on it. "Who told you?"

The governor gave her a smug smile. "You'll find there's always someone listening here and happy to make a trade for information. Now, your first shift has begun. Go help Graci with my treatment."

"Wait, wait..." Delia's panicked thoughts crashed in her mind like waves on a reef. "If I have information to trade, do I still have to be a life servant for a month?"

The governor's eyes narrowed. "That would depend on the information."

"I...I think I know who did this to you."

The governor struggled to get up, then surrendered back to the bed with a low cry of pain. "Who?!"

Delia grimaced, already hating herself for what she was about to do. "Your half-brother, Vic," she whispered. "But I'm not certain."

"Charis!" the governor yelled. "Bring Vic, Archi, and Roy Viceroy in for questioning and search their rooms!" One of the guards hurried from the room in response.

"But only Vic's knuckles were bloody, and he's the one with all the food!" Delia blurted, wringing her hands. *Poor Coli.*

"And you really think one of them would act without the others knowing?" the governor demanded, spittle flying in his vehemence. He made another attempt to get up to his knees, then cried out in pain.

Delia stood, hovering at his side. "Do you want me to help you up?"

"No! Just give me some pain medication."

Delia ran to the table and began sniffing the half-drunk teas. She stuck a finger in one and grimaced at the bitter flavor. *They gave him willow bark tea?* "Do you have broken ribs?" she called over her shoulder.

"Zelic thinks so; I'm covered in bruises," the governor answered, his voice slipping into a self-pitying tone.

"I need to prepare more medicine for you," Delia said, taking the bitter cup with her to the door. The bulbous-nosed guard didn't budge, but looked to the governor for instructions.

"Why? There's plenty left. It was too bitter," he whined.

Delia fought to hide the panic in her voice. "I didn't realize you had internal bleeding when I gave Zelic the willow bark."

"So?"

"So it can increase bleeding." *Didn't I tell him that?*

When the governor spoke again, his voice was high and tremulous. "Am I going to die?"

Yes? I don't know! Let me out of this room! "You should be fine," Delia said, borrowing a phrase and tenor she had often heard her father use. "I just don't want to give you more of this particular pain medicine."

"Oh. Well give me one of the others, then."

Others? Delia returned to the long table, reluctantly replacing the tea cup. She sniffed at more odd concoctions, some she recognized, some she did not. Their flyer must have returned with medication from a town apothecary. *Think,* she counseled herself. *What would Dad give him?*

"Hurry," the governor wailed.

Delia's panic mutated into aggravation at his petulance. "I will *not* just randomly give you one of these medicines! I didn't prepare any of them and I don't know when you had your last dose. If you want me to treat you, I need to talk to your medics and there should be some log of what you've already been given. Otherwise one of us *is* going to accidently kill you. And another thing, if your ribs are broken, you should be propped up on your back like a pupa, not lying on your stomach!"

"I want Graci back; where is Graci?" he quavered, sounding like a lost child.

"I'll find her," the bulbous-nosed guard volunteered and quickly left the room.

"It hurts," the governor whimpered.

"I can help, but I need to go to the infirmary and get the plants I harvested or at least talk to Zelic or Graci," Delia pled, picking up the willow bark tea and heading for the door.

"Don't leave. They all leave. I don't want to be by myself anymore," the governor mewled.

Delia grit her teeth. The pitiable sound of the governor weeping only added to her stress. She opened the door and stuck her head out. Only Beck and Avell remained on guard, and they both turned to look at her expectantly.

"I hear you're one of us now," Beck said with a smile that did not reach his eyes. "Congratulations."

"I need my plants from the infirmary and I need Zelic *now*," Delia said, ignoring him.

Beck shook his head. "We can't leave. Two guards is the absolute minimum outside this door."

"Well, surely it can't be policy to leave me alone in here with him," Delia hissed.

Avell snorted and turned back around. "That's *exactly* the policy."

"Close the door!" the governor cried.

Reluctantly, Delia shut it.

151

Desperation flooded her, and she rested her forehead against the door. *God in heaven, please help me. I don't know what to do.* Delia's racing mind immediately quieted, replaced with clear instructions.

After setting the willow bark tea back on the table, Delia returned to the governor's bedside and took hold of the nearest wing frame. "Your position is putting pressure on your ribs; I need to take off the wing frames, so you can lie on your back."

"No! I want them to heal! I need to be able to fly," he protested weakly.

"How far are you into your season?" Delia asked, unfastening the nearest clasp.

"Eleven and a half months," he moaned, as Delia released another clasp and carefully opened the wing frame on its hinges. His left upper wing was broken in four places and the lower in two. The outer edges of both looked brittle.

Why did they even bother with healing frames? "And the longest season on record is one year. That means this wing set isn't going to heal in time," she announced, gently removing the frame. Without the healing structure, the wing collapsed over his face.

"They destroyed my wings," he gasped, lifting his left forewing.

"Does it hurt?"

"It's still numb from the medicine," he said distractedly, trying to make his wing set lie flat.

Doubtful. It's more likely your season is ending. "You can get them lacquered back into place when your ribs heal," Delia said, shifting around the bed to remove the other frame. The right wing set wasn't as badly broken, but it, too, looked brittle around the edges. *Or did it already end?*

The door opened just as Delia set the second frame on the floor.

"What are you doing?!" Graci cried. She hurried across the room and clapped a hand over her mouth. "Oh! Your beautiful wings!" Graci looked up at Delia angrily. "It takes three medics to put the frames on; couldn't you just open them and apply your concoctions? Now we'll have to wait for Zelic." Graci found the governor's hand under his broken wing and gripped it tightly. "You must be in so much pain."

"I am; get the pain medication," the governor requested, all hint of tears gone from his voice.

Graci hurried over to the table with Delia close on her heels.

"Don't give him the willow bark tea," Delia warned.

"Why not? It works," Graci said, clutching the cup with the bitter liquid.

"It increases bleeding," Delia explained, trying to take the cup.

"His cuts aren't bleeding anymore; that shouldn't matter," Graci snapped, her voice rising as she tightened her hold on the cup.

Delia yanked the cup sideways, dumping the contents onto the stone floor. "You're going to kill him," Delia hissed. "Broken ribs and abdominal bruising mean *internal* bleeding."

Graci's eyes went wide, then filled with tears. "I didn't realize." She glanced up at the governor as the first tear escaped. "Is he going to be okay?" she whispered, her voice breaking.

"Help me get him onto his back and take his shirt off."

"But his wings..." Graci protested.

"They're not going to heal; they're numb," Delia whispered.

"Did his season end?" Graci mouthed.

"Stop whispering and bring me some medication," the governor demanded peevishly.

Graci wiped her tears on her sleeve as she crossed the large room. "Coming!"

Delia headed straight for the door and stuck her head out, relieved to see there were four guards again. "Did you send someone for Zelic?"

Beck shrugged. "Graci's back; we figured you wouldn't need him."

Delia clenched her teeth. "Fine. You and Avell will have to do."

"Have to do what?"

"Just come in here!"

The guards followed her reluctantly to the bed, stepping carefully around the discarded wing frames.

Beck let out a soft whistle.

"Why are *they* here? I don't want them helping me!" the governor protested.

"Graci and I aren't strong enough to lift you," Delia explained. "Beck, lift his shoulders. Avell, lift his hips. Graci, you hold onto his right wing set, and I'll take his left. We're going to *slowly and carefully* help him up to his knees, then help him turn to lie down on his back. *Do not* touch his ribs."

They all awkwardly climbed atop the governor's large bed, bumping each other's wings and apologizing as the governor groaned in pain throughout the entire process.

"Now, Avell stack the pillows behind him before he leans back," Delia directed.

"This wing is breaking again!" Graci warned.

Alarmed, the Governor reached out to straighten his bending wing.

"It doesn't matter; you're going to get them lacquered anyway, and it's too numb to hurt," Delia asserted, but they all flinched when the wing snapped. "It doesn't matter," she repeated. "Lean him back. Graci, take his shirt off; cut it if you have to."

Beck and Avell exchanged looks, but a glare from Delia silenced the jokes they were tempted to make.

"Back to your posts," the governor ordered in a shaking voice, perspiration covering his triangle of unbandaged forehead before Graci wiped it away.

The two guards obeyed, shutting the door quietly behind them.

Delia hurried back to the table. She sniffed the poultices, then combined them before rushing back to the bed. Large purple bruises bloomed across the governor's ribs. Delia spread the green mash liberally over each one, then placed damp bandages loosely over the top to help hold them in place.

Graci turned up her nose. "That smells weird. How long does it need to stay on?"

"Until I bring the next one," Delia said, wiping off her hands as she headed for the door. "And keep him still."

"What about the pain medicine?" the governor asked, eyeing the table.

"You're wearing it," Delia replied as she opened the door. "Don't take anything else until I talk to Zelic." Delia gave Graci one last pointed look, then left the room.

"Beck, could you wake Zelic and have him meet me in the infirmary?" Delia asked.

Beck made a face. "Is it an emergency?"

"Yes! Now go!" Delia ordered.

"Who died and made you princess?" Avell griped.

Ignoring him, Delia flew down the hallway. Her mind was still calm, but she was gripped with a sense of urgency. She knew exactly which plants she needed, and hoped the medics had not used them yet.

Inside the infirmary, a blue-winged medic was holding a wing frame open and examining the broken wing of a large blond man. She turned when Delia strode inside, heading for the office.

"Just a minute! You can't go in there!" The medic sounded flustered, and Delia guessed she was regretting leaving the office door wide open.

"Yes, I can. I'm Delia White and the governor just made me a medic," she said without stopping.

"The wildcrafter? Did your season end?"

Though she was already inside the office, Delia leaned her head out to answer. "Yes, I am the wildcrafter. And no; it's a punishment."

Delia ducked back into the office at the medic's shocked expression.

"Are her wings broken?" the large man asked.

Delia could not hear the medic's murmured response; her focus was already elsewhere. The desk was littered with the load she had delivered last night. She snatched up a medley to grind in the freshly cleaned mortar and pestle. Though it was a task she rarely did in the apothecary shop, Delia loved the feel and sound of stone grinding against stone. It was oddly soothing. She had just finished with the new poultice when Zelic entered the office, eyes puffy and hair askew.

"What couldn't wait another couple of hours?" he demanded crossly.

"Graci gave him willow bark tea."

Zelic swore. "That's it then. We have to get him off his stomach or he's going to die."

"Already done."

Zelic opened and closed his mouth like a fish. "How did you talk him into taking off the wing frames?"

"I told him we'd get his wings lacquered as soon as his ribs healed."

"And who is going to do that? We don't have anybody that knows how," Zelic protested.

"Well, we have six weeks to figure that out."

"*We*? How is this *your* problem? And why were you treating the governor anyway?"

Delia frowned. "I thought Beck would fill you in."

"No one tries to talk to me in the morning. I hate mornings. Everyone knows that," Zelic carped, rubbing his face. "When it's my turn to do the pregnancy tests, I just stay up all night."

"The governor sentenced me to a month as a medic."

"For giving the guy that assaulted you a black eye?!"

156

"That, and insulting Phasia, and Malan writing that I was a bookkeeper, and something else," Delia trailed off.

"That's ridiculous!"

"That doesn't matter right now," Delia said, taking up a cluster of field horsetail stems in her free hand. "I need you to examine the governor and see if the bruising is worse. And I need to know what medications Graci or whoever else has given him recently."

"Graci isn't even supposed to be giving him medications. Where was Neva?"

"Graci was the only one there," Delia said, pushing him back out of the office.

Zelic growled as he backed up. "Probably so she and the governor could have some *private time.*" He glanced furtively at the medic and her patient as they walked out of the infirmary, then continued out in the hall. "Graci is one of the governor's many mistresses, but the only infertile one. He forced me to put her on the medical staff when her season ended, even though she had no training."

No wonder she's so incompetent. Delia thought of the long table of medications and Graci's fawning obedience to the governor's demands. *What else did she give him?* "I didn't recognize some of the medicines in the governor's room. Did the guy you sent to buy medicine return?"

Zelic nodded, his face in a deep scowl. "I'll wake up Neva and find out what she gave him before she left Graci alone with him. I'll meet you in the governor's room." Zelic pointed to the mortar and plants Delia was carrying. "I assume this is for him?"

Delia nodded. "Field horsetail," she said, holding out the long stems with their scrub-brush tops. "Will the kitchen make it into a tea for me?"

Zelic snorted. "No. I'll make them do it," he said, taking the stems from her. "But don't treat him with anything until you talk to me first."

"Uh..."

Zelic breathed out an angry sigh. "You already did?"

"I just put the poultices that were already there on his ribs."

Zelic's tense shoulders visibly relaxed. "I made those; Neva was supposed to apply them throughout the night."

"Graci had them soaking in water."

Zelic tensed back up again until his wings shook. "I can't even yell at her without the governor punishing me." He threw up his arms in helpless rage, then stalked away.

Definitely not a morning person, Delia thought as she hurried back to the governor's room.

"Did Zelic meet you?" Beck asked as Delia approached the guarded door.

Delia nodded. "Thank you," she said, as she pushed past the guards.

"Hey!" Avell protested. "We have to do the knock first."

Delia paused with her hand on the handle. "Is there a guard on the other side of the door now?"

"No," Avell admitted, "but you can't just walk right in!"

Delia held up the mortar. "I need to apply this *now.*"

Avell began the complicated knock, but Delia opened the door and slipped past him, then quickly shut it behind her to cut off Avell's whining.

Graci leapt off the bed. "I was just checking his wounds," she lied as she straightened her clothes.

"You should wait for Graci to let you in," the governor grumbled, his face ashen.

Delia walked up to the bed, dismayed to see the poultice lying wadded up in a bandage on the floor. She looked at Graci accusingly.

"He said it itched."

The governor refused to meet her gaze.

Delia's knuckles were white as she set the mortar down on the bed beside him and began applying the new mixture. She ground her teeth while she worked until she could speak with the illusion of calm. "Your

158

life is in danger. I'm trying to save it. You need to stay still and let this medicine work." Delia turned to look at Graci who was hovering behind her. "I need a large wet bandage."

Graci pointed to the discarded poultice. "Can't you just use that one?"

Delia took a deep breath and blew it out. "No, it's been on the floor." She could hear the unnatural cadence to her voice that betrayed her suppressed anger, but couldn't seem to hide it any better.

Graci exchanged a look with the governor, then sulkily complied, the door banging behind her.

"She's going to accidentally kill you," Delia blurted.

"That's none of your concern."

"You made me a medic; it's exactly my concern." she argued as she checked his other wounds.

The governor frowned, the unbandaged portion of his forehead puckered. "Then go find more medicinal plants in the forest."

"You want me to leave you *alone*?"

The governor hesitated. "Graci will be back soon."

Delia bit back a growl as she lifted the empty mortar from the bed.

"You can go then," he added.

"Why are you letting someone incompetent treat you when your injuries are so serious?"

"You mean *you*?" the governor quipped, his ghastly color making his smile look ghoulish.

Delia's eyes narrowed as she bit back a retort. "At least don't accept any more medicine from her."

His frightening smile vanished and he stared down at his broken wings. "I was in pain."

"Let's hope her *medicine* doesn't cost you your life."

He frowned down at the green mash covering his middle. "Your poultice itches."

Delia brushed the mixture aside and examined his skin. "There's no sign of an allergic reaction. Itching can be a sign of healing; just leave it alone."

"Can't I just drink something?"

"Zelic should be bringing some tea soon."

"His bedside manner is as bad as yours," he complained. "And where is Charis? I want to know what he found and what *they* said. I should be doing the questioning." He shifted irritably, then gasped in pain.

"You need to be still," Delia cautioned as she repositioned the slipping poultice.

"I don't want to," he whined. "I need more pain medicine."

"You are a terrible patient," Delia muttered.

"Maybe you're a terrible medic," he snapped. "Maybe I should have put you in the dungeon after all."

She opened her mouth to release an eviscerating truth bomb when a knock sounded.

"That's the guards' knock; go open the door," he commanded.

Grumbling under her breath, Delia did as he asked.

"Zelic wishes to come in," Avell said formally.

"Get out of my way, Avell, before I spill boiling water all over you," Zelic threatened.

"I don't take orders from you," Avell retorted, but quickly moved out of the way.

Zelic entered gripping a tray with a steaming pot, earthenware teacup, and a pile of bandages. "Governor," he greeted curtly as Avell nearly shut his wings in the closing door.

"I need pain medicine," the governor repeated. "And where is Graci?"

"Graci is off duty," Zelic said as he set the tea tray on the table and poured out a cup.

"Tell her I want her here," the governor insisted.

"No. She hasn't slept. Lack of sleep impairs judgment."

"I decide what hours the life servants work!"

"Yes, you do. And you decided on twelve-hour shifts, remember? Graci has been taking care of you for *twelve* hours. You need to let her sleep."

"She slept," he grumbled in an undertone, but scowled at his wings rather than challenge the medic further.

Zelic glanced down at the empty mortar Delia was still holding. "You already treated him?"

Delia set the mortar down. "Your poultice was on the floor when I came in," she said, then lowered her voice. "And Graci leapt off the bed."

Zelic's nostrils flared as he walked over to survey the discarded bandage and herbs.

"It itched," the Governor said dismissively.

Zelic returned to the table, his face tightened in barely controlled fury.

"Can you replace all those plants?" he asked Delia.

"If I'm gone all day, yes."

Zelic nodded, then cast a furtive glance at the governor. "Remind me, what does field horsetail tea do?" he whispered.

"Help stop internal bleeding." Delia shut her eyes for a moment straining to remember dispensing instructions. "Two to three cups spaced throughout the day, and let it steep for at least fifteen minutes, but no longer than an hour." *I think that's right.* Before she could second-guess herself, her heart swelled with a feeling of rightness and comfort that left a catch in her throat.

"And what's in the poultice you *already* applied?" Zelic asked.

"Yarrow, witch hazel, and cottonwood leaf bud resin."

"Huh. Good work," he said, the words contrasting with his gruff tone. "Now go replace those plants."

A tiny smile flitted across her lips as she escaped the room, feeling as if a weight had been lifted from her shoulders. *Thank you, God in heaven.*

"You done?" Beck asked as she closed the door behind her.

Delia nodded.

"And he's going to be okay?"

"I think so."

The four guards seemed to collectively release a breath, their shoulders relaxing. *They care about him,* Delia realized. *He must be a better person when he's not in pain.*

"Did you get breakfast?" Beck asked.

"No, but I can eat in the forest," Delia said, wondering if he had heard her stomach growl.

"Are you sure? Tera made rolls today. If you have to be a life servant, you might as well get the benefits, too."

"Do I just go to the kitchen? Do they already know about me?"

"Probably not, but I'd be happy to go with you," Beck volunteered.

"You just want a second breakfast," Avell accused. "And your shift just started. *Mine* is supposed to be over. And *I'm* starving."

"You take her then," Beck suggested.

Avell glared at Delia a moment, then glanced at the other guards. "Fine." He stalked away without looking back.

"Well, follow him," Beck urged, shooing her away.

Delia flew after the grumpy guard, his broken, flame-colored wings making him easy to follow even when the hall became crowded. He stopped at a door that had been cut horizontally in half, the top propped

162

open to reveal a busy kitchen. A woman handed Avell a plate of heavenly smelling rolls, then he turned and walked away.

"Hey!" Delia called after him.

Avell turned back around and removed a roll from his mouth with a scowl.

"The governor made her a life servant because she threw rocks at Morph," Avell said.

"I didn't throw any rocks!"

The woman in the kitchen glared at her while Avell gave her a smug smile.

"And now you expect me to feed you?!" the woman demanded. Shaking her head, she closed the top half of the door with a slam.

This just keeps getting better. Delia frowned and flew after Avell. As she passed by him, she snagged a roll off his plate, then flew as fast as she could.

"Give that back!" Avell yelled, his words garbled by his overly full mouth.

Delia chortled as she sailed through the castle and out the open front door, grateful that there was no one waiting to catch her this time.

Chapter Twelve

It was dark before Delia returned to the castle. Replacing the ingredients to Zelic's poultices had proved more onerous than she had hoped. Her two days of previous harvesting had been done in entirely different areas. She had flown the same path as the first day, but that had made it difficult to find the second day's plants. Searching for specific herbs had sapped some of the enjoyment out of her wildcrafting, as had the knowledge that she was being forced to do it. Her lovely new spade and apparently waterproof work boots did speed up the process, but Delia returned dispirited. Coli was sure to be upset with her when she found out who got Archi in trouble, and Pearl would be livid that her bookkeeper apprenticeship might be doubted along with Delia's. Distracted by her cares, Delia missed the figure moving through the shadows of the courtyard until he blocked the front door.

"Len!" she blurted, then pulled her spade from her bag.

"I got a day in the dungeon because of you," he accused. "Couldn't you just let it go? You already gave me a black eye."

Delia gripped the spade's handle. "Well, I'm a life servant now, so you should be satisfied."

"Your season ended?"

"No, it's a punishment. Now get out of my way; I'm *working*."

"The governor made you a life servant for hitting me?"

"Among other things. Now, move!" Delia brought the spade up in front of her like a weapon and Len quickly stepped aside. She tried to open the door with one hand, but it wouldn't budge. She glared at Len. "Move further away."

"What is it you think I'm going to do?" he demanded irritably.

"I don't know, but you certainly surprised me last time."

"I'm not going to touch you," he growled. "I don't even want to."

"Then why were you out here waiting for me in the dark? And why block the door?"

"I just wanted to talk to you."

"Why?!"

"Never mind!" He walked to the edge of the courtyard before spinning around. "Happy?"

"Nothing you do could make me happy!" Delia yelled, as she stowed her spade and opened the heavy door. She wanted to pull it closed behind her, but the harshness of her words rang in her ears. Cursing, she left the door open for him and flew to the infirmary.

Inside, Zelic was pacing while another medic sat quietly in the open office, watching him.

"Finally!" Zelic said when he saw Delia. "What did you bring?"

Delia opened her bag and dumped the contents on the nearest cot. "I got more of everything."

"Good!" Zelic rifled through her plants in a frenzy. "We used all the cottonwood leaf bud resin and he's been very vocally in pain all evening. Graci made more willow bark tea and tried to sneak it to him, so I threw it all out." Zelic flung several bark chips at her. "So hide those somewhere, because I expect she'll try it again." He gathered three leaf buds and ran for the door. "Catalog the rest!" he shouted and shut the door behind him.

Delia put the willow bark back in her bag, then gathered up the bed sheet with her harvest and trudged to the office.

The medic in the office doorway waved, her gray and orange wings looking cheerful in the drab room. "I'm Caena. Your laundry is on the desk. And if you want to go eat before you catalog, I'm sure Zelic wouldn't mind." She moved aside to let Delia into the office.

Delia dropped her load on the desk and gathered up her laundry. "Thanks, but I ate in the forest," she said, stuffing her clean clothes into her bag.

"I heard you had a little trouble with the kitchen; do you want me to go for you?"

Delia sat heavily on the office stool and began labeling. "Won't they just spit in it if they know it's for me?"

Caena chuckled. "Maybe. Morph is a nice guy and he has a lot of friends."

Delia sighed. "I didn't throw rocks at him. I didn't throw rocks at *anyone.*"

"But you and Ora Sulphur planned the attack? Because the princess broke your fiancé's wing?"

Delia stopped writing and glared up at the medic. Caena's gaze was filled with gossipy delight.

"He's *not* my fiancé and I didn't plan anything!"

"But you *are* involved with the broken-winged brother, right? I heard you two were kissing right here in the infirmary."

Delia clenched the pencil so tightly in her hand that it broke. "I have *never* kissed him, and we are *not* involved."

Caena pulled a stool up to the doorway and sat eagerly. "You should tell me your side of the story; I'll spread it around."

"I don't want anyone knowing about my life," Delia grumbled, gripping the stubby remainder of the pencil.

"You should. The stories flying about you are *really bad*. It can only get better. And if you tell me, maybe the other life servants will put a mattress in your room and do your laundry and feed you."

Delia tried to ignore her and focus instead on the proper spelling of the plant in front of her.

"Where do you even sleep?"

Delia scowled, but didn't answer.

"They're saying you mated with Len White and then bludgeoned him when he broke up with you. But his black eye wasn't enough for you, so you became the governor's newest mistress in exchange for having Mr. White, Phasia, and Malan thrown in the dungeon."

Delia brought her fists down on the desk. "Who?! Who is saying that?"

Caena simpered and shrugged. "Just some of the life servants. Is any of it true?"

"No!" Delia shrieked.

"I only wondered because you keep skipping the pregnancy tests," Caena continued. "Are you worried you're pregnant? We could do a test right now."

"I am *not* pregnant! I have *not* mated with anyone! Will you please quit pummeling me with your malicious gossip?"

Caena stood, her rounded chin jutted out. "I'm not a gossip. I was just trying to help you."

"You can't possibly believe that," Delia scoffed, once again trying to return to her work.

Caena's face darkened. "I did your laundry, and it was *really* dirty! And I would have spoken up for you, but I won't now! You don't want my help? Fine! Then you can handle the infirmary by yourself, too. You get off at midnight." Caena marched across the infirmary and slammed the door behind her.

Delia fumed. She was exhausted and in desperate need of a bath. *And the cabinet is probably locked.* She reached up and pulled on the cabinet door, confirming her suspicions.

"Of course you're locked," she growled to herself. "Let's hope I don't have any patients."

Frowning, Delia threw herself back into cataloguing her harvest. When she finished she glared at the cabinet. Likely any remaining medicinal plants were inside along with all the notes on how to use them. Delia stared down at her neatly labeled plants. Did all the medics have access to Zelic's notes and those she had made yesterday? She scowled at the locked cabinet, then added the medicinal uses to each label. By the time she finished, writing with the tiny pencil fragment had cramped her hand, and she rubbed it as she read over her work. Satisfied, she removed her excellent new boots, mentally thanking Cam and promising him an apology very soon. Then she gave the locked cabinet one last impotent tug and treated her healing feet, once again wrapping them with filthy bandages. Her face seemed back to its normal size, and only her chin and lips hurt when she pressed them. She touched the tender skin of her neck, then treated the bruises there, hoping they would soon disappear. When she finished, she felt exhausted. She wandered along the rows of cots, finding them more inviting the longer she did so. *What time is it?* she whined to herself.

When the infirmary door opened, she jumped, then hid her dirty hands behind her back.

"What are you doing in here still? Where is Caena?" Zelic demanded as he walked past her carrying a clean mortar.

"She got mad and left."

Zelic swore. "So you and I end up with eighteen-hour shifts? I am *so tired* of all the infantile behavior around here. If I had any real power, I would toss Graci off my staff and bar her from seeing the governor until he's healed." He shook his head angrily as he returned the mortar to the desk and opened the cabinet.

"Did she do something else?"

"Everything I order her to do, she gets the governor to countermand, which is why my patient is alone with her again while I'm doing menial tasks!" Zelic groused as he hurried back to the door with fresh bandages. "Neva will relieve you soon. Take tomorrow off and get some sleep; you look exhausted."

It wasn't until he was gone that Delia remembered the locked cabinet. Chastising herself, she flew to the office and tried the cabinet door. A genuine smile flashed across her face; Zelic had left it unlocked. Delia changed her bandages, then stowed her catalogued harvest in the cabinet with the few remaining plants there. The majority of the cabinet was taken up with large containers of powder that Delia guessed were for pregnancy tests. Several bottles from an apothecary in Firwood were stowed inside as well. Delia was sniffing the latter to determine what plants they had used in their compounds when she heard the door. Quickly recapping the bottles and shutting the cabinet, Delia stepped out of the office.

"Uh, I was just looking for the medic, but I can come back later," Rus said, turning toward the door. He had pulled a dry shirt on, but his swim shorts and wings were still dripping.

"*I'm* the medic; how can I help you?"

Rus turned back to her, his bushy brows drawn together. "You're a *life servant* now?"

Delia bit back a retort. She was tired of answering the same question. "It's a punishment."

"For what? And how long?"

"Several things, and a month."

"Whoa. This isn't because of what that white did to your face, is it?" Rus asked.

Delia put a hand up to hide the lower part of her face. *Did it look bad? Why aren't there more mirrors around here?* "What do you need?"

"It's stupid. I can come back later." He took a few steps toward the door, favoring his left leg.

Delia sighed. "What's wrong with your leg?"

He turned back and shrugged. "I think it's infected."

"Let me see."

Rus stood near the door, hesitant. "Are you trained as a medic? Bul said you work with plants."

"I'm an apothecary apprentice; medicinal plants are my specialty."

"Oh." Rus hobbled over to the stool she indicated, then sat pointing to a scabbed wound on his calf. "One of my idiot friends stabbed me with a pencil last week. It barely even bled. Then yesterday it started hurting again."

Delia examined the wound, careful not to touch it as her dirty fingers would quickly muddy his legs. Red skin radiated out from the small scab, the swelling making his calf look slightly misshapen. "You're right; it's infected. Get up here on the cot. I'll be right back."

Delia was considering a dash to the pool when she saw the sink hidden behind wing frames in the corner. A carafe of water and block of lye soap sat next to it. Delia washed her hands thoroughly as Rus began to whistle idly.

"I'm almost done," she snapped, then felt guilty as his whistling abruptly stopped. She formed and discarded multiple apologies as she collected plants from the office cabinet and tossed them into the mortar, then grabbed the pestle and a bandage before returning to his side. Setting them on a neighboring cot, she began to grind the herbs. She could feel his eyes on her, and self-consciously tucked her chin. "Thank you for getting my shoes and soap from the bottom of the pool."

Rus' full lips turned up in a grin and he lifted his wings partway closed. "I thought you were mad that I kept your soap."

Delia shook her head. "I know you were teasing me. I just can't be...playful when I'm like this."

"You mean, in season?"

Delia nodded, grateful her task gave her an excuse not to meet his eyes. *Kind brown eyes,* she noted.

"So what are you like when you're not..." he trailed off, uncertain what word or phrase to use.

"I don't know. Less angry? Less irritated? Much less likely to yell or say rude things... or yell rude things," she conceded with a hint of a smile.

Rus chuckled lightly. "I haven't heard you say anything that wasn't deserved."

"You haven't been around me much."

"I wouldn't mind changing that."

Delia met his gaze. "Why? Are you a masochist?"

He barked out a surprised laugh. "Not particularly, no."

"Then you must not be very well informed," Delia surmised, giving her mixture a particularly violent grind.

"Enlighten me."

"No," she said decidedly.

"No?" he chortled. "Why not?"

"Because it's nice to have someone smiling at me again; I've missed it." Delia blushed, assiduously avoiding his face as she smoothed out the bandage and dumped the contents of the mortar atop it. Gathering up both sides of the bandage, she lifted it gingerly, careful to keep the herbs inside. *Why wasn't he saying anything?* She darted a glance at his face, then immediately away when she caught him looking at her.

"You're not smiling any more," Delia observed as she carried the open bandage to his cot.

"I've heard the rumors; I just thought they were too stupid to be true."

"They are stupid," Delia agreed as she carefully placed the poultice over the wound, then methodically wrapped the bandage to keep it in place. Her fingers tingled when she grazed his skin, and a pleasant scent emanated from his closed wings. She took her time tying off the bandage, touching his skin unnecessarily. *Unprofessional!* she chastised herself as she stepped back.

"So I *am* well informed, then?" he asked, his smile returning.

"Not a bit," she teased as she returned the mortar and pestle to the office. "No one who listens to rumors is ever well informed."

He snorted. "You sound like my mother."

"Wise woman. Sleep with that on and stay off your leg as much as possible. If it's still red and painful in the morning, come back to the infirmary."

"Thanks," he said, getting up. "Do you have to work all night?"

Delia shook her head. "Just until midnight; I'm almost done."

"Do you want company?"

"Yes," she admitted. "But only if you lie down again; you need to keep the wound elevated as much as possible."

He wrinkled his nose in annoyance, but crawled back onto the cot and lay down. "Better?"

"Yes."

"So why do you call Bul 'dragonwort?'"

"He didn't tell you?"

Rus grinned and shook his head. "He got mad when I asked."

"There's this ugly lily that looks like it's sticking it's tongue out at you and it gives off the scent of rotting meat; it's called dragonwort."

Rus erupted into laughter, making the cot shake with his mirth.

"When I first met him, I thought he must be carrying it or rotten meat."

"*That's* what he smells like to you?" Rus dropped his head onto his folded arms, his muffled chortles almost musical.

Delia nodded even though his eyes were shut in mirth. His light brown hair was drying in tangly waves at his neck, and she was tempted to touch them. Her arm strayed out of its own accord just as the door opened.

A middle-aged woman with charcoal wings stepped into the room and appraised them both. "Where's Caena?"

Delia retracted her arm, but Rus had already noticed it. "She got mad and left me to work her shift."

The woman grunted. "You must be the wildcrafter that the governor is punishing. I'm Neva."

"Delia."

Neva nodded, then looked at Rus. "Is he a patient?"

"Yes. He has an infected puncture wound that I'm treating with a poultice, and recommended that he come back in the morning if it's still red and painful."

Neva walked up to Rus and examined his bandage. "Which herbs did you use?"

"I'll show you," Delia offered, and returned to the office with Neva trailing behind her. Delia hurried through showing Neva the plants she had used and answering questions, hoping that Rus wouldn't leave and wishing Neva's wings didn't block her view of him.

Finally, Neva nodded in satisfaction. "Just wash up the mortar and pestle, and you can go."

Are all of the life servants going to order me around now?

Neva picked at the drying herbs in the mortar. "You really should have washed it immediately. Didn't anyone train you?"

"No."

"Well, I can do it now."

NO! Delia followed Neva out of the office, disheartened to see the empty cot where Rus had been. Neva instructed her on effective cleaning methods while Delia washed the mortar and pestle. Then they stripped the sheet off the cot Rus had used and added it to a laundry basket near the table. Neva even taught her how to administer a pregnancy test, and seemed unsurprised that Delia's was negative. Finally, Neva showed her where the cabinet key was hidden under the desk.

"There are needles and catgut for stitches next to the bandages. I would teach you about the medicines in the cabinet, but you probably know more than I do," Neva said, closing the cabinet and opening a shallow drawer in the desk that Delia hadn't noticed. "And this is the patient log. You just need to fill out your patient's name, condition, and treatment."

Delia's eyes scanned down the chart looking for the governor's name before returning to the empty line and quickly jotting down Rus' information.

"You need to list his last name," Neva said, pointing.

"I don't know it."

"Well, go ask Malan, and come back."

"Isn't he still in the dungeon?"

Neva snorted. "The day clerk wouldn't work the night shift or train anyone else to do it, so Malan was out by dinner time."

Delia breathed a sigh of relief. *Maybe he won't be irritated with me, then.* "Okay, I'll go now." Too tired to fly, Delia trudged through the castle, thinking her boots were just right for this type of walking. She listened to the clop-clop of her weary steps and took long blinks. It wasn't surprising that she ran into someone, though she wondered later why he hadn't moved out of the way.

He chuckled as she impacted his rib cage, then steadied her when she stumbled back. "You okay there? Were you sleepwalking?"

"Oh," she said blearily, blinking several times before she recognized him. "Sorry, Cam."

He grinned, his dimples showing.

Compunction hit her as her mind cleared. "And I'm really sorry about sleeping in your bed," Delia apologized, blushing. "I didn't have a place to sleep, and I thought you would be gone all night."

Cam shook his head and looked at the floor. "It was fine."

"It was really kind of you not to wake me. I hope you didn't have to stay up all night because of me, especially after your long trip."

"No, I knew where there was an empty room. I slept there."

Something about the way he said it made her think the experience had been distasteful.

"Thank you for the boots; I love them. And the spade is just perfect. I haven't worn the other shoes yet, but I'm about to."

"You're going to the pool?"

Delia nodded.

"Can you stay awake that long?" he teased.

"I *hope* so," she said, stepping around him. "And I really am sorry." She took a few steps past him down the hall before turning back. "And thank you again!"

He was still standing in the middle of the hall smiling at her. Delia's stomach did a funny flop and flutter. *Odd. Am I hungry?*

Outside the clerk's office, she listened, then held her breath and entered. There were dark circles under Malan's eyes, but he smiled when he saw her.

"I did tell you to stay away from him," he reminded her.

Though she had meant to begin with an apology, his goading made other words fly from her mouth. "You couldn't possibly have known it would turn out like that."

"No, but I knew there would be violence. How's your face?"

"It doesn't hurt anymore," she said, covering her mouth. "And I'm sorry I got you in trouble. I appreciate that you've tried to help me." She dropped her hand in a gesture of frustration. "I thought Zelic would keep my secret. I should have realized you would get in trouble."

"As I recall, you were angry that I wrote you'd been a bookkeeper. Today's dungeon nap was not your fault."

Some of the weight on Delia's shoulders seemed to lift.

A smirk twitched on Malan's face. "You weren't really going to pelt Her Highness the Princess Lexi with rocks, were you?"

Delia frowned. *Of course he knows about that.* "Maybe?" she answered honestly. "Ora said some woman had broken Talis' wing, stolen Coli's boyfriend, and was blackmailing the governor. He wanted me to distract the guard so he could get to her and break her wing. He didn't tell me he was going to *hit* the guard. I dropped my rocks when the guard got hurt. I never threw them."

"That's still pretty bad."

Delia nodded. "I know. I just got so angry that she had hurt my best friend."

Malan smiled knowingly. "Overwhelming irrational anger leading to poor decisions; I remember that feeling."

"And now I get to be a life servant," Delia said with false brightness.

"Yeah, that's how I feel about it, too."

Delia sighed. "Sorry."

"You're not the only one the governor made a life servant while they were still in season. He told me since there was no chance of my wing healing and the night clerk had just died, I might as well get to work."

Delia's eyes narrowed. "He is *not* my favorite person."

"Careful now. Any urges to throw rocks? Should I check your pockets?" Malan teased.

Delia rolled her eyes. "No, but I do need to get back to work. I forgot to ask a patient his last name and Neva wants it filled in on the log."

Malan nodded. "Neva's a stickler. What's his first name?"

"Rus."

"Big guy with orange wings?"

"Yes."

"Rus *Anglewing*."

"Thanks, Malan," Delia said, hesitating as she turned to go. "Could I...have his room number, too?"

Malan chuckled as he shuffled through the papers on his desk. "318; want me to mark it on your map?"

Blushing, Delia pulled out her map and handed it to him. "Aren't you going to tell me to stay out of his room?"

"You don't listen to me anyway," he smirked as he marked the map and handed it back.

"I'm going to start," Delia vowed.

"Then I have some advice for you: When you find a guy that smells nice, spill something on him and see how he reacts. If he gets angry, he's not for you."

"And that actually works?"

Malan smiled sadly. "That's how my dad chose my mom."

"Did you take his advice?"

Malan shook his head. "No, I did not."

Delia thought of her mother's advice to kiss as many guys as she could and colored. "Bye, Malan."

"See you later."

Delia was relieved when Neva let her go without any further tasks or training. She considered checking on Rus, but couldn't think of a sufficient excuse to wake him. At Coli's room, she knocked softly, then slowly opened the door. Coli was asleep, and didn't stir when she entered and gently shut the door behind her. The room seemed somehow larger in the dim light, and Delia swore when she realized what it was. The second bed, mattress *and* frame, had been removed. Delia exited the room as quietly as she had entered. *Now what?* Delia first tried her assigned room: it had a bed frame, but still no mattress. Groaning, she made her way to Talis' door and knocked tentatively. She grimaced when she heard him moving inside.

Talis opened the door and greeted her with a sleepy grin. "Did you come for that kiss?"

"Not now, Talis, I'm so tired," Delia complained.

His eyes widened. "Oh, your face! I heard something about a white beating you up, but I thought it was just a rumor." Talis' fingers touched her lip before she smacked his hand away.

"I don't want to talk about it! Just let me have Ora's mattress, please. You don't even have to help me drag it."

Confusion clouded Talis' face. "I already put it in your room. Right after Coli got so mad at me."

That explains the second mattress Phasia took from my room. Delia rubbed the spot between her brows where a headache was starting.

"Isn't it there?"

Delia shook her head and started to walk away.

"Delia," he called after her, then followed her out into the hallway when she didn't stop. "I didn't tell anyone that you were with Ora. I don't know how that got out. I'm sorry you're in trouble for it. I heard the governor made you a life servant; is that true?"

"Yes," Delia snapped.

"I'm really sorry. Um, what I suggested before..."

Delia gave him a warning look.

"I'm not *bothering* you. I'm just saying, if you want to escape while you still can, I'll go home with you and tell everyone we're married."

Delia stopped to glare at him. "How is that not bothering me?!"

"Because I'm not blackmailing you; I'm offering to *save* you."

"I don't need saving."

Talis touched her face again, but moved his hand before she could smack it. "And I will beat up that white for you..."

Delia rolled her eyes.

"...And Dad will give us the gray house on the hill with the big garden. And we can have Sunday dinners with your family, and you won't have to worry about your dad tromping through the woods looking for plants in his old age." He ran his fingers along a strand of her hair that had escaped her messy bun. "Your medicine is working. The medic said my wing is healing. You won't have to fly home alone."

Delia shook herself from his carefully crafted daydream and looked at his wing frame. "Is the same poultice still on it?"

"Was I supposed to change it?"

Delia sighed and took his hand from her hair. "Come on," she said, turning around, "you need a fresh dose."

Talis grinned. "You're starting to like me, I can tell."

"I am doing my *job*," Delia argued, then caught the scent of mustard. "And stop signaling me."

"I can't help it! You make me feel all...happy and hopeful," Talis admitted, his face reddening.

What is happening? Maybe I do to him what Len's stupid blue eyes do to me. "It's just pheromones."

Talis took her hand and stopped walking. "No, it's *you*. I *know* you, Delia."

Delia slipped her hand out of his and continued walking. "I'm not exactly myself just now."

"I know; you're better. You make *me* better."

Delia sighed and rubbed at her burgeoning headache. "Could you please not talk like that in front of the medic? I don't think she's the gossiping type, but still..."

"You don't want her to think the rumor about us being engaged, and you attacking the princess out of desperate love for me, is true?"

Delia smacked his arm. "If I find out you started that..."

"I didn't! I didn't! I promise," Talis laughed and danced away before she could land another hit. "Whenever anybody asks me about it, I always tell them it's absolutely...true!"

Delia flew at him, her fists raining on his chest and stomach while he laughed hysterically, then finally caught her wrists and held them to his shoulders.

"I will head butt you if you don't let go of me!" Delia shouted.

Talis chuckled. "I really don't think that's going to—oof—okay, that hurt a little."

Delia head butted him again, then clenched her eyes shut as her headache spread across her forehead.

"Did you hurt your head?" Talis asked, amusement still apparent in his tone. "I'll kiss it better."

Before she could protest, his lips brushed her forehead, making her entire head tingle. The foot she had drawn back to kick him dropped harmlessly to the floor. She opened her eyes to Talis' knowing smile.

"You want me to kiss you again. I can tell."

Do I? Mom did say to kiss as many as I could. "Let go of my hands," she requested, her vehemence replaced with curiosity.

Talis released her hands and she let them slide down his chest. It was so odd to touch him like this. The horrid jokester bully that had frequently spoiled the fun of her childhood wet his lips in eager anticipation.

"No," Delia decided, pushing away from him.

"No?!"

She walked away, a genuine smile lighting her face as she opened the infirmary door.

Neva looked up from the book in her hand. "Did you forget something?"

"I just need to change the poultice on his wing break."

Neva lifted a graying brow as Talis entered. "You put a poultice on his *wing*?"

"Zelic did," Delia answered as she breezed past the older woman.

Neva followed Delia into the office. "What's in it?"

"Chickweed." Delia retrieved it from the cabinet and dropped it in the mortar.

Neva picked up the mortar and pestle and began to grind while Delia locked the cabinet and hid the key.

"Do you know how to open a wing frame?" Neva asked.

"Yes."

Neva nodded. "Show me."

Delia bristled, the fun of tormenting Talis forgotten as she followed Neva back out of the office.

"Lie down, Mr. Sulphur," Neva directed, pointing to a cot.

Talis complied and Delia dutifully unfastened the frame and lifted the back by its hinges to expose the broken wing.

Neva cleared away the old poultice and grunted. "Stained it."

181

"What?" Talis demanded as he tried to look up over the frame.

"Hold still!" Delia commanded, struggling to keep the frame in place. "A blob of green on your golden wing is a small price to pay for healing, and it's not permanent." *Probably.*

Talis calmed and dropped his head back on the pillow as Neva dumped out the fresh herbs and began spreading them across his wing break.

"And if it is permanent, I can add a green spot to your other forewing to even it up," Delia teased. "Or polka dot all four wings if you prefer. That would look nice," she deadpanned.

"What?!"

"Close it," Neva directed, giving Delia a reproving look.

Delia did as she was told, hiding her smirk until Neva walked away with the mortar. She supported the wing frame as Talis got back to his feet.

"I think you need a green spot on *your* wings," Talis said.

"It's not so much a spot as it is the letter D. I thought it was only fair to mark you since you marked me."

Talis' eyes went wide. "Did you seriously put a D on my wing? You're kidding, right?"

"I wouldn't joke about that," she said without a hint of a smile.

Talis glanced at the wing frame then reached for the fasteners. "I want to see it."

"No!" Delia chortled as she pulled his hands away. "I'm just teasing. It's a round, green blob, and I'm pretty sure it's going away."

"*You* played a practical joke on *me*?"

Delia nodded gleefully as she backed up.

"You never did that before."

Delia edged closer to the infirmary door. "That's because practical jokes are usually mean. *This* was funny."

Talis smirked as he matched her retreat. "Or maybe you're mean now? Either way, I like it."

Delia grimaced as she reached the door. "I'm *not* mean." Her conscience smote her as she thought over her behavior since her wing birth. "Okay, I'm kind of mean, but I try to make up for it afterwards," she conceded as she opened the door, then stopped to look back at the office. "Neva? Do you want me to fill out the log?"

Neva emerged from the office with the dirty mortar and pestle in her hands. "Already done. You can go."

I needed permission to leave? "Thanks," she said, then looked pointedly at Talis.

"Oh. Thanks," he called belatedly.

As soon as his head was turned, Delia darted out into the hallway and shut the door behind her with a wild giggle. Had she laughed since her wing birth? Certainly not like that.

Talis ripped open the door. "That was *bratty*." He extricated himself from the doorway as quickly as he safely could. "And now it's time for revenge."

Delia fought the urge to squeal and run. "You have a weird effect on me."

He narrowed his eyes as he advanced. "Define weird."

You turn me into a bratty child. She shook her head as his mustard scent permeated her senses. She had never wanted to torment him when she actually *was* a child; Talis and Ora's revenge schemes were too rotten to make it worth engaging with them. When Coli's brothers had tormented her or Coli, they simply told Coli's mom. She smirked as she remembered that she had already threatened him with that this week, then frowned when she remembered why.

"You're still the same person," she said instead of answering his question.

He shrugged then winced. "Probably. But I think you're up to the challenge."

He was too close now and the mustard scent was much stronger. "Don't you mark me," she warned.

He grinned. "I make no promises."

She smacked his chest, but he only moved closer, and she found her hand resting on the spot she had hit. Part of her wanted to shove him away, but she stilled when he put a hand on her waist. His other hand toyed with her hair until it fell out of its bun in tangled waves. He ran his fingers through it, then gently touched her chin and lower lip.

"Will it hurt you if we kiss?"

"We'll never know," Delia quipped as she side-stepped out of his reach.

"Delia," he protested, but it only set her giggling as she flew away wondering at her own behavior.

Delia changed quickly in her own empty room, then took her bag and boots with her, fearing a life servant would steal them otherwise. Despite the excitement that Talis had provided, her body was reminding her that it was past time to sleep. As she walked to the pool, she briefly considered stealing a cot from the infirmary, but she doubted Neva would allow it. Even if Neva did allow it, some other life servant was sure to object when Delia dragged it to her room, screeching metal across flagstone the entire way. A wicked grin crossed her face as she contemplated sleeping in Phasia's room or stealing back her own mattress. She shook her head to dislodge the imprudent thought. The best course of action was obviously to enlist Malan's help in finding an empty room. She nodded in decision as her walk came to an end, and she opened the pool door. Humid, sulfur-scented air accosted her. She *hated* that smell. *If I ever make it off the mountain, I am never eating eggs again.* Delia's eyes widened at her unconscious use of the word *if. When I make it off the mountain,* she amended, then stepped into the malodorous room. The pool had a single occupant, and he gave her an uneasy smile.

"I'm not stalking you or anything. I just thought after what happened, maybe you shouldn't go to the pool by yourself," Cam explained.

"Listening to gossip?" Delia asked as she found a rocky shelf for her bag and boots.

Cam shook his head. "You...uh...bled on my pillow, and I noticed you were injured. I thought maybe it wasn't an accident."

Delia groaned. How had she missed that? "I'm so sorry. I'd wash it for you, but I'm not allowed in the laundry room."

"I already washed it. But why aren't you allowed in there?" he asked, his curiosity genuine.

Delia stepped into the water, her unbandaged feet immediately beginning to sting. "You really haven't been listening to any of the gossip, have you?"

"I haven't been feeling very social."

"That's right; the princess messed up your life, too."

Defensiveness, anger, then hurt animated his face in rapid succession. He was quiet, staring at the water while she waded in. He had chosen the deep end of the pool and was submerged up to his shoulders, the undulating brown and beige pattern of his wing tips reminding her of a sandy beach. She was halfway through washing her hair before he spoke.

"Did she do something to you?"

"She broke my best friend's heart, broke..." she hesitated, what was Talis to her? "Broke Talis' wing, and because I was there when Ora—that's Talis and Coli's brother—tried to break into her room, the governor made me a life servant for a month."

"You tried to break into her room?"

Delia dipped her head under to rinse her hair instead of answering. When she came back up, his expression was fixed on her.

"Were you planning to hurt her?"

Delia sighed. Cam had been kind to her, but reality was about to wreck that. "Yes. I wanted to break her wing or at least throw a rock at her," she admitted. "I didn't have the chance."

"Did you know she grew up with Tiger? That they had been best friends their entire lives?"

Delia shook her head.

"Did you know that Talis started the fight and hit Tiger twice before Lexi tried to break it up? When Talis tried to hit Tiger again, she shoved him. Talis tripped over a stool, and then fell into a table, breaking his wing."

Delia frowned. "That's not what Coli and Ora said."

"I was there...watching from a balcony."

His dark eyes were steady as he met her gaze, and she found herself starting to believe him. Delia shook her head as if to clear the image he had created.

"But they're awful people; why are you defending them?"

Cam shook his head sadly. "They aren't awful."

"I watched Tiger slam Ora against the wall; he could have broken his wings. And when I talked to the princess, she told me to get out of her way in the most alarming voice I've ever heard. She's scarier than a white without any excuse for her behavior."

Cam shook his head more doggedly now. "You don't know what you're talking about. Whites aren't scary, and Lexi *does* have an excuse."

"*I* don't know what I'm talking about? I *am* a white! And what's her excuse? Her palace is too big? Two men in love with her was not enough?!" Delia splashed as she gestured wildly.

Cam blinked as the spray hit him in the face. "*You're* a white?"

"Isn't it obvious?!"

"But your wings, and you've been really nice, well, not to Lexi, but..."

Delia spun in the water, wincing as the water dragged at her wings. "Look!" She showed him the backside of her wings. "White!" She kept her back to him as she finished her washing in jerky movements; the fury slowly eking out of her with the violence of her own scrubbing.

186

"I'm sorry," he apologized.

Was he serious? She turned back around to examine his trite expression. "Why are you apologizing? *I* yelled. *I'm* the one who tried to attack your fiancee. *I'm* the one who stole your bed and bled on your pillow. And when I said I was *talking* to your fiancé, what I really meant was that I blocked her way and called her a wing breaker. *I'm* the one who's sorry. You be something else."

His dimples creased as his eyes began to sparkle, and suddenly he was laughing, tentatively at first, but building into a braying sound as he stopped resisting it. Delia watched him, perplexed.

"Why is that funny?"

He shook his head and rubbed his eyes as he tried to quell his mirth. Finally, he mastered his amusement well enough to speak. "Thanks. I needed that."

"Needed what?"

"Uh...a good laugh? A reminder that life doesn't go the way you plan it?"

Delia's brow furrowed. "Should I be offended?"

He chuckled. "No. I'm not laughing *at* you. It's...it's hard to explain."

"Hmm." Delia turned away from him and trudged out of the pool.

"You just, you helped me get past something," he explained.

"You don't have to tell me," she called over her shoulder as she gathered up her boots and bag. "*I* owe *you*; not the other way around."

He followed her out of the water. "You don't owe me."

Delia turned to argue with him, but her brain stuttered at his bare chest. It was perfect; how had she not noticed before? Delia played through her head the first time she had met him at the pool; he had been turned away from her, she decided. She was vaguely aware that she was staring, and she slowly raked her eyes across his chiseled physique to meet his face. His almost black eyes still twinkled with amusement. *Was he speaking?* Delia focused in on his mouth as he repeated the question.

"Do you want me to walk you to your room?"

"Oh." Delia's traitorous eyes slipped to his abs, then back up again.

"Are you okay?" he chuckled.

Stop it, Delia. He hasn't even signaled you. He's just being nice. "Um, what did you say?"

"I'm going to take that as a yes," he said as he held the pool door open for her.

Did I agree to something? Her eyes slid to his chest again as she passed him, and she consoled herself that it was only natural for her to look at whatever was eye-level. *Please put a shirt on*, she thought as she looked futilely for a bag of clothing that he might have with him. That only led to a prolonged study of his perfectly formed legs. *Delia, you moth-brain, stop it! You missed what he said again.*

He chuckled, and she couldn't bring herself to ask why. Her face was heating now and she looked away each time they passed a lantern to hide it.

"If you're uncomfortable, I can go."

"No!" Delia's blush deepened as she met his gaze, then forced her eyes away before they could wander, unbidden. *Please signal me*, she thought, then immediately reconsidered. This was much worse than her penchant for blue eyes, but maybe it would go away when he was fully clothed. She peeked at his trim waist and her stomach fluttered.

Cam stopped in the middle of the hallway. "It's okay if you don't want me to know where your room is. I'll just leave you here."

Delia stared up at him, confused. "My room is 308; I don't mind you knowing."

Cam's dimples appeared as he suppressed a laugh. "We've been circling the fourth floor."

What? How much time had passed? Delia looked around wildly, alarmed to see room 405 behind her. "Um," she closed her eyes, knowing it would be easier to think if she couldn't see him. "I can't really..." Her face was flaming now, her ears feeling like two signal fires to guide lost ships to shore. "I can't think when you're undressed. I mean, you're dressed, just not enough." Delia let out a humiliated moan and turned away from him. "I know that's a normal bathing suit. It's just that you're perfect." She trailed off as she spoke, the final word only a whisper. When he didn't respond immediately, she snuck a look at him.

He was smiling, hand extended, the scent of oceanspray blossoms enveloping her in a welcome cloud. She looked down at the bag and boots she was carrying and tried to transfer them to a single hand.

"Let me," he offered, taking her bag from her, then once again extending his hand.

Does he want to carry my boots or hold my hand? Delia slipped her free hand into his, hoping she hadn't misunderstood. A tremulous thrill shot through her as he enclosed her hand in his. They walked in peaceful quiet until he stopped before a door. Delia reached out to open it, disappointed their walk was over, but Cam was already stepping inside.

"I'll only be a minute," he assured her, handing back her bag before he shut the door.

Why did he go in my room? Delia stared stupidly up at the 217 on the door. *This is his room. Why are we here? Should I leave? What did he say when he went inside? Why isn't my brain working?!* Out of sight and smell of him, her embarrassment was suffocating. She glanced down the hall, longing to run to Coli's room and hide. The door opened again before she could flee.

"Better?" he asked. He had dressed in pants and a long-sleeved shirt that he finished buttoning after he closed the door behind him.

Delia's gaze was ensnared by the little triangle of flesh until he buttoned it away. "I think I'm too attracted to you," she blurted.

He grinned. "I don't think that's a problem."

"Of course it is! I haven't said or done anything intelligent since you got out of the water," she said, starting down the hall.

He chuckled as he kept pace. "I didn't mind."

"I do!" Delia cast a sideways glance at him; grateful his beautiful body was hidden. "Why do you look like that? Do you spend your days crushing boulders into gravel with your bare hands or something?"

He dropped his head with an embarrassed laugh. "That's not a bad guess. My family owns a limestone quarry."

"For building materials?"

He nodded. "And sculpture."

You would make a perfect model, she thought, then forced herself to focus on their conversation. "Do you enjoy the work?"

"The rock is beautiful when it's polished, especially the semi-precious stone we find occasionally."

Delia heard the hesitation in his voice. "But?"

"Uh...it's dangerous. That's how the men in my family die."

"*All* of them?" Delia asked, shocked when he nodded. "Crushed by rocks?"

"Or killed by explosions or slowly suffocating from inhaling the quarry dust."

Delia's mind began to catalog all the plants that helped with breathing. "You can't treat it?"

"Nothing has worked yet."

He looked so pensive that she dropped her bag and boots to hug him, then lingered there because of the way he smelled. His hands curled around her waist, the material of her suit suddenly feeling far too thin. She pulled away abruptly, then colored at the wet mark she had left on his shirt.

"I'm sorry!"

"It'll dry."

She examined his face, looking for signs of irritation, but found none. *Does that count as passing Malan's test?* She smiled at him and started walking again.

"Isn't that your room?" he asked, pointing at the door she had just passed.

"Oh." She could feel the color rising in her face again. She had walked away from her bag and boots as well. She forced out a nervous laugh as she retrieved them and opened the door. "I'm not normally a moth brain," she said, hesitating before setting her bag on the empty bed frame. Somehow, it made the barren room look more forlorn. She set down the boots at the foot of the frame and returned to the door.

"What happened to your mattress?"

Delia gave him a grim smile. "The life servants don't like me very much."

"So they just took your mattress?"

"Twice. Three times if you count the extra bed in Coli's room."

"I thought you were hiding from whomever hurt you in my room. I didn't realize you didn't have a bed."

"Some of both," she admitted.

"You can sleep in my bed again," he offered, then colored. "I don't mean *with me*, I mean I'll sleep in Tiger's room again."

"You had to sleep in *Tiger's* room? Ugh, now I feel worse. You sleep in your bed. I'll sleep in Tiger's room."

Cam grimaced and shifted his weight. "Tiger's cousin, Wes, shared the room. I *think* he's still in the dungeon, but..."

"That's okay. If he shows up, I'll just apologize and leave. Won't be the first time it's happened." *Why did you say that?!*

"He's in the dungeon for sexual assault."

"Oh." *So that won't work.* "Don't worry about it. Malan will find me a bed."

"Who's Malan?"

"The night clerk."

Cam looked bemused. "I thought you said the life servants don't like you?"

"Most of them don't."

"Because of Lexi?"

"The guard that Ora threw rocks at is well-liked, and I made an enemy of the laundry mistress my first morning here. And Malan and the laundry mistress both ended up in the dungeon partially because of me. And then there are horrible rumors flying that some of the life servants choose to believe. So I can't sleep or eat here unless I'm sneaky."

"*And* you're a life servant for a month?"

Delia nodded. "Things are going *really* well."

Cam snorted. "I see that." He ran a hand through his short-cropped auburn curls. "You're handling it well."

"If by 'handling it well' you mean making new enemies every day, then yes, I *am* handling it well."

Cam let out an uneasy laugh. "Is that why you needed the spade? Did they make you a gardener?"

"No. I'm a medic, and I fetch medicinal plants from the forest."

"That sounds interesting."

"It is." Delia hesitated, then blurted out her offer. "You're welcome to come with me any time."

"I'd like that. Are you going tomorrow?"

"If I want to eat."

Cam grinned at her. "I have food, you know."

"Yes, but this physique," Delia said waving a hand at him, "needs a lot of food to maintain. You should keep it for your beautiful self." *Beautiful self?! I sound like Coli.*

Cam guffawed, his cheeks suffused with a rosy hue.

"Now, before I embarrass us both more, I will wish you goodnight," Delia said as she began to close the door.

"Wait. I know of someplace else you might be able to sleep. Lexi had a couple of roommates, but there are five beds in the Queen's suite."

"I'll keep it in mind," she said, shutting the door. She had begun to shiver in her wet bathing suit, and was only able to hide it by tightening all of her muscles. Now she shook while her teeth chattered.

"Goodnight," Cam called through the door.

"Goodnight," she echoed, then added in an undertone, "lovely man who makes me exceptionally stupid." It probably hadn't been wise to invite him foraging; she would likely eat a poisoned mushroom in her attraction stupor and die.

She took her time changing. She held first to the rickety bed frame, then the door handle while she rebandaged her feet. The bandages were too loose and felt lumpy in her boots when she finished, but she planned to fix them when she next had access to a stool. When she opened the door, a mattress blocked her access to the hall. Delia smiled and leaned out to check the hallway for Cam, but it was empty.

Nice and mind-numbingly attractive, she thought as she dragged the mattress into her room. She had a moment of alarm that Cam might have given her his mattress, but a quick sniff soothed her fears. *How odd,* she thought, the mattress smelled as if it had been doused with valerian. Was it from Tiger's bed? Had Coli found this smell pleasant? Delia yawned. Unpleasant smell or no, she was sleeping on it. Her limbs felt heavy as she wedged the bed to block the door. She *refused* to have another pregnancy test at 5:30 a.m., especially as it was less than three hours away. And any life servants who wished to steal her new stolen mattress or bother her in any way, would have the nearly impossible task of waking her. Delia smirked; she was going to sleep for a very long time.

Chapter Thirteen

Delia awoke with the vague recollection of someone trying to get in her room, but as the bed was still wedged firmly in place, she knew they had been unsuccessful. She smiled to herself. Perhaps the valerian-scented owner of the mattress had soporific pheromones. She amused herself by imagining Coli falling asleep dancing with Tiger. Delia briefly considered asking her friend about her ex-boyfriend's pheromones, then the previous day's problems hit her like a tsunami. Archi. Was he in the dungeon? Had he been part of the attack on the governor? Had she even been right about Vic? Would the governor lift her life-servant sentence if she was? Delia dressed quickly, then strapped on her bag; no point in leaving anything behind for the life servants to steal. She gave the mattress one last wistful look, knowing it would likely be gone when she returned.

The hallways were crowded with in-seasons complaining about the rainy weather and the abysmal lunch they had been served. Delia went straight to Coli's room, though she didn't expect to find her there. Her knock unanswered, she opened the door. Coli was flung across the bed.

"Just go away," Coli said, without turning to look at her.

"What happened?" Delia asked, feeling like a fraud and a saboteur.

Coli twisted her head, her eyes puffy and red. "Did you tell the governor about Vic?"

Delia stepped in and closed the door. She wanted so much to explain herself, to make excuses. "Yes."

Coli got up from the bed, her clothes uncharacteristically rumpled. "So *you* don't have to spend a month in the dungeon, but Archi will be there for *three*."

It was so tempting to let Coli think that; Delia's pause was a long one. "I'm sorry. Someone told the governor I was there when Ora attacked the guard. He gave me a choice of a month in the dungeon or a month as a medic. I panicked and tried to trade the information on Vic to get out of the month's punishment."

"And did you?"

"I worked a 19-hour shift yesterday, so I don't think so."

"*That's* where you've been?" Coli asked.

Delia nodded.

"So you got Archi punished with nothing in exchange."

"I told the governor only Vic had bloody knuckles, but he seemed convinced that one of them couldn't have acted without the other two knowing. I'm so sorry. I shouldn't have said anything."

"You should have talked to me first! When I asked Archi, he told me Vic and Roy went looking for the governor after he left the castle. Archi tried to talk them out of it, but they wouldn't listen. When they came back, they said they had flown all the way to Scio, but never found him."

"Did they get a month in the dungeon, too?"

"No, Delia. The governor sentenced them to *life* in the dungeon with the rapists and murderers. His own brother and cousin, but he gave them the worst punishment possible just for beating him up." Coli's bitterness was palpable.

What had Archi been telling her? "It wasn't a fist fight; he didn't even have a chance to protect himself. They knocked him unconscious from behind, then when he was helpless on the ground they beat his face, broke his wings and ribs, and made him bleed internally. He almost died yesterday. He still might."

Coli's bitterness dissolved into confusion. "But, he said..."

"I treated him myself, Coli. Whoever did that to him was vicious."

Coli opened her mouth, then closed it again. With a sigh, she retrieved her stool and sat. "Archi asked me to marry him after he explained. He wanted to leave before Vic and Roy got in trouble."

"Archi thought they were guilty?"

"They *are* guilty. After the guards found the governor's money and food in their rooms, they confessed. They both said Archi didn't have anything to do with it; that's why his sentence was only three months." Coli smoothed down her curls and sighed. "I should have just married him. Archi will probably still be in season when he gets out; he won't get stuck here, but that's too big a risk for me to take. My uncles had four-month seasons, but my dad's was only three. Now I have to start all over."

"Why didn't you marry him?"

Coli let out a humorless laugh. "Because I'm still in love with Tiger."

Delia laid a comforting hand on Coli's arm and Coli covered it with her own.

"And here I am yelling at you with your face beat up and I haven't even asked you what happened and if you're okay. I'm sorry. I'm being a bad friend."

Delia lightly touched her chin, then walked over to examine herself in Coli's mirror. The bruises on her chin and neck were fading to yellow, only the scab on her lip was really noticeable. She forced herself to recount the story, her friend's fury a strange comfort.

"They were seriously going to punish *you* for getting attacked? The governor is insane. Archi says he was a spoiled, petulant child that got everything he wanted, and he hasn't changed."

"They grew up together?"

Coli nodded. "Same estate. Archi's mom was a servant there. Archi and Vic thought their father was one of the other servants until Archi's wing birth."

"Whoa."

"Yeah, their mom wouldn't even talk about it. She just sobbed when they asked her questions. And then the guy they thought was their dad lost his temper and asked them to leave."

"What did they do?"

Coli shrugged. "They left. Slept in the stables. Vic had his wing birth two days later, and they left for the Mating Mountain as soon as Vic could fly."

"No wonder Vic wanted to go after the governor."

"He just wanted money. Did you know the governor takes half of the money he gets to run this place and gives it to his pregnant mistresses? That's why the food here is so terrible for the in-seasons. When Archi found out a month ago, they confronted the governor, tried to make him change it back to everyone getting the same food, but the governor just locked them in the dungeon for three days. Then when they heard the governor was leaving the Mating Mountain, they figured he would be taking *our food money* to his mistresses. Roy and Vic went after him to get it back. They just wanted him to stop starving us. I've lost so much weight in the past month that none of my clothes fit any more."

Delia's eyebrows lifted. She hadn't even noticed. "I can start bringing you food."

"Is the life servants' food really that much better?"

Delia snorted. "I wouldn't know. I haven't had a meal here yet. The kitchen won't feed me."

"You're *foraging* for your food?"

Delia nodded.

"Why won't they feed you?"

"Truth bombs, flying rocks, and lots of rumors."

Coli let out a pained laugh. "That's horrible! Is that why the other bed in my room disappeared?"

"Probably."

"Where have you been sleeping?"

Delia blushed. "Cam's room when he was gone, except that he came back while I was still sleeping and didn't even wake me up. And he brought me boots, water shoes, and a spade."

Coli looked down at her friend's boots. "Oh, those look...serviceable."

"They're just what I wanted," Delia said happily.

Coli examined her friend's face. "You *like* him."

Delia's blush deepened. "I am really attracted to him. When he had his shirt off last night, I had trouble finding my room."

Coli chortled. "Is he over the princess, then?"

"I don't know. He's nice to me, but I think he might just be nice to everyone. He dragged a mattress to my room last night so I could sleep there."

"Oh, that's sweet. Well, Talis will be disappointed. I think he's deluded himself into thinking you like him. I caught him telling someone that the two of you are 'practically engaged.' I got furious with him and even wrote the letter to my mom, but he swears you've been kissing him."

"I haven't kissed him! I've been treating his wing..." Delia covered her face with her hands. "And he can tell I'm attracted to him."

Coli threw her head back and laughed. "You like my brother, too!"

"No," Delia protested. "He just keeps signaling and getting too close to me!"

"Isn't that the worst?! Tiger's horrid cousin Wes smells amazing. He'd signal me just to make Tiger angry, and I swear Wes' pheromones can make me forget my own name. Not that my brother is as bad as Wes. Don't worry, I'll wave the letter I wrote in Talis' face, and then he'll behave."

"Don't do that."

"You want him to keep telling everyone that you're engaged?"

"No. Just...I'll handle it."

Coli's forehead wrinkled. "When have you ever wanted to handle my brother yourself?"

Delia blushed. "Um, it's kind of fun now."

Coli hopped up from the stool and grabbed Delia by the arms. "Are you seriously thinking of marrying him?!"

"How can I when I'm a life servant for the next month?"

"You *want* to marry him?"

"I don't know! When I'm with him, I just want to tease him relentlessly. I have to keep reminding myself that he hasn't really changed so I won't kiss him."

Coli laughed again. "You *do* like my brother!"

Delia squirmed away from her. "I don't know. Maybe."

"Well, decide quickly. The second his wing is healed enough to fly, he needs to leave. If you're not willing to go with him, tell him now so he can find someone else."

"I *did* tell him; he doesn't give up."

Coli sighed and sat down again. "He needs to make better decisions. Ora's going to be a life servant, so it's up to Talis to take over my dad's shipping business and keep my mom busy with grandchildren. If I had married Archi, I would have just taken him home with me. He doesn't want to go back to the governor's family estate."

"I can see why."

Coli nodded grimly. "But now, I have to give up Archi, Talis is deluding himself with you, Ora was sentenced to six months in the dungeon...maybe all three of us will be life servants."

Delia shook her head. "That's not going to happen. You're beautiful and you have a delightful personality. You've already found two potential mates, you'll find more. I'd offer to help you, but we both know you don't need it."

Coli grinned. "You give the best pep talks."

"If only I negotiated as well as I encourage."

Coli's smile faded. "Maybe if you talked to the governor?"

"Didn't you just say he's insane?"

Coli stood and rubbed her lips together as she carefully chose her words. "Delia, I'm going to get over Archi, and I understand why you told the governor about Vic, but don't let it be for nothing."

Delia nodded, keeping her eyes down to hide her irritation. Did Coli really think Vic and Roy's savagery would have stayed secret long enough for her to fall in love with Archi? And why was she expected to keep secrets for a criminal? Delia took a deep breath, willing herself to calm down. *This is Coli. She's your best friend, and she's had a very disappointing love life so far.* "Okay," she forced herself to say as she walked to the door.

"You should do it now," Coli prodded.

"Okay," Delia repeated woodenly, her grip on the door handle painfully tight as she opened it. She left it open, wondering if Coli was going to goad her all the way to the governor's door. She turned when she heard it shut, then let out a relieved breath that Coli had stayed in her room. Though she could see the necessity of speaking to the governor again, she didn't relish the thought of potentially losing her day off treating him nor of him flying into a temper and sending her to the dungeon. Rather than do as she was bidden, she walked down the hall and knocked on Cam's door. There was no answer, but she heard his laugh. He was just rounding the corner with a kind-looking brunette on his arm. The girl clung to him, her expression alight with charmed adoration. *Of course*, she thought. *He's beautiful, he's kind, and he's taken.*

Delia's quickly souring mood only accentuated the growling of her stomach, and she flew to the front doors without a look back. Outside, the rain pelted down in a heavy staccato. No wonder the halls were unusually crowded; everyone was forced to stay inside today.

Fine. I'll go see the governor, but not on an empty stomach. Delia took two strolls by the kitchen hoping there was some visible food she could nab. But the steady stream of life servants returning trays of dirty dishes impeded her. Lunch for the in-seasons appeared to have been some sort of soup, but the kitchen smelled of hearty stew.

"In-season lunch is over," one of the life servants informed her as he jostled by.

"I'm a life servant. I just need to get lunch before I treat the governor." It wasn't really a fib, she consoled herself; it was very likely she would be treating him when she asked about their deal.

He stopped and looked back at her. "Hmm...you're *that* one."

"Yes, but I didn't throw any rocks, I didn't attack Phasia, I didn't ask for anyone to be sent to the dungeon, and I haven't mated with anyone." *There. Surely that covers it.*

"And I suppose if I don't feed you, you're going to tell the governor?"

Maybe. "I would forage for my own food, but it's raining too hard. I've been here almost a week and haven't eaten a single meal from this kitchen." *Four days counted as almost a week, didn't it?*

"Avell said you stole his yesterday."

"*One roll*! And that's because he was supposed to take me to the kitchen and make sure I got fed. Instead he told a lie about me to ensure I wouldn't get any food at all."

The life servant narrowed his eyes. "Bad things seem to happen to any life servant who comes in contact with you."

"And now you're wondering what your misfortune will be?" Delia hadn't meant to sound threatening, but her frustration gave her voice a warning edge.

The life servant shook his head. "I'm not feeding you. Go ahead and report me. My name is Nelson."

Another life servant walked by and knocked the tray the first was carrying into his chest. "*His* name is Gray. *I'm* Nelson."

Gray sputtered as he wiped ineffectually at the soup splattered on his shirt.

Delia turned away from the pitiful display with a smile. "Thank you, Nelson."

He nodded and returned his tray to the kitchen.

Delia followed. "I'm having some trouble getting food; could you help me with that?"

He nodded again. "I *could*."

"*Will* you?"

"Tera said not to feed her," Gray reminded him, letting his tray clatter dramatically as he tossed it onto the kitchen counter.

"The governor put Phasia in the *dungeon* for refusing to wash her clothes and bedding."

Delia was tempted to correct him, but it seemed unwise when he was her best chance of food today.

"If you feed her, I'll tell Tera," Gray threatened.

Nelson opened the half door and stepped into the kitchen with Gray at his heels.

"I will! And I'll tell her you knocked my tray again, too!"

Nelson ignored his threats as he steadily filled a bowl, stuck a spoon in it, and then walked back to the half door to hand it to Delia. "When you talk to the governor, please mention that I would be happy to take over for Tera while she's in the dungeon."

Delia smirked. "Thank you." The bowl was already hot with its contents, and Delia held it gingerly around the rim to avoid being burned. She balanced it against her bag as she entered a large, empty room with a multitude of tables and chairs. Some matched the rusted metal furniture of the courtyard, but most were wooden. Delia took a seat and quickly consumed the gamey stew, not caring that it burned her tongue. When she finished, she returned her bowl and spoon to the kitchen, giving Gray a spiteful smile.

Her little triumph lent confidence to her steps, and her march to the governor's room was a steady one. At the door she faltered; not a single guard was familiar.

"I need to see the governor."

"He's not seeing anyone. They can help you at the officiant's office," a white-winged guard answered.

"Morph, that's the in-season medic that attacked you," an identical white-winged guard pushed around the first to lean over her menacingly. "Unbelievable. You try to kill my brother, then come around asking him for favors."

Delia's gaze strayed back to Morph. She could see two stitched cuts on his forehead that were only partially covered by his hair. "I am so sorry. Please believe that I did not throw any rocks at you. I had just arrived at the Old Castle, and I couldn't open the front door. I heard someone laughing at me and found Ora in the bushes. We grew up together; his sister is my best friend. He said the princess had broken my friend's heart and her brother's wing, then blackmailed the governor to avoid dungeon time. He said she wasn't really a princess. I was supposed to get you to chase me, so he could get in and break her wing. I didn't know he was going to hurt you; I never would have agreed to that."

"But you were fine with hurting the princess?!" the second white-winged guard demanded.

Delia turned to the other guard, her lips pursed with restraint. "I am often irrationally angry lately and prone to making poor decisions." She eyed his white wings. "Maybe you can relate."

Morph snorted, but his identical twin continued to glare. "If you grew up with Mr. Sulphur, then you should have already known that he is a liar, and not believed anything he said."

"He's not a liar. He's hot-tempered, mean-spirited, and foolish," Delia argued. *Just like Talis.*

Morph snorted again. "She's right. Leave her alone, Phemus, I'm fine."

Phemus pointed at Delia. "You should be in the dungeon with Mr. Sulphur, not standing here demanding to see the governor."

"I would like to check his poultice and see if I need to make a new one."

"*You've* been treating him?"

"Yes. Now, may I please see the governor?"

Phemus shook his head. "Why anyone would trust you is a mystery to me," he muttered as he gave the door a patterned knock.

Delia looked back at Morph, guilt knocking into her like a tidal wave. "I really am sorry. If your forehead still hurts, I can fix that. If not, maybe I can help you with something else."

Morph shook his head. "I'm fine."

"I'm trying not to be an awful person," Delia said, tears filling her eyes. "I want to make it up to you."

Morph cleared his throat uncomfortably and snuck a glance back at his brother. "Phemus has foot fungus," he whispered. "Can you fix that?"

"Is it peeling?" she whispered back.

He nodded.

"I can fix it."

Morph smiled without making eye contact and Delia felt a surge of relief.

"The governor will see you now," Phemus said bitterly. "But maybe I should check you for rocks first."

"I never threw any rocks," Delia hissed as she slipped by him.

On the other side of the door, the large-nosed guard gave her the tiniest nod of recognition as she entered the room. The governor was dressed in different clothes, but propped up in the same position on his bed.

"I need more pain medication," the governor said as soon as the door closed. "And I don't want it in another itchy poultice. I want something to drink that doesn't taste bad and makes the pain go away."

Sounds like a problem only Pearl could solve. "Zelic said I had to check with him before I gave you anything else."

"I'm the governor, and I'm ordering you to get me more pain medication."

Delia glanced over at the table that had been littered with medications before, but it was bare. *Zelic's efforts to keep Graci from medicating the governor?* "I'll look at the log and see what I can give you, but I want to discuss my sentence first."

"What about it?" he snapped. "I have given you an order and I expect you to obey it."

Did the petulant little boy that got everything he wanted ever grow up? Delia walked to his side taking slow, deep breaths to control her temper. When he opened his mouth to speak again, she spoke before he could. "Where are you experiencing pain?"

"Everywhere!"

The swelling on his face had gone down, revealing handsome features discolored with bruises. "I'm going to examine you," Delia announced as she lifted his shirt. His purple bruises had darkened to near black and weren't spreading. "This looks better."

"It looks awful! It feels awful."

"Does it hurt more than yesterday?"

"No," he conceded sulkily.

"Good." Delia lowered his shirt. She was going to have to recruit Zelic to resist his demands, and she didn't want to have this discussion in front of the medic. "Since Vic was guilty, doesn't that mean my life-servant sentence is over?"

"I didn't agree to that," he snapped.

"What *will* you agree to?"

"Everyone knows what you did. If I reduce your sentence, everyone will have to know *why* it was shortened."

"So, more gossip and hatred? I'm already accustomed to it."

"The *life servants* hate you now. If everyone knows you got Vic thrown in the dungeon for the rest of his life because you were angry that he kissed you, won't the in-seasons hate you, too?"

"That isn't why!" Delia protested, her heart sinking.

"If you can bear the infamy, your sentence can be over as soon as you train all of the medics."

And how long will that take? "Fine."

"*And* if any of the medications I need aren't reachable by the other medics, I'll expect you to continue to provide them."

"You realize you're talking about itchy poultices and bad-tasting teas?"

The governor glared at her. "I know they help, I just don't like them. Will you get them or not?"

"As long as I'm still here," Delia conceded.

"Then we have an agreement. Now get me that pain medication before I lose my temper and have you thrown in the dungeon alongside Archi."

Delia cringed at the reminder. "Is there any chance you might shorten Archi's sentence?"

"Why? Are you offering to serve it for him?"

"No."

"Then get me my medicine! Now!"

Delia hurried from the room, catching the look of pity the large-nosed guard gave her as she exited. Had she made a mistake? Delia imagined all the in-seasons looking at her the way Coli had, and shuddered. Surely it was still better than a month of being a life servant.

"Morph," she said as soon as the door shut behind her. "Do you know where I can find Zelic?" It was odd that the guard she had wronged felt like her only ally among the four outside the door.

"He's in the infirmary," Phemus snapped. "Shouldn't you know that?"

Morph gave her a slight shrug and she forced down an acidic retort. If the in-seasons started speaking to her the way Phemus did, truth bombs and violence would ensue. *How long did Coli say Archi has been on the mountain?* Delia couldn't remember. *And Vic has been here just as long, but what about Roy? How many friends do the three have?* Delia clenched her fists, ready for the fight to come. Each person that passed her in the hallways was a potential foe, and she began to imagine the arguments that she might have with each one. *Stop. This isn't healthy*, she chided herself.

"You look ready to kill!" Talis commented chattily as he drew up beside her. "Not me, I hope?"

"Why, Talis? Have you done something worthy of death?"

Talis grinned. "See, you never would have said that to me before. You're way more fun now."

"Yes. I'm a riot," she deadpanned.

"So, have you given any more thought to my pro..." he left off abruptly at Delia's death glare. "I mean, my suggestion."

"Did the princess actually break your wing or did she just push you away from Tiger and you tripped?" As she expected, Talis' fury was instantaneous.

"I wouldn't have tripped if that reeking floozy hadn't shoved me! She comes prancing into the middle of a fight knowing she's the cause of it! Tiger and Coli were practically engaged!"

"Like us?"

Talis' face flushed with guilt before he hid it and took her hand. "Then you accept?"

Delia pulled her hand away and stopped walking to face him. She hesitated only a moment before launching into the painful necessity. "I don't like your temper, Talis. We've never gotten along. We only do now because I'm not myself. We may be physically compatible, but we aren't *emotionally* compatible. So stop telling people we're together so you can find someone to marry you."

Talis' blue eyes were stormy as he absorbed her words. He opened his mouth, then clutched her shoulders and pulled her in for an unexpectedly gentle kiss. Delia's hostility melted away under his touch and she marveled again at the effect he had on her. His hands slid up to her face, their feather-light touch caressing her cheeks as he prolonged the kiss. She could hear snickers and whistles as people passed them, but her agitation was simply shut off. Her fingers climbed his shirt front while her face flushed at her own boldness. He was pulling away now, and a tiny whimper escaped her before she could stop it.

Talis chuckled and kissed her forehead. "Maybe we're *so* physically compatible that the rest doesn't matter."

That's not right; is it? He was walking away before she finally remembered to breathe. Everyone in the hallway seemed to be watching her with amusement. Flames of embarrassment scorched her face, and she let her hair fall forward as she hurried away.

It was a relief to hide inside the infirmary. The steady grinding of a mortar and pestle could be heard coming from the office, and Delia found Zelic seated inside.

"You have the day off," Zelic reminded her.

"The governor commanded me to bring him pain medication that doesn't taste bad."

Zelic groaned. "He can't have more morphine yet, and it tastes awful anyway. These herbs are ready," he said, holding out the mortar.

"He said no itchy poultices."

Zelic sighed and dropped the mortar with a heavy thunk. "He's *safer* when I keep Graci away, but *so* much more difficult to deal with."

"I noticed."

"Why were you talking to him, anyway? Did he send for you?" Zelic asked.

Everyone would know soon enough; she might as well tell him. "I went to see if he was going to reduce my sentence in exchange for the information I gave him."

"That's a dangerous game to play."

Delia nodded her agreement. "Especially as he's going to tell everyone what information I provided."

Zelic let out a low whistle. "Are you still a medic, then?"

"Until I train all the other medics."

"And who decides when that task is done?"

Delia grimaced. *Probably should have specified that.*

Zelic gave her a pitying look. "You're no good at this game."

Ignoring his comment, Delia walked over to the cabinet and rifled through her wilting inventory, pausing with a gnarled reddish bud between her fingers.

"Does the kitchen have honey? With enough of it, I can mostly hide the taste of cottonwood leaf bud resin."

"I have no idea. You'd have to ask."

Delia frowned. "Tera has instructed the kitchen staff not to feed me. Even if I tell them it's for the governor, I'm not sure they would believe me."

Zelic muttered an oath. "Life-long servitude is a poor excuse for emotional regression."

"And yet..."

Zelic took the bud from her fingers, grabbed two more from the cabinet, then picked up the mortar and pestle. "Indra will be back from her lunch break soon. You can leave when she arrives." He was halfway to the door when he came hurrying back. "I forgot bandages. Hand me some, will you?"

Delia took some out of the cabinet and handed them to him.

"And lock that, please," he called over his shoulder on his way out.

Delia retrieved the key, but set it on the desk while she treated her feet and wrapped them in fresh bandages. She locked the cabinet, then paced the infirmary. Her idleness gave her too much time to think, and her mind kept drifting back to the hallway kiss. She vacillated between stern determination that it would not happen again and eager anticipation of the next kiss. Smiling, she touched her lips. *Everyone should kiss like that.*

When the infirmary door crashed open, she jumped briefly into flight. The woman who had refused to give her rolls stomped into the room, her muddy white wings quivering in rage.

"Where is my honey?!" she demanded as she began searching.

A small part of Delia wanted to laugh, until the woman marched into the office. Delia followed at a brisk pace, wincing as the portly woman yanked violently at the locked cabinet.

"Open it!" she commanded.

"There isn't any honey in there. Zelic left to find some to sweeten the governor's medicine."

"Oh, he found it all right! That traitor Nelson gave him all of it! Now open this cabinet before I break it!"

Delia backed away. All the carefully catalogued medicinal plants and apothecary bottles would not withstand the violence of her search. "Not unless you calm down."

"Oh, *I* need to calm down? This from the girl who tried to kill Morph?"

"I didn't even try to *hurt* him. Now get away from that cabinet before you tip over the governor's medication and make it all spill out. If he has to wait for another flyer to bring him more morphine, you can bet you'll spend that same time period in the dungeon."

A flash of fear crossed the woman's face before she hid it. She stepped purposefully out of the office, smoothing down her hair with a ruddy hand.

"This isn't over. You tell Zelic that he had better return my honey jar as full as I left it or he will be eating in-season meals for the rest of his life! And you! Don't think you can get food from my kitchen again. *Nelson* is no longer on my staff." The woman spat his name as if she were expelling an errant bug that had flown into her mouth.

Delia glared at her until the infirmary door slammed behind her, then she hurried in to check the cabinet. One of the apothecary bottles had indeed tipped over, its contents creating a growing puddle. Delia swore as she quickly righted the unlabeled bottle. The liquid had the sharp scent of alcohol, and she hoped it wasn't an expensive tincture. The mess, except for the lingering smell, was almost cleaned up when a voice behind her made her jump.

"What happened? What did you spill?" Zelic asked, setting down the mortar with a glass jar inside it.

"*I* didn't spill anything. Some woman from the kitchen came in here screaming for her honey and shook the cabinet, certain it was inside. She said that if you didn't bring back her honey jar just as full as you found it that you would be eating in-season meals for the rest of your life. I am not allowed to eat at all."

Zelic's mouth was tight as he took several deep breaths. When he finally spoke, it was through his teeth. "What did she knock over?"

Delia held out the apothecary bottle. "This one. I was hoping it was just alcohol."

Zelic took it and peered inside. "It's a tincture of cannabis. Or it *was*."

Delia hurried past him to wash her hands while she assessed her symptoms. Was she feeling unusually calm and relaxed? Her father had only sold dried cannabis, and Delia had never had occasion to use it. When she returned to the office, Zelic was holding the bandages she had used to mop up the spill.

"Were they clean?"

Delia nodded. "Can you still use them?"

Zelic frowned. "Probably not. I was saving it for when we ran out of morphine. Speaking of which, it's almost time for the governor's next dose." Sighing, he grabbed a bottle from the cabinet, the empty bottle of cannabis tincture, and the glass jar he had brought in with the mortar.

"Is that the honey?"

Zelic nodded. "The governor decided he wants all of his medicine flavored with honey."

"Someone is going to be unhappy."

"*Someone* is about to get locked in the dungeon," Zelic said. "And where is Indra?"

"I don't know. The screaming woman from the kitchen was my only visitor."

Zelic huffed an angry breath. "That was Tera."

"I figured. Nelson asked me to tell the governor that he would be happy to take over the kitchen while Tera's in the dungeon."

Zelic snorted. "I'll pass along the message. If Indra shows up, tell her she's on pregnancy test duty for the next month."

"And *I*," Delia said as the door closed behind him, "am working on my day off." How was she supposed to train all the medics when two of them wouldn't even work their own shifts? Growling, Delia finished the cleanup, then returned to pacing. *At least it's rainy*, she thought. If she had been missing a foraging-for-fun trip, infirmary duty would have been intolerable. Maybe the cannabis was affecting her. The only scent she could detect was alcohol, but she propped the infirmary door open just to be safe.

When Zelic finally returned, he brought the blue-winged medic who had told her she wasn't allowed in the office.

"Indra has decided to work her shift after all," Zelic announced.

"I just didn't want to get caught in the middle of a Tera tantrum," Indra explained wearily. The words had the sound of multiple repetitions.

"Yes, so nice of you to leave that for Delia to enjoy," Zelic said as he returned the empty bottle, bandages, and honey to the cabinet.

"Tera already hates her," Indra whined as she gestured at Delia. "Tera *likes* me. When she makes a dessert, she always makes sure I get some."

"I'm sure those desserts will be very comforting when you're getting up at four in the morning all month," Zelic commented. "Delia, you can go. Sorry you didn't get a day off. Do you want to schedule training sessions with the staff?"

"Oh. Um...I think I need to find plants in places you can walk to first."

"Better yet, can you transplant some medicinal plants to the castle garden? You can train the staff on those. Save the walking tour for me," Zelic suggested.

"That's a really good idea," Delia said, surprised she hadn't thought of it. "Where is the castle garden?"

"Hidden and guarded. I'll talk to the head gardener and get him to make space for you. I can take you there tomorrow."

"Is there a drying room? It's okay to keep the herbs in the cabinet if we use them quickly, but otherwise, they're going to molder... or get soaked in cannabis tincture," she added wryly.

"Ha," Zelic replied with no trace of humor. "No, that won't be happening again. Tera is in the dungeon and demoted, Nelson is now the head chef, and the honey stays in the medicine cabinet until the governor is recovered."

"Wow."

"Yes, she who messes with the governor's pain medication is richly rewarded," Zelic said.

"She who refuses to indulge the governor's mistress is also rewarded," Indra grumbled.

When Indra ignored her questioning glance, Delia turned to Zelic.

"Neva used to be head medic. The governor demoted her when she refused to put Graci on her staff," Zelic admitted.

"That's how he got the job," Indra added, her eyes narrowed in spite.

"It's not as if I campaigned against Neva. I didn't want Graci on the staff, either," Zelic protested.

"But you weren't willing to go to the dungeon to keep her out," Indra sniped.

Zelic took a deep breath and blew it out. "Yes, Indra, you've figured me out. I exist to satisfy the whims of our governor."

Delia left before she heard Indra's reply, but was already pitying Zelic for having to respond to whatever it was. She was grateful no one but Zelic would be wildcrafting with her; having to tromp through the forest with Indra and Caena would have been miserable.

Delia wandered through the halls, oddly disconcerted with her free time. Most of the residents seemed to flock in and out of the ballroom, but Delia was determined not to experience the musical cacophony and pungent scents of *that* room again. The remainder of the in-seasons were swimsuit-clad and traipsing to or coming from the pool. At least no one but the life servants were glaring at her. Longing to go outside, Delia checked to see if the rain had let up, but large drops still bounced off the courtyard paving stones with punishing velocity. Sighing, she pulled the door closed and began wandering again. Neither her sister nor Coli were in their rooms. Her own room was now completely empty. Someone had taken the bed frame along with the stolen mattress. Delia let out an angry huff and slammed the door of her useless room. Desperate, she knocked on Talis' door, but felt relief when no one answered. Eventually, she wandered back toward the ballroom, eyeing the clusters of chattering in-seasons smiling and laughing at conversations she couldn't quite hear. Her perusal of the crowd stopped abruptly on Len's serious face, his searing blue eyes meeting hers in something of a challenge. She glared at him and turned away, but he was already coming toward her. Cursing, Delia walked rapidly, hoping to disappear around the corner before he caught up to her.

"Delia!"

Delia rolled her eyes as she turned around. "What?"

Len was closer than she had expected and she stepped back instinctively.

"I'm *not* going to hurt you," he snapped.

Delia watched him warily. "What do you want?"

"I want you to dance with me."

"What?! No. Why would you even want to?!"

He stared at the floor and took a calming breath. "It's not because I'm interested." He touched his black eye that was beginning to yellow. "You cured me of that."

"Funny, you cured me of my interest as well," she snarled.

His hands tightened into fists. "You made all the girls here afraid of me," he growled. "Not one of them will dance with me."

"*I* didn't do that," Delia seethed. "Gossip and *your* violence did."

He took a step forward to point a finger in her face. "You can fix it! You *should* fix it. If you dance with me, they won't be afraid."

Delia smacked his hand away and backed up. "They *should* be afraid! Either you can't control yourself or you *like* being violent!"

Len grabbed her wrist. "You're the one who's violent! I'm a calm person!"

"Yeah, I can see that," someone retorted.

Len turned to look at the speaker while Delia dug her stubby nails into Len's hand to free herself.

"Ow!" Len yelled as he grabbed her other wrist and forced her hands apart.

Two blue-winged men came up on either side of Len, the shorter of the two speaking. "You can let go of her right now and walk away, or Everes and I can make you."

Delia used Len's distraction to knee him in the groin. He grunted in pain, releasing her wrists as he fell to his knees.

"Or she can handle it herself," the speaker added wryly, his wide mouth spreading into a grin.

"Thanks anyway," Delia said, rubbing her wrists with a frown. She was going to have more bruises.

"You must be Delia White."

Delia gave the two men a wary nod as Len rose to his feet, eyes blazing.

"I suppose you'll get me another night in the dungeon for that," Len said, his voice strained.

"I didn't *get* you the first one! Can't you *ever* take responsibility for your own actions?"

The taller man, presumably Everes, edged protectively between Delia and Len.

"Time to go," the shorter man said, dropping a hand on Len's shoulder.

Len threw his shoulder back, freeing it from the shorter man's hand. He glared at the two men, muttered an expletive-laced insult, then walked away, his gait uneven.

"If he sics the guards on you, tell them Damus and Everes Blue were witnesses."

"Thanks." Delia could hear the flatness of her tone and knew it gave them the wrong impression. "Really. That was..." *Kind? Courageous? Unnecessary?* "...nice."

Damus chuckled and exchanged a glance with Everes. "We've done our chivalrous deed of the day...even if it wasn't wanted."

Delia shook her head, her face heating. "No, it's good that there are guys like you. I'm...grateful." *And embarrassed.* "Bye," she blurted, hurrying away. Delia headed back into the crush and noise of the crowd. She couldn't risk meeting Len in an empty hallway, not in his current state of frustrated rage.

"Nice meeting you," Damus called after her, his voice a little too wry for sincerity.

Delia idly rubbed her wrists as she dodged happy people eager to interact with one another. She frowned as they brushed against her, disliking the contact. *Can I really not have a relationship with another white?* Her interactions with her sister had certainly been strained, but not violent. Delia rubbed her wrists again. *Maybe it's just Len.* She hoped it was, and the sudden urge to experiment and prove that it was *Len's* problem rather than a *white* problem overcame her. Breathing through her mouth and covering her ears, Delia forced herself inside the ballroom. Spying pale wings in the crowd, she flew closer, disappointed when she discovered their owner was a tall, pretty blonde with a joyous smile. *Not even a white*, she thought. Scanning the dancers, she found a pair of white wings, then realized it was Pearl. Her sister looked smugly amused as she spun through the air with a brown-winged male. *Maybe she hasn't given up*, Delia thought, silently wishing her sister well before another flash of white caught her eye. Delia dodged through the crowd until she stood behind the white-winged man. He was shorter than average, only a few inches taller than she was. His head was closely shaved, displaying a collection of whorls that must be miserable to manage if he ever let his hair grow longer. She leaned forward and breathed through her nose, inhaling the scent of sun-warmed sand. His white wings were marbled with olive green, and they twitched whenever he made a caustic remark. His companion snickered and made vulgar gestures. Repelled, Delia was turning away when the lewd companion noticed her.

"She's mateable, Dom. Why don't you dance with her?"

Dom turned, his boyish face creased in a frown as he looked at her. "You don't like the music?"

Delia shook her head, her hands still clapped over her ears.

"Do you want to go out in the hall?" he asked, his crass companion chortling.

Delia nodded, wondering exactly how foolish she was being as she followed him out of the ballroom. He stopped just beyond the chatting clusters, his face weary rather than hopeful as Delia dropped her hands.

"I'm a white," he blurted, his low voice querulous. "Is that going to be a problem?"

Delia turned and showed him the back of her wings.

"You're a white, too?"

Delia nodded.

"Are you mute?"

"No, I just don't enjoy shouting to be heard." Even outside the ballroom, the music and conversation spilling out were clamorous.

He jerked his head, inviting her to follow, and walked to the end of the hall near a lantern. "Better?" he asked. They could still see the entrance and its enthusiastic conversationalists, but the din was more bearable.

Delia peered down the adjoining hallway to ensure Len wasn't waiting. Her shoulders relaxed when she saw only strolling couples. "Yes, thank you."

"Do you want to dance here?"

Delia's face colored. "I don't really know how."

A smirk pulled up one corner of his mouth. "I don't like dancing, anyway."

"Then why go to the ballroom?"

"You mean the dance hall?" he corrected.

Delia was tempted to pull out her map and show him the proper name, but resisted. Instead, she grit her teeth and nodded.

He grimaced, his long eyelashes casting shadows on his freckled nose. "Why go anywhere in this lousy castle? I'm trying to find a mate."

Delia lifted an eyebrow at his word choice. "*Mate,* not wife?"

He threw back his head with an irritable sigh. "I've been spending too much time around Skinner."

"The nasty guy in the ballroom?" she guessed, wondering if he would correct her a second time.

Dom snorted. "Yeah. I know him from home."

"Friend?"

He shrugged. "Kind of. You know what it's like. It's nice to be around anyone who knows your actual personality and is willing to tolerate your current one."

Delia nodded. *Maybe that's why I enjoy Talis now.* Her mind began to replay their kiss on continuous repeat while she fought to focus on the conversation. "One of my *friends* from home actually prefers me this way."

"Why?" Alarm registered in his brown eyes as he heard his own incredulous tone. "I mean, you seem... nice," he backpedaled.

Delia grinned at his discomfiture, then sobered with an unsettling thought. *What if it isn't just Talis? What if I just enjoy tormenting people now?* "I *was* nice. He isn't. He likes it better when I'm like him."

His light eyebrows climbed his tanned forehead. "That's a doomed relationship."

"I know that," she snapped.

He narrowed his eyes. "Doesn't seem like you do."

Delia bristled, then forced herself to calm down. Her own fiery temper was going to sink the experiment if she couldn't control herself. "I'm here with you, aren't I?" The words sounded more like a challenge.

"Why *are* you here? Hasn't anyone told you to stay away from whites?"

"Yes," she said, ignoring his first question. "I see you're not heeding the advice, either."

He snorted. "So we're just going stand here provoking each other until one of us gets mad enough to walk away?"

The grin had crept back onto Delia's face. Leaning in abruptly, she kissed him.

His complete shock delighted her and she found herself wanting to giggle. *It's not just Talis that brings this out in me!*

"Why did you do that?"

Delia shrugged. "I wanted to."

"So are we...?"

Not wanting to answer the question, Delia leaned forward and kissed him again, this time lingering until the hallway smelled of a lazy afternoon at the beach. His kisses were tentative and sweet. She clasped his arms to steady herself, then slowly pulled away.

"You're not violent," she said, a pleased smile wreathing her face.

"Not to women. Only a sad excuse for a man hurts a woman."

Delia grinned and kissed him again. "I like you," she announced.

"Well, I hope so. You *have* just been kissing me. And I don't even know your name."

"It's Delia."

His brows contracted and he took a step back. "You're the girl that got Roy and his cousins locked up."

"They almost killed the governor," Delia protested, feeling the futility of doing so even before the words left her mouth.

"He uses his power to make others suffer. We need a new governor; we had one for a day, but *you* attacked her, and she decided to leave."

"She wasn't better!"

Dom lifted his arm and wiped his mouth in disgust before stalking away.

Well. At least he wasn't violent.

Delia stood still as the scent of the beach dissipated, and she began to feel the weight of her bargaining. "They're both awful," she muttered. "And I only attacked her verbally."

"What?" a passing girl asked. "Were you talking to me?"

Delia shook her head and flew. She was done with people. Done with rumors. Outside, the rain was still drizzling, but she flew out into it until her wings were too drenched to fly; then she slogged through the mud of poorly kept trails. Holly grape pricked her through her pants as she trudged. Squatting down, she dug up the spiny plant, then cut off the roots. At least she would be making things right with Morph. She walked on, muddy spade in one hand and muddy roots in the other. Her hair was plastered to her head and her clothes soaked through as she tried to find her way back to the Old Castle. The trails intersected and dead-ended without giving her a sight of the stone facade, and her frustration grew as the light faded. When it was fully dark, the rain finally stopped and a chilly breeze rustled the trees. Delia's wings and extremities were numb before she found the right path back to the castle. Her teeth chattered as her uncooperative fingers stowed the rain-washed spade and root so she could open the door. Inside, she shivered miserably as she dripped her way into the clerk's office.

"Why were you outside? You must be freezing!" Malan said, standing as she entered.

"Someone took the bed and frame out of my room and Coli's," she said, the chattering distorting her words. "I need a room off the record."

"I know of one room, but you're not going to like it."

"I don't care. I just need a place to sleep."

Malan grimaced. "Archi and Vic's room is empty."

Delia groaned. "I don't want to even *think* of the rumors that would start."

Malan nodded sagely. "If I give you an unassigned room, the day clerk might reassign it. Prisoners' rooms are a safer choice...as long as no one lets them out early. The governor *definitely* won't let his brother out early. And the day clerk won't reassign Archi's room until someone gets all of their belongings out of it."

"What about Tiger's room?"

"Wes was never officially sentenced. Now that the princess is gone, someone will let him out soon."

"Fine," Delia said wearily. "What's their room number?"

"Archi and Vic have room 413. You want me to write it on your map?"

Delia shook her head as she turned to go. *The less evidence the better.*

Room 413 was brightly lit, but devoid of all personal property. Delia briefly wondered who had packed up Archi and Vic's belongings and brought them to the dungeon, but immediately decided it had to have been Coli. Awash in guilt, Delia removed her sodden clothing and changed into her swimming suit with difficulty. Her shivering and numbness colluded, making her lose her balance repeatedly. She laid her wet clothing out to dry across the little table and stools, tucked her bag and boots under the table, and hoped anyone who found her belongings would assume the room had been reassigned to a new arrival. She glanced at the two rumpled beds that ruined her ruse, then stripped one and wadded the bedding beneath it, kicking at the wad until it was no longer visible. She made the other bed neatly, the scent catching her attention as she fluffed the pillow. Delia inhaled deeply, then tossed the pillow away with irritation. It was *Vic's* bed. She rubbed

222

her temples in frustration, her icy fingers only making her feel colder as she attempted to view the room from someone else's perspective. *Not enough*, she decided, retrieving her bag. She removed her wrinkled clean clothing and hung it from a tidy row of hooks, then flung her nightgown across Vic's bed. *Better.* As a final touch, she dumped her dirty laundry out and kicked it about the room, hoping she was spreading her scent. With a satisfied nod, she left for the pool.

The hallway outside the bathing pool was puddled and sparsely populated with flirting loungers. Delia kept her wings closed tightly, hoping to pass for anyone other than herself. She kept her head down as she crept into the warm water. The room was nearly full of shrieking, splashing bathers, and Delia had to fight the urge to snarl whenever one of them came near. Someone called her name, but she had no intention of owning it in such a crowded place. Instead, she drifted behind a tall man with broad, open wings that shielded her washing from much of the room. His scent was oddly familiar. She looked up at his brown hair, then his yellow and black wings, but couldn't place him. He wasn't speaking or washing. Delia edged around his wings to peer at his face. His even features were handsome, but the intent expression on them was unsettling. She followed his gaze to a set of hot-pink and blue wings that made Delia gasp; they looked just like her new sister-in-law's wings.

"Do you know her?" the tall man asked.

Delia shook her head.

His dark, calculating eyes slid off Delia and back to the girl. "Then why did you gasp?"

The willowy girl was turning now, her lovely face a duplicate of Dina's. She was alone, and had just finishing washing, but her path to the shallow exit was blocked by Bul and his friends. Rather than ask them to move, Dina's twin waited, her cheeks coloring at the predicament.

The tall man walked over and pushed the voluble Bul out of the way.

"Hey!" Bul shouted. "What's your problem?"

"You're blocking the lady's way," the tall man said, holding out a hand to Dina's twin, whose blushes redoubled at the attention.

"Thank you," Dina's twin said, hesitantly taking his hand.

"You're welcome. I'm Wes."

Wes! Tiger's cousin? That's why the smell was familiar!

"Ria," the twin replied, and let Wes guide her out of the water, still holding her hand.

Delia wasn't finished washing, but she followed them. Someone called her name again, but she pretended not to hear. Out in the hallway, she had to run to catch up with Wes and Ria's long strides.

"Do you have a roommate?" Wes was asking, the air thick with his valerian scent.

"Not anymore; my sister got married last week," Ria answered.

"Do you mind if I dry off a little in your room? I wouldn't ask, but someone left my balcony doors open and my room is ice cold."

"I wish my room had a balcony," Ria said. "My room at home did."

"It's nice until it rains and gets your mattress all wet," Wes commented. "I'm not sure where I'm going to sleep tonight."

Ria stopped in front of a door with a blushing smile. "This is my room."

Wes pulled her in for a kiss while reaching around her to open the door.

Even if Dina was awful and Ria wasn't quite family, Delia still felt an obligation to protect her from Wes. "Wes just got out of the dungeon," she blurted. "For sexual assault."

Ria stiffened in his arms, but Wes lifted Ria and backed her into her room.

"Dina isn't here to protect you, but I will. Dina married my brother. So you and I are family."

224

"Just ignore her," Wes said, closing the door.

"Wait," Ria said just before the door shut.

Delia could hear a murmured conversation through the heavy door, then it opened and Ria slipped out.

"Dina only wrote me a short note to say she had arrived safely and to give me her address. Is she okay?"

"She's fine. My brother is going to build them a house overlooking the ocean."

Ria smiled. "We grew up in a beach house; she'll like that."

Delia shifted uncomfortably. "Are you sure you want Wes in your room? He has a bad reputation."

Ria colored. "I didn't ask him in."

"Come back to the pool with me, then."

Ria hesitated with her hand on the door. "It's so crowded. I don't really like it there. And I promised Wes I would be right back."

"I don't think that's a safe promise to keep."

Ria looked torn. "He says he didn't assault anyone; that it was just a misunderstanding."

"Let's go find out if he's telling the truth," Delia suggested, starting to walk away.

Ria took a couple of steps and then hesitated. "I should tell him I'm going."

"We'll make it quick," Delia said, taking a few more steps, speeding up as Ria reluctantly joined her.

"How are we going to find out?"

"Malan, the night clerk, knows everything," Delia assured her. "He'll tell us."

Ria's pace slowed. "Maybe I should just go back. You can find out and tell me later."

"Ria, the man pushed his way uninvited into your room. He doesn't want to dry off, he wants to sleep in your room."

Ria colored. "But if he doesn't have a place to stay..."

Delia let out a huff of frustration. "He wants to mate with you. Right now."

Ria stopped walking altogether. "You can't know that."

"His intent was pretty obvious."

Confusion flickered over Ria's pretty face. She turned to look back the way they came, then once again followed Delia. At the clerk's office, Ria stopped in the doorway while Delia stepped up to the desk.

"Malan, I need to know why Tiger's cousin, Wes, was in the dungeon."

"Wes Swallowtail sexually assaulted the princess. You're not involved with him, are you? Because he's worse than Len White."

"No." Delia tipped her head subtly to draw his attention to Ria.

A look of understanding flashed in Malan's eyes and he cleared his throat. "Mr. Swallowtail likes to seduce women, then when he gets them pregnant, he openly jeers at them and shares intimate details of their time together. Three unfortunate women have been his very public victims. You *do not* want to get involved with him. Luckily, you're not his type. He prefers tall brunettes," Malan finished, fairly shouting his last words. Sighing, he added quietly, "she's gone. Nice of you to look out for your sister-in-law's twin, though."

"Thanks, Malan," Delia called over her shoulder as she chased after Ria. When Delia caught up to her, Ria hid her face in her hands. Delia placed a consoling hand on her arm. "If I had known he was that bad, I would have interfered at the pool."

"He's in my *room*," Ria cried, her voice betraying her hidden tears.

"I'll get him out," Delia promised.

"*How?*"

Delia smirked. "I'm a white. Repelling people is what I do."

226

Ria slowly dropped her hands, her eyes swimming. "I don't want him to see me."

Delia nodded. "You go to room 413 and wait for me. I'll take care of it."

"Thank you," Ria whispered, then hurried away.

An eddy of decimating words and cold sarcastic fury churned in Delia's head. Instead of knocking, she threw Ria's door open, startling Wes up from the two pushed-together beds.

"Where's Ria?" he demanded.

"Safe from you."

"You interfering little..." Wes finished his sentence with crude profanity.

"Yes, we women are so annoying, aren't we? We just keep forgetting that we only exist for your gratification."

"I wouldn't gratify myself with you if you paid me."

"And I'm crying on the inside that I won't be the victim of your ruthless attention. I guess I'll just have to console myself with letting all the women on the mountain know what a psychopath you are."

His handsome features twisted in wrath. "No one will listen to you; everyone hates you. I know who you are."

"And yet, you're standing there alone."

Wes stepped forward menacingly. "I'm not alone."

Delia let out a hard, mirthless laugh. "You will *always* be alone; replaying your cruelties in your head is the closest you'll ever come to companionship." Delia stepped back into the hallway just as a noisy group walked by. She inserted herself into the center of them and kept pace, pleased to discover the pool was their destination. The girls in the group glared at her, one engaging in a whispered conversation that ended in a snicker. It was a small price to pay for a safe exit.

Back in the bathing pool, Delia finished washing while listening to Bul's tireless boasting and off-color jokes. Rubi would splash him or smack his arm occasionally, which resulted in uproarious laughter from the entire group. Delia stood just outside their grouping, hoping the proximity would make her seem less approachable to the rest of the bathers. She had caught a few dark looks from random occupants when she had reentered the pool; news of her tattling on Vic had obviously spread. It was a relief that Rus still smiled when they made eye contact. When she climbed out of the pool, he followed.

"Sorry I didn't stick around the infirmary; I figured you were busy."

Delia nodded. "I was."

"My leg's getting better," Rus said.

Delia looked down at it and frowned. "You should let me treat it again; it's not healing like I hoped it would."

He looked down at his leg. "It feels better."

"Just the same, you should sleep with a poultice on it tonight," Delia advised as she stepped out into the hall.

Rus followed her, his limp still perceptible. "Do you want to do that now?"

Delia walked slowly so Rus could keep up. "I have a few stops to make, then I can."

Rus' hopeful expression dimmed, his limp suddenly more noticeable. "I'll meet you at the infirmary."

"Actually, if you don't mind, I could use an escort."

"You need a gimpy escort?" he chuckled.

Delia gave him a rare smile. "You just have to stand there and look menacing. And I may not even need you."

Rus flexed his upper body and scowled. "Like this?"

Delia was grinning now; his scowl somehow made her feel more comfortable. He wasn't as tall as Wes, but he was more muscled. Delia forced her eyes away as she felt her brain begin to stutter. What was it with her and brawny chests? "That will work," she managed to say.

They walked a few paces in comfortable silence before Rus spoke again. "Am I scaring away the guy that hurt you?"

Delia shook her head. "No, I've made new enemies since then."

Rus squelched a grin. "How did you do that?"

"Have you met me?"

He chuckled. "Just the in-season version of you. Do you make this many enemies when you're not in season?"

"Definitely not. There were two bullies I didn't get along well with, and I fought with my brother and sister occasionally."

"You're a triplet?"

"No, a quadruplet. One of my sisters is too sweet to fight...except when she was in season."

"That has to be weird."

Delia nodded heartily as she came to a stop outside Ria's door. "There may still be an angry man in here," she warned before throwing the door open. The room reeked of valerian, and Delia rolled her eyes at Wes' petty revenge.

Rus coughed and his eyes began to water. "Is this your room?"

"No, it's Ria's." Delia hesitated as she realized she didn't know Dina and Ria's last name. She left the door open and started down the hall.

Rus followed, fighting a coughing fit. "Who made the stench?"

"Wes Swallowtail."

"And why did he do that in Ria's room?"

Delia sighed and explained what had happened.

"So your new sister-in-law asked you to look out for her twin?"

Delia shook her head. "I only had a couple of days to get to know Dina, and we didn't get along at all. I think she would rather have died than ask for my help."

Rus hid a smile. "Yeah, I heard her lose her temper at the pool once; she's intense."

"Ria's not like that at all," she assured him, and knocked on Archi's door. "Ria? It's Delia." Delia opened the door a crack. "You okay?"

"Yes," Ria answered, opening the door with one hand while she swiped at tears with the other. "Is he gone?"

"Yes, but he marked your room. You're welcome to sleep here tonight, though."

Ria colored. "Oh no, I need my things. But, thank you." Ria gave her a hesitant hug, then slipped past her, her blushes redoubling when she saw Rus. "Thank you," she repeated, then bolted down the hall.

"Should we go with her?" Rus asked.

"I'm not sure," Delia admitted. "I don't know how tenacious Wes is."

Rus grimaced. "Well, if you believe rumors..."

"Which we don't," Delia asserted.

Rus pressed his lips together.

Delia rolled her eyes. "Fine...what's the gossip on Wes?"

"That he prefers easy targets—like lonely girls who don't put up a fight."

Delia and Rus exchanged a look, then followed after Ria. Despite her shorter legs, Delia quickly outpaced Rus' limping jog. She expected to see Ria at the bottom of the stairs or down the hallway, but she couldn't see her distinctive hot-pink and blue wings anywhere. At Ria's door, Delia knocked rapidly, then fought to catch her breath. When there was no answer, she tried to open the door, but it didn't budge.

"Ria?" she called, rapping so hard that her knuckles smarted.

The door opened a couple of inches and Ria peered out. "I thought you were Wes!"

"You shouldn't be alone," Delia blurted as her relief surged.

"I know. Could you sleep here? I know it smells like Wes, but the smell in your room..."

Delia snorted. "It's not my room, and I don't mind. I think I slept on Wes' mattress last night anyway."

Ria's eyes went wide, her mouth falling open.

"It's a long story," Delia assured her.

"Everything okay?" Rus asked. His limp was pronounced now and his expression spoke of repressed pain.

Delia winced in sympathy. "I shouldn't have asked you to escort. I'm sorry." She glanced briefly at his visibly damp wings before closing her own. She took Rus' calloused hand, and laid his muscled arm across her shoulders. "Lean on me," she directed, blushing at his closeness and the warmth of his skin.

"It might be easier if I rest my arm on your head."

Delia glared up at him. "I'm not *that* short."

"Yes, you are," Rus chuckled.

Delia shook her head at him, then turned back to Ria who was watching them with amusement. "I need to take him to the infirmary, then I'll be back."

"You'll sleep here?"

Delia nodded. "Just barricade the door with one of the beds."

"Okay," Ria agreed. The door shut and the sound of metal screeching across flagstones began almost immediately.

"I can walk on my own," Rus asserted, taking a few hobbled steps with her.

Delia squeezed the hand she still hadn't released, then slid her other arm under his wings and across his bare back. "Lean on me," she repeated, her face turning strawberry red. "I'm stronger than I look."

Rus tentatively shifted his weight. "Do you boss all your patients around like this?"

"All three of you? Yes."

Rus snorted. "So why did you sleep on Wes' mattress?"

So you did hear that. "The life servants and I are playing this fun game where they take any mattress I might sleep on."

"That doesn't sound like a fun game. Why are they doing that?"

"The laundry mistress started it when I was rude to her. Whoever is doing it now is probably angry that she's in the dungeon, or thinks I threw rocks at the princess' guard."

"So you just find an empty room and sleep there?"

"When I can't find a better option? Yes."

Rus' brows contracted. "Then whose room did you hide Ria in?"

Delia flinched. "Prisoners' rooms are ideal because I don't have to worry about the day clerk reassigning them."

"So you slept in Wes' room?"

Delia shook her head. "No, a friend dragged Wes' mattress to my assigned room, but then a life servant took it *and* the bed frame. My room is completely empty."

"So whose room are you using now?"

No...I was hoping you would drop that. Delia sighed. "The night clerk said it was my best option, partly because no one would expect me to sleep there." She could feel his eyes on her, but she kept hers on the floor as they walked.

"You're not..."

"It's Vic and Archi's room," she admitted.

He blew a low whistle. "It's a good thing rumor hasn't picked up on that yet."

Delia groaned. "I didn't want Archi to get in trouble. I only told the governor about Vic so I wouldn't have to be a life servant for an entire

232

month. And I know some people think I'm a lousy rat for telling, but I think Roy and Vic meant to *kill* the governor. They nearly succeeded; he still might die. What kind of person beats an unconscious man so viciously, then leaves him to bleed to death?"

Rus was silent for a time. "Rumor has it you were involved with Vic."

"Rumor is stupid. I met him, he tried to kiss me, I told him not to, and he did it anyway. When I got angry, he called me a *psychotic prude.*"

"Then how did you know he attacked the governor?"

"His knuckles were bloody, he had a lot of food, and a friend overheard him talking about how furious he was with the governor. It was just a guess."

Rus fell into a reverie, his face pensive.

Delia gave him a few minutes to mull, but then could bear it no longer. "You don't want to talk to me anymore, do you?"

Rus frowned. "I didn't think there was any truth to the rumor that you got Vic a life sentence."

"He got *himself* a life sentence. He and Roy beat a man nearly to death and robbed him. How is that *my* fault?" Delia tried to keep the edge out of her voice, but it kept creeping back in. She could feel Rus' back muscles tensing up at her words.

"I didn't say it was. I just thought it was all made up."

Delia stopped before the infirmary door and looked up at him. "What *exactly* about the truth is bothering you?"

Rus lifted his arm off her shoulders and took a step away, forcing her to drop her arm as well. "What if Vic didn't do it? What if they have the wrong guys in the dungeon?"

"They don't. Roy and Vic confessed."

"But you didn't know that. You got them in trouble on a guess, just to help yourself."

"Not *trouble*. Nothing would have happened to them if they hadn't been guilty," Delia argued.

"I watched the guards drag them out of the dance hall in front of everyone."

Delia's arguments died on her lips. *Had Coli been with Archi then? No wonder she was angry.* "Oh. So that's it, then? We're not friends any more?" She swallowed around an annoying lump that had found its way into her throat.

Rus sighed and looked at the floor. "We can still be friends."

But you're no longer interested. "Fine, friend. Let's get that leg treated." Delia held the door open for him while he limped through.

Indra looked up with a sulky expression, then reluctantly stood, book in hand. "Are you going to treat him?"

At Delia's nod, Indra sat back down and resumed reading.

"Lie down," Delia directed Rus, escaping to the office before he could comply. Inside, she hastily gathered plants, brushing impatiently at her face when a few tears fell. *I barely know him; what does it matter?* She stayed hidden inside the office while she ground the herbs into a wet mash. When she emerged, she wrapped his leg as fast as she could, avoiding touching him as much as possible.

"Finished," she announced, not making eye contact even when he stood in front of her.

"I do still want to be your friend."

Delia said nothing, feeling uncomfortable as he turned and limped across the room. "Indra, do you want to wash the mortar and pestle or help Mr. Anglewing to his room?"

"I'll wash them," Indra grumbled, setting her book aside.

"I really don't need help," Rus protested as Delia once again held the door for him. When he limped through it, she took up her place at his side. He reluctantly laid an arm across her shoulders, and they made their way to his room without speaking. At his door, he lifted his arm and she began to walk away.

"Thanks," he called after her.

Delia didn't answer, only increased her speed. Her stomach was grumbling, and making pleasant conversation with her new roommate while hungry seemed impossible. She swung by the kitchen and knocked at the half door.

A blue-winged woman with a kind face opened it. "You must be Delia. There's not much left," she apologized as she poured a green liquid into a bowl. "But I do have cookies."

Delia thanked her as she took the steaming bowl in one hand and the warm cookies in the other. Then she sat in the empty dining hall, and felt annoyed by her own eating sounds. When she finished, the blue-winged woman took her dish with a smile. Delia wanted to thank her for smiling at her, but decided it sounded too awkward. She trudged back to her stolen room, changed, and gathered up all her belongings. If Ria changed her mind, Delia would simply have to risk an unassigned room. She couldn't go back to Vic and Archi's room; it would only fuel her infamy. She walked down to Ria's room with all her wet clothing hanging heavily over one arm, her muddy boots and water shoes in the other.

"Ria, I'm back," she called outside the door, concerned knocking would only frighten her and too encumbered to do so easily.

"Delia?" Ria called through the door.

"Yes."

The unpleasant scree of metal on stone sang out into the corridor, then Ria opened the door. "Oh, you brought all your things."

Delia flinched as a wave of Wes' scent floated out. "I hope that's okay. The life servants take what I leave in my actual room. It doesn't even have furniture now. So I just go wherever there is an empty bed."

Ria shut the door behind her. "So that wasn't your room that I waited in?"

"No."

"Why would the life servants do that to you?" Ria asked, grimacing as Delia laid her wet clothing out on the table. "Maybe you could take those to the laundry?"

"Basically, all the life servants are mad at me for things I didn't do, and I'm not allowed to use the laundry."

Indecision flickered over Ria's pretty face. "Will I get in trouble if I put your dirty clothing with mine?"

"I don't know," Delia answered honestly. "You wouldn't get in *official* trouble if they noticed, but the laundry ladies might take their revenge."

"What will you do with your dirty clothes if I don't?"

"Wash them in the lake when I'm finished with my life-servant duties."

"You're a life servant?!"

Delia nodded. "It's a punishment. I'm a medic until I finish training the other medics in medicinal plants."

"Are you an apothecary apprentice, too?"

"My dad trained all four of us. Some days he needed the help, but most often I think he just liked the company."

A spasm of pain pinched Ria's features, then fled. "Your father is a nice man."

"Nap's nice, too—when he isn't in season. He'll be good to Dina."

Ria's eyes filled with tears, and she quickly turned her head away. "Let's go to the laundry now when no one is there." Ria opened the door, the blessedly fresher air of the corridor wafting in.

Delia quickly sorted out her dirty laundry and collected her sodden clothes. Out in the corridor, Ria was just disappearing down the stairs. Delia left the door open to air the room, and hurried after her. At the laundry room, Ria waited outside the closed door anxiously waving Delia in.

"It's empty," Ria whispered. In the far right corner, there's a laundry pile with my name on it. Just add your clothing beneath mine."

236

Delia darted inside. The humid room was half large vats of water and half drying racks. Against the back wall, eight neatly labeled piles of clothing awaited the morning staff. In the far corner, she found the pile labeled "Ria Agrias" and stealthily added her own clothing. She rearranged the pile until it looked almost the same as it had before, then darted back out.

Ria let out a startled shriek at Delia's sudden appearance, then glanced around to see if anyone had noticed. Down the hall, a black-winged man turned to stare at them, and Delia groaned as she recognized him.

"You're not supposed to be in there," Holis smirked, walking toward them. "Now what should I charge you for keeping your secret?"

"Do you have any money?" Ria asked Delia in a panicked whisper.

"No, but I can handle this."

"You can handle what? Me?" Holis chuckled. "I don't see a bar of soap, so I assume you intend to give me another taste of that acid tongue of yours." As he drew closer, his lip curled in distaste, and he gave Ria an evaluative sniff. "Are you with Wes?"

Ria shook her head, her cheeks aflame.

"He marked her entire room after I told him to leave it," Delia informed him.

Holis snorted. "You really know how to make friends."

"Yes, I'm almost as infamous as you," Delia retorted.

"We don't have any money," Ria said, her voice barely above a whisper.

Holis smiled smugly as he leaned forward. "I'm sure we can come to another arrangement."

Delia pushed him back. "Do you ever consider how completely repulsive your words are *before* they come out of your mouth?"

Holis grinned. "Are you implying that *you* think before you speak?"

Delia growled as she marched back into the laundry room and retrieved her clothes from Ria's pile. Back out in the hall, Holis was openly laughing.

"Happy?!" Delia demanded.

"I am amused, but I would have preferred to get a few life-servant meals out of it," Holis admitted.

"*That's* what you wanted?!" Delia hissed.

"Of course. What did you think?" Holis gave her a wicked smirk before turning back down the hall.

Delia muttered a string of expletives while Ria wrung her hands.

"Are they still going to take my clothes? Or wreck them? Is he going to tell on us? Can you give him life-servant meals? Maybe you should."

Delia took Ria's arm and pulled her into the laundry. "We'll just wash them all ourselves."

"But I don't know how," Ria protested.

"Fine. You watch. I'll wash." Delia inspected the vats until she found one that had the slick feel of soap, then dumped all their clothes in. The vat was deep, and she soon discovered her sodden clothing sunk. She soaked her shirt trying to retrieve it before finding what looked like a giant wooden spoon against the wall.

"What if you wreck them?" Ria asked, staring anxiously at her floating clothes.

Delia fought to control her temper and her tone. "Then I will apologize."

"The last inn we stayed in wrecked two of Dina's sweaters. She was so angry, she made them give us the room, food, and laundry for free."

That's not hard to imagine.

"Which was actually a good thing because we didn't have any money left from selling our jewelry, and Dina didn't want any of the in-seasons staying there to know that we're poor." Ria let out a little gasp. "Dina *did* already tell you that?"

238

Delia nodded in the dim light. "She told Nap what happened with your father."

Ria spun a few pieces of clothing around the surface of the vat with a single finger. "It's strange that he isn't our father. Dina and he are just alike. I'm more like our mother, though we both look like her."

Delia took up a washboard and began to scrub, hoping her silence would encourage Ria to keep talking.

"I wouldn't have guessed he could disown us so completely. I frustrated him, but he was so proud of Dina. I still write him letters, but he never replies."

"I'm sorry."

Two giggling girls entered the room, ignoring them as they dumped their laundry at the back wall, then took paper and a pencil from a shelf Delia hadn't noticed. They scrawled their names, then dropped the papers atop their piles. "I still can't believe he asked you to marry him," one of the girls teetered. "You just met him, *and* his wing is broken!"

"I know! He's a great kisser, but..." Her words trailed off as they left the laundry room.

Delia flushed. *Probably Talis.* At least she needn't feel guilty for her experimental kiss with Dom.

Ria continued swirling her clothing, with two fingers now instead of one. "So why are you a life servant?"

Delia rewarded Ria's confidence with a full report of her misadventures on the Mating Mountain, even the parts that caused her shame. Ria listened with rapt attention, her occasional gasp the only sound that interrupted Delia's narrative.

"Are you going to marry Talis if his wing heals in time?"

"If I did, it would be for the wrong reasons, and I don't think we'd be happy together once my season ended. So, no," Delia concluded.

Ria was silent while she helped Delia hang their clean clothes on the drying racks, then abruptly cleared her throat when they finished. "Could I maybe meet him?"

239

Delia's mind had drifted to Morph and his brother's fungal infection. "Who?"

Ria dropped her chin to let her rich brown locks cover her face. "Talis," she whispered.

"Oh." Delia frowned in thought. It wasn't necessarily a *bad* idea, but it was hard to imagine Talis being a good husband to Ria. *Or anyone,* she admitted to herself.

Ria tucked her hair behind her ear and made eye contact. "Because then I could live near Dina, and our children could play together." Ria's voice broke and she cleared her throat before she continued. "Dina's the strong one. She said I could come live with her and Lord West, so I didn't worry, but now…"

"Lord West is the guy who wouldn't marry her?"

Ria nodded miserably. "He seemed so nice. And he was kind to me. When Dina told him I was allergic to the wool blanket on my bed, he sent someone to fetch me a new one from town. It seemed like everything was going to be okay for the first time since Dina's wing birth."

"I'm sorry."

Ria wiped her face. "I can't read people. I get fooled all the time. Dina always fixes it."

Delia hesitated, choosing her words carefully. "Talis isn't the nicest person. Being married to him might be too high a price to pay for being near Dina."

"But *you* considered it…to be near your family."

I'm still considering it, Delia thought, but said nothing as she walked to the shelf with the paper and pencil. The paper was a random pile of scraps of various sizes, and the pencils two mere stubs that it appeared someone had been chewing. Corralled between the two was a pile of pins. With a slight grimace, Delia picked up the larger pencil stub and wrote *Coli Sulphur* on a yellowing, triangular fragment, then used a pin to attach it to Ria's clothes. Selecting a brown, curling paper, she wrote *Pearl White,* and pinned it to her own.

"Will that work?" Ria asked.

Delia shrugged as she stowed the pencil stub back on its shelf. "Probably better than writing our own names if Holis tattles."

Ria frowned unhappily. "Do you think he will?"

"Don't worry about it. I'll handle it," Delia assured her as they walked to the door. "Will you check and see if anyone is out there?"

Ria nodded, then slipped through the door. A few minutes later, the door opened. "It's empty now."

Delia followed her out, her mind churning possibilities.

Chapter Fourteen

The scent of Wes, though decidedly unpleasant, once again soothed Delia into a heavy sleep. She awoke to Ria shaking her.

"You have to get up for the pregnancy test," Ria pled.

Delia merely turned her head away. "I never do," she mumbled into the pillow.

"But you'll get in trouble. They already pounded on our door."

Delia groaned. "No one knows I'm here."

Ria let out a frustrated sigh, and hurried out the door. Before it shut, Delia was already dreaming of giant thistle plants with Wes and Holis faces instead of blooms. In the dream, Delia took out her spade and began to chop away at the spiky stems, but the spade suddenly spoke to her. Delia stared down at it, surprised to see Cam's face on the handle. "Hi," he said. Delia dropped the spade with a little shriek that woke her. She stared at the walls of Ria's tidy room, then her perfectly made bed with a delicate pink coverlet. Delia crawled clumsily out of bed, kicking wildly when the ugly gray blanket clung to her foot. She cursed at it, only to have her Wes-scented hair fall into her mouth. Delia gagged and spat it out, then yanked her hair into a messy bun. The overwhelming valerian stench of the room had slightly dissipated, but her nightgown and even her clean clothing had absorbed the smell. Delia changed furiously, livid that she now smelled like Wes' mate. Muttering vague threats against him, she hid her belongings under Ria's bed, then strapped on her bag as she hurried from the room. The halls were virtually empty, but as she drew near the dining hall, sound crescendoed into a clamorous din. It was easy to pick out Ria's hot-pink and blue wings in the crowd and the large yellow and black wings sitting next to her. *Wes!*

Delia flew to their table, angry words surging from her mouth before she even landed. "Get away from her! How many times do you need to be told she's not interested?!"

Wes laughed into the sudden silence. "I know you're disappointed that we can't be together, Delia, but I choose Ria."

Delia let out a noise of pure rage, but Ria stood and caught her arms before she could leap at him. Ria's face was flushed, her eyes filled with shame and panic. "Don't," was all she said.

"See? She's protecting me," Wes goaded as people began to murmur.

Delia felt a hand on her arm and turned to see Rus with Bul not far behind.

"What's the problem?" Bul asked.

"It's not a problem," Wes said. "I've had them both; now I've made my choice. Delia isn't taking it well."

The room hushed again as Delia moved Ria aside to face her accuser. "You've never even touched me," Delia hissed as she strained against Rus' firm grasp.

"You seem really upset about that," Wes grinned, gratified at a few low chuckles from the crowd.

"Oh, shut up, Wes," Holis called from across the room. "You marked Ria's room out of revenge last night when Delia kicked you out of it."

"That's true," Ria affirmed, her chin wobbling.

The room erupted into jeering laughter. Wes protested, but his words were largely unheard. He stood, raising his voice in his defense until someone threw water on him. Two more cups' worth splashed his face before Wes left the room sputtering and swearing.

Delia flinched at the spatter, but kept her eyes on Holis. "Why?" she mouthed. Holis shrugged, then got up and left the room. Delia felt Rus' grip loosen on her elbow, and she turned to look at him. *Did you change your mind about us?*

"Are you calm?" Rus asked.

Delia pulled her arm free. "I'm never calm."

Bul chortled. "You really can't get along with anyone, can you?"

"Because Wes is a such a sterling example?" Delia snapped, but her eyes were on Ria, who was brushing at the drops of water on her expensive-looking blouse. "Are you okay?"

Ria gave her a watery smile as a tear slid down her cheek.

"I'm sorry I didn't get up with you. I thought he'd leave you alone in public."

"It's okay," Ria said, her words too soft to be heard in the cooling clamor.

"I have to work today, but you can come with me," Delia offered.

"We can stay with her," Bul volunteered.

"Ria, this is Bul and Rus," Delia said. "They're bratty, but they're decent guys."

Bul beamed.

"I'm not bratty," Rus argued.

Ria murmured a greeting.

"Yes, you are," Rubi said as she joined Bul, slipping an arm around his waist.

Rus made a face at her, and Bul snickered.

"Ria, do you want to stay?" Delia asked.

Ria's face flamed. "I'll be fine," she mumbled.

Rubi let go of Bul and came to Ria's side. "I'm Rubi. We were just about to go to the pool. Do you want to come with us?"

"No, we weren't," Bul said, his expression confused until Rubi shot him a look. "Oh, yeah, I forgot. We're going to the pool."

Rubi turned to Delia. "We'll look out for her."

Delia took in Ria's uncomfortable smile, followed by looks of assurance from Rubi, Rus, and Bul. "Okay. I'll be back before dark." She gave Ria's arm a little squeeze before she left the dining hall.

At the kitchen, Delia stopped to get a life-servant breakfast, then took it directly to Holis' door. He grinned broadly when she handed it to him. "This isn't bribery, this is a thank you. You didn't have to speak up for us, and I appreciate that you did."

He shrugged lightly with the warm plate in hand. "It was the decent thing to do."

Delia's eyes narrowed as she considered him. "I may have been wrong about you."

Holis smirked. "Want to come in and find out?"

Delia rolled her eyes and flew to Coli's room. She peeked inside when no one answered, but the room was empty. *Hopefully, that means she's feeling better*, Delia thought as she hurried to Pearl's room. Her sister answered her door briskly, but her face betrayed disappointment. *Who was she expecting?*

"You returned my shoes filthy, so I hope you're not asking for another favor."

Delia grimaced. "I thought I might be going home, and I knew you'd prefer dirty shoes to no shoes at all. Was I wrong?"

Pearl frowned. "No. What do you want?"

Delia shifted her weight, her disillusionment palpable. They hadn't always gotten along, but she missed her sister's concern and support. "You're not going to ask why I wanted to go home?"

"No. The guards came by looking for you *three times* and Coli told me the rest."

"Oh. Sorry. They didn't bother you about being a bookkeeper, did they?"

Pearl's gray eyes flashed. "Yes, they did. And a medic bothered me about it this morning. I *told you* not to tell anyone. You should have listened. If we both end up life servants, it's your fault! Now *what do you want?*"

Delia flinched. Writing her sister's name to tag her own clothing had seemed like such a good idea last night. "I washed my clothes and Ria Agrias' last night and put them on the drying racks with your name and Coli's because Holis saw us and threatened to tell."

Pearl's glower softened. "Ria, Dina's twin?"

Delia nodded. "Wes Swallowtail is harassing her, and I'm trying to keep him away."

"Is she like Dina?"

"Not at all."

"Are you friends?"

"I think so." Perhaps it was the receptive expression on her sister's face, but Delia found herself blurting out things she had not meant to say. "She's lost without her sister. She wants me to introduce her to Talis, so she can live by Dina and have their kids play together."

Pearl's eyebrows shot up. "But Talis is a jerk."

Delia fought the urge to defend him, her traitorous brain choosing this moment to once again replay their kiss. "When Dina thought she was going to marry Lord West, Ria was going to live with them."

Pearl shook her head dismissively, her tone acidic. "He's not a Lord yet. He's just an aristocratic creep that came here to seduce the *peasant* girls." Pearl's hands were fisted, her knuckles white with the strain.

"Did you know him?"

"Yes," Pearl hissed through her teeth.

"Did he try to seduce *you*?"

Pearl's face flamed so brightly her freckles disappeared. "I don't want to talk about it," she said, and abruptly shut her door.

Delia stared at the door for several seconds, digesting her sister's words, then made a mental note to ask Coli about it. She was walking away when Pearl opened her door again.

"Thank you for the marshmallow root," Pearl barked, then punctuated her gruff words by slamming the door.

"You're welcome," Delia replied to the empty hall.

Her last errand *could* wait until she returned from foraging, but Delia was worried she had already taken too long to respond to Morph's simple request. She held her breath as she pushed open the infirmary door, hoping neither Caena nor Indra would be working, but they both eyed her as she stepped through the door.

"Well, if *she's* here, then I'm not needed," Caena said, looking aggrieved as she headed for the door.

Delia blocked her way. "I am here to put together a poultice for *one* patient and then I am leaving. Zelic assigned me to find medicinal plants to transfer to the garden today."

Caena sniffed, then returned to her stool beside Indra as Delia headed into the office. Delia ground herbs, then washed the mortar and pestle, all the while trying to block out Indra and Caena's gossiping.

"Phasia still swears she'll have her revenge. She said she's going to find every last bit of Delia's clothing and tear it to shreds," Caena said eagerly, casting glances at Delia as she spoke.

"Phasia's gone buggy if she thinks the governor won't put her back in the dungeon for that. She's already lost her position; she needs to calm down," Indra replied, looking regretfully at the closed book in her lap.

"And I heard Phasia has been looking for Delia's clothes in all the young men's rooms' Delia frequents, but there are so many, she doesn't have time to check them all."

Delia removed the wet mortar and pestle from the sink and dripped it across Caena on her way to return it to the office.

"My book!" Indra cried, clutching it protectively to her chest.

"You did that on purpose!" Caena shrieked as she jumped to her feet.

"Of course I did," Delia snapped. "Stop spreading lies about me or at least have the courtesy to only do it behind my back!"

"You should be grateful I tell you!" Caena yelled while Indra rubbed at the cover of her book where a stray drop had marred it.

"Sorry I got water on your book, Indra," Delia said, then slipped out the infirmary door, narrowly resisting the urge to slam it. Instead, she muttered about gossips all the way to the governor's room.

Her relief upon seeing Morph standing guard outside the governor's door was immense. Phemus was once again behind him, but she didn't recognize the other two guards.

"The governor can't be disturbed," Phemus said loudly.

"I'm not here for him," Delia retorted as she looked at Morph.

Morph's eyes widened with understanding. "I'm taking my break," he announced to the other guards.

"Morph! You need to stay away from her! She already tried to kill you once!" Phemus called after his brother.

Morph followed Delia into the staircase and out of the guards' sight and hearing.

"This poultice will help," Delia said, taking it out of her bag. "He can wrap it to his feet tonight, but he needs to spend some time every day barefoot in the sunshine and keep his feet dry as much as possible.

Morph smiled and unwrapped the brown poultice, sniffing at it experimentally.

"I'll make him a new one in a couple of days. It will probably take a week to clear it up."

"Morph!" Phemus called as he rounded the corner.

Panicking, Morph slid the poultice in his pocket and put a hand over it to hide the bulge. "I'm fine, Phemus."

Delia took the opportunity to fly the other direction, Phemus' urgent conversation blessedly indiscernible. She didn't want to hear any more rumors, conspiracies or lies. *Why do people even talk if all they're going to do is spew ugliness and cruelty?* Curious and condemning eyes followed her as she flew through the Old Castle, whispered conversations trailing out behind her like a wake. She burst through the outer doors, cold sunshine and birdsong embracing her as they drew her irresistibly into the forest. She flew until the anxious weight of false accusations fell from her and she was blissfully alone.

When the light began to wane, Delia reluctantly returned to the castle. Wildcrafting had soothed her as always, but the returning weight of her cares wore away her ease before she passed through the front door. Inside the infirmary, Zelic was pacing with a frazzled air, but stopped abruptly when she entered.

"Caena says you dumped the entire mortar full of water over her head so she couldn't finish the rest of her shift. Indra was terribly put-out that she had to work alone without breaks and she says you ruined her book. However, I saw her book, so I know *that's* not true. And Graci almost gave the governor a killing dose of morphine this afternoon. Neva is taking an unusually long dinner break, and I need to check on the governor and Graci before she kills him and I kill her." Zelic ended his long-winded speech with a huge breath of air.

Delia hid a smile at his threat of violence. "Go, then. I have herbs I can catalog before we do transplants with the gardener."

"It's late. He won't go out there with us *now*," Zelic protested.

She opened her bag and waved a chamomile plant at him with its roots wrapped in a damp bandage. "It would be wasteful not to."

Zelic made a noise of frustration as he hurried out the door.

Delia openly grinned and began to unpack her bag. He was certainly a high-strung person to begin with, but when he became agitated Delia found him unaccountably delightful. It was a shame he wasn't still in season. Neva returned before Delia finished cataloguing and slowed the process by asking detailed questions about all of the day's findings.

When Zelic returned, he had Graci in tow. "Neva, I need you to spend the rest of your shift with the governor. I just gave him his morphine dose. Delia, Graci is going to train with you for a few days."

"I can't harvest much if I'm grounded," Delia complained as Neva left.

Ignoring her, Zelic entered the office and moved all her catalogued herbs to the cabinet, locked it, and pocketed the key. "Graci, you're in charge of the infirmary until I return. If anyone needs medicine, stall them or tell them to come back later."

Graci murmured a sulky assent as Zelic pointed to Delia's bag. "You have all the transplants in there?"

Delia nodded and followed him out of the infirmary. When the door closed behind them, Zelic spoke.

"You're babysitting her," he said in a hushed voice, slowly growing louder as they walked further away. "She is a constant danger to the governor. She is too dim-witted and eager to please. The moment she has access to the medications, she gives the governor whatever he asks for. My restrictions, chastisements, and training seem to have no effect. If she is *in* the castle, the governor will demand she nurse him, and then it's only a matter of time before Indra or Caena are careless with the key, and Graci will sneak in to get him some pain medication. I simply can't have her here. Just take her hiking and wear her out. You may show her plants that can do the governor no harm as long as they look nothing like plants that *can do him harm.* You are a valuable resource, and I hate to waste your time this way, but it is the only excuse the governor will accept for having Graci gone, and I literally don't think I can keep him alive if she remains here."

Delia sighed. She couldn't argue with that and still respect herself.

"And please try not to goad Caena. I know she's an awful gossip, but she's a competent medic," Zelic added.

"I only dripped a little water on her lap after she implied I'm promiscuous," Delia complained.

"Well, now she'll be certain that she was correct and spread it all the more," Zelic chided.

"That's not logical!"

"There are some people that aren't worth the conflict. Their sense of justified escalation is boundless, and their revenge is never complete. Caena is one of them. Phasia is another."

"Perfect," Delia deadpanned. "Anyone else I should goad?"

Zelic chuckled. "Phemus? Tera?"

Delia groaned. "I need to get off this mountain."

Zelic stopped in front of a door to the left of the kitchen. "This is the life servants' dining room. The head gardener is probably still at dinner. You're welcome to come in, but you may not like the reception."

"I'll pass. I need to check on someone in the in-season dining room anyway.

Zelic nodded and opened the door, the scent of fish wafting out before he closed it behind him. Delia passed the kitchen, exchanging challenging looks with Gray, and entered the in-season's dining hall. She spotted Ria surrounded by Bul's friends, and felt a swell of gratitude. They had combined two tables so their group of six could cluster together. Ria was seated between Rubi, and Bul's dark-haired friend.

"Did Wes bother you today?" Delia asked without preamble.

Ria started and looked up at Delia. "No. I haven't seen him since breakfast."

"You have to ask? We told you we'd take care of her," Bul protested over the top of Ria's soft words.

"Thank you," Delia said, then reached around Rus to take his empty plate, earning a glare from Rubi's unpleasant friend. The latter opened her checkered wings and leaned into Rus to prevent Delia from reaching between them again. Rolling her eyes, Delia opened a side pocket of her bag and dumped a pile of tiny wild strawberries onto Rus' plate. Then, she set it down on the other side of him, purposely allowing her arm to brush his.

Rubi's friend eyed Delia's earth-stained fingers. "They're dirty," she complained.

"Those are the smallest strawberries I've ever seen," Rubi remarked, picking one up. "Do they taste the same?"

"Much better," Delia assured her as she turned to go.

"And they're not poisonous?" Bul asked.

Delia turned back to glare at his impish grin. "Of course not!"

"Just checking," he said as he tossed two in his mouth. "They're good!" he exclaimed, clearly surprised.

Delia rolled her eyes and left the dining hall. It had taken several patches of wild strawberries to gather so many, but she was happy to have a way of showing her gratitude. Outside the dining hall, Zelic and a short, stocky man that reminded Delia of a mole were waiting.

"Kip, this is Delia," Zelic said.

"You can't transplant at night," Kip blurted. "It has to be done in the early morning or at latest early afternoon on a cloudy day. And tonight is especially cold; it might even frost." He shook his head with an aggrieved air, his soil-colored wings quivering.

Delia opened her bag and showed him the contents. "Then what should we do with them?"

Kip lifted out each of the three plants with reverential gentleness and cradled them in his arms. "I'll put them in the growing room with the seedlings. This is chamomile," he said, touching the small daisy-like blooms, "but what are the other two?"

Delia pointed to the larger plant with tightly budded cluster flowers. "That's yarrow. It will want a sunny spot and it likes to spread." Delia touched a long, pointed leaf on the third plant. "This is valerian. It likes wet soil, and this one was growing in the shade."

Kip nodded his head, unconsciously holding the plants closer to his chest. "I'll transfer them to the gardens," he said, and began to walk away.

"Wait," Zelic protested. "I'd like to keep the medicinal plants together to avoid confusion."

Kip's forehead furrowed. "But they won't all be happy in the same spot."

"Will you want my medics traipsing all over your garden?"

Kip looked horrified. "I don't want them in my gardens *at all.*"

"Then how will we harvest them for medicine?" Zelic demanded.

Kip hugged the plants to his chest, then looked down and repositioned them. "I will harvest them when necessary."

"You don't know anything about medicinal plants!" Zelic protested.

"I know enough." He looked at Delia appraisingly. "She can teach me."

"The governor wants the *medics* trained to harvest medicinal plants," Zelic argued.

Kip shook his head, his mouth puckered tightly. "Not in my gardens," he assured them, then quickly walked away.

Zelic groaned and rubbed his face.

"So I need to train the medics in the forest *and* Kip in the gardens? How many are there anyway?"

Zelic shook his head. "Only the gardeners know. I'll talk to the governor. You're done for the night. Your shift with Graci starts at ten tomorrow morning. I'll make sure she's in the infirmary waiting for you." He walked away with a swift, agitated pace, his striking yellow and black wings flowing behind him.

Delia glanced at the nearby kitchen door where Gray gave her a smug grin. "Hope you're not hungry."

Delia's forest dining had been adequate, but a hot meal sounded lovely. She stepped closer to see around Gray, hoping to spot Nelson or the kind blue-winged woman.

"Nelson's not here," he said, guessing her intent. "And if you complain about me, I'll make sure someone spits on every meal you get."

An apropos truth bomb tickled the tip of her tongue, and she bit it to stop the offending words. Delia forced herself to look at him with clinical eyes. His greasy, thinning hair splayed inadequately across a shiny bald spot. Her gaze skipped over his snarling face and snagged at the bulge beneath his Adam's apple. "You have a goiter. You should have Zelic or Neva check it out."

Gray shifted his collar to hide it. "It's fine. You're just used to looking at your own scrawny neck."

Does he think that's an insult? "Thank you?" Before he could say anything else unpleasant, Delia walked away, congratulating herself for not responding in kind.

"It's a lovely neck," a familiar voice said.

Delia turned to look at Talis leaning against the doorway of the dining hall.

"Would you mind if I kissed it?"

Delia shook her head and continued down the hall, but a flurry of shivers ran from her neck to her arms. She could hear Talis' steps behind her, and she slowed to let him catch up.

"No, you don't mind?" he asked, one hand holding his wing frame steady.

Yes. "How's the wing?"

"Healing. Should be perfect for our wedding next week."

"*Our* wedding? What about all the other girls you've asked to marry you?"

Talis' face lit with glee. "You're *jealous.*"

"I'm not jealous," Delia argued, her voice sounding sullen to her own ears.

"Don't worry, no one's said yes, and you're still my first choice."

A happy warmth suffused Delia's heart and cheeks. *You didn't get along with him before you were in season*, she reminded herself. *You didn't even like him.* She glanced up at his smiling face. *Maybe he's changed?*

"I heard the governor shortened your punishment."

She frowned and looked down at the stone floor. "Did you hear why?"

"You turned in Vic? Yeah, I heard about that."

Delia snuck a glance at him. "That doesn't bother you?"

"I'm a little mad at myself for not thinking of it before you."

Relief filled her, her clenched shoulders relaxing. "What would you have asked for?"

"To be allowed to marry before my wing healed."

She stopped in front of Ria's door. "And *whom* would you have married?"

Talis grinned and put a hand on the doorframe as he leaned in. "I *love* that you're jealous."

Delia let him get within inches of her lips, then opened the door to escape him. *Don't complicate things by kissing him again,* she chided herself. She glanced around the tidy room, relief filling her as she saw the clean clothes piled on both their beds. *Thank you, Coli and Pearl!*

"Oh, so we're playing that game again?" Talis grinned, following her into the room. "So this is where you've been hiding out!" Talis suddenly grimaced in disgust. "Smells awful. Wait, is this Dina's sister's room? The one Wes marked?"

Delia nodded. She detached her bag and set it on the floor, then began to look for her water shoes.

"That rumor sounded so fake! Did Holis really shame Wes out of the dining hall?"

"The people who threw water on him definitely helped, but yes."

"I'm sorry I missed that," Talis laughed as the scent of mustard suffused the air.

"Stop that!" She glared at him while she fished out her shoes from beneath the bed.

"I'm fixing it! What you mean is *thank you*."

Delia smacked him on the calf.

"If you wanted to touch my leg, you only had to ask," he teased, chortling when she threw a shoe at him.

"Watch the wings!" he laughed.

Delia retrieved her shoe missile, then set her soap on the table with her bathing suit. "I need to change."

Talis backed up into the hallway. "You realize the life servants will figure out that you're sleeping here from the rumors? That bed will probably be gone by tomorrow, if not tonight."

Delia groaned. *That means I can't leave my belongings in here, either.*

"Hey, who are you?" a challenging male voice called from the hallway.

Talis stood up straighter. "Delia's fiancé. Who are you?"

Delia smacked Talis' chest. "Stop telling people that!"

"I'm Sal. Why don't you move so Ria can get into her room? She has a headache."

Talis and Delia stepped back as Ria slipped into the room, holding her head. Sal, Bul's dark-haired friend, took up a protective stance just outside the door facing the hallway.

Talis shot Delia an amused glance over the shorter man's head. "Are you standing guard?"

"Yeah." Sal's brown wings spread wide to block entrance or exit through the open door.

Ria dropped her hand from her forehead and shot Delia a pleading look. "Can you make him go away?" she mouthed, then dimmed the solar lantern.

"I can take it from here," Talis said.

Sal snorted. "Your wing is broken. You won't intimidate Wes."

Talis' voice was tight with irritation. "And you will?"

Delia rolled her eyes. "*I* will. Thank you for your help, Sal. I'll stay with her."

Sal turned to look at Delia. "That white beat you up, and he's half the size of Wes. I'm staying here."

Delia glowered at the painful reminder and shut the door.

Ria turned the lantern back up. "He thinks we're a couple, but he smells like rotting beach seaweed," she whispered, distressed.

"Did you tell him?"

Ria shook her head. "Bul, Rus, and Rubi are nice, but they're all paired off. Sal latched onto me at breakfast and hasn't let go."

Delia frowned. "Who is Rus with?"

"Rubi's friend, Cia."

"Checkered wings?"

Ria nodded.

Delia flinched. *That was fast. How could Rus choose her?* Delia let the sounds of an irritable conversation between the two men outside the door distract her from the flash of pain.

"Would Sal stay if he knew you weren't interested?" Delia asked.

"I don't know. I'm just going to go to sleep; you don't think he'll stay all night, do you?"

"I can make him leave right now, but I can't do it in a nice way," Delia warned.

Ria shook her head. "He's been kind to me. I'll figure it out tomorrow."

Something hit the door, making both girls jump. Delia hurried over to the door and opened it a crack, then threw it open and hurried out into the hallway.

"Stop it!" Delia yelled just as Sal swung at Talis, his fist connecting with Talis' dimpled chin. Talis reeled back and Delia ran to steady him, but he was already lunging for Sal. Delia caught his arm, her voice rising to a shriek as the two men converged. "You're going to break your other wing! Do you want to be a life servant like Ora?"

Talis' eyes were blazing, but he stopped straining against Delia's hold.

Delia turned her glare on Sal. "Ria isn't interested. You smell like rotting seaweed to her, but she's too nice to tell you."

Talis snorted derisively.

Sal looked stunned, then peered sadly into the darkened room. Frowning, he lifted his shirt to wipe the blood from his nose. "Good thing *you're* not too nice, *Thistle*."

Talis lunged forward again and Delia threw herself between them.

"Sal, go *now*," Delia hissed through her teeth.

Sal muttered a string of expletives as he walked away.

Delia turned back to Talis. "Fighting? Again? Did you start it?"

Talis rubbed his jaw and didn't answer.

"They're going to put you back in the dungeon," she warned, glancing at the spectators that were now drifting away.

"Doesn't matter," Talis growled. "Squatty little weasel knocked my broken wing into the wall."

Delia glanced up at his wing frame with alarm. "Are you in pain?"

Talis nodded.

"Infirmary, now," she commanded.

"What about Ria?"

Delia looked back to where Ria stood in the doorway, her face white. "Barricade yourself in. I'll be back."

Ria obediently shut the door; the sound of metal screeching on rock immediately followed.

Satisfied, Delia grasped Talis' upper arm and began to march him along.

"Slower, Delia, I can't keep my wing steady."

With a huff, Delia changed sides, supporting his wing frame as he walked. "If you just ruined your chances of going home, I'm going to be *so* mad at you," she muttered.

"Why? Were we going home together?" His tone was challenging, still laced with anger.

Maybe. "Just because I said I didn't want to mate with you, doesn't mean I don't want you to be happy."

"Because we're such good friends?" he asked wryly.

"Because I care about you, moth-brain!"

Talis stopped walking. "Care about me *how*?"

"You know *how*. Don't be stupid!" Delia tried to get him walking again, but he resisted.

"My wing's not going to heal, Delia! I don't want to keep wearing this stupid frame and get stuck here as a life servant. Just take it off. Help me fly back home tonight. We'll tell my parents we're married. No one has to know."

"*I* will know!"

"You know it's completely unfair that the king and the governor control all the marriages. Isn't it enough that we want to marry each other?"

"Did I *say* that?!"

Talis' face hardened, and he stood up straighter. "Then why am I wearing this miserable thing?" Talis knocked the wing frame out of her hands, then gasped in pain.

"So you can heal and get married!" she growled at him as she once again steadied the wing frame.

"I was only doing that for you!" Talis swore under his breath. "I know you like me, Delia. My parents like you. My sister loves you. This

260

is the wisest choice for both of us." He put a tentative hand on her cheek. "Come here."

Delia allowed him to pull her closer, his tender kisses sweeping her lips, her cheeks, then trailing down her neck with insistent fire. Appreciative whistles erupted in the hallway, and she pulled away, her face flaming.

Talis chuckled happily, and they continued their slow walk to the infirmary. Delia's face slowly cooled, but her thoughts tumbled like seaweed in the surf. When they came to an empty hallway, Talis glanced behind them, then leaned down to whisper.

"The new officiant won't marry us while my wing is broken, but he'll sell me a blank marriage certificate. We can forge the rest of it."

Delia shook her head as Talis placed soft kisses on her cheek and ear. "I have to finish training the medics. Just let your wing heal in the frame until then."

"And then you'll leave with me?"

Instead of answering, Delia turned her face toward his, accepting the kisses that made her feel lovable and hopeful.

"Sleep in my room tonight," he whispered against her lips.

Delia drew back, startled. "No."

"Why not? If you're pregnant, they'll have to let you go. It won't matter if you're done training them."

Delia shook her head. "I can't just mate with you."

"Delia, it's not going to be any different a few days from now. My wing won't be healed enough to get married. If you want the forged certificate first, I'll go buy it now."

Delia started walking again, forcing him to keep pace while she held his wing frame. "We're taking care of your wing right now."

"I'll get it afterwards, then," Talis said as they arrived at the infirmary.

Inside, Graci stepped out of the office. "I can't get into the cabinet and neither can you."

Delia sighed in annoyance. "Didn't Zelic come back?"

Graci's lower lip protruded out in a sulk. "The governor requested *me*, but Zelic went instead. *He* has the key."

"Lie down, Talis," Delia directed, helping him keep the wing frame steady. As soon as his stomach hit the cot, Delia unfastened the frame. "Oh, it shifted." The fight had dislodged the frame so that it was pinching off one of the main blood vessels flowing into Talis' broken wing. "Graci, I need you!"

Graci hurried over and kept the broken tip of his wing stationary while Delia removed the frame, cursing herself for the slow trip to the infirmary. When the frame clattered to the ground, she minutely examined the break.

"Where is the pain?"

"My whole wing was aching, but it's getting better."

"Graci, get Zelic. I need to get into the cabinet *now*."

Graci nodded, and hurried out the door as Talis lifted his head off the pillow.

"What's the matter? Do I have another break?"

"No, but the frame was cutting off the blood supply to your wing."

"That sounds bad. Is it still going to heal?"

Delia twitched. "Probably."

"But not as good a chance as before?"

Delia frowned, then forced herself to meet his eyes. "Not quite as good, no."

"Just leave the frame off, then. Let me see if I can fly with it."

"No, I'll treat it and put the frame back on. Trying to fly now will jeopardize your wing's healing."

Talis shook his head and started to rise. "We could leave in the morning."

"Talis! I can't hold your wing steady when you move. Lie back down!"

Talis shook his head. "No, it's not going to heal in time. I'm just going to fly with it broken. It'll hurt, but I can do it." Talis rose up to his knees while Delia desperately tried to keep his broken wing in place.

"Please stop!"

Talis climbed off the cot with Delia flying after him to stabilize his wing. But as he began to walk away, she had to let the broken wing go. For one moment, his wing tip stood straight, seemingly healed along the green-splotched break. When it fell, Talis grimaced, his eyes shut as perspiration broke out on his forehead.

"No!" Delia cried out as she landed.

Talis swallowed, then opened his eyes. His voice strained as blood leaked from the break. "I'm going to go buy our marriage certificate now. Go pack your clothes. We'll leave tonight."

Tears sprang into Delia's eyes. "I can't leave the infirmary unattended."

"When they come back, then. I'll pack and go see Ora. Say your goodbyes to Pearl and Ria, then meet me at my room. We'll say goodbye to Coli together."

Panic made Delia's heart beat frantically in her chest. "My punishment isn't over; I can't go."

"If they come after you, Dad's lawyer will take care of it. I'm sure they'd let you off with a fine."

"I...can't."

Talis' brows knit. "What do you mean?"

"I can't do this. This is going to be a bad relationship the moment my season is over. We barely tolerated each other before. When I'm back to myself, our physical attraction won't be enough. And I won't even be your wife."

Talis frowned. "You're making a mistake. You were always happy at home. You love your family. You love Hamlet. You'll step right back into your life. And we don't have to tell them we're not married. *Think*, Delia. Nobody that wants you now will want you when your season is over. I know what you're really like, and I still want you."

"That's not flattering," Delia growled.

"But it's realistic. This is your best chance and mine. Leave with me tonight." Talis held out his hand, the mustard-scented air thick with tension.

Delia shook her head.

Talis let his hand drop with a hard laugh, his words bitter. "You'll probably end up a life servant, you know. At least you'll keep Ora company. I just hope you can live with yourself if I die trying to get down the mountain without you." Talis turned to go, his broken wing tip swinging out and back. He sucked in a jagged breath, waiting for the pain in his wing to subside before he moved again.

Delia's anger battled her pity, the latter winning out. "You should ask Ria."

"What?"

"I think Ria would go with you and pretend to be your wife."

"Because of Dina?"

Delia nodded. She watched Talis walk to the door and tried to ignore the wistful longing to chase after him. "Talis," she called after him.

He turned slowly, his broken wing tip moving only slightly.

"You be nice to her," she said fiercely.

One side of Talis' mouth lifted in a weak smirk, then he was gone.

Delia hurried to the doorway and watched him walk away. It still didn't feel like a mistake letting him go, but it wasn't something she wanted to do. When he disappeared into the stairwell, she pulled the door shut. Talis' words played on a loop in her brain: *Nobody that wants you now will want you when your season is over.* The words stirred her wrath and she clung to it, finding the anger easier to bear than the pain and crippling fear. She marched up and down between the cots, reciting to herself every rotten thing Talis had ever done until she felt thoroughly wise in her decision. She had just begun a second recitation when the door opened and Zelic stomped into the room.

"Where is your patient?" he demanded.

"He refused further treatment."

Zelic kicked one of the cots, making it screech a few inches across the stone floor. "Perfect!" he yelled. "Graci is with the governor, he's ordered that the medicine cabinet remain unlocked, and that Graci be in charge of treating him from now on."

"Is he really that stupid?!"

Zelic kicked the cot a few more inches, then pulled it back into place. Delia followed him as he walked into the office, unlocked the cabinet, and threw it open. "Help me Graci-proof this cabinet," he ordered. "Anything she might use to unwittingly harm him."

Delia complied until his arms were full. "What are you going to do with them?"

"It's best if you don't know."

Delia followed him to the outer door and opened it for him.

"Thank you," he barked. "If Graci shows up and wants to know where the morphine is, play stupid. Offer her a poultice."

Delia frowned.

"And next time I have carefully kept Graci away from the governor, *don't* send her to the governor's room to fetch me."

Delia let the door close behind him with a deep sense of chagrin. She should have left Graci with Talis and fetched Zelic herself. Guiltily, she picked up Talis' wing frame and stacked it neatly against the wall, then retreated to the office to make patient notes.

It was an hour before Zelic returned, calmer and vaguely smug. "From now on, any plants you bring in that aren't Graci-safe go directly to me. The governor may not have a healthy sense of self-preservation, but I will *not* be the head medic that let one of his charges dose the governor to death."

"I'm sorry. I should have come for you myself," Delia conceded.

"Was it Talis Sulphur?"

Delia nodded. "His wing frame was pinching off the blood supply to his wing."

"How did *that* happen?"

"He, um, knocked it against a wall," Delia lied.

Zelic's eyes narrowed as he studied her face. "Did he try to fly with his broken wing?"

"Not while I was watching."

"It will be less painful if we cut the broken tip off. If he shows he can fly with it damaged, he could still be married."

Hope flared in Delia's chest before she crossly argued it down. "I'll let him know," she offered.

"Since Graci won't be leaving the governor's side, you're back on wildcrafting duty tomorrow: transplants and cuttings both. Look for ground access routes; you'll be taking Neva with you the day after."

Delia nodded her agreement, then hurried out the door and flew to Talis' room. When her anxious knock received no answer, she opened the door. The room was dark and empty. Delia flew up and turned on the solar lantern, spilling light into the mustard-scented room that was completely devoid of belongings. Heart sinking, Delia turned the lantern off, then flew to Ria's room. The pile of clean clothing was still on Delia's bed, but Ria's bed had only a neatly tucked sheet. All of Ria's clothes were gone along with her pink blanket. Delia shut the door and sat heavily on a rusted stool. Somehow the loss of her new roommate stung as much as losing Talis. She pulled a strand of loose hair around to her nose, enjoying the mustard scent in the Wes-reeking room. Then the door began to open. *Maybe they didn't leave yet!* Delia leapt to her feet, but when she pulled the door open, Phasia stumbled into the room with a startled shriek.

The angry words tumbled from Phasia's lips before she had even caught her balance. "You can't prove I was going to do anything! This isn't even your room! *You* don't belong here!" Phasia yelled as she pointed a red finger in Delia's face.

Delia mastered the urge to smack her hand away. The woman was twice her size and had already tried to break her wings. She clenched her teeth as if they could filter her words. "You need to leave or I will go talk to the governor *right* now," Delia threatened, her hand still on the door.

Phasia's furious face turned purple. "You got me thrown in the dungeon! You made me lose my place as head laundress!"

Another truth bomb bloomed on Delia's tongue, but she bit it back. "You need to leave," she repeated.

"If you go to the governor, I'll..." Phasia began as she glanced around the room, her eyes catching on the pile of clean laundry. A cruel smile twisted her faded features. "I'll destroy everything you own."

Delia swallowed. She didn't have money left to replace *anything*. Wicked glee crinkled Phasia's wrinkled face as she saw the effect of her threat. Before Delia could stop her, she lifted a yellow top from the bed and tore it in half with a deranged giggle.

"How did you like that?" Phasia asked, tossing the remains to the floor.

Delia let her verbal venom fly. "Your life is beyond wasted; every day you become a worse excuse for a person than you were the day before."

Rage again twisted Phasia's features and she set into the pile of clothing with a flurry of destruction. Delia grabbed her bag off the floor and her bathing things from the table, then flew from the room. She was almost certain none of her remaining belongings would survive, but she flew hard anyway, landing at the governor's door winded.

"Phasia is ripping up all my clothes," she panted to the four guards clustered outside.

Beck winced while one of the other guards shook his head. Delia didn't recognize the others.

"I'll take care of it," Beck volunteered.

Delia flew back to Ria's room, checking periodically to ensure Beck was still following, his white wings waving behind him like flags as he ran. Delia landed just outside the door, her eyes snagged by the pile of torn clothing on the floor. Phasia was yanking angrily at a pair of sturdy brown pants. She had popped off the buttons and ripped all the pockets, but her efforts to tear them in half were frustrated. No clothing was left on the bed. Beck ran past her, catching Phasia by the elbow before she could do any more damage. The woman whirled on Beck, striking him with her captured arm before she realized who had her.

"Oh!" Phasia's vehemence faded with the single word. "She...she tried to attack me again, Beck. I was just..." Phasia looked down at the pitiful remains of Delia's clothes. "I *had* to...because she...she tore up *my* clothes, so it's only right that I..."

"Oh, Phasia. You know you have to go back to the dungeon for this," Beck said, sincere regret lacing his words.

"No!" The word turned into a sob as Beck pulled her from the room. "You can't believe her! She's a *liar*!" Phasia shrieked and leapt at Delia, only to have Beck tow her back.

"Phasia, you're just making it worse for yourself. You know I have to report this."

"But Beck, she says the most horrible things to me, and then I just can't control my temper. It's like I'm in season again," Phasia blubbered. "Please don't put me back in the dungeon!" She continued her plaintive cries as Beck led her into the stairwell, but Delia could no longer make out the words.

The remnants of Delia's clothes littered the floor. She sorted through them first with hope, then dawning despair. Aside from the brown pants Phasia hadn't finished destroying, nothing appeared salvageable. She searched the room until she located the extracted buttons, then stowed them in her bag, wishing she had thought to bring a needle and thread. She took one last look at the pitiable pile, then flew up to turn off the lantern. Someone else could clean up Phasia's havoc.

She didn't have the energy to fly to Coli's room; the triple loss after a long work day had drained her. She trudged through the castle, grateful that her boots made her footfalls as heavy as she felt. She kicked Coli's door lightly instead of knocking, then leaned against it, waiting. When no one answered, a lump grew in her throat. She walked on to Pearl's door, knocking this time, but with the same result. Delia opened the door, soothed by the typical disarray of the room. She changed quickly into her bathing suit, dashing tears from her cheeks. *They're just clothes*, she reminded herself. *And you chose not to go home with Talis; you can't be sad about it now. And you barely know Ria. You're fine. It's fine.* Despite the pep talk, the tears kept falling. Defeated, she sat down on Pearl's stool and sobbed. When her cries quieted to sniffles, she poured her heart out in prayer. She knew God was perfectly aware of her difficulties, but she told him anyway, drawing strength from the quiet peace that was his answer. Drying her tears, she packed her meager belongings into her bag and set out for the pool.

Red eyes cast down, Delia avoided interaction through the sparsely populated halls. She looked up briefly when she entered the pool, but Holis' was the only face she recognized. He gave her a smirk, then drifted to her side when she waded into the water.

"Wes been giving you trouble?" he asked.

Delia shook her head and began to wash.

"Someone break your heart?"

Though his tone was sympathetic, Delia could read the amused curiosity in his eyes. "Have you come to wreck our truce or reinforce it?"

Holis chuckled. "I'm just bored."

"It's not a good time to bother me."

"Is it ever?"

Delia snorted. "No. But Phasia did just rip up all my clothes, so tread lightly."

"Aw, I can't believe no one told me! I *hate* being a pariah."

Delia rolled her eyes at him and dunked her head under the water. When she came up, he was already talking again.

"So you caught her in the act? Did you tell the guards? Is she in the dungeon again?"

Delia glared at him as she lathered her hair. "Yes."

"To all three?" When Delia nodded, Holis pumped his fist. "Yes! That's a whole week of life-servant meals for me."

"You bet on her destroying my clothing?"

"No, I bet that she'd be back in the dungeon within the week."

Somewhat mollified, Delia rinsed her hair. When she stood upright, Holis grinned at her.

"Want to go get life-servant meals right now? I'll let you borrow one of my shirts."

She was tempted to reject the offer, but the idea of a clean shirt to sleep in was appealing. "I might keep it for a while," she warned him.

"I might let you."

Delia narrowed her eyes at him. "This isn't going to be a romantic relationship."

"But if you wear my shirt and have a meal with me, people will think it is."

"Why would you want that?" Delia demanded.

"I have my reasons."

Delia examined his symmetrical face with its perfectly straight nose and high cheekbones. *Maybe? No,* she chastised herself. "This isn't going to be a physical relationship, either, if that's what you're thinking."

Holis smirked, but said nothing while she finished washing. As she climbed out of the water, he followed her.

"So we're eating, then?" he asked.

"Depends on the shirt."

He snorted, but kept pace with her. At his door, he stepped inside and came back with a soft gray shirt. "It'll be too big, but you can pretend it's a dress."

"Thanks." She slipped it into her bag, then started toward the kitchen.

"You're not going to wear it now?" he asked, following her.

Delia stopped and turned to face him. "Is that a problem?"

Holis frowned. "It doesn't help my illusion."

"How can it possibly help you to convince anyone that we are together?"

He hesitated. "You and I both have image problems right now; appearing to be a couple could help."

Delia bristled, then began walking again with angry strides. "And what's my image problem?"

Holis smirked. "You get all your boyfriends thrown in the dungeon."

"That's not true!"

Holis shrugged. "What people are saying about me isn't true, either."

"You *haven't* impregnated a bunch of girls?"

A smug grin enveloped his face. "No, that's true."

"Ugh, you're despicable. How can you be proud of that?" Delia demanded as she stopped in front of the kitchen's half door.

"Seven beautiful women were willing to mate with me. I'm the envy of the male life servants," Holis bragged as he knocked.

"Men are horrible. How could you use those poor women and abandon them to raise your children alone? And what sort of man admires that kind of abuse?"

The half door swung open and Nelson smiled at them. "That sort," Holis said, pointing at him.

"What are you accusing me of?" Nelson asked good-naturedly.

Delia glared at both of them.

"Just gambling," Holis lied fluidly. "Did you hear about Phasia?"

"I'm surprised it took you an entire hour to collect on our bet," Nelson commented, then handed out a plate with some sort of fish and mushroom casserole. "Do you want dinner, too?" he asked Delia.

"Yes."

Nelson handed her a plate of the steaming mixture. "Sorry about your clothes. The laundry has a bin of abandoned clothing if that's all you've got," he said, nodding at her bathing suit.

"Thanks."

Nelson nodded, then gave Holis a meaningful look before shutting the half door.

Holis grinned as they walked into the empty dining hall. "Did you see that? It's working already."

Delia waited until Holis sat down, then sat several tables away.

"I thought we were eating together," he complained.

"Do you really want me close enough to kick you? Because I want to."

Holis' expression soured. "I thought you might appreciate my honesty."

"Not when it reveals you're an even worse person than I thought you were," she snapped, then took a bite of the fishy casserole.

"How can I be worse? I got Wes to leave Ria alone, didn't I?"

"Thank you for that," she said through clenched teeth. "But you just finished *bragging* about all the poor women that you sent home, pregnant and humiliated. You haven't an ounce of empathy or shame. How can you be so cruel?"

"Not everything is the way it looks."

"Sometimes it is," Delia said in an undertone.

Holis' expression darkened. "You don't know me. You know nothing about my life."

"So you're implying that there's something that justifies what you've done, *including* boasting about it?"

"You're such a hypocrite. Where's your empathy for all the people you've sent to the dungeon? Have you kept a tally? Everybody else has. *Seven* people, Delia, two who will *never* get out. How do you live with that?"

"They made their *own* bad choices and they are dealing with the consequences!"

"Yeah, so are my seven."

Delia wanted to vomit up every bite of her dinner. She pushed her plate away and stood. "Truce over. We are *not* going to be friends." Delia fumbled with the clasp of her bag, her fingers trembling with rage.

"I didn't want to be your friend anyway. I was just figuring out how to make you my number eight."

Delia hurled his shirt at him, feeling a degree of satisfaction when it landed in his food. "Don't speak to me again," she hissed, then stomped from the room. The horridness of the day swirled around her like a riptide. She needed to get out of her wet bathing suit and into something clean. Growling at the necessity, she turned toward the laundry room. She gave everyone she passed a challenging stare, welcoming the confrontation. She needed a release: violence or digging in the soil would do. Since it was cold and dark outside, she might have to make do with the former. Her fists tightened, straining the blood from her knuckles. *Who could I hit and not get dungeon time?* Bul would let her, but Rubi wouldn't like it. Nap would have let her, she thought, then fought a wave of homesickness that stole her breath.

Inside the laundry, steady drips from newly drying clothes seemed too loud as she weaved between vats and drying racks searching for the abandoned clothes bin Nelson had mentioned. She finally found it beneath a rotting wooden desk. The bin was labeled "Unclaimed," and it was quickly evident why no one had bothered to claim them. Delia had always preferred comfortable clothes over fashionable ones, but the bin seemed to hold neither. She sorted through all sorts of scratchy fabrics, unpleasant patterns, and ruined clothing. Near the bottom, she found brown overalls and a stained white shirt. Snatching them out, she sniffed them suspiciously, then held the clothing against her for size. They were too large, but she could make them work. Yanking her dirty clothing out of her bag, she replaced it with her new findings. Then she tackled her dirty pants and shirt, scrubbing furiously until thoughts of violence waned. Finished, she strode through the castle, her wet clothes flung over her arm, evidence of her open defiance of Phasia and her minions.

In the clerk's office, Malan started, and quickly hid a partially completed sketch of a woman's face beneath his record book.

"Is that Psyche?" she asked.

Malan colored. "Yeah. Birthday present." He cleared his throat. "Sorry Phasia got to your clothes. She has to stay in the dungeon until she repairs all of them."

Delia thought of the shredded pile on Ria's floor. "I don't think they're repairable; she was thorough."

"Then she'll be there a while."

Delia waited for a sense of satisfaction or sated rage to fill her, but she just felt numb. She simply wanted her clothes back. "Any chance they'll stop taking my mattress now? Or let me use the laundry?"

Malan shook his head. "The new laundry mistress is Phasia's friend."

Delia's shoulders sagged.

"But I know room 408 will be empty until morning."

Delia sighed. "Thanks, Malan." She gave him a weak smile and left. She stopped at Pearl's room, but her sister wasn't there. Delia searched her sister's strung out belongings until she found a needle and thread. Flinging her wet clothes over Pearl's table, she sat and sewed the buttons back onto her brown pants. Everywhere a pocket had been torn away, the material was darker, making the pants look strange. Delia thought of the torn pockets likely sitting in Phasia's dungeon cell and wondered what she would attach them to. The horrors that woman would likely create from the vestiges of her wardrobe were not something she wanted to see. Shaking her head, Delia finished her task, collected her wet clothing, and went to Coli's room in hopes of borrowing a nightgown. When Coli didn't answer, Delia leaned her head against the door and briefly considered theft.

"She's in the dance hall."

Delia looked over to see Cam just down the hall, standing outside his door.

"Can I ask something weird?" she blurted.

He chuckled, his twin dimples making her stomach flutter. "Sure."

"Can I borrow a shirt to sleep in?" The words sounded so much worse out loud than they had in her head. Flushing, she started to walk away. "Forget I said that."

"It's not a problem. Let me grab one." Cam entered his room, and Delia fought the urge to run. Heat spilled down her neck and tipped her ears bright red. When he reemerged and started walking toward her, she found herself stuttering.

"I-I didn't want to sleep in someone else's bed naked." *Oh no, what just came out of my mouth?!* "Not that anyone else would be there; I don't even know whose room it is. I sleep someplace new every night." *Not better! Stop talking!*

"Did someone take your mattress again?" Cam asked, his forehead wrinkled in concern as he handed her a beige shirt.

"They took my bed frame, too. There's nothing in my room." Delia felt something warm on her cheek and reached up to brush it away, smearing the moisture. *I'm crying?!* She swiped furiously at her cheeks and tried to will the lump in her throat away. "But at least I have room for my boots in my bag now, because the laundry mistress ripped up most of my clothes." Delia's voice broke on the last word and she cleared her throat in a vain attempt to hide it.

"Do you want a hug?" he asked, holding his arms out.

She wanted to tell him no, her lips even formed the word as she found herself stepping into his hug. The comfort was so immediate that it proved her undoing. She sobbed into his shirt, clutching at him like he was a life raft with one hand and holding her wet clothes away from him with the other.

"How can I help?" he asked when her sobs quieted to sniffles.

Delia let out a feeble laugh as she pulled away and mopped at her face. "I'm fine."

"It's not a weakness to admit when you need help. You helped me when I needed it. I owe you."

Another feeble laugh that sounded too much like a sob broke from her. "You found me a mattress, got me shoes, a beautiful spade, and you even let me sleep in your bed when you must have been exhausted. You can't possibly owe me."

One dimple appeared as he gave her half a smile. "You helped me be happy again; I'll owe you forever."

The stupid tears were back. Delia shook her head and turned away from him. Her time on the mountain had felt like an unmitigated disaster. Had she really done something good? "Sorry," she said, "I'm just a mess tonight."

"I'm making a trip to town again soon. Want me to buy you some child-size clothing?"

Delia gave him a watery smile for his teasing. "I don't have any money left."

"If you take a load of mail down or agree to bring mail or supplies back, the governor's head officiant, Erynnis, pays you. It's not a lot, but enough to buy a few things."

"I'm still a life servant; I can't leave."

"Hmm, I forgot about that. That's probably why I never see you."

Or you're too busy being adored by your girlfriend, she thought, but merely nodded. "Thank you again for the shirt, and letting me fall apart on you." She gestured at his chest, noticing the wet spots there with chagrin. "Sorry about that."

He looked down and brushed at the spots. "Don't worry about it. And you can keep the shirt."

Delia's lip trembled, the horrid tears clogging her throat again. Nodding her thanks, she hurried away. She found room 408, then walked past it twice, waiting for the hallway to empty. When the couple a few doors down finally stopped kissing and said their goodnights, she slipped inside. The untidy room smelled like goat milk, but the sheets looked relatively clean. She draped her wet clothing over the table, undressed, hung her suit on an empty hook to dry, and then changed into Cam's shirt. Crying had made her eyes feel grainy, and she took long blinks while she moved the bed to barricade the door. Sinking onto the lumpy mattress, she tucked her nose into the sleeve of Cam's oceanspray-scented shirt and immediately fell asleep.

Chapter Fifteen

The next morning felt infused with new hope despite the goat milk smell that had leached into her drying clothing. She quickly packed up her belongings, moved the bed, and abandoned her borrowed room. The halls were filled with drowsy girls sleepwalking toward the infirmary, and Delia felt wicked delight in avoiding the compulsory pregnancy tests. She stashed her still-drying clothes in Pearl's room, hoping her sister wouldn't be irritated. Then, she grabbed a life-servant breakfast of odd-smelling porridge and ate by herself in the in-season dining room. When she finished, she burst outside just as the sunlight was beginning to pierce the forest trees. Singing to herself, she traipsed through the forest finding ground routes to medicinal plants for her coming training sessions with Neva and Zelic. After a forest lunch, she took to the air, scouting new areas of the mountain for transplants. The brown of her overalls was too light to match the rich, volcanic soil, but they were easy to move in, and only dragged like sails when she flew fast. Her resulting meandering speed returned her to the castle just before dark. A few couples lingered in the courtyard, the mild chill of the evening only drawing them closer together. Delia recognized Cam, the adoring brunette glued to his side. He looked up as Delia flew past. She gave him a self-conscious wave that he returned, then she darted into the castle. Caena glared at her when she entered the infirmary, so Delia catalogued her few finds quickly and placed them in the unlocked cabinet, then left without saying a word. In the clerk's office, Malan was sketching again, but hid it more fluidly this time.

"No arrests today," he announced regretfully.

Delia sighed. "Could we just pretend I'm a new arrival, make up a name, and give me a new room?"

"Not without me going to the dungeon again when they find out."

Delia grimaced.

"But there is a groundswell of pity for you now that everyone knows Phasia destroyed your clothes."

"I don't want to be pitied."

Malan shrugged. "It's better than being hated."

Delia frowned. "I just need to know where to find Kip the gardener."

"You have plants for him?"

Delia nodded.

Malan glanced at an ancient watch with a cracked face. "He's probably in his bath."

"And where is that?"

Malan colored. "Oh, you can't go there. It's the men's hours at the life-servant pool, and not many of them have bathing suits."

Delia's sudden blush matched his own. "Could you tell me where the growing room is, then?"

"That I can do." Malan held out a hand for her map.

Delia took it out of her bag, brushed off a few flecks of soil, and unfolded it.

Malan reached over the desk to take it from her hand and marked a blank edge of her map, deep within the castle. "We don't map out the life-servant areas," he explained. "It's easier to keep the in-seasons out of places they don't know exist. And if the growing room is locked, you can leave the plants in Kip's room." Malan wrote 230 on her map. "But he might lose his temper if you do that; Kip's a little funny about plants."

Delia smirked as she took back the map. "I noticed that. Thanks, Malan."

Each time Delia looked up from her map on the way to the growing room, she noticed people looking at her, but not with the vague or marked hostility that she had come to expect. The men seemed to fall into the curious or disapproving category, but nearly all the women gave her pitying looks of solidarity that only increased as their eyes traveled down her dirty overalls. Delia looked down self-consciously. Her pant legs from the knees to the hem were muddy, and quickly stiffening as they dried. She looked like what she was: a migrant day-laborer who had not been paid. She met a few gazes and recognized the suppressed horror there; she was living their nightmares. Delia chuckled to herself. *This* wasn't the miserable part. Coming home dirty with a few rare finds was always satisfying. Being hated, persecuted, and feared was what she found difficult to bear. For a moment, Delia squinted her eyes and imagined all the people gone. The castle seemed peaceful, almost welcoming. Living here wouldn't be so bad. It was the *people* that made her suffer. Delia slowed as she entered the life-servant section of the castle; there were fewer people, but much more disapproval. She found the growing room door and tried the handle, but it was locked.

"What are *you* doing here? This area is for *real* life servants, not the temporary ones."

Delia turned to see a stout, white-winged woman with meaty fists pressed into her ample hips. "I'm doing my *job*."

The woman harrumphed. "I know what you did to Phasia, and I won't let you do it to anyone else."

Delia's hands closed into fists as her eyes narrowed. "What is it you think I'm going to do? Stand there while someone tears up the rest of my clothes? Fly away when they try to break my wings?"

"You know what you did!" The woman enunciated each word, leaning further forward as she did so.

Delia glared up at the woman as she bent over her menacingly. *Why does everyone have to be taller than I am?* "Yes, *I* do. And clearly *you* don't. So get out of my way before I have to tell the governor that his pain-relieving plants died while some delusional woman threatened me."

"I am not delusional!" The woman's mouth pinched together in an angry circle, then spewed a blob of spittle onto Delia's cheek.

"You *spat* on me?!" Delia wiped her arm across her face, leaving a smear of dirt. Outrage summoned a truth bomb to the tip of her tongue. "You're too repellent and gullible to have any real friends..." she began.

"What did you say?!" the woman interrupted.

"Margi, do you really want to join Phasia in the dungeon?" Startled, both women turned to look at the unexpected speaker. Beck warily approached Margi, a pained expression on his face.

"*Me*?! She's the monster standing here threatening and insulting me!"

Beck sighed loudly as he stepped between them, facing Margi. "Apologize so I don't have to report you."

"*She* should be in the dungeon," Margi yelled, trying to step around Beck.

Beck groaned as he grabbed Margi's arm. "You know you can't spit on people, no matter *what* they say to you." He gave Delia a pointed look as he pulled Margi away.

"You didn't see me spit on her! I made sure no one was looking!"

Delia snorted, tempted to yell the rest of her truth bomb at the foolish woman's back. But one look at the faces of the life servants that had quietly clustered around her changed her mind. She stepped forward slowly, giving them the opportunity to move out of her way. With a few head shakes and muttering, they finally cleared a path, then followed her to Kip's door.

"Are we having a parade?" Delia asked sarcastically as she raised her hand to knock.

"You're looking for me?" Kip called from the back of the crowd, which parted and slowly dispersed as he moved forward, hair and wings dripping on his dry clothes. "You have more plants?"

Delia nodded and unlatched her bag, lifting out three more transplants for the garden.

"Wait, don't tell me!" Kip took the plants eagerly, sniffed them, and petted the leaves. "Is this a mint?" he asked, pointing to a plant with variegated leaves.

"Lemon balm. Likes sunny spots, and it will spread."

Kip sniffed it again. "I *can* smell the lemon," he said, then pointed to a prickly plant with budded yellow flowers. "Is this holly?"

Delia nodded. "Holly grape. It grows everywhere around here, but I didn't know what would still be accessible in the snow."

Kip shivered as if reliving the winter. "We have a covered garden if it will grow in the shade."

"It will," Delia assured him.

Kip touched the barbs that rounded each leaf and winced before focusing on the third plant. "This looks like a weed," he said as he patted a green mat with white-petaled flowers

"It's chickweed, and it likes to spread, but not as bad as the lemon balm."

"And where will I put you two so you don't crowd the others?" Kip asked the plants as he happily walked away.

Delia smiled after him until the weight of unfriendly stares reminded her where she was. With a little jump, she flew out of the corridor, grateful to have a swift means of escape. She kept going until she landed at Pearl's door. When she knocked, her sister opened the door and gave her a brief hug, then invited her inside.

"I can't believe she tore up your clothes in front of you. I think I would have thrown a chair at her head."

"I didn't want to end up in the dungeon; I can't even get down the stairs without gagging. And besides, Phasia's twice my size and she already tried to break my wings once."

Pearl blew out an angry breath. "I'd rather keep my clothes and go to the dungeon for a day or two, but I'm much tougher than you are."

Delia recognized the usual bait and rolled her eyes, but let her sister continue uninterrupted.

"The clothes you left are dry, and you can have my yellow shirt. Coli has a nightgown and a dress for you. She said she'd leave them on her bed, because she'll probably be out with Mel."

"Who's Mel?"

"You haven't talked to her in a while?"

Delia shook her head.

"You two should talk. I don't think she's mad at you anymore. Mel— her new boyfriend— is hilarious; even I laugh. Oh, and Talis and Ria got married."

Married? Delia fought and failed to keep her face blank. *Did the bribed officiant actually marry them?*

Pearl's brow furrowed. "They didn't tell you? Coli only knows because he left her a note. You're not sad about it, are you? Not after he tried to blackmail you?"

Yes. "No. He's Ria's problem now."

"Good. Dina can help keep him in line."

Delia snorted. "I hadn't thought of that. They're going to fight."

"You shouldn't enjoy that thought," Pearl scolded her as she handed her the clothes. "And just so you know, I have a boyfriend now, too."

Delia's eyebrows shot up. "The guy with the brown wings you were dancing with?"

The smug smile was back. "Probably."

"What's his name?"

"Zaret. We're going to dance again tonight if you want to meet him."

Delia held up a dirty hand. "I need to wash, and then I should get to bed. I have work early tomorrow."

Pearl frowned. "I'm still mad you're doing that."

"You make it sound like I'm doing it for fun."

"Because it *is* fun for you! You're always happy out digging."

"Unfortunately, that's only part of it. I get back, and the life servants spit on my face, rip up my clothes, and take my bed."

Pearl's face wrinkled in disgust. "Someone spat on you?"

Delia pointed at her cheek. "Right here. Just minutes ago. Still think I'm having fun?"

"You should go wash," Pearl conceded. "You can meet Zaret later."

"Thanks for the shirt," Delia said, and stepped into the hallway.

"And Delia?"

Delia turned around.

Pearl gave her a wry smile. "Wait a few days before you infuriate another life servant."

She's teasing. Calm down, Delia told herself as a wash of fury spread through her. "Yes, because all of their decisions are my fault," she snapped sarcastically.

"Hey, I just gave you my shirt. I'm entitled to a little brattiness."

Delia clutched her sister's shirt, trying to resist the urge to throw it back at her. "If you're feeling humorous, maybe you've reached the end of your season."

Pearl's eyes widened, then narrowed. "That was mean."

"Better to infuriate you than a life servant, right?" Delia gave her sister a false smile and walked away. She had only taken a few steps before her guilt smote her and she turned around. Pearl was standing in the hallway watching her.

"I'm sorry," Delia said, her voice still irritable, though the words were sincere.

"You think my season is ending?"

Delia shrugged. "You hugged me and your voice sounds more like normal."

Pearl flew down the hallway past her sister. "Then I'm getting married tonight. Go wash fast!"

"Doesn't that decision involve *two* people?" Delia called after her, but her sister didn't stop to answer. Pearl's urgency was contagious, and Delia flew to Coli's room instead of walking. When Coli didn't answer her knock, she opened the door and was pleased to see the nightgown and dress waiting for her on Coli's bed. Rather than take it with her, Delia changed into her bathing suit and left her belongings there, then flew to the pool.

When she stepped inside the pool room, cheerful shouts of "Thistle!" came from the far side. Bul and Ruby waved her over, and Rus nodded. Cia's grip on Rus' bicep tightened, her face lit with smug malice. Sal glowered, then turned his back on her. Delia gave them all a quick shake of her head, her mouth tightening into a grimace that was meant to be a smile. Wading in, she washed quickly, scrubbing her cheek until it was red. Then she dunked her head, letting the slowly moving water cleanse away her irritation along with the grime. When she stood up, a man her own height with a broad nose grinned at her.

"Hi! Thistle, is it? I'm Malachi. My friends and I are going to visit a lake tomorrow and I wondered if you wanted to come. They'll be other girls there, so you don't have to feel uncomfortable. You could come meet them right now if you like." He turned to the side to indicate a group of people watching eagerly.

Delia resisted the urge to snort. "I have to work tomorrow."

"Oh, I get it." His pale green wings lined with brown drooped. "Sorry to bother you."

"No," Delia grabbed his arm, belatedly wondering why she was doing so. "The governor made me a temporary life servant as a punishment. I really do have to work tomorrow."

"Oh. I'm sorry."

"And my name isn't Thistle. That's just a rude nickname someone gave me because he finds my in-season personality abrasive."

"Ohh. I'm sorry. What is your name?"

"Delia. Delia *White.*" *Why are you still holding his arm? Let go!* Delia forced herself to let go of him. He had a soothing smell, like chamomile.

He laughed nervously, the sound slightly grating, and ran a hand over his dark curls. "Could we start again? That didn't go very well."

286

"It went fine, but I have to go. My sister thinks she's getting married tonight." She wanted to touch him again, but she made her hands stay at her sides as she turned and walked away. *What's the matter with me? He's not even attractive,* she argued with herself. *His wings are attractive,* she amended, surreptitiously sniffing her hand to see if the chamomile scent remained. Disappointed she could only smell her own soap, she glanced back at him. He had turned and was wading back to his friends; the green panels on the backside of his wings were the fluorescent color of seedlings edged in black— like rich soil. She found herself smiling as she hurried back to Coli's room. Her cursory knock brought an unexpected answer.

"I'm changing! Just a minute!" Coli hollered through the door.

Delia stood there for a full minute, dripping, then knocked again.

"Don't be impatient!" Coli snapped.

Delia's mouth twitched. "You know you're not going to be ready soon. Just let me in so I can get dressed, too."

"Oh, Delia!" The door opened and a half-dressed Coli waved her in, then quickly shut the door. "Pearl is losing her mind. You have her convinced that she's going to become a life servant any second, and she's probably already in the governor's office telling the officiant to start without us."

Delia was just pulling on her brown pants with the missing pockets when Coli tossed a white dress at her.

"Wear that instead. I'm giving it to you, anyway."

"Why does it matter?" Delia complained as she complied. "Why are you even changing; weren't you in the ballroom?"

"It matters because it might be the last time we see Pearl, and I was completely sweaty, but each new thing I put on gets sweat on it, then I have to change again!"

Delia straightened her new dress and put a hand on Coli's shoulder. "As long as we don't look or smell dirty, she won't care."

Coli frowned. "I know that."

"Then what's really the matter?"

Coli blushed. "Mel's coming. He's my new boyfriend, and I really like him, and I want him to be there with me, and thinking about marrying me...so I need to look perfect."

Delia hid a grin. "You always look perfect."

"I do not! Just look at this! I sweated through the left arm already!"

"Then just keep that arm down."

"We're going dancing after," Coli whined.

"Then he'll be expecting you to sweat."

"But not before we even start dancing!"

Delia hid her mirth with a cough, then grabbed her friend's arm. "Come on. You look great."

Coli resisted a few steps, then allowed herself to be dragged from the room.

"Where's the governor's office?" Delia asked.

The question pulled Coli out of her sulk. "This way." Coli began to fly with Delia hurrying along beside her, her wings too wet to get off the ground. Coli looked back and landed. "Sorry, I forgot your wings were wet."

"Tell me about Zaret. Did Pearl really just tell him to marry her and he agreed?"

Coli chuckled. "Probably. He's liked her since she first arrived, but Pearl only wanted to be friends. A few days ago he got a girlfriend. Pearl got jealous and realized she *did* like him, so she made him break up with his girlfriend, and they've been together ever since."

Delia snorted. "Where is he from?"

"Only a half day's trip down the coast from home."

"That's perfect."

Coli nodded. "I know. I wish Mel lived closer to home. It's the only thing wrong with him. Otherwise, he's the best person I've ever met." She stopped outside a grand set of doors and knocked.

One of the doors opened a crack, the prominent-nosed guard from the governor's room asking what they wanted in his rumbling voice.

"Pearl White's wedding."

The nose withdrew, and the door swung wide enough for them to pass.

Inside, Pearl stood next to a ginger-haired man whose brown wings looked just like two crunchy autumn leaves. Coli looked around the room, her disappointment evident. "Mel should be here," she whispered.

"Finally!" Pearl turned to snap in the young officiant's face. "Start now," she commanded.

The officiant's expression became mulish, but Zaret smiled and whispered something to him that made his expression soften. Pearl rolled her eyes, but leaned closer to Zaret, her arm tucked in his.

"He handles her perfectly," Coli whispered. "He seems to find all her bossiness charming and always manages to smooth over difficulties she has with others. He's been doing that the whole time she's been here, even though they weren't together until recently."

Pearl turned to glare at them and Coli pressed her lips together.

The officiant was hefting a large open book. "I know you already told me your names and I wrote them here, but I'm supposed to ask you as part of the ceremony," he explained, then hesitated to squint at his own handwriting. "Are you Zaret Leafwing of Tidewater?"

"Yes." Zaret smiled as he looked down at Pearl's hand on his arm and covered it with his own.

"And are you Pearl White of Hamlet?"

"Yes," Pearl answered, her tone only a little frightening.

"Please come forward."

Pearl tipped her head irritably to indicate they were close enough.

"I'm supposed to say that, too," the now flustered officiant explained. "Do you, Zaret, of your own free will and choice seal this woman to you for life, and if it be God's will, for eternity?"

Zaret's broad smile lifted his ears. "I do."

"Do you, Pearl, of your own free will and choice seal this man to you for life, and if it be God's will, for eternity?"

Pearl's grip on Zaret's arm tightened. "I do."

"Then by the authority given me by our governor, who has his authority from King Danaus IV, before God and man, I pronounce you sealed together as husband and wife for life, and God willing, for eternity." The officiant turned the heavy book in his arms, momentarily losing his grip on it until Zaret helped him regain it. "Please sign the book," he said, then looked around with alarm.

Pearl's head tipped back and she let out a sigh. "You left it on the throne."

Coli squelched a giggle as the officiant fetched his writing instrument, his face red and dotted with perspiration as he handed it to Zaret. They were all silent while it scratched across the paper. After Pearl signed, the officiant handed her the marriage certificate and took possession of the book.

"Congratulations," the officiant said, and wrestled the book closed, the fancy metal writing instrument hitting the floor with a clang. "Um, it's time for you to go."

One of the guards unfastened the bolt on the balcony doors and pulled them open. The chill night air drifted in with the sound of crickets. The couple turned toward their guests, Pearl giving them both a swift, but intense hug while Zaret held his hand out with a smile.

"You must be Delia," he said as he shook her hand, his palm soft against her calluses.

Pearl looked at him with pride, then pulled him toward the balcony. Before they flew, Pearl looked back at them. "Write me letters," she ordered. "Both of you." Her severe expression slipped into a giddy grin as they leapt into the air.

"You really think her season is ending?" Coli asked as they shuffled through the door the guard was holding open.

Delia shrugged, her happiness for her sister tinged with a sense of loss.

In the hallway, Coli launched herself into the arms of a portly man making his beige wings flap to regain his balance. "Mel! Why didn't you come in for the wedding?"

"How can you ask that?" he teased. "Did you not see my dazzling appearance?" He stood straighter, sucking in his gut as he tossed his straight, brown hair. "This beauty takes time."

Coli threw back her head and laughed, then kissed him on the forehead, his shorter height evident as they stood side by side. "Delia, this is Mel."

"I feel like I'm in the presence of a legend," Mel joked. "You are the talk of the castle and the favorite topic of my lady love. It's an honor to meet you." He bowed facetiously rather than shake her hand.

Delia glanced at Coli's eager face and tried to hide her irritation. "Thanks?"

"You should come dancing with us, so you can see this woman's angelic grace," Mel rhapsodized as he danced a giggling Coli around the hallway.

"I have to work in the morning."

Coli stopped dancing and frowned at her. "You should come for just a little while. It's not very late."

"I hate it there. And I don't know where I'm sleeping tonight."

Coli stepped away from Mel and took Delia aside. "I'm worried about you. You're not socializing. Come meet Mel's brothers; I think you'll like them."

Not likely, since I don't like Mel. "I don't really have time for that."

Coli sighed. "You have to *make* time for it or you'll be keeping my brother company for the rest of your life."

Delia knew Coli meant Ora, but her traitorous brain revisited her time with Talis instead.

"Delia, I'm serious. Let me help you find a boyfriend while I'm still here."

"You're *leaving*?!" Mel looked farcically shocked.

Coli shook her head, rolled her eyes, and continued her appeal to Delia. "You need someone around from home that can tell people how wonderful you are." Sensing Delia's waning resistance, Coli tugged on her arm. "Come on. Just meet Mel's brothers and dance a few songs."

"Wet wings," Delia reminded her.

Coli towed Delia down the hallway while Mel tagged behind them. "You can floor dance or choose someone with huge wings and he can fly for both of you."

Mel snorted, and Coli shot him a quelling look.

Delia looked down at the white, woolen dress that fell below her knees. "Won't that give the spectators below an uncomfortable view?"

"Yes!" Mel blurted. "Which is why she gave it to you."

Coli turned to swat at him, and he chortled as he dodged her. When she turned back to Delia, she took up her friend's arm again with a sigh. "Just keep your legs together, and *no one* will see anything."

Mel skipped to Delia's other side, shaking his head vigorously.

"Fine," Coli said, pretending to be irritated, despite the chuckles that kept breaking through. "Just floor dance, then."

Mel switched to absurdly enthusiastic nodding and Coli laughed.

"You'll probably like Mel's brother Tyro the best because he's pretty, but Ryd is nicer."

"I don't know if I should be more offended that you noticed my brother's beauty or that you think he's not that nice."

Coli released Delia's arm to comfort Mel in his feigned sulk. "You know I prefer your darker coloring, and you have to admit Tyro is a bit..." Coli hesitated.

Mel clapped his hands over his ears. "Don't say it! If you impugn my brother, how shall I marry you?"

Coli stopped mid-step and mid-giggle. "He proposed!" she crowed to Delia. "Oh! It's official! I shall be a bride!" Coli danced around in a display of silliness that baffled Delia. It was obvious she was teasing Mel, but Delia couldn't fathom why she felt comfortable doing so.

Mel's face was red, but he recovered himself enough to play along. "Tis true! A mere slip of the tongue and I am engaged!"

"And now you shall never be free of me!" Coli agreed as she embraced him. "Should we return to the governor's office now?"

Mel sucked in a breath and swallowed before he could speak. "After we promised Delia an evening of entertainment? Surely we could not be so rude."

Coli nodded. "You're quite right. Manners before marriage, certainly." She took Delia's arm again and pulled her along.

"What was *that*?" Delia whispered as Mel lagged behind.

Coli shrugged, then whispered back: "Marriage scares him; maybe if we joke about it, he'll get used to the idea."

Delia snuck a look at Mel. His eyes were wide and he stumbled as he walked. *He's more likable when he's too confounded to put on a show*, she decided. "I don't think he's used to it yet."

"I don't have time for subtlety. He's the one I want."

Delia's eyebrows climbed her forehead. "How long have you known him?"

Coli shook her head. "It doesn't matter. I've made up my mind."

Delia snorted. "Then I guess it's happening. Happy unofficial engagement."

"Thank you. I knew you'd understand."

The cacophony of the ballroom enveloped them, making whispered discussions impossible. Delia resisted lifting her hands to her ears with difficulty, knowing Coli wouldn't allow it. Instead, she tightened her jaw, making the blood rush past her ears and dampen the sound. The commingling scents of the dance floor varied from pleasant to nauseating in the space of a few steps, and Delia began breathing through her mouth to avoid the latter. Coli had spotted her quarry, and led Delia through the tangle and crush of people with practiced skill. Polite touches followed by her brilliant smiles and words of pardon seemed to part the sea of bodies and wings that clogged the floor of the ballroom. Delia tried to imitate her, but her false smiles seemed to cause alarm rather than accommodation. Resigned, she let Coli continue to tow her until they stood alongside the eclectic band, their out-of-tune and makeshift instruments wailing to be put out of their misery. Delia's hands were halfway to her ears when Coli turned to her and shouted.

"Delia, this is Tyro and Ryd."

Delia dropped her hands and nodded, pinching her mouth into a semblance of a smile. Ryd looked just like Mel, his second chin showing when he smiled. Tyro's eyes were absurdly blue, and he lifted his dark brows as Delia stared at him. He said something she couldn't hear, then offered her his hand.

Coli and Ryd chuckled as if Tyro had said something amusing, and Delia gave Coli a questioning glance. Coli nodded toward his proffered hand, and Delia took it. Tyro was taller than his brothers, but still only medium height. He pulled her closer and shouted something about the hallway in her ear. Delia nodded, then allowed herself to be pulled back across the crowded room.

In the hallway, he released her hand and turned to face her. "So, what's Coli been saying about me?"

That you're not as nice as your brothers. "Not much."

"Come on, you can tell me," he coaxed, leaning closer and running a hand down her arm.

"Were we going to dance or something?"

Tyro chuckled. "Look, I don't want to insult you, but I'm not interested."

"Then why did you bring me out here?" Delia demanded.

"So I could find out what Coli thinks of me. You *are* her best friend, right?"

"You are her *boyfriend's* brother, right?"

Tyro shook his head. "She's not serious about Mel; how could she be? This is just a game. Tell her it's working; I want her."

"I think I'll go tell Coli *and Mel* right now," Delia threatened, and turned to go back into the ballroom.

Tyro pulled her back. "Mel knows he's just a placeholder for me. He's seen how she flirts with me. He's not stupid enough to think a tall, beautiful blonde with a big inheritance wants *him*."

Delia yanked her arm away. "Then I'll just have to convince him otherwise."

Tyro tried to grasp her arm again, but missed as she darted into the crowd. "Hey, stay out of it; this isn't your business," he called after her.

Delia closed her wings tightly, but kept her arms out to knock anyone out of the way that got near her. Scents assaulted her nose in a sickening blend that reminded her of a compost heap contaminated with meat. Once again breathing through her mouth, she returned to Coli and Ryd.

"Where's Tyro?" Coli asked. Delia couldn't hear her words in the continuing cacophony, but read her lips.

"We need to talk," Delia yelled.

"You need to *dance*," Coli yelled back.

Delia grabbed her friend's arm and yanked her away from the band.

"Tyro wants you and your 'big inheritance.' I think he's convinced Mel that you're only toying with him so you can get Tyro," Delia bellowed.

Coli blanched, then her face tightened with fury. "*That's* the problem?! I'm going to kill Tyro."

"Don't give him the satisfaction. He'll probably like it anyway," Delia shouted.

"I have to find Mel!"

Delia nodded as Coli plunged into the crowd. Delia picked her way along the periphery, ears covered. One man tried to talk to her, but she merely shook her head. One woman backed into Delia's elbow, knocking her against the wall.

"Oh! Sorry!" the woman shouted. "Are you all right?"

Delia turned to glare at the woman and recognized Cam's girlfriend with an unfamiliar man's arms around her. *That's not Cam.* Forgetting to breathe through her mouth, Delia sucked in cilantro-scented air.

"I think she's okay," the man said, his hands shifting possessively at the woman's waist as he nuzzled her hair. Delia's eyes followed the movement, then shot an accusatory glance at the cheerful brunette.

"You *are* okay?" Cam's girlfriend asked, concern darkening her pale blue eyes.

Rubbing her bruised elbow, Delia nodded and moved forward. She emerged from the ballroom, dodged the conversationalists clogging the mouth of the room, and sped up the stairs, then down the hall, wet wings bouncing painfully with the movement. At Cam's door, she hesitated, composing and discarding conversations. *She's cheating on you! Unless she has an identical sister.* Delia frowned. She hadn't considered that. *That is the most logical conclusion.* Disheartened, Delia sagged against his door. She envied Coli her certainty. Coli's words *he's the one that I want* repeated in her head. "You're the one that I *like*," she whispered, then dragged herself away. At Coli's door, she knocked before entering, then collected her belongings along with Coli's donated nightgown. On her way to Pearl's room, she stopped by Cam's room again. With his borrowed shirt in hand, she knocked at his door. She didn't want to give it back, but she needed a pretext. She took one last sniff of the shirt, then straightened her arm as the door opened. Cam stood there shirtless, rubbing the sleep from his eyes, and Delia's carefully composed speech disintegrated. She held out his shirt mutely, her eyes riveted to his chest.

Laughing, he took the shirt and put it on. "I thought this was my gift to you?"

Delia's eyes found his face and she flushed scarlet. "Thank you."

"Do you want it back, then?" Cam asked, lifting the bottom of the shirt to expose his chiseled abs. When she didn't respond, he dropped the shirt hem.

Delia shook her head to dislodge the image. "I'm sorry. Did you say something?"

Cam chuckled. "Was there something else you wanted? Or did you just come by to give my shirt back?"

"Oh. I didn't wash it; do you want me to wash it?"

Cam sniffed at his shoulder. "No, it's fine."

"I..um, have a weird question for you...does your girlfriend have an identical sister?"

Cam gave her a bemused smile. "Holly? Yeah, she has an identical twin."

"Oh. That must be who I saw, then." Deflated, Delia turned away. "Sorry to wake you up."

"You *saw* her? Where?"

Delia turned back. "The ballroom just now."

Cam shook his head. "That had to be Holly. Her sister just gave birth to sextuplets." His brow furrowed and he bit his lip. "Are you sure it was her?"

"I think so."

Frowning, Cam went back into his room, then returned wearing shoes. He managed a grim smile and nod before he marched toward the ballroom, wearing his suspicions like a cloud of grief.

Delia was sorely tempted to follow, but she doubted having a witness there would be comforting. She wondered at her previous eagerness to tell him of Holly's cheating—especially after the princess had cheated on him, too. Delia groaned. He was probably going to have trouble trusting women after this. She made her way to Pearl's room, alternately wishing there was some painless way of delivering bad news and fantasizing about comforting Cam. Her sister's room was blissfully untouched by vengeful life servants. Delia almost smiled as she wedged the bed against the door, then changed into Coli's nightgown. But when she crawled onto her sister's bed, her mind replayed her awkward conversation with Cam over and over until she felt thoroughly disgusted with herself. When sleep finally came, her dreams were angst-ridden with life servants who spat on her every time she said the wrong thing. She awoke groggily to the shaking of the bed. Someone was throwing their weight against the door, making the bed screech and shudder.

"Hey, this is my sister's room now. Whoever you are, you need to get out," a male voice said.

Swearing under her breath, Delia changed and packed up her belongings in the faint light of the lantern. The banging against the door had stopped, but she could hear a conversation just outside the door.

"The front desk guy said he'll send a guard, and just to wait here for him," a female voice said.

Flaming moth wings! Just go away so I can leave!

"You're exhausted. Go sleep in my room; I'll take care of this," the same male voice said.

"You're tired, too, Elis. And I don't want to carry my bag any more," she said, then laughed. "Are you sure there's actually a person in there? Maybe someone pulled the furniture to block the door with string or something."

298

"No, I can smell her and she was making noise while you were gone," Elis said.

"*Her?*"

"Can you smell anything?" Elis asked.

"No," she admitted.

"Then it's a girl."

A tentative knock sounded. "Hey, if you're scared or something, you can come out. We won't get you in trouble," Elis' sister said.

Elis huffed. "I will."

Hating her options, Delia pulled the bed out of the way and the door creaked open. A man blocked the doorway, his orange wings backlit from the hall.

"Can you see her?" the female voice whispered behind him.

"Yeah, she's even smaller than you." Elis took a step into the room. "It's okay. You can come out."

"I could if you both *moved*," Delia said, warily.

"Why were you blockaded in here?" Elis asked, taking a step closer.

"This was my sister's room. She got married last night. I didn't think they would reassign the room so quickly."

"Ooh, that makes sense," Elis' sister nodded, still blocking the doorway. She was only a little taller than Delia, but her dark brown and orange wings were open. "But don't you have your own room?"

"The life servants took all the furniture out of my room and ripped up most of my clothes."

Elis' sister gasped and clutched her bag to her chest. "And no one stopped them?"

Delia shook her head.

"So you don't even have a place to sleep?" Elis' sister asked.

"I just look for an empty room each night."

Elis' sister gasped again. "No wonder you barricaded yourself in. Elis, we have to help her."

Elis sighed. "Emi..."

"Her sister just left, Elis! There's no one to help her," Emi protested.

"If you want to help me, just let me go and don't describe me to the guard when he comes."

Emi stepped out of the doorway and into the room. "Of course."

"Thanks," Delia said. "And I don't recommend asking the laundresses for fresh sheets; that's how I got into this situation." Delia slipped out into the hallway, then groaned as she saw Beck walking toward her.

"I knew it," Beck crowed.

"Well, what do you expect? My room hasn't had a bed for days," Delia demanded irritably as she walked right past him.

Beck turned and kept pace with her. "I knew Phasia took a couple of mattresses out, but I didn't think anyone else was doing it."

"They took *all* of the furniture out of my room, Beck. It doesn't even have a bed frame. I have to find a new place to sleep *every* night. They even took the extra beds out of my friends' rooms. "

Beck looked perplexed. "I didn't realize they were doing that."

"And I didn't mean to be cruel to that woman last night, but after she *spat on my face*, I couldn't keep my mouth shut."

"I wouldn't have handled that well, either," he admitted. "I keep forgetting you're a white."

"How can you forget?! I'm constantly in trouble!"

"I was, too," Beck chuckled. "It's just that you're so colorful and you never seem like a genuine threat to anyone."

"Thank you?"

Beck chortled.

Delia stopped in front of the infirmary door. "So am I in trouble? Or can I go to work? I'm training Neva today."

Beck held up his hands. "No trouble. But check your room before you pilfer someone else's tonight," he advised as he walked away.

"Why?"

"Because there might just be a bed in there," Beck called over his shoulder.

"Thanks, Beck." Delia smiled grimly after him, then pulled open the infirmary door.

"You're late," Neva observed as she crossed to the door.

Caena gave Delia a catty smile, but Indra stayed hidden behind her book.

Delia stepped back to let Neva out. "Sorry. I had a problem."

"Let's not lose any more daylight," Neva urged as she increased her marching speed.

Delia hid her amusement. She doubted Neva was in any shape to hike for longer than a few hours, let alone the entire day. Then she glanced down at Neva's footwear and reconsidered; her boots were practical and had evidently seen heavy use.

"I like to hike when I have a chance, but I don't have many," Neva explained when she noticed Delia's gaze. "Once you train me, maybe I'll have more opportunities."

As the day wore on, Neva's enthusiasm and energy didn't wane, despite the limp that showed up around lunch time that Neva assured her was nothing. An hour later, Neva found a walking stick and was able to keep going. When they exhausted all the plant sites that Delia had scouted, Neva asked her to identify every bit of flora on the way back. By late afternoon, Neva needed long breaks, but masked them by stopping to quiz herself on various plants Delia had already shown her. Though Neva had brought her own food, she delighted in Delia's meal foraging and wanted to taste everything Delia ate. It was the most animated Delia had seen the phlegmatic woman. When they returned to the castle just before dinner, Delia was a little sad to lose her company.

Forging on to the infirmary, she greeted Zelic and handed over the day's finds, carefully separating anything dangerous to the governor for Zelic to hide away. After she catalogued the new plants and answered Zelic's questions about them, she turned to go.

"Wait," Zelic requested. "I'm guessing Neva is too exhausted to finish her shift?"

"Probably. She didn't complain, but she was moving slowly and painfully by the time we got back."

Zelic nodded. "I need you to watch the clinic while I hide the new finds that I don't want Graci getting into."

"Fine."

"And I need you to come back in four hours so I can treat the governor again...unless you want to do it."

"No, thanks."

"As long as Graci is the governor's 'personal nurse,' we're short-staffed," Zelic explained.

Delia frowned. "That doesn't bode well for my punishment ending early, does it?"

Zelic grimaced. "No. We really need another medic." He gathered up half her findings and headed for the door. "But you're not training me until noon tomorrow, so you can sleep in." He stood awkwardly at the door until she opened it for him.

"Aren't you going to need help putting them away?" Delia called after him as he hurried down the hall, magnificent yellow and black wings bouncing.

"No," he shouted without turning around.

Delia shrugged, then headed for the sink to thoroughly wash her dirt-stained hands. Before she finished, the infirmary door opened. She turned to look, her hands still covered in soap.

"You!" Margi shouted, her frizzy gray hair contrasting with the red of her face. "You got me thrown in the dungeon just like Phasia! *You* should be in the dungeon; *we* didn't do anything wrong! You're the one that can't control herself! And I *do* have friends! And I'm *not* stupid!"

Delia rinsed her hands quickly, with her body twisted around so she could watch Margi. "How can I help you?" She meant the words to sound calm and professional, but they came out mildly threatening.

"I won't let you touch me! It's your fault my back hurts from that horrible dungeon mattress anyway!" Margi's words ended in a whimper, both hands now bracing her lower back. She was surprisingly chubby for a life servant, but her skin sagged as if she had recently lost weight.

Delia dried her hands, but kept her distance. "Zelic should be back soon."

"Good! Because I don't trust you!" Margi climbed on the nearest cot with her feet atop the pillow so she could watch Delia. "You hurt people!"

You spit on them! Delia congratulated herself for not saying the words out loud, then walked sideways to the office, never turning her back on Margi. She was probably being overly cautious, but the woman had such a desperate, unhinged air about her; Delia didn't want to give her the opportunity to graduate from spitting to wing breaking. Inside the office, she shut the door, then began to pick through the cupboard and then her bag for pain-relieving poultice ingredients. If Margi refused to use it, she would take it to Neva. When she began to grind the herbs with the mortar and pestle, Margi began shouting again. Sighing, Delia opened the door to check on her unwilling patient.

"What are you doing?! I can hear you making noises in there!"

Delia brought the mortar and pestle out with her, continuing to break down the plants with the scraping noise of rock against rock. Standing eight feet away, she tipped the mortar, so Margi could see what she was doing.

Appeased, Margi's alarm settled into a sulk. "We had one of those in the kitchen. Tera used it to make mint tea; but she wouldn't let me have any."

"Do you work in the kitchen?" Delia asked, hoping to calm her into chatter.

"Not any more. Tera kicked me off her staff." Margi's sulk quickly morphed back into anger. "She said I was eating too much when I cooked, but she's fatter than me! Now I work in the laundry, with my *friend*, Phasia."

Delia gritted her teeth to resist responding.

"And she is *never* going to fix your clothes. She just keeps ripping them into smaller and smaller pieces."

Words erupted through Delia's clenched jaw. "And *I'm* the awful person? She takes my mattresses, destroys my clothes, and tries to break my wings, but you still think *I'm* the one wronging *her*?"

Margi leapt off the cot, the pain making her gasp. "You know you attacked her! And you made her lose her job and got her put in the dungeon!"

Delia backed up, gripping the mortar like a weapon. "All I ever did was say rude things to her after she was incredibly rude to me. Just the same as I did after you spat on me. I can't make anyone lose their job or go to the dungeon. You and Phasia broke the rules and the governor and his guards imposed the consequences. You should be blaming yourselves."

Margi shook with rage as she advanced. "I am *not* sorry I helped Phasia take your mattresses or your furniture, and I am going to keep doing it! The governor may not punish you, but *I* will!"

Delia took another step backwards, her grip on the mortar tightening. "How can you think the governor hasn't punished me? I'm an in-season life servant! I'm only here listening to your absurd ranting because he *is* punishing me!"

A shrill whistle startled both women, and they turned to look at Zelic standing in the doorway.

"Why did you blow the whistle?! I didn't touch her," Margi shrieked. "I didn't even spit on her yet!"

Zelic shook his head, then held out his hand for the mortar. Leaving Margi a wide berth, Delia walked over and gave it to him while Margi continued her increasingly incoherent tirade. "Just go," he told Delia.

Delia looked down at the brownish mixture in the mortar. "It's a pain-relieving poultice; she has a backache from sleeping on a dungeon mattress."

Zelic sniffed it. "Willow bark?"

"And some valerian to help her sleep."

Zelic nodded, then pushed Delia through the still-open door as Margi advanced. "Margi, you stay here," Zelic insisted.

A guard Delia didn't recognize was coming down the hallway. He gave Delia a suspicious glance, but Margi's shrieks followed by a second whistle pulled his attention. He ran into the infirmary, white wings trailing behind him. Delia was tempted to stay and eavesdrop, but the frequency with which Margi kept repeating her name soon convinced her otherwise. She hurried to her room, holding her breath before she opened the door. Inside was a bed and mattress with bedding and a pillow. A gleeful noise of joy escaped her as she slipped inside. Behind the door, there was even a table and stool. She danced about the room as she changed into her bathing suit. She didn't quite dare to leave her belongings in her room, so she dropped her bag in Coli's empty room. Unable to resist, Delia walked slowly past Cam's door, straining to hear or smell anything from within the room, but was disappointed.

The lure of dinner had emptied the halls and the bathing pool. Delia luxuriated in her private bath, lingering even after she was done washing. A few blossoms and bits of plant detritus floated away from her on the subtle current. Her stomach growled softly, but without urgency. She had stopped too frequently to eat edible plants with Neva to be truly hungry for dinner. *Maybe I should do this every day.* The thought was delightful until she remembered *why* she was here. With a determined frown, she left the pool. It was time to get serious about finding a husband. Her resolve remained until the sight and sound of the complaining herd of in-seasons leaving the dining hall enveloped her. She moved with them up the stairwell, envying those who flew over her head. She needed to figure out how to wash without wetting her wings. A man with vivid yellow wings brushed against her, then looked down at his wet shirt sleeve with irritation. *You just failed Malan's test,* she thought. She could hear a conversation about what dinner ought to be, and another behind her about how Vic and Roy were heroes for beating up the governor. Delia looked back and met Dom's disapproving eyes while Skinner made a lewd comment about her body. Growling, she pushed between the people in front of her to get away from them.

"Hello again," a familiar voice said, followed by a trilling laugh.

Startled, Delia realized that she had inadvertently inserted herself between Emi and Elis. "Sorry," she apologized, "just trying to escape someone."

"I'm sensing that's a theme with you," Elis snarked, his boyish face contrasting oddly with his wry smile.

Emi laughed, then abruptly sobered. "Oh, that was rude, wasn't it? Maybe I shouldn't laugh at that." Her pretty face contracted while her large, brown eyes widened in alarm.

"It's fine. I guess it's true," Delia conceded. She glanced back again to assure herself that Dom and Skinner were no longer behind her.

"Did you find a place to sleep tonight?" Emi asked, then cringed as if immediately regretting her question.

"I think so. One of the guards put furniture back in my room. So as long as no one took it while I was bathing..."

Emi let out a sigh of relief. "Good! I have been so worried for you."

"That's kind of you."

Emi flashed her a radiant smile as she turned to go up another flight of stairs. "Oh! I guess we'll see you later."

Delia waved as she stepped out into the hallway. Emi returned her wave while Elis shot Delia a quizzical glance. He was attractive, but his wary look seemed more of a threat assessment than interest. *He probably found out I'm a white.* Shaking off that little irritation, Delia stopped at Cam's door, arguing with herself about knocking. In the quieter hallway, she could hear the steady drip from her wings, her hair, and her suit. Looking down, she sucked in a breath at the puddle forming beneath her shoes, then hurried down the hallway to Coli's room to change and retrieve her bag. She scanned the room for something she could use to dry the puddle, but short of applying dirty clothing, she didn't have an option. Which reminded her, tonight would have to be a washing night. Donning her brown pants with the missing pockets and Pearl's shirt, she returned to Cam's door and used her boots to disperse the water. The end result was worse than the puddle. A morass of child-size muddy footprints decorated the flagstones. Taking out her dirty clothes, she turned them inside out and knelt to mop up the mess she had made. She was almost finished when the door opened. A self-effacing joke was rolling off her tongue when she looked up to see Holly.

"Oh! Did you fall?" Holly asked.

"No..." Delia began, but Holly was already speaking.

"Cam, there's a girl on the floor outside your door."

Nooooo!

Delia jumped to her feet just as Cam joined Holly in the doorway.

"I just dropped something," Delia lied, waving her muddy clothing at them while her face flamed. "Well, bye." Delia hurried down the hall, mentally kicking herself. *Why am I so awkward around him?!* She berated herself all the way to the laundry, then tromped inside and flung her clothing into a soapy vat, ignoring the two people already there.

"Hi again! I took your advice about the laundry ladies, so I'm washing my travel clothes myself," Emi said, holding up her wet clothing over a steaming vat, her infectious smile beaming.

Elis glowered from a stool nearby. "They're not mad at *you*, Emi; they'll wash your clothes for you."

"Oh, hush. You're awfully grumpy for sleeping all day," Emi chided him.

"My room smells horrible. I had to sleep with the door open, and people kept walking by. 'Hahahaha, oh Rus, you're so funny, hahahahahha,'" he mocked, the unpleasant laugh sounding very much like Cia's.

Delia snorted. "Is your room on the third floor and has two beds?"

Elis nodded.

"Wes Swallowtail marked that room when the girl staying there turned him down."

"What does that mean? What is marking?" Emi asked.

"He released his pheromones over and over. Some guys use it to mark girls as their mates," Delia explained.

"No! Are you serious?" Emi asked, her dark eyes wide.

"Then they should make that Wes guy sleep in his stench. I'll take his room," Elis grumbled.

Delia smirked. "He's not a pleasant person."

"Obviously," Elis agreed.

"And he's twice your size," Delia added.

Elis frowned.

Emi trilled a laugh as she hung up her clothes. "So much for that plan."

"Can we go to the dance hall now?" Elis whined.

"I just need to figure out how I tag these as mine," Emi said, searching around the drying racks.

"Over there," Delia said, pointing to the shelf with paper and a pencil.

"Thank you," Emi said, humming as she crossed the room.

"So you're a white," Elis said quietly. "That's why you don't get along with the life servants."

Delia shook her head irritably. "Some of them are looking for a fight. They hate their lives; they feel punished, and they want to punish others."

"Is that how you feel?" he asked.

Delia scowled. "No."

"How *do* you feel?" His blue eyes bored into her, perceptive and judging.

"Annoyed by this conversation," Delia snapped.

The humming stopped. "What did I miss?" Emi asked.

Elis cleared his throat. "Nothing."

Emi walked over, her eyes bouncing between them. "Do you two want to have a private conversation? Because I can go."

"No," Elis said, jumping up from his stool. "Let's go."

Emi put her neatly written name on her drying clothes. "Well, nice to run into you again," Emi said. "It's Delia, right?"

When Delia nodded, she continued.

"We're going to the dance hall now if you want to come with us."

Elis dropped his head with a sigh.

Delia pointed at the soapy vat where her clothes were soaking. "This is going to take a while. But thanks."

Emi flashed another dazzling smile before she passed through the door Elis held open for her. Delia's responding smile faded at the wary frown Elis shot her as he shut the door. Delia growled, wishing she had splashed him when she had the chance. She grumbled to herself as she scrubbed her soiled clothing. She had thought she was prepared for the disadvantage of being a white, but the reality aggravated her to exhaustion daily. Delia vented her savage feelings by flinging her soapy clothing into the rinsing vat, splashing water all over the floor. Considering what the room was used for, it was rather a marvel that the floor had been dry in the first place. *Or perhaps the result of a lot of effort.* She squelched her flash of guilt in rationalization while she rinsed, then went looking for a mop while her clothes hung on the drying racks. She found the mop in a corner and cleaned up the mess she had made, thinking how much she could have used the mop outside Cam's door. *And why is Cam still with Holly? Wasn't she cheating on him? Why does he keep choosing unfaithful women? Choose me!* The mopping became more vigorous as her agitation grew, until she had accidentally cleaned the entire laundry room floor. Cursing herself, Delia shifted Emi's name label until it appeared to cover her clothing as well, then left, banging the door behind her. At the kitchen half door, she rapped irritably.

A woman she didn't know swung the door open. "Do you need travel rations?"

Did they offer that? Could she be getting food from the kitchen for foraging days? "I didn't realize that was an option."

"Only if you're getting married tonight."

Oh. Delia frowned sulkily. "I'm not."

"Then you have to wait until breakfast for more food. But maybe your young man has some saved?"

Delia shook her head angrily. "I don't have a *young man*. I worked all day and now I'm hungry. Could I please have my life servant meal now?"

The woman's mouth formed an O. "Are you Delia White?"

"Yes."

The woman stared at her until Delia was tempted to say something rude.

"I don't think very much of what they say about you is true." She spread her white wings so Delia could see them; her lower wings were freckled green and gold like Delia's sisters, but her upper wings were topped with bright orange. "The life servants were awful to me, too. So I'm going to help you." The woman began piling orange mash onto a plate. "You can go share this with a young man. The governor keeps them starving up here, so a good meal goes right to a hungry man's heart. Any time I can get away with giving you extra, I will." She nodded as she handed Delia a plate piled so high with food that she needed both hands to keep it from tipping. "We'll get you married yet."

Delia sniffled, then felt tears trailing down her cheeks. "Thank you."

"But don't let anybody see you walking around with that plate. Hide it!"

Delia scurried into the empty dining hall and set the plate down on the nearest table, then unlatched her bag. It would be a little messy, but the plate just barely fit inside if she held up the top flap. Walking with one hand beneath her bag to support the plate and the other holding the bag open, the food was barely hidden. As she passed by the kitchen, the woman nodded her approval and Delia beamed a genuine smile at her. Each time she passed someone in the hall, she peered down at the food as if she were searching for something in her bag. When she reached Cam's door, she hesitated. If Holly was still there, could she bear to share with both of them? Delia knocked, then held her breath. When Cam opened the door, she let it out.

"Have you been crying again?" Cam asked, looking concerned. He was wearing the shirt she had slept in, and Delia wondered if it smelled like her.

"Oh, no. I wasn't. I mean, I was, but not for a bad reason. I'm fine."

"Okay," Cam chuckled, but the sound was forced.

"Is she still here?"

"Holly? No." Cam's expression darkened.

"Good!" Delia said, then stepped forward, forcing Cam to back into his room.

"What are you doing?"

"Could you help me?" Delia asked, dropping the flap so he could see the overfilled plate.

"Wow. That's a lot." He reached in to help her lift it out, smearing food on both their hands and wrists. When they wriggled it

311

free, Cam let go, and Delia set the plate on his table. Cam licked his fingers. "It's good, too."

"A nice lady in the kitchen gave me enough to share."

"And you're sharing it with *me*?"

"Why not? You've been very kind to me."

Cam smiled, making both dimples appear. "Do you have a spoon or something?"

Delia's face colored. "I'm sorry, I forgot. I'll be back." Delia hurried through the door, the sound of Cam's chuckle following her down the hall.

Back at the kitchen half door, she gave a frantic knock. When it opened, the woman laughed. "I know. Forgot forks. I'm getting senile." She handed Delia the utensils wrapped in a cloth napkin.

"Thank you so much!"

"Is it working?"

"I can't tell yet," Delia admitted.

"Well, hurry back!" the woman encouraged, making shooing motions at her.

Delia ran, her damp wings jostling painfully until she slowed to a speedy walk. Cam's door was still open, so she stepped hesitantly inside, the napkin-wrapped utensils extended. Cam stood awkwardly by the table, an uncomfortable expression on his face.

"Maybe you should share it with someone else," Cam said, his eyes riveted on the food.

"No." Delia shut the door, pulled out a second stool, and sat down. When he didn't move or speak, she began unrolling the napkin to retrieve a fork.

Cam chuckled. "You can't just say no."

"I just did." Delia glanced up at him, then couldn't remember what she had planned to say next.

Cam scratched the back of his head and sat down, a rosy hue heating his face. "Remember how you said you thought you were too attracted to me?"

Yes. Instead of answering, Delia stuck her fork into the mound of food and put it in her mouth. It tasted like yams and dill, and she briefly wondered if the castle garden had dill plants.

"There's such a thing as being pheromone drunk, and I think you might have it. I don't want to take advantage of that."

What? Delia's face flashed scarlet and her fork clattered onto the table. "You're not taking advantage of me. Every chance you get, you help me out. You remind me of my sister, Chloe, or my dad. You're just a good person. And while your pheromones are pleasant, it's your incredible physique that messes up my brain...and maybe the dimples, too. But I *do not* feel inebriated or unable to make good decisions, and if you keep your shirt on, I should be just fine. Now pick up that fork and eat before I stab you with it."

Cam's mouth fell open, followed by a surprised chortle. "Okay." He picked up the fork and began to eat, shooting her bemused glances as they ate silently.

The sound of her own chewing seemed enormously loud inside her head, even her swallows felt audible in the silence. "Please talk. I hate the sound of me eating."

"Thank you for the food. I was hungry."

"That must mean it's time for another trip to town."

Cam shrugged and stared at the table until he swallowed the food in his mouth. "I don't really feel like it."

"Why not?"

Cam chuckled without humor. "Someone advised me to use food to lure a mate."

Does he know that's what I'm doing? Delia dropped her gaze and waited for him to continue.

"And I don't much like what I've been catching."

Does that include me? Delia panic-reviewed their conversations. He had offered her food before, but she had never accepted it.

"The Princess Lexi and Holly were both involved with someone else while we were together." He shook his head. "Maybe I just like duplicitous women."

"Does that mean you and duplicitous Holly are no longer together?"

He nodded grimly. "She likes her other boyfriend more."

Yes! "Maybe you should let your next girlfriend pick *you*, instead."

One dimple showed in his left cheek. "Did you have someone in mind?"

"You know that I do! Don't you dare be coy about it."

Cam laughed like a donkey braying for a full minute before he sighed. "How do you do that?"

Delia watched him with a puzzled smile on her face. "Do what?"

"Make me laugh when I'm depressed."

Delia shook her head. "I wasn't trying to be funny."

"I think that's why it's so effective. Thank you." Cam fell into a reverie.

"I can hear myself eating again," Delia warned.

Cam chuckled. "Will it help if I eat louder?"

"No. Tell me about your family."

"Uh, I'm an only child, but I grew up with plenty of cousins. When we weren't helping our parents at the quarry, we'd have dirt clod wars on the slag heaps. I've still got a scar from when one of my older cousins accidently threw a rock." He leaned forward and lifted the hair off his forehead to display a one-inch scar. "It was a good childhood, except for when someone died."

"How often did that happen?"

"Only a few times. My grandpa, two of my uncles, and a cousin."

Delia stopped eating to look at him. "I'm sorry. That must have been awful."

Cam nodded. "But my parents are great. And my best friend, Elissa, could always make me laugh."

Delia felt a surge of jealously. "Is she here?"

"No, she left before I got here."

Delia forced her muscles to relax. "You miss her."

Cam shrugged. "It's only been a couple of weeks, and she already wrote me a letter. She's all giddy because she's pregnant and throwing up constantly."

Delia snorted. "She sounds enthusiastic."

Cam chuckled. "You have no idea." He took another bite and studied Delia's face until she blushed under the scrutiny. "What about your family?"

"I'm a quadruplet; two sisters and a brother. Did you meet Pearl or Nap?"

Cam shook his head.

"They weren't themselves anyway."

Cam nodded sagely. "My mom's a white. She told me what it was like for her and her sister."

Delia choked on her food.

Cam stood up. "Are you okay? Do you need some water?"

Delia shook her head and coughed until her lungs felt empty. "Just went down the wrong way," she croaked out.

Cam hovered a moment longer, then reluctantly sat. "Did I surprise you?"

"A bit," she conceded, her voice still rough.

Cam smiled. "She has a theory for how you can tell what an in-season white is really like."

Delia lifted her eyebrows, waiting for him to explain.

"Oh, I'm not going to *tell* you," he teased, "that would skew my results."

Delia fought down the urge to punch him. "How very scientific of you."

He chortled. "Are you going to kill me? Because that expression says you're thinking about it."

"Murder? No. Violence? Yes."

He chuckled and slid his stool back, muscles flexed to move if she lunged.

"Oh, I'm not going to do it *now*. That would be too obvious and not at all terrifying."

He laughed again, though the sound was not entirely comfortable. "Should I be scared?"

"Of course." Delia braved another bite, reminding herself not to breathe as she swallowed.

Hesitantly, he followed her example, watching her warily. "It's really fun to tease you, probably because it's also stupid."

"It's good that you realize that."

He chuckled. "Seriously, how worried should I be?"

"Oh, I'm not going to *tell* you, that would skew my results." Giddy laughter bubbled up Delia's throat, but she managed to swallow it down as she flung his words back at him.

"Okay, I deserved that," Cam conceded as he watched her.

A tiny smile graced Delia's mouth. "Yes, you did."

Cam's dimpled smile answered her own. "You're interesting."

Delia tipped her head. "Thank you?"

"Oh, it's a compliment. Holly's nice, but the most interesting thing she did was cheat on me."

Delia frowned. "That's not the good kind of interesting."

"No, it's not," he agreed and resumed eating. "You didn't finish telling me about your family."

"My dad's an apothecary and we all help out in the shop...helped out," she corrected. "My brother is hilarious, Pearl is brilliant, and Chloe is so kind. We fight, except for Chloe, but we laugh a lot, too. Chloe gets her gentle sweetness from my dad, and the rest of us are a lot like our mom."

"She sounds like an interesting lady."

"She is." Delia's brow puckered as she thought of her mom preferring her dad's in-season personality.

"Sounds like you miss them."

"I do...even though Pearl just left. I have a great family." *Except Dina.*

"And if you end up living too far away to visit?"

Delia abruptly stopped chewing, then swallowed hard. "Where are you from?"

"Wallowa. It's only two days to the east flying, but ten days by wagon."

Delia swallowed again even though there was nothing left in her mouth. Her throat felt desperately dry. "I'm from half a day's flight to the west. It's a little coastal town called Hamlet."

"That's at least two weeks of traveling by wagon between Wallowa and Hamlet."

Delia slumped on her stool.

"And over two mountain ranges," he added. "One of which isn't passable most of the winter...unless you have wings."

"That's not ideal," Delia admitted as she set her fork on the empty plate.

Cam scraped his fork around the plate, gleaning the remainder and sliding it into his mouth before he spoke. "Is it too far?"

Delia studied his expression while his gaze focused on the plate. He dragged his fork back and forth until she put her hand over his to stop him. His dark eyes met hers.

"Inconvenient isn't the same as impossible," she said.

Dropping his fork, he flipped his hand to hold hers. "So...did you decide about that girlfriend candidate?"

Delia's mouth twisted up in a partial smirk. She stood and leaned over the little table. "I'll claim you." She stretched until it felt like the table would topple, but managed to drop a quick peck on his lips before the table shifted loudly on the flagstones. Blushing, she released his hand, then stumbled over the stool. She picked up their empty plate, but somehow sent the forks clattering to the floor. Cam retrieved them, then stood before her with an enigmatic grin.

"What?" she asked, simultaneously wiping her mouth and using her tongue to check her teeth.

He set a gentle hand on her cheek as he bent down and kissed her. The sweetness of it was so disarming that the plate was quickly forgotten and slipped from her fingers. Cam caught it before it fell and set it firmly back on the table. The scent of oceanspray blossoms curled around her and she let her hands settle against his chest. When he broke the kiss, she breathed out a happy sigh, then started as she remembered the plate and looked down at her empty hands, then the table. "You caught it. Thanks." She reclaimed it from the table, stacked the forks atop it, then looked at him with a shy smile. The forks once again clattered to the floor.

Cam chuckled as he picked them up and placed them back on the plate. "Are you *sure* I don't make you pheromone drunk?"

She swatted his chest reflexively and he chortled, then took the plate from her hands again.

"I *do* have to take that back to the kitchen," she protested.

"Yes, but I want to kiss you first."

"Oh." A smile ghosted across Delia's mouth as she shifted her weight. When his hand cradled her face this time, she leaned into it and kissed his thumb. The little moan he made as he claimed her mouth thrilled through her. *This* was her new favorite thing. When he broke the kiss this time, she had to fan her wings to keep her balance. He handed her the plate and forks, and she looked down at them dumbly, momentarily forgetting why she had wanted them. He piled the cloth napkin on top.

"There. Unless you want me to take it back?"

Delia shook her head. "But maybe it can wait?"

Cam chuckled. "I would like that, but it's not a good idea." He brushed his fingers across her cheek, then dropped his hand.

"Why not?" Delia asked, irritation bleeding through the simple words.

Cam smiled. "Because my father taught me to put women on a pedestal and treat them like they're the most important person in my world."

"And you're not supposed to kiss the pedestal women?"

Cam grinned, and toyed with a strand of her hair. "I can kiss them, but anything more than that is an act of selfishness."

Delia's brows contracted as she mulled his words. "But not forever."

"Until one of the pedestal women becomes my wife."

Delia colored and dropped her gaze to the dirty plate. "Okay," she said. "But I'm not sure that pedestal thing is healthy."

Cam shrugged. "That's how my father treats my mother."

"But...*perfect* things belong on pedestals. And up there, maybe you don't see their flaws or you pretend they don't have any. Then when the flaws show themselves, you're disappointed."

"My dad says: 'Treat your wife like the flawless gift you know she can be, and she won't disappoint you.'"

Delia shook her head. "I have flaws. I'm going to disappoint you."

Cam took the plate and set it back on the table. "You're missing the point." He took her hands in his. "My dad married a white. My mom has flaws just like anybody else. My dad *treats* her like he doesn't see them."

Delia rubbed her fingers across the thick callouses on his hands. "I guess my dad does that, too. I've never heard him criticize my mom."

Cam nodded happily. "That's the way it should be."

Delia's nod was slower as she recalled the criticism she had received from the other men she had kissed. "I think so, too."

"Glad we agree." He lifted her hands to his mouth and kissed each one. "Now we should go somewhere public."

"You want to kiss in public instead?" she teased.

Cam chuckled and released her hand to grab the plate. "How about if we take it back together?"

They walked to the kitchen holding hands and exchanging goofy smiles. Delia wondered if everyone they passed could tell they had been kissing; she had the ludicrous urge to loudly confirm their suspicions. At the kitchen, she took the plate from him and knocked. When the top of the door swung open, it was Gray that glared out at them sourly.

"What?" Gray snapped.

Delia looked around him, hoping for a sight of the white-winged woman, but Gray only moved to block her view. "Just returning this," she said, handing him the dirty plate.

"You know, most of the life servants try to eat at standard times, so they don't overtax the kitchen. It's almost nine. Dinner was *three* hours ago," he complained.

Delia's eyes widened. "I have to go back to work."

Cam's brow puckered. "Now?"

Delia nodded. "I have to relieve my boss for a while. See you tomorrow?"

320

Cam's shoulders and wings drooped, though he nodded. Delia gave him a genuine smile, hope lighting her face as she turned away. She hurried toward the infirmary, then turned back for one more look. Cam was scowling at Gray, who was leaning out the half door and speaking vehemently. *Fantastic.* She flew back quickly.

"...alone in the dungeon," Gray snarled.

"I doubt that."

"Doubt it all you want, it won't make it less true!" Gray retorted and slammed the kitchen half door shut.

Delia resisted the urge to hit the door, focusing instead on the unhappy expression on Cam's face. "I'm a little infamous," she admitted.

"How many of the life servants are treating you like that?"

"Not all of them."

Cam shook his head. "That shouldn't be happening. Maybe you should talk to the governor about it."

"He tends to dole out punishments when I talk to him, so I think I'd rather avoid that."

Cam's brows knit in consternation.

"I have to go to work anyway."

"Why did you come back?"

To rip out a patch of Gray's greasy hair and make him swallow it. "Oh, I just...wanted to kiss you goodbye." It wasn't a bad save, but she blushed furiously at her boldness.

A subtle tightening of Cam's jaw betrayed his agitation, but he bent down and gave her a quick peck on the cheek.

Delia frowned, a hand flying up to cover the spot he had kissed. It felt almost dismissive. "Don't be bothered by Gray. The guy he hates is in charge of the kitchen now, and he probably blames me."

"That doesn't excuse..." he trailed off, his head lowered, mouth pulled tight.

321

"We can talk about it later, but I really have to go now." Delia backed up a few steps. *What did Gray say?!* "See you tomorrow," she repeated.

Cam made a noncommittal noise and turned away.

No! It had been such a blissful, hope-filled dinner; it couldn't be ruined already. Delia grit her teeth and marched away. Gray had been wise to slam the kitchen door so quickly when he saw her coming. She spent her walk to the infirmary fantasizing about what she would have done if he had not.

Zelic was waiting just inside the infirmary door. "Glad you remembered. The governor already sent Graci to fetch his medicine *twice.*"

"Sorry," Delia grumbled.

"And you have a patient." Zelic nodded across the room.

Delia turned to see Malachi waving at her from atop a cot, his lovely green and brown wings splayed out over the sides. "Why didn't you treat him?"

"I *tried* to. He just kept saying he'd rather wait for you."

Delia grimaced. "How long has he been here?"

Zelic snorted. "A while. I think he has a bad case of *subterfuge.*" He lifted his eyebrows meaningfully before closing the door behind him.

Delia approached her patient warily, noting the lack of obvious illness or injury.

"Hi again. Sorry if it's weird to wait to see you. I was just hoping to talk to you again, and I haven't seen you at the dance hall, so I figured this was the best place to find you. But not because I'm stalking you or anything, I just really thought it would be nice to get to know you, and I also have this rash." Malachi lifted his pant leg revealing a scarlet rash that reminded Delia of spilled jam. "It itches, but stings when I touch it."

Delia gave him a pitying glance. "When you went to the lake, did you walk through any vegetation with your legs bare?"

"Yeah."

"Were the newly sprouting leaves reddish and in clusters of three?"

"Uh..." He closed his eyes and squinted.

"With little yellow flowers?"

He opened his eyes. "I remember yellow flowers. Do they look like little stars?"

Delia nodded. "That's poison oak."

Malachi's mouth fell open. "But everybody else walked through it. I'm the only one with the rash."

"That won't last long," Delia predicted.

Over the next hour, six more members of their group showed up in the infirmary, including a sobbing yellow-winged girl that had tucked the poison oak flowers behind her ear and now had a rash blooming across her face. Since most of the group had sent affected clothing to the communal laundry, Delia expected to see more cases of the miserable rash. She quickly exhausted the medicine cabinet's supply of witch hazel and rubbing alcohol, then sent Malachi to the kitchen for baking soda. Unfortunately, Gray refused to part with any. By the time Zelic returned, Delia had a stress headache and hands so parched from washing that they were ready to crack and bleed. After her harried recounting of the past hour, Zelic laughed.

"This happens all the time. We just wash their clothes very carefully, and tell them not to touch their rashes."

Delia blinked incredulously. "You don't treat them?"

Zelic shrugged. "I didn't know rubbing alcohol helped. The governor says buying poison oak remedies from local apothecaries is a waste of money. His predecessor only kept a little on hand for the life servants."

"But the rashes are so miserable."

"They can be," Zelic conceded as he absently scratched at his arm. He turned to face the four remaining patients. "We don't have anything left to treat your rashes. Take all your affected clothing to the laundry tomorrow morning and tell them they have poison oak oil on them. Touch them as little as possible so you don't give yourself more rashes. If any of your blisters start oozing pus, come back."

The patients slid off their cots with grumbled complaints and made their way to the door.

"But I'll have more medicine by tomorrow night," Delia blurted.

Zelic shot her a look, but stayed quiet until the door closed behind the last patient. "You shouldn't promise that. You're training me tomorrow, so your search area will be limited."

"I'm training you at noon. That gives me the whole morning to find what I need."

Zelic shook his head. "I don't think I ever had your enthusiasm for this job."

Delia scowled. "I'm not enthusiastic about the job. I just don't like people suffering when I can help them."

Zelic chuckled. "Is there a difference?"

"Yes!"

"Okay," Zelic said, laughter evident in his voice though he pressed his lips together to hide his smile.

Delia rolled her eyes and stomped out of the room, Zelic's laughter breaking free just before the door shut completely.

"This isn't enthusiasm," she argued with the almost-empty hallway. "I'm just enduring my punishment well. That's what I'm supposed to do."

An uncomfortable hitching laugh interrupted her. "I talk to myself, too," Malachi admitted.

Delia frowned and continued walking while he fell into step beside her.

"Bet you're glad you didn't go to the lake with us now."

"If I had gone with you, you wouldn't *have* a poison oak rash."

Another hitch of laughter erupted. "That's true! I didn't even think of that." Malachi let out a musical hmm. "So, do you want to go dancing?"

"Right *now?*"

He nodded eagerly.

"No. I have to work early tomorrow."

Though he kept smiling, his voice took on a bit of a whine. "Again?"

"That's how being a life servant works. I'm essentially a slave until my punishment is over."

"Oh. That's awful."

Definitely not a source of enthusiasm, Delia thought as she came to a stop outside her door. "Well, goodnight." Delia held her breath as she opened the door. *Please let there be a mattress!* She let out a happy sigh when the room was just as she had left it.

"Would you maybe like to dance tomorrow, after work?"

"I have a boyfriend." *I think.*

"Oh!" he hitched yet another nervous laugh. "That's not surprising."

Delia looked at him sharply, but there wasn't a trace of sarcasm in his open, unattractive face.

"Well, thank you for helping my friends and me." He nodded once, then hurried down the hall.

Delia watched him go, a bemused expression on her face. She wasn't tempted, but it was lovely to be thought a prize and treated kindly. She said a quick prayer of gratitude that people like Malachi existed, and as she drifted off to sleep, hoped to be more like him.

Chapter Sixteen

Delia awoke to a sense of rightness that was only partially marred by the memory of Gray's tirade and Cam's reaction. She was tempted to seek Cam out, to try to smooth over whatever aspersions Gray had cast her way, but she had work to do. Hopefully, the damage could be undone when her workday was finished. Dressing quickly in her missing-pockets pants, she flew through the castle and into the courtyard. The streaming sunlight told her she had slept longer than she intended, so she flew faster than was comfortable and settled for a convenient breakfast of mushrooms, though she despised their earthy flavor.

Lunch was well underway when she returned, and she flew over a sporadic collection of in-seasons sunning themselves while they ate. She self-consciously ran her forearm across her sweaty forehead, leaving a streak of dirt that matched the soil embedded beneath her nails. Dom caught her eye, his gaze quickly sliding away as if he had not seen her. Emi waved enthusiastically and nudged her brother, but Elis' attention was riveted on the gray-winged girl that sat beside him. Delia returned Emi's wave, then hurried through the castle. Zelic stood impatiently tapping his foot outside the infirmary.

"I'll just be a minute," Delia lied as she pulled open the infirmary door and went inside to catalog her cache.

"Can't you do that later?" Zelic followed her into the office, his tone peevish.

"You sound like you just woke up," Delia commented as Neva pushed into the office to survey the newest herbs.

"This office is too small for three people," Zelic griped as he left.

Delia jotted down her findings as quickly as she could, but Neva's questions, once again, slowed her down. When she finally finished, Zelic was stretched out on one of the cots, sound asleep.

"Should I wake him?" Delia asked.

Neva patted his leg until he made incoherent noises. "You'll be irritated if you miss your training."

327

Zelic threw himself off the cot with a dubious noise of assent and stumbled toward the door. Delia followed, leaving him plenty of space for his misplaced steps and occasionally out-flung wings and arms as he steadied himself. He stopped just beyond the courtyard and spun around irritably.

"Well? Where are we going?"

"Why are you so horrifically grumpy?" Delia asked, stepping past him to lead the way.

Zelic waited until they were sufficiently advanced down the path to have outpaced any listening ears. "Governor had another bad night," he grumbled, squinting against the sunlight dappling his face. "And I am officially out of excuses as to why Graci can't administer his medicine. If I *say* that she's a moth-brained ninny that has no right to practice medicine, then he'll put me in the dungeon and make Graci the head medic."

"Graci?! Why not Neva?"

"Because Neva won't give him extra morphine, either."

"Is his pain worse?"

"No. He's showing signs of addiction, though."

Delia sighed. "Are you weaning him off of it?"

"I'm trying. It's not going well."

Delia frowned. She had seen morphine addiction before. Mr. Fritillary's wife was an addict. Her revolving menagerie of illnesses—some real, some imagined—were always secondary to the insistent pain that she claimed only morphine could relieve. Her father had stopped supplying it when he realized the problem, but Mrs. Fritillary would simply goad her husband until he rode to a neighboring town and bought more. After an overdose nearly killed her, Delia's father had started supplying Mrs. Fritillary with the drug again, but in small quantities and diluted with placebos. Delia glanced around her for suitable placebos just as a flurry of cottonwood seeds floated past her. Following their trajectory, she located the towering tree.

"If you still have honey left, you could substitute black cottonwood twig tea. They're both bitter; maybe he won't be able to tell."

Zelic scowled as he brushed a cottonwood seed from his hair. "He will when he doesn't get euphoric."

"Tell him he's built up a tolerance to the drug," Delia suggested, then flew up to gather twigs and buds from the gnarled giant.

Zelic glared up the twenty feet of rough trunk to where Delia stood on a thick branch. "Am I supposed to climb it when I need more?"

"I'll find a smaller one later," she assured him, snapping one more twig before she flew back to his side.

Zelic's silence as they resumed walking the trail seemed to denote acceptance, and Delia began to relax by degrees. By the time she was showing him how to harvest the third plant of the day, Zelic seemed to have regained his better humor. But Delia hadn't truly minded his temper; it had been nice to be the calmer person for a change, not unlike spending time with Pearl, who always felt like a coiled spring, even before her wing birth. *I wonder if they're happy? Has pregnancy given Pearl back her personality yet?* Delia smiled involuntarily at the thought of being an aunt and playing with her nieces and nephews. Then the stark reality of Cam living two weeks away from her family smote her. She had implied she didn't mind. *Was that true?* She tried to picture the overland journey with young children, camping along the way. *Depends on how many children we have,* she decided. Her face grew warm at the thought.

"Do you need to rest?" Zelic asked.

Delia pulled her mind back into the present. "No." She looked up at the darkening sky. "We should go faster, actually." She was fairly certain she could find their way back in the dark, but it didn't seem wise to test her memory at Zelic's expense.

Zelic's pace had been so much faster than Neva's that they had managed to almost complete the same circuit, despite losing the morning hours. Zelic griped about his feet, but never lessened his pace. They returned to the castle only an hour after dark. Back in the infirmary, Zelic catalogued their finds with Delia reminding him of uses when he failed to list them. Caena stood just outside the office listening, but looking through Delia as if she weren't there whenever they made eye contact. *Better than gossip*, Delia thought with a grim smile.

It wasn't until Delia returned to her blissfully untouched room that she remembered her drying clothes and the fact that she had failed to tell Emi. Unpleasant words of self-condemnation flitted through Delia's head as she put on in her bathing suit, and continued as she walked to the pool, soap in hand. She was tempted to stop by the laundry first, but her soil-encrusted hands were too dirty to carry clean laundry.

The door to the pool was once again propped open with a rock, the sulphur smell reduced to a subtle background scent. Delia surveyed the semi-populated room, searching for an empty spot of water with no boisterous splashers nearby.

"Aw, Thistle has come to say goodbye to us!" Bul called out from the far side of the pool, Rubi pressed against his side. "We're getting hitched!"

"You're welcome to come to the wedding," Rubi added politely, her dark eyes sincere.

Delia glanced at Cia and Sal's twin glares from either side of the happy couple. Rus had his back to her, Cia's possessive hand gripping his shoulder.

"Thanks, but I'll probably have to work...congratulations." Delia could tell it wasn't the right tone or expression to go with her words and attempted a face-tightening smile to compensate.

"Thanks," Rubi chirped.

Bul flinched at Delia's forced smile. "That's a nice murderous expression."

Rus turned to see Delia's face, but was immediately pulled back around by Cia's white-knuckled grip on his shoulder.

Delia scowled. "I'm happy for you, both of you. I just can't make this..." She made a sweeping motion of her head, "...cooperate."

Rubi smiled sympathetically.

"Just don't go frightening anyone else with that face," Bul teased. "No one deserves that."

"No one deserves your stench, either," Delia snapped.

Rus and Sal hooted with laughter while Rubi whispered something to Bul.

"I was just teasing you," Bul griped. "Besides, I smell like *steak*." He turned to kiss Rubi, then lingered until his friends began to whistle their approval.

Rolling her eyes, Delia waded into the water, for once grateful that her small stature made her disappear in a crowd. She washed quickly, then managed to leave the pool when Bul's group was too distracted to notice. She wished them well and appreciated their kindness, but was grateful they were going. She rarely kept her temper for long around Bul, and probably owed him an apology even now. Their uneasy friendship was difficult to maintain and, without Bul's gregariousness, it certainly wouldn't have lasted this long.

At the laundry, her clothes were missing from the drying racks, as was Emi's name tag. Delia groaned. How could she have forgotten to tell Emi? *Cam*, she reminded herself. *Cam is why you forgot to tell Emi.* "Please be in the abandoned clothes bin," she said aloud as she crossed to the desk and pulled out the box. The brown overalls and stained white shirt were all she recognized.

"No!" she growled, then let fly one of the curse words that was trumpeting in her head. Retrieving the cast-offs, she ran to her room, her dread weighing her down as much as her sodden wings. She flung the door open, her gaze flitting about the room before it registered that her bag, boots, Coli's nightgown and dress, and the day's dirty clothes were all still there. *No more taking chances*, she told herself sternly as she dressed in the overalls and stained shirt. Her missing-pockets pants were all that she had left of her own clothing as she had worn Pearl's yellow shirt today. She packed her remaining belongings, strapped on her bag, then picked up her dirty clothes. She was tempted to barricade herself in the room, but she hadn't yet seen Cam today, and she knew he would be hungry.

She rapped smartly at the kitchen half door, perversely hoping Gray would answer so she could demand to know what he had said to Cam. But it was the white-winged woman who smiled out at her.

"I'm Sara, by the way," she said, and filled a plate without being asked. "And I'm very sorry Margi took the last of your clothes down to Phasia to shred."

Delia's nostrils flared as she processed the information. *So Margi got out of the dungeon and immediately began tormenting me again?*

Sara held out the heaping plate and looked pityingly at Delia's overalls. "Pol—he's over the dungeon—was too slow to stop her, but Margi *is* locked up again." She sighed as Delia took the offered plate. "I'd give you something of mine, but I very much doubt we're the same size." Sara chuckled and patted her rounded tummy.

"Thank you, Sara," she replied belatedly, then repeated her words when Sara handed her forks and a napkin.

"Don't lose hope. Keep feeding your young man and you'll get a proposal any day now."

Why would I wait for him to propose? Delia wondered, but merely nodded and turned away. She thought of Coli's schemes to get Mel to marry her and wondered if they were working. She couldn't imagine herself playing any such games. If she decided she wanted Cam, she would just tell him so. Delia smiled with grim amusement. She and Pearl were more alike than she had realized.

Without a free hand, she hit Cam's door with her elbow, then kicked it with her boot when there was no response.

"I'm putting a shirt on," Cam called from inside.

Delia's face pinked at the thought, her expression betraying disappointment when he opened the door fully clothed.

"Whoa," Cam said, taking the plate from her and setting it on the table. "That's even more than last time."

"She feels bad for me because Margi got more of my clothes and took them down to Phasia to rip up."

His brows contracted as he took the dirty clothes from her and started to drape them over a chair.

"Just toss them on the floor; they're caked in dirt."

"I'll just put them with my dirty clothes." He retrieved his bag and folded her clothing neatly inside before tucking the bag back into its corner.

Delia hid her amusement as she unlatched her own bag and sat down. "Don't you ever throw dirty clothes on the floor?"

"Uh...no."

"Really? Not even when you were young?"

Cam shook his head. "There was always a hamper on the porch. Dirty clothes aren't even allowed in the house."

"Oh, the quarry dust. I forgot."

Cam nodded as he sat.

"Sorry."

Cam unfolded the napkin and took out a fork. "It's okay. The upside is I'm tidy."

"I'm...not," she admitted, watching his face for a reaction.

Cam chuckled. "I kind of figured that."

"And you don't mind?"

Cam grinned. "It's all part of the services I'm willing to provide to my pedestal woman."

Delia let out a surprised snort. "You're really serious about that?"

Cam nodded and took a bite, then shifted it in his mouth before swallowing hard.

Delia sampled the casserole and immediately considered spitting it out. "Tastes like bitter dirt."

Cam began pulling the mass apart with his fork. "I see mushrooms and leafy greens in some sort of yellow mash."

Delia pushed the plate to his side of the table and set down her fork.

"You're not going to eat it?"

Delia shook her head.

"Have there been any cases of food poisoning today?"

Delia smirked. "Not that I know of."

"And the life servant who gave this to you actually likes you?"

Delia's smirk morphed into irritation. "Yes."

"Then I'm eating it." Cam dug into the distasteful dish with enthusiasm, only the creasing around his eyes betrayed the nastiness of it.

She watched him eat, increasingly amused at his suffering. "You should come foraging with me tomorrow; I'll show you what you can eat."

Cam gagged subtly, his eyes watering as he forced down another mouthful and swallowed several times. "You don't have to train anyone tomorrow?"

Delia shook her head. "I don't think so. I'll probably just be harvesting transplants for the garden."

Cam took out his canteen and drank thirstily before returning to the plate.

"You don't have to finish it."

Brows knit, he attacked the remaining pile.

Delia fought back a giggle. His bronzed face had paled and his gagging was becoming more frequent and noticeable. "Stop! You're going to make yourself vomit."

"I'm fine," he lied, hiding a portending belch.

Delia laughed outright and pulled the plate away from him. "Stop! Your pedestal woman demands that you stop."

Cam set his fork down.

Delia grinned. "Will that always work?"

Cam swallowed, his expression still queasy. "Maybe."

Another laugh broke free from her, one that sounded like her old self. Sitting there in his spartan, stone room with the pleasant scent of oceanspray tickling her nose, she felt peaceful. A warmth in her chest seemed to grow as she looked at Cam, still struggling to keep his meal down. *He is a good man,* she thought, *the kind I'd like to marry.* Unbidden, her eyes filled with happy tears as the warmth expanded to envelop her whole body. She knew what this feeling was. Like the instructions on how to save the governor's life, God was communicating with her.

"What if your pedestal woman demands that you marry her?"

Cam's head came up, his eyes wide. "Are you...?" The rest of his question was lost to a gagging cough that ended in a stream of vomit, semi-neatly deposited atop the dirty clothes inside his bag.

Delia stood, concern warring with humor. "Can I help?" He groaned, then the disquieting sound of vomit again filled her ears.

When he was finally able to stop, he cleared his throat. "That was *not* my answer," he said, his voice guttural and halting. He closed his bag, concealing the repulsive contents, and shakily stood. "I'm so sorry. I'm going to go wash this out."

"Let me," Delia offered, trying to take the bag from him as he moved to the door.

"No," he argued. "It's too gross."

Delia blocked his way. "Your pedestal woman demands that you let her help."

An embarrassed smile eased his expression and he laughed feebly. "I'm turning into Elissa."

Delia frowned, unreasonable jealousy surging through her.

Cam caught her expression and shook his head. "She throws up a lot. At her wing birth, she vomited all over herself and me right in the middle of class." He chuckled as he looked down at his besmirched bag.

"I teased her a bit at the time. Seeing me humiliate myself like this would delight her."

Delia's frown lessened as she fought to make it go away entirely. "She sounds...

interesting."

"She is. Now, before the smell of my puke makes me dry heave, could you let me out of the room?"

Delia crossed her arms, still blocking the door. "You didn't answer my question."

Cam blanched and wiped his mouth. "Could we please have this conversation after I get cleaned up?"

Delia narrowed her eyes, considering, then turned and opened the door, preceding him into the hallway. "But I *am* going to help you," she announced.

"You can take the plate back."

Delia darted back into the room to retrieve it, belatedly remembering her bag. She strapped it on quickly, then ran to catch up with him. "Wait," she requested. When she caught up to him, she lifted the top of his bag and slid the remaining food inside with a sickening plop, before once again covering it.

Cam grimaced and swallowed. "I'd really rather just clean this up myself."

"They're my clothes," Delia pointed out.

He shook his head. "That only makes it worse. Please just let me do it alone."

"If *I* had thrown up on *your* clothes, would you be comfortable letting me clean it up by myself?"

Cam frowned. "No."

"I'm not comfortable, either."

Cam laughed uneasily and stopped walking. "I'm really not equipped for this much humiliation in one night. The kindest thing you can do for me is to say goodnight, and when you see me tomorrow, pretend it didn't happen."

Delia tipped her head as she watched his face. His ill pallor was giving way to ruddy embarrassment. "I don't want you to pretend for me. You tried to fill your empty stomach with too much unpleasant-tasting food that may or may not be spoiled; throwing up was the natural result." She shrugged. "It happens."

He ran a hand over his face. "Not to me."

"Sounds like you were overdue, then."

He chuckled ruefully and resumed walking.

"And it's not as if I haven't humiliated myself plenty around you: getting caught sleeping in your bed, forgetting where my room was, crying snot all over your shirt, your girlfriend catching me cleaning the puddle I made outside your door..."

"Is that what you were doing?"

Blushing, Delia hurried on without answering his question. "Isn't that just the sort of thing that happens when you *really* like someone? You want to be around them and impress them, but the overwhelming attraction disables your brain. In fact, if you hadn't humiliated yourself soon, I would have worried you weren't truly interested."

Cam guffawed a great belly laugh that forced him to stop walking and returned the queasy color to his face.

"Are you going to vomit again?"

Cam's laugh died out. He shook his head, but then yanked the bag open, his stomach once again heaving its contents.

Delia laughed wryly and patted his arm. "Your retching might as well be a love song."

Washing the dirty clothes and bag were strangely pleasant, though punctuated with Cam's dry heaving. They shared embarrassing stories from their youth and laughed at their mutual humiliation. Returning to his room, they laid out Delia's clothes to dry and she hugged him goodnight, mutually agreeing that post-vomit kisses were unappealing.

Delia floated to her own room, the giddy sensation creating a lift that didn't require wings. As she climbed into her door-braced bed, the thought of vomiting love songs spread a grin across her face that only faded slightly as she began to dream.

Chapter Seventeen

Delia dreamed of Cam gorging himself on forest mushrooms. She tried to shriek when he reached for a deadly conocybe, but her voice made no noise. She struggled to run to him, but her body seemed frozen in place as he smiled at her. He tossed the deadly fungus into the air, then caught it in his mouth. He chewed as Delia watched in horror. As he grabbed for another, she awoke tangled in her blanket. Her usually slow return to coherency was bypassed by the lingering terror of her nightmare. She dressed in last night's clothes and hurried to Cam's room. The flight to his door somewhat cooled her sense of urgency, but the staccato of her knock was still frantic. She waited impatiently, and even considered barging in, before the door finally opened.

"Hi," Cam yawned, distorting the greeting. "Is it morning already?" He rubbed the sleep from his eyes and blinked rapidly.

Delia dropped her bag and flung herself at him, wrapping her arms tightly around his neck. "Don't eat mushrooms in the forest."

Cam emitted a sleepy chuckle, his arms slipping under her wings to encircle her waist. "Wasn't going to."

Delia leaned back to evaluate his complexion, then heaved a relieved sigh at his returning color. "Are you going to throw up again?"

Cam considered as he lowered her to the ground, then shook his head. "I'm starving, though. Is it breakfast time?"

"No idea. But no castle food for you today."

"Just forest mushrooms?" he teased.

Delia smacked his arm, and he laughed merrily. "I had a very bad dream about you poisoning yourself. So don't eat anything unless I give it to you."

"Okay," he agreed.

Delia retrieved her bag, then pulled out Coli's nightgown and dress. "Can I leave these here?"

His eyes went to the nightgown, and Delia blushed crimson. "Not because I...I just need a place where the life servants won't take them."

Cam cleared his throat to hide the chuckle perched there and pointed at an empty hook on his wall.

Delia hung them up, careful not make eye contact. She could feel her flush spreading down her neck. "Well," she laughed awkwardly, "let's go."

Outside, the birds were singing their dawn song as first light filtered through the tall evergreens. The cool morning eased the heat in Delia's face until she felt herself again. Taking deep breaths, her shoulders relaxed from their clenched position.

"I didn't realize you were such an early riser."

Delia shrugged. "It's a good time to forage."

Cam grinned, his dimples showing on both sides. "My mom is going to love you. She's always up at dawn with some project or another. She says it's the best part of the day. Last summer, she..." he trailed off and came to a stumbling halt.

A slow smile spread across Delia's face as she stopped beside him. "Did you make a decision?"

He looked down at her, wonder on his face. "I guess I did."

"Are you saying yes, then?"

He laughed to himself. "I guess I am."

"That's enough incredulity. It's not *that* surprising, is it?"

He chuckled and scrubbed a hand over his face. "No. It's just fast, and I was determined that *this* time..."

Jealousy surged and Delia wished she could punch the princess right in the middle of her terrifying face—then fly away very fast.

"...I would be more cautious and take it slow."

"I'm still a life servant," she reminded him. "I can't get married until the governor releases me from my punishment...whenever that might be."

"Do you think he's going to make you serve the full month?"

Delia frowned. "Possibly. But I don't want to talk about this here." They had reached the edge of the empty courtyard.

Cam looked around with some confusion. "Where *should* we discuss it?"

"Anywhere else." Delia threw her arms out at the forest. "This is my escape. Now, let's go find our breakfast." She jumped into the air, the cold breeze tugging at her wings. She heard his chuckle before he was flying at her side.

"And what are we eating?"

"Mint first," Delia decided.

Cam breathed into his hand. "Does my breath still smell bad? I can't tell."

Delia smirked. "It's to settle your stomach so you don't puke any more love songs today."

Cam guffawed, losing altitude until he recovered, face flushed. "You're going to tease me about that forever, aren't you?"

"Forever and ever," she agreed, taking his hand. It felt lovely in her own, and combined with the forest, her world was at peace.

She felt a little guilty about it, but she spent most of the morning finding food for Cam, promising herself that the afternoon would be dedicated to wildcrafting. But the afternoon came, and she found herself lingering at the lake, grinning at his braying laughter and enjoying the sunshine while they grazed on trillium leaves and wild strawberries. *This is what life is supposed to be*, she thought, her joy so complete that she hugged him to hide the tears welling up in her eyes.

"I'm so happy with you." Her voice warbled a bit and she cleared her throat to steady it. "Everything is better."

Cam emptied his handful of tiny strawberries into his mouth, then checked the cleanliness of his hands before returning her hug. "Sorry, wasn't ready."

Delia counted the seconds in her head, waiting for him to echo her sentiment. When he said nothing, she released him and turned away to hide her disappointment. "I should get to work." She slipped her spade out of her bag.

"We should talk first."

All of her fears rose up in a rogue wave that sent her emotions tumbling. *Breathe. Maybe it will be okay.* She sucked in air, hating the little gasping noise she made.

"The more I think about us going back to Wallowa, having children..." he shook his head, "the worse I feel."

Delia took a few involuntary steps away from him, as if the distance could lessen the pain. "You don't want to marry me?" She had meant to sound calm, but the words were an angry challenge as she turned to look at him.

He shook his head. "No, I do. It's just that...something doesn't feel right."

"Is this about the gossip? What did Gray say to you?"

Cam's hands were up in a placating gesture. "That's not it. I didn't even really believe him."

"So you only *partially* believed him?"

He struggled for words, his face imploring. "I just wanted to make sure what he said wasn't true."

Delia's assessing hmm was full of disbelief.

"I've been cheated on twice and I was oblivious." He clutched at his dark curls, the hair atop his head barely long enough to grab. "I'm paranoid now."

She could feel her blood pounding in her temples as she fought to keep her voice civil. "Ah, so Gray said I was mated to someone else?"

He opened his mouth, then shut it, his gaze falling to the ground.

"*Several* someone elses?"

"You don't want to hear it. And I know it's not true now. This isn't what I wanted to talk about."

"How could you ever think it *was* true?!"

"Let's discuss this later when we've both calmed down."

"I'm a white! I don't calm down!"

Cam put a hand on her arm, but she immediately shook it off. "I know that you do. And later you'll realize this is just a misunderstanding. I already talked to Coli. I know Gray lied. I'm not worried about that. I *am* worried that some part of the decision I unconsciously made this morning is wrong. I didn't listen last time I had this feeling, and I've regretted it ever since."

"You mean with the princess," Delia guessed, her petty jealousy once again piqued.

Cam nodded grimly.

"So you felt like this *after* you got engaged to the princess?"

He shifted his weight, his wings twitching.

"And it was because you had made a bad choice?"

"Yes, but I don't think *you're* the bad choice."

"Just our getting married is?!"

He compulsively clutched and released his hair, ripping out a few strands by the roots. "I don't know. I don't think so."

"Let me know when you figure it out." The venom dripping from her words as she launched herself into the air was almost palpable. She wanted to scream at him to stay away from her or maybe just fly back and cry in his arms. How could he feel bad about something that brought her so much happiness? *If I know it's right, why doesn't he?* She endured the long flight back without giving into the urge to look behind her. It would be infuriating if he had followed her, but decimating if he had not. *Better not to know*, she decided. She passed over areas knowing there were plants there she needed to harvest, but if she stopped, would he? Would he assume it was time to talk about why he didn't want to marry her? Her stomach lurched at the thought. Was he even behind her? She looked back before she could control herself, but she saw nothing. Despair seemed to dampen her wings, and she skimmed the treetops before forcing herself to fly higher. *It was just too soon. Why did I say anything?* And why did he talk about his mom loving her as if it was a foregone conclusion that they would meet? She growled to herself in answer. If anyone knew how to recover from mentioning marriage too soon, it was Coli. She would find her friend, make her recount her entire conversation with Cam, murder Gray, and then somehow fix everything. A grim smile twitched her lips as she thought of harming the slandering life servant. *Maybe just a truth bomb*, she amended, *in front of everyone he knows*. She chastised herself for her malicious thoughts and flew faster. Even with the cool wind in her face, she could feel perspiration trickling down her back. A good bath was in order, but not until after she had some answers. At the castle, she shoved past anyone even remotely in her way, earning irritable outbursts along her path. She checked Coli's room and even the pool before she consigned herself to the painful necessity of entering the ballroom. She flew into the room, deftly dodging dancing couples as she searched for Coli's golden wings and hair. But it was Coli's ringing laugh between cacophonous songs that helped Delia locate her. Mel was gulping water at her side, apparently imitating the drinking habits of some sort of animal. Coli's laughter was near hysterical while Tyro glowered nearby.

"Mom!" Mel sputtered between gulps, "Mel poisoned me!"

"I didn't say that," Tyro snarled. "I knew it was just another one of your stupid pranks."

"I'm dying," Mel squealed as he clutched his neck and fell to the floor.

When Coli tipped her head back for another peal of laughter, Tyro gave his brother a surreptitious kick. Mel scrambled to his feet, one hand clutching his thigh.

"You're not funny," Tyro growled.

Mel gestured to Coli, who was still shaking with laughter and dabbing tears from the corners of her eyes.

Delia fastened her hand around Coli's wrist. "I need to talk to you."

"Okay," Coli agreed, her breath still hitching with laughter as she allowed herself to be towed through the crowd. "I'll be back," she promised Mel.

When they reached a quieter hallway, Delia stopped and spun on her friend. "What did Cam ask you and what did you tell him?"

Coli sighed. "He shouldn't have even told you we talked."

Delia crossed her arms over her chest. "Well, he did."

"You're not going to like it, Delia. You'll be happier if you don't know, especially if you're hoping to get together with him."

"We *are* together. This morning we even agreed to get married."

"Delia! Why didn't you tell me?"

Delia shook her head. "You're never around when I'm not working."

Coli inclined her head in agreement. "So why does it matter what we talked about?"

"Because now he feels "bad" about our decision, like he did after he got engaged to the horrid princess."

"Ohhh." Coli drew out the word with a low breath as she looked at the floor.

"And everything seemed fine until that spiteful kitchen servant talked to him. So I need to know: *what* did he say?"

Coli clenched her eyes shut and grimaced. "That the governor will never let you go because you're his newest mistress and you're infertile, so you'll never have to leave. And that if the governor finds out Cam is spending time with you, he'll lock Cam in the dungeon."

Delia sucked in a gasp, her face hardening in fury.

"I told him it wasn't true, that you haven't mated with anyone, and that you don't even *like* the governor."

"His season was over before I even met him and he already *has* an infertile mistress!" Delia blurted, then pressed her lips together. "I shouldn't have told you that."

"You should tell Cam that."

"I thought you said he believed you!"

Coli shrugged. "I don't know him. He *seemed* like he believed me, especially after I told him about the guys you *did* get involved with."

"Coli!"

"Isn't that better than him thinking you're secretly with the governor?"

Delia scowled in begrudging agreement.

"And I told him what you're really like: how kind you are, that you take care of people without them asking, and that you're funny."

"Thanks," Delia said, still frowning.

"It was a good conversation—after the initial awkwardness. He really likes you. Did he ask you to marry him this morning?"

Delia's face lit with a brief smirk. "I asked him last night what he would do if I demanded that he marry me."

Coli erupted in surprised laughter. "You didn't!"

"And then he threw up."

Coli chortled hysterically. "Just because the question stressed him out?"

Delia shook her head with a slight smile. "He may have consumed a large quantity of bad food before I asked."

Coli laughed so hard she had to steady herself against the stone wall. "And I thought my teasing acceptance of Mel's accidental proposal was bad."

"No, I'm clearly winning," Delia said wryly. "How are you and Mel? And why is Tyro still hanging around?"

Coli frowned. "Because he's the most conceited and manipulative man alive. Every time I get Mel convinced that I love him and that I really want to marry him, Tyro finds some way to twist it around in his head. I'm trying to talk Mel into coming home with me, because I can't bear a lifetime of dealing with his brother."

Coli continued complaining as a wave of homesickness hit Delia. She thought of the two-week journey from Wallowa, then shook it off. *I'm not going to Wallowa,* she reminded herself. Rather than being a distressing thought, it seemed to settle into her, like it belonged. *So was I wrong about Cam?* The peacefulness within her seemed to dissolve into confusion.

"...So now every time Tyro decides to torment us with his presence, I encourage Mel to tell me about all the pranks he and Ryd have played on Tyro. They're hilarious—nothing as mean as what Talis and Ora used to pull—and the retelling usually drives Tyro away. He's being really tenacious today; if you wanted to truth-bomb him, I wouldn't mind."

Delia looked past Coli back toward the entrance of the ballroom and grimaced. "I will if you really want me to, but I should be working or at least trying to make things right with Cam."

"You think you can talk him out of a bad feeling?"

Delia groaned. "I'm going to try. He's such a good person and I feel so happy around him."

Coli gave her a brief hug. "Good luck. I'm off to do essentially the same thing."

Delia hurried away with renewed purpose and hope. If Wallowa wasn't right, did that mean her hometown was? Sharing a house with Dina sounded horrific, and it would be odd to live in the same town with Talis after their brief relationship. *But could it work?* Delia mulled the possibilities as she left the castle, keeping watch for Cam while she finally began her workday. She retraced her path to the lake and back again without seeing him, but managed to procure medicinal plants and cuttings along the way.

Back at the castle, she handed off her transplants to a delighted Kip and catalogued the remainder with the ever-inquisitive Neva. No longer satisfied with each plant's properties, Neva wanted to know where she had found each one. After explaining as best she could without a map, Delia cautioned, "But all of these could be dangerous for the governor if Graci got into them." Neva nodded sagely. "I'll give them to Zelic. He said to tell you that you're training Caena and Indra tomorrow after breakfast."

"That sounds...perfectly monstrous."

Neva coughed out a low chuckle as Delia turned to go. "Do you want some advice?"

Delia turned back around. "Yes."

"Praise Indra's efforts and they'll both pay better attention." Seeing Delia's doubting expression, she added, "Indra lacks confidence and Caena is competitive."

Delia evaluated the older woman thoughtfully. "Do you miss being the head medic?"

Neva scoffed. "No."

"But you were good at it." It wasn't a question, and Neva's shifting silence was all the confirmation Delia needed. "Thank you for the advice."

Neva merely nodded, her attention focused on cleaning up the soil Delia had inadvertently scattered across the desk. Frowning, Delia glanced in her bag and found a similar mess. Then her eyes caught on her dirt-embedded nails and filthy hands. She stood irresolute a moment, the pull to find Cam stronger than the need for a bath. Ultimately, vanity won out. Delia left the infirmary and went directly to her room to change. Inside, her bed was made and a sprig of broadleaf lupine graced her pillow.

"Pedestal woman, indeed," she whispered to the empty room. She lifted the purple blossoms to her nose and inhaled their sweet scent. She was *definitely* going to talk him out of his bad feeling. Delia changed into her bathing suit in a rush, then stopped by Coli's empty room to stash her boots and bag before flying to the pool. The door was closed, Rus' rock kicked aside. Delia held her breath and opened the door, letting the steamy, sulphur-scented cloud dissipate as she shifted the rock back into position. Finally, she breathed in, bracing herself for the nasty scent. Instead, the air smelled like oceanspray blossoms. Delia stepped eagerly inside, giving the pool's lone occupant a tentative smile.

"Are you still mad at me?" Cam asked.

Delia dragged her eyes away from his perfectly sculpted muscles, her mind trying to make sense of his words. "What?"

Cam chuckled and stepped deeper into the water until only his head and shoulders were visible. "That was unfair of me," he conceded. "I was just hoping it might help you forgive me."

Delia stepped into the water. "I'm sorry for losing my temper. And thank you for the lupine and making my bed; that was nice."

Cam grinned, his dimples appearing as his eyes twinkled. "I think I figured it out."

"Figured what out?"

"The bad feeling."

Delia frowned, then steeled herself against the coming conversation. Somehow, she would convince him.

"It's the quarry. I don't think I'm supposed to go back. And I thought first maybe I could just do something else in town, but my family would insist. And then our kids would grow up around the mine, and they would get hurt and they would die before their time, and I just can't live with that."

Though she had been prepared to argue, his words drained all her fight and confusion away, especially his use of the word "our." *Our kids*, she repeated to herself as he continued.

"Mining is all I ever trained for, but I could get a job with the flying guard or as a crown agent until my season ends. After that, I'm not sure what I'll do." He stared down at the water, running his arms along the surface of it. "I used to want to be a doctor."

"What will your family say?"

He ran a hand through his wet hair. "They'll..." he chuckled ruefully, "they'll hate it so much. But I can't raise kids there; I just couldn't live with myself if something happened."

Was that why I felt peaceful about not moving to Wallowa? "Then, you're not taking back your unconscious decision to marry me?"

Cam smiled. "I consciously choose you as my forever pedestal woman."

Delia swam to him and wrapped her arms around his neck, despite the bar of soap in her hand. "Too late. I already demanded that you marry me. All that's left for you is to agree."

Cam laughed as she kissed him. "Okay, I agree," he conceded as his hands encircled her diminutive waist.

They kissed until an appreciative whistle sounded from the doorway, startling them apart. Delia turned to see Damus entering, a wry grin on his broad mouth. She blushed furiously as she swam back to where she could touch. Damus' brother Everes walked up beside him looking quietly amused.

"Why are we stopping in the doorway?" Emi asked, then peered around Everes' shoulder.

"Oh, hi!" Emi greeted her, grasping Everes' arm as he moved toward the water. Her brother Elis followed, looking annoyed.

"Don't stop on our account," Damus said. "It's not like it's a public pool. I assume you don't need any help this time?" Damus asked.

Delia shook her head, her face still scarlet as Cam moved to her side. The shallower water exposed his lovely chest, and the pool conversation quickly became garbled nonsense to her addled brain. She could still hear Emi's ringing laugh, but the remainder of her senses were all fixated on Cam. He took her still-dirty hand in his rough one and looked down at her, his face both proud and adoring as words rumbled out through his throat. *Uh-oh, what did he say? Do I need to answer?*

"You're engaged!?" Emi squealed, splashing over to embrace her. Alarmed, Delia released Cam's hand and held her breath until Emi deemed the hug was finished. "That's so exciting! When did this happen?"

"Um..." Delia looked back at Cam. "This morning?"

Cam grinned, his dimples sinking deep into his cheeks as he nodded.

"Are you getting married tonight? Oh, wait, you can't! When will the governor let you get married?" Emi asked with genuine concern.

Cam's dimples disappeared and Delia's smile tightened into an artificial one that looked more like a grimace.

"Emi..." Elis chided.

"What? Should I not ask that? I'm sorry!"

"Congratulations," Damus said as Everes nodded what appeared to be the same sentiment.

"Maybe if we all go ask the governor together, he will let you go," Emi suggested.

Damus snorted.

Delia shook her head emphatically. "That's a great way to end up in the dungeon."

"Oh. Why would he do that?" Emi turned to look askance at Everes. She lowered her voice and glanced conspiratorially at the door. "Is he a *bad* governor?"

Elis rolled his eyes. "Of course he is, Emi. He starves the in-seasons while the life servants get fat."

"I've had enough to eat," Emi argued.

Elis glanced at his slender sister. "A pea would fill you up."

Emi laughed with good humor, and Delia foolishly turned back to Cam's chest, quickly losing the thread of the conversation. Wings closed, she tucked her shoulder into him, her eyes drifting up to the day's worth of stubble that shadowed his jaw. She lifted her hand, wanting to touch it, and saw the dirt embedded under her finger nails. Self-consciously, she took a step away from Cam and began to wash.

Emi was alternately teasing her brother and Everes while Damus cracked jokes. Cam laughed when they did, but took a step back each time. Delia moved when he did, amused at his apparent discomfort. By the time she finished washing, they were nearly on opposite sides of the irregularly shaped pool with only Emi trying to include them in the conversation.

"You don't like them?" Delia whispered.

"I like them. Damus and Everes are Elissa's brothers."

"You grew up with them?"

Cam shook his head slightly. "Their dad, the day clerk, had several mates. Have you met Psyche?"

Delia scowled.

He chuckled quietly. "I'll take that as a yes. She's their sister, too."

"*Psyche* is Elissa's sister?!"

He nodded. "Different mother, though."

"How many siblings do they have?!"

Cam looked up at the ceiling as he thought. "I can't remember, but it's a lot."

Delia turned to stare at Damus and Everes. "So they all grew up without a father?" she whispered.

"I think so."

Delia imagined her life without her dad and blinked back tears. *My life would be completely different,* she realized. She brought her gaze back to Cam. *He'll be a good dad,* she thought, and peace filled her mind. Taking his pruning hand, she pulled him out of the water, glancing back at his damp chest often enough to trip twice. Each time, Cam steadied her.

"You okay?"

Delia flushed. "I'm not clumsy, I'm just distracted."

"You need me to put a shirt on?"

"No!" Delia's flush turned scarlet at her own vehemence. Damus chuckled, and she looked back to see the whole group watching her with amusement. Elis' reproachful gaze was the only exception. "We're going now," she announced unnecessarily. Cam let go of her hand to retrieve his bag.

"Bye!" Emi called cheerfully. "Let us know when your wedding is!"

Delia left without answering, but Cam waved and nodded.

"You don't like them?" Cam teased as he pulled a shirt out of his bag and slipped it on.

Delia let out a disappointed sigh at the eclipsed view, then belatedly recalled the question. "I *like* them; they're nice. I just didn't like the *question*," Delia groused.

"About when we're getting married?"

Delia nodded. "I'm training Caena and Indra tomorrow, then I'll have trained all the medics except for Graci, and she's always with the governor. I think I have to train the gardener, too, but so far he won't even show me where the garden is." She dug a groove in her soap with her thumbnail.

"But the governor *is* going to let you leave, right?"

Delia eyed him, seeing the worry etched in his forehead. "Coli told me what Gray said to you."

Cam looked away. "I shouldn't have even listened to him."

Delia glanced around, waiting until there was no one near them, then stepped closer, her voice low. "I shouldn't tell you this, but for your peace of mind, I'm going to. The governor's season ended before I even met him. And Graci? *She's* his infertile mistress. He just wanted me to get him out of pain. And now that he's addicted to the morphine he's getting from local apothecaries, he won't want my poultices. He may like that I supply the infirmary with free medicinal plants, but I don't think he cares enough about the people here to really let that influence him. When I've trained all the medics like he asked me to, I think he'll let me go."

Cam let out a big breath. "Okay, good. That makes me feel better. I didn't believe the rumors after I talked to Coli, I just..."

"It's okay," Delia patted his arm, then became distracted with the feel of the muscles beneath her hand.

"Did you want dinner?" Cam asked, humor lacing his voice.

"Huh?" Delia looked around, realizing they had come to a stop in front of the closed kitchen half door.

Cam chuckled. "Are you hungry?"

Delia released his bicep, her face hot. "Um, no. You?"

Cam shrugged.

"You haven't eaten since I got mad at you at the lake, have you?"

Cam gave her an uncomfortable smile. "You said not to eat anything from the forest unless you handed it to me."

Delia nodded. "I did say that. And you skipped the in-season dinner because you were waiting for me at the pool?"

Cam shifted uncomfortably. "It was probably just soup, anyway."

"Okay, then. Get dressed. It's not dark yet," Delia ordered and began walking away before she realized Cam was slow to follow.

Turning around, she caught him giving the kitchen a last look of longing. "You want the food here? Even after last night's fiasco?"

Cam shrugged. "The forest is fine. I'll go get dressed."

Delia stopped him with a hand to his chest, then dropped it quickly before her brain went fuzzy. "See, this is where the pedestal thing worries me. Our life together can't be all about what *I* want. That just makes me feel selfish and controlling. Neither of us will be happy." She rapped sharply at the kitchen door, relieved to see Sara was again on duty. "Dinner, please, Sara," Delia requested, then thanked her when she handed over another heaping plate.

Sara eyed Cam, then grinned at Delia approvingly. "It's working!" she whispered much too loudly as she handed over utensils and a napkin.

"It *worked*. We're engaged," Delia confided.

Sara jumped up and down with a squeal that belied her years. "Oh, I'm so happy for you! I just knew it would work!"

"Thanks to you," Delia smiled.

Sara fumbled with an unseen handle, then opened the lower portion of the kitchen's half door. "I just have to hug you," she explained.

Delia handed a bewildered Cam the plate, then returned the older woman's enthusiastic hug.

Sara pulled back and wiped a few tears with the back of her hand. "This is how it should end for all of us."

Sorrow for Sara, for all the life servants smote Delia, and she futilely searched for something comforting to say. "Thank you, again," she said, feeling the inadequacy of the words before they were even out of her mouth.

"Oh," Sara warbled, the back of her hand catching another errant tear. She bustled back into the kitchen and shut the lower door behind her. As she reached for the upper door, Delia could see the cascade of tears coursing down Sara's ruddy cheeks. Delia opened her mouth, prepared to blurt the first thing that came to mind, but Sara closed the door before anything did.

"Is she okay?" Cam mouthed.

"I don't know," Delia mouthed back. "Should I knock again?"

Cam shrugged, tipping the plate, then steadied it before the contents could slide off.

"Or maybe we should just go sit down and eat," Delia suggested. "Here," she said, taking the plate from him, "you shouldn't be seen with that."

"So," he began as they walked toward his room. "You were beguiling me with life-servant food?"

Delia blushed as he grinned at her. "I thought that was obvious."

Cam chortled. "It was a solid strategy."

"Until you threw it up, yes."

"Even then."

Delia rolled her eyes at him."Yes, cleaning up vomit together was a bonding experience," she said wryly. *It actually was*, she laughed to herself. "Will you be throwing up this plate as well?"

"That depends."

"On?"

"Do you have some dirty clothes I can vomit on? It really makes the experience better."

Delia snorted and tried to elbow him, but he danced out of the way.

Back in his room, they ate slowly, enjoying their teasing conversation. When they finished, she looked at him warily. "Are you going to keep it down this time?"

He looked around the floor. "Well, I don't see any dirty clothes here, so..."

Smirking, she threw the napkin at him and he caught it with a grin. "What are we doing tonight?" she asked.

"Anything you want."

Delia shook her head resolutely. "No. Anything *you* want. What would you like to do?"

He gave her a dimpled smile. "Dancing?"

She fought a grimace. "Does it have to be in the ballroom?"

He shook his head. "Not if you don't mind my humming."

"I haven't heard you hum. Are you good at it?"

"Nope. That's why you haven't heard it."

Delia's eyes lit up with amusement. "How bad are you? Will people throw things?"

He shrugged. "There might be some vomiting."

"Yours?"

"Theirs."

Delia chortled; the deadpan wittiness too difficult for her to maintain. The floodgates open, she was quickly hysterical. Balancing upon the stool became a challenge. He stood to steady her, then pulled her to her feet. Their laughter quieted as he bent for a kiss, lingering until she reached up to twine her hands around his neck.

"Should I stand on something?" she murmured against his lips.

He chuckled as she climbed atop the stool, making them the same height.

"Too tall?"

"Just right," he whispered, nuzzling her ear.

Goosebumps ran all down the right side of her body, and her breathing hitched. "Best to save that for after the wedding."

He chuckled and returned to her lips, kissing her until she forgot how to stand and sagged against him. "Okay." He lifted her down from the stool and kissed her forehead. "We need to stop."

Delia let out a ragged sigh. "You're right." Picking up their plate, forks, and napkin, she turned to the door and only stumbled a little on her way out of it. In the hallway, she turned back. "Meet you on the patio for dancing after I change?"

Cam grinned. "Are you forgetting something?"

"I don't think so."

Turning back into his room, Cam gathered her dried clothing along with Coli's donated nightgown and dress, then brought them out to her without a word.

Delia colored. "Oh, yes, clothes would help...with the...changing." She covered her face with the pile of clothes he had just handed her. "And hopefully, I will stop embarrassing myself soon."

Cam grinned. "It's nice. Kind of like a love song."

"It's definitely your turn to sing one."

"I'm humming, remember? On the patio, right after you change."

"It had better be awful."

Cam laughed as he shut his door.

Chapter Eighteen

Cam's humming was only mildly tone deaf, assuming Delia had correctly identified the song he was trying to hum. His dancing, conversely, was superb. When their wings were dry enough, they spiraled up into the twilight sky until they met the treetops, then danced among them. Back on the patio, they caught their breath and watched the stars.

When Delia's neck began to ache, she snuggled into his chest. "We should do this every night, even if we only have time for one dance."

"As long as we can fly," Cam agreed.

"No, even after, since I probably only have a week or so left." *I will so miss flying.*

"Doesn't really seem fair that pregnancy will end your season."

Delia lifted her head and extricated herself from his arms. "No, it's logical. My body will need to redirect its resources, and it's safer if I'm not risking crash landings." Delia thought briefly of Nap's fall and frowned.

"We can wait if you want."

"And risk not having children? No, thank you. Besides, I'm eager to have my personality back." Delia marched over to the castle door and yanked it open.

"Wow, stronger than you look."

Delia gave him a pleased smile before continuing into the castle. "I have to do laundry now. Want to keep me company?"

"We need to get you some more clothes."

"Don't bother. I have more at home and a near endless credit at a local shop."

Cam frowned. "I can support you. You don't need to move back in with your family."

Delia stopped walking to stare at him. "When you said you wanted to be a guard or crown agent until your season ended, I just assumed that I would stay with my family."

"I can send you money. We can have our own home."

"Or you can save what you earn and we can have our own home when your season ends."

Cam's brows knit together in consternation.

"If we were going to Wallowa, we would be living with your parents, wouldn't we?"

"But I would be working at the family business."

"And I will be working at mine." Delia set a hand on his arm. "I love wildcrafting. I even did it here *before* the governor forced me to. And I plan to do it wherever we live."

"Professionally?"

"I think someone should stay home with our children, but otherwise, yes."

Cam blinked several times. "I hadn't considered that. Do you want me to stay home with our kids?"

Delia shrugged. "If you want to. I can support us. Or we can move somewhere without an apothecary and start our own shop. It can be *our* family business." Warmth enveloped her as this idea took seed.

Cam nodded. "I like that. It feels right."

Delia took his hand and squeezed it. "I love this moment that we're having, but I have to work early tomorrow and I really need to wash my clothes tonight."

He chuckled. "Reality's not very romantic."

Delia started walking again. "Sure it is. When we're romantically scrubbing the dirt out of my clothes, maybe we'll hold hands in the soapy water." A wry grin lit her face. "And then you can hum again."

Cam chortled as he followed her. "One tone-deaf love song coming up." He commenced humming loudly, drawing the attention of everyone they passed. When a young woman covered her ears, they broke into hysterical giggling that petered in and out while they did laundry. When Delia finally went to sleep, her face ached from smiling.

The next morning was decidedly less pleasant. The pattering rain soaked the trio of medics within the first hour, and Indra turned her ankle by the second. Caena grudgingly helped her fellow medic walk, but kept up a steady stream of malicious gossip until Delia was tempted to feed her something as poisonous as her words. Instead, she utilized Neva's advice and praised Indra's efforts until Caena fell into silent, sullen envy. Delighted, Delia pocketed salmon berries to thank the older medic. She quickly found herself filling every available space with thank-you gifts, because Indra preferred to eat the food she had packed from the castle kitchen and Caena regarded all the edible plants that Delia indicated with suspicion. Considering her earlier temptation, Delia couldn't blame her. They returned to the castle in the early afternoon with all parties relieved it was over.

Back in the infirmary, she found Neva sketching the medicinal plants in the cupboard and eager for Delia's feedback.

"Since we don't have a reference guide, I decided to make one," Neva explained as she chewed the salmon berries Delia had brought her. "I'll paint the drawings later."

Delia looked at the crude drawings and pointed out several inaccuracies.

Neva's weathered cheeks colored slightly. "I'm not an artist."

"Malan is. Maybe he could do the drawings?"

Neva cleared her throat. "I'll talk to him. Now, what plants did you find today?"

Delia unloaded her medicinal harvest and spent the next hour answering Neva's questions as well as helping her create the written portions of the reference guide. Delia's wet clothes were making her itch, but Neva's enthusiasm seemed to build rather than subside. Delia finally left when a life servant came in with a nosebleed.

Finally free, Delia was removing her mud-stiffened clothing before her door was even shut. A cluster of pink purslane flowers were draped across her pillow with a note. Stripped of her filthy clothing, Delia lifted the bouquet and inhaled the sweet scent, then peeled off the remaining leaves and ate them. The note read:

Delia,

Since you're working today, I took a courier job to Firwood. I'll be back tomorrow. Don't be mad. You know we need the money.

Cam

p.s. I promise not to eat any mushrooms.

Delia frowned, letting the note drop back onto the bed. She didn't disagree with his decision, but she regretted the loss of his company. Though they hadn't been together very long, spending time with him had become a very pleasant habit. Now sulky and slightly irascible, she put on her bathing suit and marched down to the pool, glaring at anyone who met her gaze. The door was propped open and Delia hurried in, colliding with someone on his way out.

Gripping her upper arms roughly, he set her aside before releasing her. "Watch where you're going," Len growled before his eyes lit with recognition. "Did you do that on purpose?"

"Of course not," Delia snapped. "I'm engaged now."

His cool blue eyes evaluated her. "Congratulations."

"Thank you," Delia said, her tone making the pleasantry sound like an insult.

Len shook his head, then walked away.

She shivered, looking down to see the red marks he had left behind on her arms.

"Did that white bother you?"

Scanning the pool, Delia found the yellow-winged man who had asked the question. She shook her head as she covered one of the red marks with her hand,.

"Are you sure? I'll beat him up for you." Smiling, he assumed a boxing stance.

Delia peered down at his good-natured face unable to tell if he was joking or not. "I'm fine."

"You have to be careful around whites; they don't know how to be gentle."

Delia glared at him. "*I'm* a white."

"Oh." He backed away. "Sorry, no offense. I couldn't tell." He glanced from her wings to her face several times before turning away to wade deeper into the pool. The other bathers moved further away as well.

Rolling her eyes, Delia waded into the water, watching the other in-seasons shift their positions as she moved. They were all watching her, some openly, some subtly. She forced herself to wash at a normal pace, refusing to show her discomfort at their wariness, but her scowl deepened with each moment of hushed conversation.

I'm still a person! And I didn't feel the least bit violent until you all began acting like you're bathing with a bear! The shouted words in her head did nothing to alleviate her irritation. She finished washing and exited the pool with a furious scoff. *It shouldn't matter that Cam's not on the mountain*, she argued with herself. *And you know he's coming back.* This last assurance she repeated over and over, going so far as to change in his room to feel closer to him. She was comforted by his scent, the clothes he had left behind, and his tidily made bed. She was tempted to crawl into it, to sleep away the time she had to be away from him, but she had things to do. Steeling herself, she picked up her bag of foraged treats and set about delivering her thank-yous: wild strawberries for Sara, peppermint to calm down Zelic, more foot fungus medicine for Morph, dandelions for Malan to use as paint, wild carrots and thistle roots to feed Coli, and a flowering stalk of skunk cabbage for Beck. Though she had planned to bring the jocular guard some food, imagining Beck wielding the powerful stench of the yellow flower had filled her with silent laughter. When she gave it to him, he chortled and held his nose, his eyes alight with mischief.

Finally finished with her altruistic errands, she felt socially exhausted, but emotionally sated. An early bedtime was appealing, but having clean clothes to wear was more so. Sighing, she dragged herself through her laundry, recalling vomit love songs and imagining her life with Cam. Such pleasantries sped the work, and she was laying out her clothes to dry in his room only a short time later. The temptation to sleep there returned, but she resisted, knowing he would let her sleep and simply find another bed for himself. Wistfully, she inhaled his lingering scent, then abandoned his room.

Early the next morning, she knocked at his door with irrepressible enthusiasm. An entire day without him had been more difficult than she had anticipated. When he didn't answer, she called his name, then burst into the room. Everything was as she had left it, except the scent of him had faded some. The smell of the laundry soap from her drying clothes was more prevalent now.

"It's fine," she said to the empty room. "I'm sure it's fine. He'll be back soon." *He is coming back. He is. Nothing is wrong*, she continued in her head. Numbly, she followed the steady stream of girls in the hallway until they came to a stop outside the infirmary. Surprised by her location, Delia began to turn away, but Caena had already seen her.

"Well, it's about time!" Caena called from the doorway, the pencil she held in her hand arched back like a scorpion about to strike. "Now we'll finally get an answer: is she or isn't she?"

Some of the girls in the line tittered at Caena's rude speculation, and Delia wondered how long it had been since Caena had been one of them. *Not more than five years*, she decided.

Caena's face twisted into a malicious smile. "Come to the front of the line, Delia. I'm sure no one needs this test more urgently than you do. In fact, what a clever way that would be to get out of your punishment." Caena motioned her forward while the entire line turned to stare at Delia.

The fury she had been tamping down flared and her pity for Caena evaporated as truth bombs began to tickle her lips. "You...you're being unprofessional, Caena." The strain to resist cruel words was physically taxing and Delia longed for a stool to sit down.

Wrath darkened Caena's face. "Oh, am I? I'm sorry," she said insincerely. "I thought you *liked* truth bombs."

And that was all she could stand. "Oh, I do. Let me share one: this thin veneer of friendliness you wear like a bad wig hides a conniving sadist. It's a good thing no one wanted to marry you or you might have created a scourge of children just as malevolent as yourself."

The line erupted in soft gasps that quickly gave way to whispered conversations, but Caena was silent, mouth open. Delia took a few steps backwards before she turned to leave. Even then, she glanced back to make sure the medic wasn't coming after her. Caena hadn't moved, but her mouth was now pinched closed, her face splotched scarlet. Delia grimaced at her own cruelty as she walked away. *That wasn't kind*, she chided herself. *Even if she is horrible. Now you'll just have to apologize to her.* Delia groaned; that was the worst punishment she could imagine for herself. *Later,* she promised with a twinge of guilt.

She had meant to find the gardener and train him, but she found herself outside taking deep breaths and trying to calm down. It was still dark and decidedly chilly, a steady drizzle dampening her wings as she stood in the courtyard. Flicking the water from her wings, she forced herself back inside the castle with a sudden epiphany: it had *rained* yesterday. It was still raining today. Had Cam even made it to town? Was he stuck there waiting for the weather to improve? Alarmed, she imagined him shivering and wet, too far down the mountain to get back to the castle, but still too high up to reach a town with his sodden wings. She conjured and discarded a dozen improbable rescue plans before she found herself sitting in the in-season dining hall with a bowl of broth in front of her. Dazed, she looked around her at the partially filled room, then back at her soup. As there wasn't a spoon, she lifted the bowl and drank the contents. It wasn't unpleasant, but certainly inadequate. *Can I still get a life-servant meal if I just ate the in-season breakfast?* Resolving to ask, Delia picked up her bowl and stood to leave, only to have a life servant wrench it from her hands.

"You can't take that out of here," she scolded. "And where's your spoon? Did you hide it in your pocket?"

Delia stared at her incredulously. "I didn't get one."

Around her the room quieted as the life servant took out her whistle. "Hand it over. Don't make me call a guard."

Delia pulled out the lining of her overall pockets, her anger boiling up into words that threatened to spill over.

"Well..." the life servant said, wavering.

"She didn't have a spoon; she drank it," Dom barked from across the room.

Was he watching me? Delia turned to look at him, but he only shook his head and looked down at his bowl. His friend Skinner leered at her. Frowning, Delia turned back to the accusing life servant, but she was already carrying a load of dishes toward the kitchen. Mildly alarmed at the trouble the woman might cause, Delia quickly left. Returning to her room, she scoured her bag for overlooked thank-you gifts. She was tempted to eat the scattered berries she found, but instead, she marched back into the dining hall and held them out to Dom.

"What's this?"

"It's a thank-you."

"Are they poisoned?"

Delia rolled her eyes. "Yes, I'm poisoning you in front of everyone."

Suspicion still plainly written on his face, Dom took a single salmonberry and popped it in his mouth.

"Hey, give me some," Skinner complained, reaching for her hand.

Delia pulled her hand away, then dumped the remaining berries into Dom's empty bowl.

"This doesn't change anything between us," Dom informed her.

"I know that," she snapped. "I'm engaged. I just wanted to thank you."

Dom grunted and began eating. Skinner made a lewd suggestion, and Delia hurried away before she heard anything else.

Irritated but determined, she opened the door to the life-servant dining room and glanced around. The room was sparsely populated, and its few occupants glared at her until she left. Next, she tried Kip's room and the nearby growing room, but the first was empty and the latter was locked. Frustrated, she flew to the clerk's office.

Malan showed her the portrait of Psyche, her hair now a dandelion yellow. "It's a little bright for her hair, but I like it anyway. If you get me some more pigments, I might be able to talk a friend of mine into making you some clothes."

"Your friend wants pigments, too?"

Malan shook his head. "My friend wants a new room, I want pigments, and you need clothes. None of us have money, so we barter."

Pity for Malan and all the life servants filled her. "I'll see what I can find."

"Thanks. Now, how can I help you?"

"I need to find Kip; he's the last person I need to train."

Malan glanced at his ancient watch. "He'll be out in one of the gardens gathering food for lunch."

"How many gardens are there?"

"Lots. And they're all secret. Your best chance is to leave him a message in the kitchen or wait for him there."

"How long until he comes back?"

Malan shrugged. "Probably a couple of hours."

"Hours?!"

"Some of the gardens are miles away. Kip starts out early, but the mud will slow him down."

Delia blinked at him. If Kip had transferred her medicinal plants to more than one garden, training him would not be as simple as she had planned. "Why are they so spread out?"

"Probably so the in-seasons don't steal all the food."

Delia huffed out a breath. "Thanks," she muttered, then added, "really" when her grumpy tone sounded too insincere.

Malan nodded and returned to painting by dandelion.

Delia made her way to the kitchen, grateful to spot Nelson behind a plump woman who had opened the half door. "I need to talk to Nelson," she blurted before the woman could speak.

Nelson looked up, then came to the door wiping his hands on his apron. "Did you want breakfast?"

Delia shook her head. "When Kip stops by, would you tell him I want to train him today?"

Nelson's eyebrows climbed his broad forehead. "Okay. Where should I say he can find you?"

Delia groaned inwardly. The only place in the castle that was even vaguely appealing was Cam's room, but there was nothing to do there. She could work in the infirmary, but Caena was there and Delia wasn't ready to apologize yet. She could wait in her room and try to sleep, but the anxiety she was feeling for Cam and his safety probably wouldn't allow her to. With a sigh, she resigned herself to a lost day.

"I changed my mind. Tell him I'd like to train him tomorrow. Ask him where and when he'd like me to meet him."

"Okay," Nelson repeated.

"Thank you." This time she managed to make the words sound reasonably sincere.

Before she left the castle, she stopped by Cam's room again though she knew it was illogical to expect him to return today. *He's at a comfortable inn,* she told herself, *snoring into a pillow.* Did he snore? She hoped he did. Chloe snored and the sound was oddly comforting, lulling Delia back to sleep on the rare occasions that something had managed to wake her. She stared into his empty room long enough to feel self-conscious, then meandered out of the castle to find paints in the forest.

The continuing drizzle made her flight a short one, but she was careful to fly near a path so she could walk back to the castle when she was done. She collected various wildflowers, a few tubers, and some friable bark. When she began to shiver, she dug up a small foxglove and a columbine to add to Kip's secret gardens, then trudged back to the castle with only her feet dry and warm. She looked down at her trusty work boots and thought of Cam. Her mind painted a picture of him huddled under an oak tree trying to stay dry and casting a look of longing at a cluster of death cap mushrooms. She shook off the image with a literal shake of her head that flung water side to side. *Now he's having lunch in a cozy restaurant. And the food is so good, he's going to eat until his stomach aches.* She smiled to herself as she entered the castle. She stepped into the clerk's office, but stopped in the doorway when she saw an older man with blue wings behind the desk instead of Malan. *Day clerk,* she reminded herself. *And Psyche, Elissa, Damus, and Everes' father.* She examined him curiously until he looked up with a cross expression.

"You're not new. What do you want?"

"Malan's room?"

"We don't give out the room numbers of life servants to in-seasons."

Delia frowned. *Malan does.* "Maybe you could make an exception since I'm also a life servant."

369

The clerk gave her a brief glance. "No," he said simply, returning his gaze to the papers in front of him.

Delia huffed in annoyance. She was tempted to wring out her shirt to increase the size of the puddle forming beneath her, but resisted the pettiness. *He's probably not the one who will have to mop it up anyway.* Instead she went in search of Kip, hoping the rain had driven him indoors prematurely. When her searching proved fruitless, she returned to her room. She had just removed her boots when she noticed something wasn't right with her bed. Her wings were too wet to fly up and make the lantern brighter, so she stole one from the hallway. Holding it over her bed, she shivered. Black ants swarmed her bedding, a solid line of them extending across her floor to disappear into the wall. Closer inspection revealed both crumbs of food, soil, and larvae scattered across her unmade bed. Quickly retrieving her boots, she fled to Cam's room. Its emptiness gave her a momentary pang, but that was quickly swallowed up in her relief to have somewhere ant-free to change and sleep. *It had to be Caena*, she thought, regretting her decision to postpone her apology. She shivered again, her paranoia creating the sensation of ants crawling on her skin. It was a common hazard for her, spending so much time digging, but she loathed ants. They were so quick to bite her, attaching their tiny jaws to her skin with ferocious tenacity until she scratched them off. Even then, their bites took weeks to heal, the result of a mild allergy to their venom.

Well, I won't be using that room again, Delia promised herself as she changed into her bathing suit. Thoughts of revenge kept popping into her head, but she shut them down as soon as they appeared. Ever-escalating cycles of retaliation made everyone suffer; she had experienced that often enough with her siblings to know better. Besides, she couldn't be certain it was Caena.

At the pool, Delia washed quickly, dunking her head often and splashing unnecessarily to block out the sound of Cia's alarming laugh. Cia and Rus weren't the only other bathers, but Cia was clearly putting on a show for Delia's benefit: alternately fawning over Rus and shooting her malignant glares. Delia's eyes slid to the conspicuous couple involuntarily as Cia slapped Rus' arm, threw back her head, and made a noise that sounded like an angry seagull. Delia grimaced and looked away. Though Cia was successfully irritating the entire pool—including Rus— she wasn't engendering the envy she so clearly desired. Delia could pity Rus now; his rejection and subsequent choice no longer stung. She left without glancing their way again.

She returned to Cam's room and dressed, letting her long wet hair dampen the back of her shirt. Grabbing her bag of plants and makeshift paints, she once again went searching for Malan and Kip. The latter she caught returning to the castle thoroughly soaked and grumpy until she handed over the transplants. Then his eyes lit up in the customary way and he even agreed to train with her the following day at noon. She found Malan in the life-servant dining room just before his shift, but he shook his head subtly when he caught her gaze, so she waited for him in the hallway.

"Sorry," he said when he finally came out.

Rather than answer, Delia reached into her bag and showed him the many-hued flowers, tubers, and bark.

"Those are perfect!" He glanced around him, then motioned for her to follow. At a door, he held out his hands for the plants, then quickly took them inside. He reemerged moments later, wiping his hands on a stained rag, and carefully closed the door.

Is he trying not to wake someone? Delia resisted asking, suddenly wondering if some of the life-servant rooms were shared or if that had even been his room. Malan walked briskly away, and after a short hesitation, she again followed.

He glanced around before speaking in an undertone. "If certain people know I have paints, they'll wonder if I have paper. And then they'll wonder if I *took* the paper from somewhere else. And since I *may* have done that, it's best if the paints stay secret." Malan grinned at her.

Delia shook her head, uncertain whether she wanted to scold or pity him.

"Now, I have to get to work, but I will talk to my friend about sewing you some clothing."

"I'm not sure I'll be here long enough for that."

"Did the governor release you?"

"No," Delia admitted. "But I've done what he asked." *Except for training Graci.*

"The governor...doesn't always do what he says he will."

Delia felt a flash of frustrated anger and fought to remain calm.

"And if Mr. Crescent doesn't get back soon with that morphine, who knows what the governor will do to him."

"That's Cam's courier job?! He's getting the governor more *morphine?!"*

Malan glanced around the entry, nodding awkward smiles to their inadvertent eavesdroppers. "Let's go inside," he said, stepping into his own office.

The blue-winged man behind the desk grunted. "You're late." His gaze fell on Delia as he stood and walked around the desk. "She asked for your room number, but I didn't give it to her."

Malan gave the older man a tight smile. "I don't mind if she knows."

He snorted as he left the room. "Does Psyche know that?"

Malan gazed after him without answering. "He didn't want to be my father-in-law, but *still* acts like one," he mumbled.

Delia shook her head to dislodge the momentary distraction. "Are you *sure* Cam went to buy morphine?"

Malan settled behind the desk. "It's hard to keep a secret here."

Like you and Psyche? "You manage."

Two spots of color appeared on his cheeks, his eyes suddenly wary.

"The *paper*," Delia mouthed.

Malan let out a breath as the two spots of color faded. "I don't know what you're talking about," he asserted, then softened his statement with a conspiratorial smile.

Delia tried to return the smile, but her face wouldn't cooperate.

"Don't worry. The rain will let up, Mr. Crescent will bring the morphine, and the governor will be feeling artificially generous and happy. Ask him to release you then."

Delia frowned, but gave him a shallow nod before leaving abruptly. *How could Cam get more morphine for the governor after I told him he's an addict?* She wanted to yell at him, to tell him he should know better, but instead she paced inside Cam's room, pulling at her damp hair. When that failed to soothe her, she sought out Zelic, grateful to find him alone in the infirmary.

"Did you know he sent someone to get more morphine?" she blurted without preamble.

"If the *he* you mean is the governor, then yes. Your fiancé woke me up hideously early yesterday to tell me."

"He did?"

"He claimed he was just *checking* to see if I needed anything else from the apothecary, but you *told* him about the governor's addiction, didn't you?"

Delia swallowed, her throat suddenly tight and dry.

"Normally, that's a bad thing, but in this instance, you probably saved the governor's life...*again*. I sent Mr. Crescent on his way with a note for the local apothecary."

Delia let out a heavy breath and sat on the nearest stool.

"But don't be sharing any more information about patients with him. We have a duty to protect their privacy."

Delia grimaced. "I know that."

"Good. Did you train Kip yet?"

"Tomorrow. Does the governor still want me to train Graci?"

"I'll ask. If he says no, I'll recommend that your punishment be over."

"Thanks, Zelic."

Wandering back to Cam's room, Delia retrieved her sodden clothes from the corner, a slight smile lighting her face as she realized how much Cam would hate that she had tossed them there. The thought led immediately to sorrow that he was gone, then anxiety as to where he was. *He's fine,* she repeated to herself. *He's*...she tried to picture some cozy inn with soft feather beds and hearty meals, but her mind was not cooperating. All she could see was Cam shivering beneath a sheltering tree and snacking on poisonous mushrooms—destroying angels this time. She shifted her muddy load and hurried through the castle to the laundry room. *Don't think about it,* she instructed herself, then repeated the advice her mother frequently gave her: *If you can't do anything about it right now, then you're not allowed to think about it.* Delia circled the interior of the castle twice, waiting for the last of the laundry ladies to vacate the room. When they finally departed, she rushed through washing the day's work clothes, then laid them out to dry in Cam's room. She needed a distraction, something to keep her from worrying. She needed Coli. Groaning inwardly, she made her way to the ballroom, but the room was empty. Even the corner where the musicians huddled with their broken and makeshift instruments was abandoned. Following the few people she found in the hallway, she ended up in the in-season dining room amid the cacophony of many conversations, most of them the sour sound of complaining. Harried life servants handed out bowls of mushroom soup while in-seasons carped about its inadequacy or the lack of places to sit. Delia searched the room for Coli's golden head, spotting her between Mel and his brother, Ryd. Tyro stood a short distance a way, glaring at the trio.

Delia composed greetings in her head as she approached. She tried to smile pleasantly when Mel recognized her, but abandoned her efforts when Coli met her gaze.

"What happened?" Coli demanded.

Delia's forehead crumpled. "He went to town yesterday morning and he's still not back, and it's raining, and I'm worried he's stranded somewhere shivering and eating poisonous mushrooms," she admitted.

"That sounds fun," Mel quipped. "Let's do that tomorrow."

Coli hushed him with a hand over his mouth. "Cam's not a moth brain. He's probably waiting comfortably in town until the rain lets up."

"But it was raining when he left; what if he never made it to town?"

"He could still glide down with wet wings. I'm sure he made it to town."

Delia clutched her forehead. Coli's assurances were soothing, but not enough. "I need a distraction."

"I can be distracting," Ryd offered. "I juggle." He reached for his tablemates' spoons, but Mel snatched his away.

"Badly," Mel asserted. "You juggle badly. And in a room full of soup and wings, that's not a good idea. Now, what the lady is in need of is one of my famous stories."

Coli laughed while Ryd groaned and replaced Coli's spoon.

"When I was a boy, I was astoundingly beautiful," Mel began.

Ryd rolled his eyes. "And tall...you forgot tall."

"Thank you, brother," Mel added. "I was tall and so breathtakingly handsome that the other children naturally reacted with adulation."

"Naturally," Ryd deadpanned.

"But Tyro," Mel glanced knowingly at his other brother, "was consumed with jealousy."

Tyro looked away, but glowered, obviously listening.

"He followed me everywhere, learning to walk like I did, laugh like I did; I even caught him stealing my clothes. But the only time he could manage to be the center of attention was when I wasn't there."

375

"Wait, where am I in this story?" Ryd asked.

"Shh, don't interrupt my masterful storytelling."

"So I don't exist in this one?"

"Of course you do," Mel chided, then turned back to Delia. "Ryd was also there."

Ryd scoffed.

"One day, I decided to make a rope swing for the other children, including Ryd. And I climbed high into a tree with the rope clutched in my beautiful mouth. The children cheered, amazed that someone so attractive could be doubly blessed with such physical prowess."

Delia snorted, pulled into the story despite her worries.

"But just as I clutched the perfect branch upon which to knot my rope, Tyro could bear my superiority no more. He grasped the other end of the rope that trailed on the ground beside him, and yanked."

"I didn't pull it!" Tyro argued, abandoning all pretense of ignoring the story. "You just fell."

"Down I tumbled to face the envious treachery of such a brother, who quickly dropped the rope and feigned ignorance."

"I didn't pull it!" Tyro repeated, watching Coli's reaction.

"This is a *real* story?" Coli clarified.

"*All* my stories are real. This one ended with a broken nose, a few missing teeth, and two broken legs that kept me out of school for the rest of the year. When I returned, Tyro had finally achieved his goal. He was the tallest, most beautiful boy, and all the children's adulation belonged to him."

"He pulled you out of the tree?!" Coli's gaze jumped between the brothers until Ryd gave her a confirming nod. Coli stood, her eyes narrowed as she stared Tyro down. "You could have killed him!"

"It wasn't that high," Tyro argued. "And I didn't pull the rope. He just fell. He's clumsy."

Coli's jaw jutted outwards. "Don't talk to me anymore. I don't care if we're going to be related. We're done."

"He's *lying*," Tyro protested.

Coli held up a hand to stop his further protests. "Mel, we're getting married tonight. And Tyro," Coli speared him with a ferocious glare, "you're not invited."

Smirking, Delia and Ryd followed as Coli marched out of the room with her startled groom in tow.

"*That* was a good distraction," Delia conceded.

Mel tittered nervous laughter. "Do you think he believed us?"

Coli stopped walking, her grip on Mel's arm going slack. "*Believed* us? I wasn't putting on a show for him. I'm *serious*. You know I love you and I know you love me; I'm not waiting around watching Tyro manipulate you any more."

Face frozen in alarm, Ryd stealthily walked backwards until he disappeared around the corner. Delia watched him go with amusement. A part of her recognized that she should give the couple some privacy, but her curiosity was too piqued to move.

Mel bent to one knee. "But you, my love, are so worth waiting for."

Coli clutched his face in both hands. "Stop it. Be serious for just a minute. I love you and I'm sure about us. If my feelings and potential regrets are truly your only concerns, then you have nothing to worry about. I will happily go to the officiant's office right now and I will marry you. But don't ask me to keep waiting so I can be sure; your fear is going to turn me into a life servant."

Mel turned toward Delia, his eyes alight with humor, but Coli forced his gaze back to her. "No," she chided. "No jokes. I want a straight answer. Will you marry me right now?"

Mel swallowed, his Adam's apple bouncing.

"You are worth loving," Coli proclaimed fiercely. "Regardless of what your dysfunctional family may have taught you."

"Hey," Ryd protested from around the corner.

Coli snorted. "Not you, Ryd."

"Thank you," Ryd replied.

"I need an answer," Coli continued. "Yes or no?"

"Yes?" The word was breathless, almost strangled.

"I'll take it," Coli announced, hauling him to his feet. "Go talk to the officiant. Delia, get our travel rations. Ryd, pack up Mel's stuff. I'll pack up mine and meet you all in the governor's office."

Mel turned to go, but Coli didn't release his hand. Pulling him closer, she kissed him. "Don't talk to Tyro before the wedding, please. You can tell him *after*."

"Yes, my queen."

Coli grinned at him, watching him go, then turned away with a sigh.

"So *that's* how it's done," Delia teased.

"Don't jinx it. This is a minor miracle. One that I will not have delayed because you're not back with the rations."

Delia scoffed. "I've seen you pack. I have plenty of time."

"Not today!" Coli yelled back as she flew down the hall.

Chuckling, Delia hurried toward the kitchen. With Sara's help, she obtained double rations, then met Ryd and a visibly sweating Mel in the governor's office.

"Is this the bride?" the elderly officiant asked.

The answering chorus of no's had him frowning and mumbling something about courtesy.

Mel wiped the perspiration from his face with an already damp sleeve. "She's coming." He tried to laugh, but the sound that came out sounded more like a desperate wheeze.

"She's not a fast packer," Delia explained, handing over the rations. "I'll go help her."

378

"No need!" Coli panted as the guard let her through. She smoothed down her golden curls and took her place by Mel, hastily clutching his hand.

The elderly officiant knit his graying brows, but began the ceremony. When Mel asked him to repeat a question the second time, the officiant took a long breath, the joints of his hands turning white where he clutched the ornate sealing book.

"Just say 'I do,'" Coli whispered.

"Uh," Mel laughed nervously and again mopped his brow. "It's hot in here."

"Do you wish me to continue?" the officiant asked in clipped tones.

Coli gave Mel a less-than-subtle nudge.

"Oh, uh, yes, continue," Mel faltered.

"Do you, Mel, of your own free will and choice seal this woman to you for life, and if it be God's will, for eternity?"

Mel sucked in a stuttering breath. "I do."

Coli's voice was filled with glee as she spoke the same words. She giggled as Mel seemed to have difficulty remembering how to sign his name in the officiant's book. When the officiant handed him the wedding certificate, he stared down at it, impervious to Ryd's teasing.

"Is he going to be okay?" Delia whispered when Coli hugged her.

"He'll be fine; he's married to *me*."

"Good point. Are you going to say goodbye to Ora?"

Coli's eyes went wide. "Please don't tell him I almost forgot. We'll go now." She grabbed hold of Mel's arm, startling him out of his stupor. "We have to say goodbye to Ora," she announced. "Then we'll leave."

Delia and Ryd trailed in their wake, increasingly uncomfortable at the physical affection they were showing each other. When Mel and Coli stopped to engage in a serious kiss, Delia turned around.

"Are you going to go tell Tyro now?" Delia asked Ryd.

"Not until they leave—whenever that might be," he mumbled, his face red as he glanced at the amorous couple again.

"What if they run into him *before* they leave?"

"We should probably prevent that," Ryd said.

Delia nodded her agreement.

"Um, they're going into Mel's room."

Delia turned back around just as Coli pulled the door shut. "Well, that's..." she cleared her throat, "...uncomfortable."

Ryd chuckled. "It really is."

"Maybe we should go find Tyro and keep him occupied?"

"Let's do that," he agreed readily, bolting down the hallway as if he were being chased.

His brisk pace forced Delia to jog to keep up, her still-damp wings jostling uncomfortably as her wet hair slapped her back. Ryd finally stopped in the ballroom where the musicians were warming up with random snippets of music that didn't blend well together. There were only a few in-seasons waiting impatiently for the dancing to start, and one ostentatious male flipping and diving through the air above them. When he landed, Delia recognized Tyro and his cocky strut as he strode toward them to a smattering of applause.

"Is this where you try to convince me that they actually got married?"

Delia bristled. "No, this is where I mock you for your inability to accept reality."

"I knew it! I knew he couldn't go through with it," Tyro crowed. "And I suppose she wants me to come console her now?"

Delia snorted, tempted to recommend he try it.

"No, no, no," Ryd blurted. "That's not a good idea."

"Why? Is he with her?" Tyro laughed derisively. "Trust me, if *he's* her only company, she'll want me there."

Delia shook her head. "How can you be this oblivious?"

Tyro leaned down until only inches remained between them. Delia caught her breath, irritation instantly warring with attraction at his nearness and his lovely blue eyes. The corner of his mouth lifted in a smug grin.

"What woman can resist this?"

She wanted to smash his face and break his perfectly straight nose. She forced her fists to open and instead shoved him away from her. "*All* of them."

"Please. If I wanted you, you would already be mine."

Disgust and fury were making her incautious. The desire to lead him to the evidence he would not accept tempted her once again. "I'm *engaged.*"

"Yeah, well, you weren't when they introduced us. And honestly, I could probably still get you now."

Her hands were fisted again, her desire for violence increasing. She considered truth-bombing him, but he might be the one person who was impervious. Frustrated, Delia shot an imploring glance at Ryd.

"Don't be a jerk, Tyro," Ryd protested.

"I'm not being a jerk, I'm being a realist. You two should try it some time. Now are you going to tell me where they are or should I just go looking?"

Don't let him spoil Coli's wedding day, she reminded herself. *That's all that matters.*

"Uh, that's not a good idea, Tyro," Ryd repeated.

"Stop trying to help him. That relationship is doomed to fail. She might not marry me, but she definitely won't marry Mel."

At her tipping point, Delia's mouth moved of its own accord: "She just did, you conceited mass of idiocy. You think this pretty exterior entitles you to every whim, but until you learn to hide your pomposity and delusions, you're going to be alone."

"Same to you, little scorpion. Why don't you crawl back in your hole with your make-believe fiancé?"

Delia's eyes widened in apoplectic rage, her whole body trembling with the urge to attack him or divulge Coli and Mel's current location and activity. Maybe both.

Ryd winced. "He's not make-believe."

"Have you met him? No? That's what I thought." Tyro shook his head. "You should keep better company, brother." Tyro walked away and Ryd followed.

"Really. You don't want to find them. I'm saying that for your benefit as much as theirs," Ryd cajoled, grasping his brother's arm.

Tyro pulled away. "There's nothing you can say that will stop me."

Ryd stopped at the mouth of the ballroom, belatedly realizing they had the attention of every other occupant. Even the musicians had stopped their warm-up exercises to listen. The suppressed quiet of the room weighted Delia's steps as she walked across it with the clomp of her work boots punctuating each step.

"We tried," Ryd said when she reached him. "Do you think we should warn them?"

Delia raised a single eyebrow, inviting him to reconsider his words.

Ryd laughed nervously. "Uh, yeah. That's not a good idea." He looked up as the musicians renewed their warm-up exercises. "We could dance if you want."

"I'm *engaged*," she snapped.

"Oh, right. Sorry. *I* believe he's real."

Though he sounded sincere, the idea that she had to defend Cam's existence was perfectly maddening. Wrath charged through her like lightning striking water. "I'm going to go now," she managed, grateful when he didn't follow her. Back in Cam's room, she paced until she burned off most of her anger. Then she lay down, certain she wouldn't be able to sleep. And then the guilt hit. Not because she wished she had been kind, but because she wished she hadn't descended to Tyro's level. The ugly invective he utilized instead of conversation made her feel worthless, and she was furious with herself for participating. Restlessly, she kicked at the blanket. She didn't want to apologize to him, she just wanted to feel unsullied. Frustrated, she turned her face to the wall and whispered a prayer, pouring out a torrent of emotions that soon coursed over her nose to dampen the pillow. Eventually, pity for Tyro began to replace her anger, along with the reminder to apologize to Caena. Tomorrow, she promised herself.

Chapter Nineteen

"Five thirty, testing time! Ladies report to the infirmary!" A booming voice hollered from the hallway.

Delia stirred, intending to go back to sleep until she remembered her promise. Caena was certain to be in the infirmary. Delia winced, anticipating a repetition of the day before. Bolstering herself with the knowledge that she would feel better once the apology was over, she dressed quickly and marched to the infirmary. The sight of Caena at the front of the line filled her with equal parts reluctance and dread as she approached.

"Sorry," Delia mumbled when she reached her.

Caena looked past her to speak to the next woman in line. Mildly annoyed, Delia waited for Caena to look at her, say something, or even mark her present on the check-in list. Instead, Caena continued to pretend she wasn't there, asking for the name of the next woman in line.

"It's not my turn," the woman protested. "It's hers." She nodded at Delia.

Caena merely shook her head. "She's just a life servant that enjoys tormenting others. It's best to ignore her."

Scoffing, Delia stepped out of line. *Better than having her imply I'm pregnant*, she reminded herself. And she did feel better. The apology that had nearly choked her coming out seemed simple and easy to say now, despite Caena's insulting words and behavior. If Tyro were suddenly to appear, maybe she would apologize to him, too. Yet, when she made it outside without seeing him, she was undeniably relieved.

The rain had finally stopped and Delia watched the stars disappear in the dawning light. *He'll be back today*, she thought, suddenly wanting to squeal and giggle like a child. *I get to be with Cam today!* Indulging a whim, she flew toward Firwood, hoping to meet him halfway. After three fruitless hours, punctuated only by short stops for food, she was forced to turn back. When she finally met Kip for training back at the castle, she was tired and cranky despite the sunny day. The gardener had wanted to blindfold her before leading her to his hidden gardens, but she had flatly refused, instead agreeing to be sworn to secrecy. Only one of the gardens was near the castle; its proximity to the graveyard likely kept the in-seasons from looking too closely. The garden itself was partially covered by a rotting wooden lean-to with moss and flowers growing from the roof. From the air, it merely looked like a funeral garden; empty ground made pretty until more bodies were buried there. The second garden he led her to was more than an hour away on foot and flanked by an icy stream. The well-used trail appeared to end at a small fire pit; the continuing trail was blocked with blackberry brambles. Delia flew over the thorny vines while Kip tackled them with his thick gloves. The many tiny tears she had detected in his brown wings no longer surprised her. In the gardens, each of her transplants seemed to be adjusting well and Kip was eager to learn harvesting techniques for the medicinal plants. Since the long treks between gardens afforded them so much time, she regaled him with the plants' uses as well. As they returned to the castle, Kip amused her by asking about nearly every plant they passed, though his interest rarely went beyond whether or not it was edible. As the castle neared, Delia indulged visions of her happy reunion with Cam, forcing Kip to repeat his questions when her thoughts proved louder than his words. At the castle, she sped to Cam's room and eagerly threw the door open. She scanned the empty room for any sign of his return, but found none. Thoughts of Cam dead or dying somewhere on the mountain again flooded her brain.

"He's fine," she told the empty room. "He's just flying slowly, because he's so weighed down by...one small bottle of morphine." Delia scowled. *He has a reason*, she told herself, *and it's not because he's dead*. Her mind once again played visions of him eating poisonous mushrooms, this time deadly galerinas. "Stop it!" she scolded herself. In a fit of pique, she yanked off her dirty clothes and flung them into the corner. Unsatisfied, she retrieved them and threw them again. Clumps of drying mud skittered across the floor as her clothing hit the wall. Wincing, she cleaned up the mess she had made, then once again changed to her bathing suit— the monotony of her new routine felt especially trying.

"What if this is it? What if this is the rest of my life?" *And he never comes back, but I keep waiting for him,* she added silently. Numbly, she made her way down to the bathing pool and washed mechanically, ignoring the other bathers. A sliver of hope had her rushing back to Cam's room, but it was once again empty; its tidiness was marred only by her filthy clothes and boots on the floor. Sighing, she dressed in still-damp overalls and ambled off to the infirmary. Zelic was with a patient, so she meandered into the office. Neva's medicinal plant guide sat on the desk. Delia thumbed through it, spotting new errors and correcting them. She was deep into her editing task before Zelic interrupted her.

"No in-seasons allowed back here," he chided.

"Funny," Delia deadpanned without looking up.

"Seriously, only medics can be in the office."

Shaking her head, Delia ignored him.

"Are you going to leave or do I have to summon a guard?"

Nonplussed, Delia stared up at him. Zelic held his whistle to his lips, but her bemusement only grew. "Are you actually going to blow that?"

Sighing, Zelic dropped the whistle back into his shirt pocket. "I was trying to be *fun*."

At Delia's perplexed head shake, he continued.

"Beck says I'm 'no fun,' and I should try a practical joke or two."

"That's what *this* is?"

Zelic frowned. "I thought you liked practical jokes; didn't you tease Mr. Sulphur that the green spot on his wing was permanent?"

"Neva told you?"

Zelic nodded. "Anyway, I was just trying to tell you in a *fun* way that you're no longer a medic; the governor released you from your sentence."

Tears pricked Delia's eyes and clogged her throat. Until she heard the words, she had not realized how worried she had been that the governor wouldn't. "Thanks," she croaked out. "Thanks for asking him." Turning back to Neva's guide, Delia made another correction.

"Shouldn't you be running out of here to give the news to your fiancé?"

"He's not back yet."

"Yes, he is."

Delia's heart pounded as she again looked up at Zelic. "What? When?"

Zelic held up a green glass bottle. "He just delivered this."

Delia knocked over the stool as she stood. "Did you tell him I was here? Is he waiting?"

"No, I wasn't done with my patient, so he just handed me my order. I put it in my pocket, and..."

Delia rushed past him, missing the rest of his sentence as she ran, cursing her wet wings that kept her from moving faster. In the hallway, she nearly collided with several people, ignoring their disgruntled remarks as she hurried on. At Cam's door, she forced herself to stop and knock; her hand visibly shook as she waited for the door to open. When nothing happened, she pounded on the door, her fist aching.

"Cam? Cam? I'm coming in." Delia opened the door, a soft cry escaping her when she saw the room was *still* empty. *Where is he?* Though her logic urged her to wait where she was, her irrational worry drove her to search the castle. When she didn't find him at the pool or in the dining hall, she returned to his room, willing him to be there. She forced herself to knock again before she threw open the door and growled her frustration at the empty room. Her eyes slid over the neatly made bed, her clothes hanging with Cam's shirts from the hooks, and her bag in the corner. Shaking her head, she slammed the door, then immediately opened it again. *Did I make the bed?* She didn't remember making it. *And where are the dirty clothes I threw on the floor?* Glee replaced her irritation. He had been here, even cleaned up after her. Where would he go next?

"To find me," she said aloud. She trotted happily down the hall and rounded the stairs, then burst into her own room ready to greet him. Someone had stripped her bedding, ants and all, though a few stragglers darted anxiously across the stone floor in search of the others. She shivered reflexively as she shut the door. *Where else would he go?* He had been to the infirmary, but obviously hadn't seen her in the office. *He must think I'm still out foraging!* She hurried out of the castle and stopped in the courtyard, searching among a sea of brightly twitching wings. The sun caught and augmented their colors, making metallic sheens gleam. Autumn hues caught fire in a familiar pair of wings, and Delia ran to them. Cam stood gazing eagerly out into the forest, his feet shifting periodically as he scanned the skyline just above the trees.

"Searching for a pedestal woman?" she asked breathlessly.

Cam turned, an enormous grin spreading over his face. "No, I already found her."

Delia laughed joyously as he picked her up in a tight hug. She tucked her face into his neck, the scent of oceansprays delighting her senses as she struggled to contain her tears. "I missed you," she whispered.

"You missed my cleaning services," he teased.

Delia wriggled to be let down, her feet dangling in the air. "Sorry I made a mess of your room; somebody anted my bed."

Cam chuckled as he set her down and took her hand. "I saw that. They were surprisingly difficult to eradicate."

"You didn't get them all," she said, allowing Cam to lead her into the castle.

"Are you complaining?"

"No! Just explaining why I'm not sleeping there tonight."

Cam chortled. "Okay. Where *are* you sleeping?"

Delia looked up at him, her face pink. "At home, with you?"

"You can leave? The governor released you?"

Delia nodded happily. "Zelic just told me."

"So...are we getting married tonight?"

"Unless you're too tired and need to sleep. We could get married in the morning instead. I could sleep in Coli's room if it hasn't been reassigned yet—she got married last night."

"Good for her. But, I think I could make it to Firwood tonight."

Delia's grin widened, her cheeks beginning to ache with the strain of it. "Okay, but I don't have money for a room at an inn."

"I do, but we won't need it."

Delia swallowed down disappointment. "Okay, we can camp."

Cam stopped at his door and opened it. "We should talk."

Delia frowned, trying to keep alarm at bay as she sat down at his table. "About what?"

Cam sat across from her, his hands held out for her to take them. Tentatively, Delia slid her hands into his, feeling the roughness of his callouses. When he didn't answer right away, she shifted uneasily, scouring her memory for an unresolved problem. "I didn't fail your mother's test, did I?"

Startled, Cam shook his head and pressed her hands. "Not at all. And it's not a test, it's a theory. My mom says you can tell what kind of person a white truly is by how they act when they calm down. If they apologize, take responsibility, and try to make things right, then they're a good person being temporarily tormented by their hormones."

Delia panic-reviewed her time with Cam; had she apologized enough? Did any of her failed attempts to make things right with the life servants count? She withdrew her hands from his as a lump lodged in her throat. Did he think she was a good person? "Are you worried that I'm not?"

"Delia, how can you think that? You're so hilarious and kind that I couldn't even tell you were a white."

Delia's acute relief made her eyes fill with tears that she rapidly blinked away. "Then what do we need to talk about?"

Cam clasped his hands, released them, then clasped them again. "Getting stuck in Firwood for a couple of rainy days may turn out to be a really good thing for us. The apothecary's apprentice just got married and isn't coming back. He was grumbling about it when I stopped there. After I told him about my amazing wildcrafter fiancee, he offered *us* the internship. I told him I had to ask you first, but I found a place for us to live just outside of town in case you said yes. I flew mail down to town and back up as well as fetching supplies for seven different people. With the money they paid me, I have enough to cover rent until Mr. Elfin—that's the apothecary—pays us. And we would only be a day's trip away from your family, and a day closer to mine." Cam held his breath, his expression hopeful as he waited for her response.

"That's amazing," Delia breathed, relief pouring through her. "I'll miss my family, but that's so much better than staying with them while you join the flying guard." *And I really don't want to live with Dina nor have to see Talis regularly.*

Cam let out his breath with a whoosh. "I'm so glad you said that! I was worried you wouldn't want to live in Firwood or have to keep working."

"No, it's perfect," Delia assured him. "It's just one internship we're sharing, right?"

Cam winced slightly. "Sort of. You're paid labor, I'm not. But he said once I'm trained, he'll pay me. Hopefully, I'll be fully trained and getting paid before we have children. But I'll do odd jobs in the evening or whatever it takes so we have enough money to live. I'll figure it out."

Delia reached across the table to touch his face. "That's not something you have to figure out on your own. We're in this together."

Cam looked down as he cleared his throat, then sniffed. When he looked up again, his eyes were bright with unshed tears. "You are the best pedestal woman I could imagine."

Delia sprung around the table to hug him. He slid his arms under her wings to return the embrace.

"You know, when I'm sitting, we're about the same height," he said with a barely suppressed chuckle.

Delia tugged at his hair before kissing the top of his head. "That was so bratty; didn't we already discuss how dangerous it is to tease a white?"

"You *said* that, but I'm still waiting for consequences."

Delia gave him a playful growl as he stood and backed away as much as the small room would allow. "I'll give you consequences," she threatened, launching herself at him.

Chortling, he caught her as she kissed him roughly, then pulled away. "How about that consequence?"

"That was terrible, but I haven't quite learned my lesson."

Delia's violent kisses quickly devolved into a more passionate variety, until Cam opened the door behind him.

Surprised, Delia released him. "Why did you do that?"

"Uh, I think it's time to get married."

Delia took a big breath, willing the warm buzz throughout her body to die down. "Okay. Let's pack."

As neither one of them had many belongings, the process was short. Minutes later, they both stood, bags in hand, double-checking the room to ensure they left nothing behind.

"Do you need to say goodbye to anyone?" Cam asked.

Delia thought through all her thank-you gift recipients; her goodbye had been implicit with each one. She considered briefly Emi's request to let her know when the wedding would be. *Social nicety, not actual request*, she decided. Silently, she wished the exuberant woman well.

"I don't think so. Ora is still in the dungeon, but I can't bear the smell and he and I aren't really friends." *And Phasia, Margi, Tera, Archi, Roy, and Vic are there.*

They stepped out into the hall, Cam pulling the door closed behind them with a resounding thunk. The sound echoed through the empty hallway with a tone of finality.

"Somehow that made it more real," Delia said, excitement pinging through her.

Cam chuckled as he took her hand. "And you're sure you want to do this?"

"Sure about *you*?" Delia looked up at him, the peaceful feeling once again spreading throughout her chest. "Very sure."

Cam grinned as he leaned down to kiss her. "I meant about not waiting until morning."

"Oh." Delia colored, but gripped his hand tightly as they began to walk. "Though it would be nice to prove you exist, I really don't want to be here any more."

Bemused, Cam chuckled. "Okay. Who thinks I'm imaginary?"

"Coli's awful brother-in-law, Tyro, and maybe his brother, Ryd, and probably anyone else who heard about it."

"But we don't care what they think?"

"No, we do not. Or at least not enough to parade you around yelling, 'See! He does exist!'"

Cam chortled as several people nearby turned to look. "Maybe they'll tell everyone else."

Delia shook her head. "No one spreads good news about me. They'll say I was ranting and raving in the hall while dragging a ridiculously attractive man against his will."

"*Ridiculously* attractive?"

Delia nodded vehemently. "As evidenced by my complete inability to speak or navigate when your shirt is off."

Cam smirked. "I'm going to be tempted to abuse that."

"Don't you dare! We'll end up lost in the forest eating false morels."

Cam hesitated, his fist raised to knock at the officiant's closed office door. "Maybe we should eat first or at least get travel rations."

"Are you saying you have an irresistible urge to remove your shirt?"

Cam chuckled, opened his mouth to speak, then closed it again as a deep blush suffused his face. Rather than answer, he knocked on the door.

"Uh, okay. Just a minute," a voice fumbled from inside before the door opened a couple of inches and the officiant from Pearl's wedding peered out at them. "Did you want to schedule a wedding?"

"No," Delia said, tamping down the urge to snap at him. "We want to get married right *now*."

Opening the door further, the officiant looked behind them with consternation. "No guests?"

Delia shifted uncomfortably. *Maybe I should have invited Emi after all.*

"No guests," Cam confirmed.

The officiant's scrutiny fell on Delia. "You're the in-season life servant. I can't marry you without the governor's approval."

"He released me today. I'm not a life servant any more."

"Uh-huh. That's why you're trying to sneak away during dinner with wet wings?"

"I'm *not* sneaking away! And they're almost dry." Delia scowled at him and fanned her wings. In the excitement, she had forgotten they were damp.

The officiant shook his head mulishly.

"Go ask the governor if you don't believe me."

"I can't leave my post. You'll just have to come back tomorrow."

As the door began to shut, Delia put her boot in the door to stop it, but Cam gently pulled her back.

"One more night won't matter. It's not worth having a fight with the officiant."

Delia fought the urge to yank her arm away. "It's worth it to me. He sells wedding certificates to people who can't get married. I can get him to marry us."

"Do you want me to pay him?"

"No!"

"Do you want to blackmail him?"

Her wings drooped. "No."

"So you just want to yell at him until he whistles for a guard?"

Delia stamped around in a circle letting out a frustrated cry that rose in crescendo. Cam pressed his lips together, but his dimples betrayed his amusement. When she stopped, his chin shook with the effort of not laughing.

"You think this is funny," she accused. "My room is crawling with ants, the governor could change his mind at any moment, most of the people here *hate* me, and you're laughing."

Cam shook his head resolutely. "I am *not* laughing."

Delia scrutinized him. "You were."

"Not out loud." He collected her in his arms, smiling down at her. "I'll sleep with the ants tonight; you can sleep in my room. We can have dinner together..."

"And then you'll throw up."

Cam chuckled. "We can forage for dinner."

Delia looked longingly down from the balcony. The front door was still propped open, a fresh breeze ruffling the moth-eaten tapestries hanging in the entry.

"If I go out those doors, I don't think I can bear to come back."

As she watched, a life servant walked out the open door carrying a tray covered in sloshing bowls of brown liquid. Soup again. Nelson wasn't feeding the in-seasons any better than Tera, maybe worse. Delia scowled and Cam released her.

She shook her head, touching his arm reassuringly. "It's not you. It's the stupid soup." Delia took a long breath, then blew it out resolutely. "I need to talk to the governor."

"About soup?" Cam teased.

Delia scoffed and took his arm, towing him along until his steps became less reluctant.

"Is this a good idea? If you're concerned he's going to change his mind, why give him an opportunity? Tomorrow morning the old officiant will be on shift. He'll know that the governor has released you. He'll marry us."

Delia was shaking her head before he finished talking. "We shouldn't have to wait. I've been here for weeks and every day something new goes wrong. But today I can salvage. Today can be a fresh start." Delia slid her hand down to his. "And if I start saying grumpy things, just squeeze my hand."

Cam squeezed her hand, a wry smile lighting up his face.

"You're hilarious," she deadpanned, and gave his hand an impatient tug.

"Yes, I am."

Delia pulled him along until they stood in front of the governor's guarded door.

"Look, it's the roll thief. Remember, boys, if she isn't stealing your food, she's probably about to pelt you with a rock," Avell sneered. Two of the guards smirked, but slid their hands to their clubs. Cam stepped forward, his free hand fisted.

"Avell," Beck cajoled, pushing him from behind, "are you trying to behave as badly as you smell?"

"I don't smell!"

The other two guards tittered. "Yes, you do," one of them said in an undertone.

Leaning subtly closer, Delia inhaled, the unmistakable scent of skunk cabbage flowers wrinkling her nose. Beck gave her a conspiratorial wink, clearly delighted with her thank-you gift. Delia cleared her throat in an attempt to remove all traces of humor from her voice.

"I need to see the governor."

"No," Avell retorted. "You're not a medic any more. You can go talk to the officiant like everyone else."

"The officiant is the problem. He thinks I'm still a life servant and won't marry us."

"Erynnis or Sminth?" Beck asked.

"Erynnis knows; he's the one that told *me*," one of the guards said.

"I'll go deal with Sminth," Beck offered, stepping forward.

"Then I'm on door for the rest of the shift," Avell asserted, stepping back.

"It's not your turn!" one of the other guards complained, shoving him.

Beck rolled his eyes as their bickering escalated. "If the governor hears you, he'll put you both in the dungeon."

"I called it first!" Avell griped with a mighty shove that knocked the two guards into each other.

"Enjoy the dungeon," Beck called cheerfully as they started down the hall. When they were out of Avell's hearing, Beck glanced back at the guards and chuckled. "I should feel guilty, but I really don't."

"Did you hide the skunk cabbage in his room?" Delia asked.

Beck shook his head, chuckling. "I rubbed it all over his clothes and bedding. He thinks some in-season marked his room."

Delia frowned. "He'll just hate the in-seasons more now."

"Not possible. He's already experiencing the maximum amount of loathing. Besides, the guy that smelled like that skunk flower left before you got here."

Delia scowled at the memory. "I think I got his room. It's why I stripped my bedding and brought it to the laundry."

Beck chortled. "That's right! I remember one of the laundry ladies ranting about having to change the sheets. I guess she never changed them."

"Great. Mystery solved," Delia said wryly as Cam again squeezed her hand.

Beck patted her shoulder, making both Delia and Cam flinch. "I know it didn't turn out well for you, but it *is* funny. Maybe you and Mr. Crescent can laugh about it later." Beck nodded to Cam.

"Maybe," Cam acknowledged, giving him a wary smile.

"Sheesh, you force a guy to take a nap one time," Beck teased. "Don't make him take naps," Beck advised her.

"Wasn't planning on it." Delia flashed Cam a puzzled expression, but he merely shook his head.

Beck rapped briskly at the officiant's door, rattling the handle when he didn't receive an immediate response. "Sminth? You in there? It's Beck."

The door opened wide. "I was just trying to avoid...oh, her," Sminth said, frowning.

"She's all right. And she's not a life servant any more. The governor released her today after she finished training Kip."

"You *heard* him say her punishment is over?" Sminth asked.

"Yep. I have door duty today and the governor is not a quiet man."

"You're sure?"

"Yes, he complains very loudly."

"I better not get in trouble for this," Sminth said as he began fumbling with a ring of keys. When they followed him to a door at the back of his office, Sminth scowled. "Take them around through the hallway. Only officiants go this way."

"And mistresses," Beck quipped as he shooed Cam and Delia out. He led them to the governor's office door, gave it an odd-patterned knock, then grinned when Phemus opened the door. "Been marked yet today?"

Phemus growled in response, his scowl deepening as he saw Delia and Cam. "*You're* marrying *her*?"

How's your foot fungus, Phemus? Delia thought as Cam clasped her hand tighter.

Beck pushed the guard aside and beckoned Cam and Delia to follow."Be nice; it's her wedding day,"

"She's no princess," Phemus muttered as they passed. The second guard, his brother Morph, gave him a light shove and a quelling look.

Delia's free hand tightened into a fist, which she considered burying in Phemus' gut until Cam spoke.

"Thank goodness," Cam intoned.

Disarmed, Delia looked up at him. *He means it. He prefers me to a princess.* A wondering smile crept across her mouth. *A horrid princess,* she conceded. *But still, a princess.*

Sminth stood at the throne, a large book splayed over it. He was leaning down to write awkwardly, cursing when he made an error. "Your names and where you're from," he demanded.

"Beck White of..."

"Beck!" Sminth scribbled out the B he had just written. "Erynnis is going to kill me."

Beck chortled unrepentantly.

Sminth glared at Cam. "Don't tell me your name actually begins with a B."

Cam shook his head. "Cam Crescent of Wallowa."

Sminth wrote without looking up. "And Delia White from where?"

"Hamlet."

Muttering under his breath about the need for a table, Sminth hefted the ornate book and assumed a reverential manner. "Do you, Cam, of your own free will and choice seal this woman to you for life, and if it be God's will, for eternity?"

"I do."

Delia grinned at his unreserved answer and the certainty in his face.

"Do you, Delia, of your own free will and choice seal this man to you for life, and if it be God's will, for eternity?"

Giddy bubbles rose up her throat in a wave of uncharacteristic laughter. "I do."

"Then by the authority given me by our governor, who has his authority from King Danaus IV, before God and man, I pronounce you sealed together as husband and wife for life, and God willing, for eternity. Sign the book." He turned the bulky book in his arms, awkwardly holding it with one hand while he retrieved his pen from his now ink-stained shirt pocket. Cam carefully signed his name, then handed the pen to Delia, who scrawled hers. When she returned the pen, she hugged Cam as a ridiculous squeal escaped her.

"Okay," Cam chuckled. He returned the hug and kissed her lightly before guiding her to the balcony doors that Morph had just opened. "Let's get out of here before anyone can change their mind."

"Wise," Beck approved, nodding happily.

Morph gave them a wordless smile as they stepped out onto the balcony.

"Are your wings dry enough?" Cam whispered.

"To fall slowly? Sure." She laughed at Cam's look of alarm. "We're foraging first, remember? This breeze will finish drying them."

"Wait!" Sminth called.

Cam and Delia both tensed and leapt up to the railing, out of the officiant's immediate reach.

"Your wedding certificate," he explained, waving it at them.

Beck chortled. "You nearly escaped without it."

Cam took the certificate with a look of chagrin, before carefully stowing it in his bag. The sun had fallen behind the trees, casting long shadows across the courtyard where a smattering of in-seasons were finishing their meager dinner.

"Did you just get married?!" Emi called.

"Congratulations!" Everes called from beside her.

The cheerful salutation echoed around the courtyard as the diners turned to watch them descend into the forest. The day was officially salvaged. *It's the first day of our forever.* Delia grinned at Cam as her heart warmed with the truth of that thought.

Epilogue

"Shh! Don't hum so loud," Delia warned, a tired smile softening her words.

"That *was* my quietest hum," Cam chuckled as he twirled her around their tiny yard. "I promise they won't wake up."

Delia yawned involuntarily. "You said that last night, but Tris was awake when we went back inside."

Cam's yawn echoed her own. "Yes, but she didn't wake her brothers and she went right back to sleep, so it doesn't count."

"Okay," Delia agreed sleepily, another yawn interrupting her. She laid her head against his chest, her fuzzy slipper-clad feet stilling as a soft snore escaped her.

Looking down at his sleeping wife, Cam shook with silent laughter and kissed the top of her head. "Should we go inside now?"

Her head lolled on his chest, but her eyes remained shut. "No, we're dancing," she objected, and began to sway. "Why aren't you humming?"

"You said it was too loud."

"I don't remember saying that. You should hum...it's my love song," she murmured sleepily.

He resumed humming, the tuneless song almost immediately interrupted by another snore. With a quiet chuckle, he lifted her into his arms and carried her back inside.

"I love you, Cam," she whispered, snuggling into his chest.

"I love you, too."

"Sorry I fell asleep again."

Cam grinned as he set her down. "I think I was humming a lullaby anyway."

Delia giggled, then covered her mouth, listening for the wail of waking babies. Instead, a restful trio of infant snores sounded from the nursery. Relaxing back into her husband's arms with an enormous smile, they resumed their dance.

The End

Acknowledgments

This book would have been a mess of errors and inconsistencies had I been left to my own devices. Melody Shellman, editor extraordinaire, thank you for the time and assistance you have given my books.

Dawn Zaugg, Laura Pederson, Kim Hovinghoff, Kris Taylor, Susie Johnston, James Talbot, and Karalee Kochevar: your encouragement and enthusiasm kept me going. Thank you for all the fabulous suggestions and corrections.

Kara Wren Perry, you were entirely pivotal to this book. Without you, it simply would not exist. Thank you for your guidance, assurance, and tolerance.

And to my readers, thank you for giving my stories a slice of your time. Writing them is a cathartic joy, but your praise is an enduring delight.

Made in the USA
Columbia, SC
14 November 2021

48882277R00226